# AMONG THE HILLS

REGINALD FARRER

# AMONG
# THE HILLS

WATERSTONE · LONDON

Waterstone & Co. Limited
49 Hay's Mews
London W1X 7RT

First published in Great Britain 1911.

This edition first published by
Waterstone & Co. Limited 1985.

ISBN 0 947752 35 8

*Front cover:* 'Mountain Stream' by G.E. Libert
Reproduced by courtesy of the
Board of Trustees of the Victoria and Albert Museum

*Back cover:* Geranium Sanguineum T.1107 from
Florae Danicae vol. 7. 1794. Copyright of the Trustees
of the Royal Botanic Gardens, Kew © 1985.
Reproduced with permission.

Cover Design by Carol Brickley at Boldface.

Printed and bound in Great Britain by
Richard Clay (The Chaucer Press) Ltd,
Bungay, Suffolk.

Distributed (except in USA) by
Thames and Hudson Ltd

These solemn heights but to the stars are known:
But to the stars and the cold lunar beams,
Above the sun arises: and alone
Spring the great streams.

# Contents

|  |  |  |
|---|---|---|
| | MAP | 8 |
| I. | TOWARDS THE HILLS | 9 |
| II. | THE GRAIAN ALPS | 14 |
| III. | A LITTLE LATER | 40 |
| IV. | THE COTTIAN ALPS | 73 |
| V. | THE BACK DOOR OF THE MARITIMES | 116 |
| VI. | THE ANCIENT KING | 146 |
| VII. | OVER THE WALL OF FRANCE | 172 |
| VIII. | THE COURT AND GENEALOGY OF THE SILVER KINGS | 201 |
| IX. | THE GATE OF THE SOUTH | 230 |
| X. | ROCCA LONGA | 283 |

# AMONG THE HILLS

## CHAPTER I

### TOWARDS THE HILLS

THE high snows are down by now, and all the children of the hills are sleeping. Over the Yorkshire Garden winter lies dark ; in the autumnal desolation I can think of no more consoling task than to remember the bygone joys of summer. For beautiful things, perhaps, are never quite so perfectly beautiful as when they have passed beyond the untrustworthy criticism of eyesight into the safe guardianship of memory. This is a hard saying ; but I fancy I detect a meaning in it. For, into the actual seeing and enjoying of a thing there always enters the personal element of the moment ; and, with the personal element, incompleteness. One sees too much, or one is tired, or one is cross and hungry ; or one cannot notice the world because of the plants that abound in it. A thousand different reasons combine to make the visual impression crowded and unsatisfactory ; one cannot seize it and incorporate it ; the whole thing is too big for us at the time. But distance and absence clarify the view ; wipe out the confusing touches, and reduce the chaos to a composition of bare essential lines. The

Alps or the jungle are never so near, or so clear, as when one is standing on the shores of Pall Mall or the Mediterranean. Therefore, for the effective remembering and appreciating of summer, nothing is so essential as the presence of winter.

Joy remembered is not present grief made keener ; very far from it ; the memory of sun and warmth and delight makes the present cold winter of one's discontent a great deal more endurable. Or, rather, perhaps, one gets away from it, on those blessed wings with which we are all provided, if we care to use them. Thought of past summer, too, is assurance of summers to return again ; in memory one learns to appreciate impermanence ; as summer is gone, so winter must go, and the cycle be revolved eternally. Winter and such-like seeming deaths need only be commas in a sentence as interminable as one of Walter Pater's :—νιφοστιβεῖς Χειμῶνες ἐγχωροῦσιν εὐκάρπω θέρει. Therefore will I avert my own eyes from the dank dead herbage, the mildewed weeds, the fallen brown leaves that have buried the Yorkshire Garden from view, and will sail forth upon a voyage of reminiscence, to beguile the dark weeks that yet must elapse before the world begins its obvious activities again. And to all my faithful that so choose I gladly issue this ticket of invitation to accompany me ; always premising that this large handsome ticket is not transferable ; neither by loan nor hire. But to be purchased with honest cash, and kept upon the drawing-room table.

This, then, is what I will do for all those who rightly value me ; I will carry you away upon the wings of

memory (and if those wings, like an aviator's, occasionally fail, or flop you into seas of error, it shall not be
for lack of care or safeguard on my part), I will lead you
up to the wild rocks and little mountain lakes where the
children of the hills abound ; I will show you the place
and the habit of each, and record such deductions and
experiences as I myself have acquired from seeing them
at home. For very many are the failures that are due
to no other cause than ignorance of such matters, combined with misdirected zeal for the welfare of a plant
whose natural inclinations are too rarely indicated in
any book of botany or horticulture. Sometimes, indeed,
you may find a brief word or two as to the situation
(" wood " or " marsh ") preferred by a given plant ; but
it is rarely that such words give any actual guidance, and
more often they are absent altogether.

Therefore I think that there is a place waiting on your
shelves for a book that shall try to give you some
information as to the plants *in situ* ; even though that
information shall be limited and partial. For it is only
small strips and patches that I know ; or, rather, as I
should say, that I have visited. For—" know," what
does one ever have time to know in life ? I do not even
*know* my own garden yet ; it is always a nest of surprises.
How then should I claim to know the enormous and
incalculable Alps, on which my feet may have gone
roaming for a day or a week ? No, but without claiming
any knowledge, there are a few things I have seen there,
among the many millions that I have not.

And the things seen I will therefore record, asking

you to remember that my field of exploration, though large and wide and showy in appearance, is really, when I contemplate it, only as one grain of sand among the vastnesses of the world.   For I am merely going to take you now for a cheap little humble trip of six weeks or so, round the Graian, Cottian and Maritime Alps.   It is but a tiny instalment ;   and to what does its value amount ? The Pyrenees are as yet white blanks on the map of my mind ;   not a leaf or stone can I show you of the Balkans, nothing of Eastern Austria, and above all nothing, nothing whatever of those Himâlyas that I suppose I shall never be able to visit,—unless, indeed, you all purchase this volume with an avidity unequalled in the memory of man or publisher.   However, it is a poor thing to sit down and do nothing, simply because one can't do everything.

But there is one special thing I have to say before we set off.   And that is that in the ensuing notes I mean quite often to be guilty of forgery.   For I am going to take you to see some extremely rare and precious plants ; I have no intention of making these chapters so plain a guide that unscrupulous depredators, nurserymen and others, may be able, in the light of my words, to go straight out and exterminate the species of which I talk. This book wants to be a cultivator's help, not a collector's. Therefore, though in some cases (where dealing with plants of wide distribution) I shall make no bones about the identity of the hills in which I find them, when I come to anything particularly precious I may, perhaps, shroud its habitat in mystery.   Nor shall I tell you when I am doing this.   But of course my warning does not mean

that I shall play fast and loose with facts. I am
writing to show you how and where the plants grow;
absolute accuracy of description is my aim, and it would
destroy my whole purpose if I described a sun-loving
high granitic alpine as occurring low down on limestone
in the shade.

And my notes on locality must also be taken merely
as cultural suggestions, and not as dogmas. I describe
how and where the things do grow; it by no means
follows that they *must* grow in similar conditions at home,
nor that they can *only* grow in such conditions; for, on
the same rock in the Alps you may easily find two plants
of which the one will thrive with us like a groundsel in any
sort of decent soil and situation, while the other dies as
obstinately as an allegory on the banks of Nile, no
matter what exquisite care you may take in reproducing
its native stones and soils and aspects. However, with
all due reasonable deductions, it undoubtedly does help a
gardener enormously, to have seen his plants in the circumstances that they naturally choose; so now come along
and see them.

# CHAPTER II

## THE GRAIAN ALPS

PERHAPS I may spoil my market by this opening ; and yet, though all that comes after may be, by contrast, bathos, I cannot resist beginning our tour with the most resplendent display of mountain flowers that I have ever seen in my life. You shall have, on the Mont Cenis, a *Répétition générale* of almost all the glories you will subsequently meet, raised to the tenth degree of splendour and prodigality. For the benefit of those who have no maps, and would not bother about them if they had, I may as well explain the situation of the Graian Alps. From the Lake of Geneva along all the north of the Lombard Plain to Domodossola runs the enormous wall of the Pennine alps, from the Dent du Midi, Weisshorn, Dent Blanche, Matterhorn, Mischabelhoerner up to the mass of Monte Rosa. Below this, on the Italian side runs the curling valley of the Dora Baltea, down to Turin, and this, in its turn, is walled in on its lower side by the lesser but still magnificent rampant of the Graian Alps, which sweeps round across the Western corner southwards, beginning roughly parallel to the Northerly range, from the bulk of the Grand Paradis to the Mont Cenis. Immediately under this lies the deep valley of the Dora Riparia, and when the mountains rise again on the south, they are the Cottian Alps, running almost straight down in a series of ripples, broken only by the unexpected pyramid of Monte Viso, until the valley of the Stura intersects the ranges, where the Maritime Alps cross the Cottians at right angles and prevent their further progress. And the Maritimes wall in the Riviera, stretching full across the South, from Enchastraye through the "*Massif*" of the Argentera, to the Col de Tenda, on the eastern side of which they fade away into the Ligurian Apennines, gradually dropping towards the Gulf of Genoa.

That is to say that the plain of Turin is engirdled by a semi-circular wall of mountains ; the Pennines along the north, the Maritimes in the South, the Graians and then the Cottians running round to connect the two. It is the circuit of this amphitheatre that I offer you. The Flora, take it all in all, is perhaps the richest there is any chance of seeing in the European mountains. Though I have not yet ransacked the Grand Paradis, I know that it is a centre for such first-class rarities as *Valeriana celtica* ; the main mass of the Graians give a general display surpassing everything I have ever dreamed of ; the Cottians, among their gaunt chines, hide *Primula cottia, P. Bonatii, Gentiana Rostani, Fritillaria delphinensis, Saxifraga valdensis*, and other plants entirely peculiar to the range. And, when at last you reach the Maritimes, you are on still nobler ground. For their high granitic ridges are the sole dwelling-places of *Saxifraga florulenta* and *Viola nummulariaefolia*, while as soon as you have dropped down on the Mediterranean slope, and got off the granite on to the limestone, you enter on the only earthly territory of *Primula Allioni ;* and the special field of three most precious Saxifrages, *cochlearis*, and the two royal varieties of *S. lingulata.* To say nothing of many minor marvels : *Iberis garrexiana, Moehringia papulosa, M. sedoides, Phyteuma Balbisi, Asperula hexaphylla, Aquilegia Reuteri*, and the blazing fires of *Lilium pomponium.*

The first comment I have to offer on the Mont Cenis is that of Mrs. Prig. For "there ain't no sich a person." Which lambs could not forgive the disillusionment ; " no, Betsy, nor worms forget." Likewise " which fiddlestrings was weakness to expredge my nerves " when I discovered that this mountain, which almost all my life I had longed to visit, was nothing more than a geographical myth. Nor is there even a Mont Cenis Tunnel. For the Tunnel undermines the Col de Fréjus, and the Pass of the Mont Cenis lies many miles to the East, climbing between the Rochemelon and the Ciusalet. It seems to have been, indeed a strange vagary of our ancestors to name their passes after mountains that they did not even pretend existed. Wild geographical confusion resulted ; people expected to find, somewhere near every given pass, the mountain from which, apparently, it took its name. And when they did not find it, they invented it ; feeling that if they couldn't see a peak of some twelve thousand feet or so, it must be by art-magic, as the peak could not fail to be there, seeing that down below there was a pass called after it.

I am not romancing. Witness the history of Mont

Iséran. The famous Col de l'Iséran must obviously have a Mont Iséran somewhere near, before it can become its Col: so says the logical mind of man. Accordingly, from the beginning of the nineteenth century geographers have always given glowing descriptions of Mont Iséran, which, it appears, is a magnificent pyramid of granites, giving birth to the Arc, the Isère and the Stura. This eminent peak towered, upon maps, to the height of more than thirteen thousand feet. It continued so to tower, through several generations, until in 1859 Mr. Matthews was inspired to go and have a look at it. He got to the place where it towered; lo and behold, there was nothing there. Nor could he find anybody who had ever heard of Mont Iséran in those parts, much less set eyes on it. He was not unnaturally surprised, as a thirteen thousand foot peak is usually at least visible to the naked eye, whatever its other defects may be. The long and the short of it was that Mont Iséran had never existed at all, except on paper; where it continued its haughty career even as late as a French map of 1890.

However, I survived my disappointment about the Mont Cenis, and determined to go there, although it did not exist. I was fired by descriptions of botanists, who had found it the most gorgeous theatre of the Alpine flora; and decided that, for the first time in many years, I would go really early to the Alps, and see the glory of the flowers at its best. True it was that, from the accounts, one need not expect to find any species of eminent rarity, but the general show of lovely and interesting alpines was said to be quite dazzling; and,

after all, a district that gives one *Campanula cenisia,*
*C. Allioni, Viola cenisia, Eritrichium, Petrocallis, Primula*
*pedemontana, Androsace glacialis, pubescens, Vitaliana*
and *carnea,* to say nothing of all the typical high alpines,
need not be sniffed at by any collector—unless he demands to tread on *Saxifraga florulenta* at every step, and
to find great auks laying eggs all over the place among
tufts of *Primula Allioni.* So I tore away the usual ties
that keep one at home, and alighted, on June the 22nd, on
the platform of Modane.

How justly one hates Modane when one is merely
passing through, and there has to undergo the harassment
of the Customs. And how I loved Modane when I stepped
from a stuffy train that morning into the freshness of young
daylight among the mountains. On all sides rose the
peaks, the snow was only beginning to go, and the air
had a crystalline tang that seemed to breathe of spring
itself, and all the wonderful things that arrive on the
skirts of spring. There is a public motor which carries
one up the pass to the Hospice (whence another can convey you down again the other side to Susa). Into this
I stepped, and we were whirled away through the clear
sunlight. It is about sixteen miles from Modane to
Lanslebourg, where the ascent begins, and all that time
the high-road goes undulating up and down in the valley
of the Arc, and there are flowers all the way, although
the precious beauties do not, of course, begin as yet
to appear. Gradually wonderful peaks unfold across
the river ; bit by bit they are revealed to be only the
buttresses, gargoyles and bastions of the Dent Parrachée,

whose whole angry splendour is not revealed until you look back from the village of Termignon. Far away at the head of the valley are more snowy spires, the mountains over Bessans and Bonneval, to the left of which used once to tower Mont Iséran. At last one runs into the long main street of Lanslebourg, and comes to the midday rest.

Lanslebourg, which is still in France, lies immediately at the foot of the Pass, which now rises sharply to the right out of the valley of the Arc, up the wooded wall of mountain, in a series of great zigzags, towards the snows that are still lying low on the hillsides and among the brushwood. In the forests round Lanslebourg itself there are many pleasant treasures. Most conspicuous of all in June, is *Atragene alpina*, which here seems to occur in forms more splendid and clear-coloured than usual, sweeping over the bushes in veils, and hanging down in showers of big blue stars. It is so beautiful here that sometimes its flowers remind one of *Aquilegia glandulosa* itself. And the vigour of it! Up through a living bush it pokes and pierces, to come at last into the sunlight. And then that one little thready wooden stem breaks out into a cataract of growth like a green sheet tossed over the shrub or tree beneath, and throws its blossoms here and there and everywhere in a riot of magnificence. Or perhaps it takes some dead pinetree, and makes itself a complete shroud for the corpse, winding it in showers of verdure and long trails of celestial crosses. Or runs in and out among the bushes like a smouldering fire, erupting into blossom here and there as roses emerge in an English hedgerow.

Always and everywhere round Lanslebourg it is of a pure and perfect beauty, although in other districts I have seen its flowers duller and heavier in the tone of their blue. However Atragene is always a thing of the daintiest charm, although at Lanslebourg it even surpasses itself. I can recommend it thus heartily, and name the place without reserve, because the Atragene is quite safe from eradication. Never was there a plant with so devilish a running root. I spent the whole of one grilling day in the forest at Lanslebourg, trying to discover seedlings that might prove less entirely hopeless to collect than the grown plants. And though I did succeed in finding a few, they were but a very small percentage among my disappointments. You light on the nicest little apparent youngling with only two leaves; and you say to yourself " ha-ha." And you begin to dig for it with a glad heart. And you find that it has an underground rootstock that runs along for three or four yards, deep among stones, and ultimately merges into some full-grown specimen that you had carefully avoided. Not to mention that forest soil, as hard as nails, and packed with roots, can be the most exasperating medium to dig in. I was exuding crossness at every pore by the time I had got my fill of Atragene.

Nor was I soothed by tap-rooted *Ononis rotundifolia* (which did yield seedlings though); and still less by *Pyrola rotundifolia*, which here occurs abundantly in the darker woodland, and repeats on a rather smaller scale the tiresomeness of Atragene. Indeed, I am not sure that it does not surpass the alpine Clematis; for Atragene does

at least have a decent bunch of root-fibres when at last
you succeed in arriving at them ; whereas the Pyrola
meanders feebly about underground with a few slack
white threads which seem to have nothing satisfactory
or coherent in their natures. Even worse than this
species, though, is the almost impossibly difficult *P.
uniflora*. This, even after the most exhaustive search,
has never seemed to me to have any real roots at all.
Therefore I was the more consoled and delighted at Lanslebourg, when I found it growing in slaty silt by the path-
sides in the wood, and producing, to my astonishment,
normal masses of compact roots exactly like any other
decent plant's. I collected these clumps with ease and
joy ; they are now thriving in their pots with a heartiness
almost as great as I had forecasted from their habit, and,
at any rate, many leagues removed from the mimpish
gloom in which dwindle the ordinary plants one has
of *P. uniflora*, with only one feeble long white piece of
cotton by way of a root.

Leaving Lanslebourg, the road mounts quickly, in
wide sweeps, past the last hayfields filled with Pheasant's
Eye Narcissus (an inferior form, so far as I saw it), through
the pine-forest that clothes the side of the mountain. At
once the air grows nippier with the breath that comes
down from the snow, and in five minutes begin to appear
the flowers of the uplands. White Pinguiculas and
*Primula farinosa* are everywhere, by the roadsides, and
over damp rocks and slopes ; *Saxifraga aeizoon* is in
clumps on the ledges, but will not be in flower for several
weeks to come. And then, at a turn in the roadway,

*Gentiana verna* takes possession. In patches, in mats, in blobs and stretches, the dazzling azure of it is scattered over the roadside grass with a careless profusion that seems almost ostentatious. It is universal in a few minutes more, growing by the yard of solid colour. One kicks oneself, in bitterness of soul, remembering the parsimonious pieces on which one prides oneself at home. It nearly offends one's sense of decency to see it thus luxuriating here in such unbridled splendour, quite forgetting that it is a difficult capricious plant. But the arrogant gorgeousness of it takes one by the throat, and crushes out every feeling except pure awe. Every instant it grows more abundant. Not only is it a carpet along the roadside, but now it enamels the open glades of grass, and one sees it glimmering like dim heavens, up and up the sunlit stretches of the woodland. Never had one conceived of it as tolerating copses ; yet here, wherever a ray of light can penetrate the forest, there are wide beds and masses of it, spattered with their stars of blossom so thickly that as one passes they make mere sheets of indiscriminate azure in the twilight of the wood.

Hepaticas are there, too, in their myriads, if one had time to alight and collect them ; and in barer places *Gentiana acaulis* opens trumpets like the sky at midnight ; and over all these, shoots up that form of the mountain pine which is called *uncinata* because its cone-scales turn back in odd definite hooks. As the road rises the wood grows thinner, and *Gentiana verna* yet more shamelessly abundant. The motor has to stop at intervals and have cold water poured over it. This gives one the chance to wander down a little into grassy glades where *Primula farinosa* lies like a vesture of pink, while in the dappled light of the sparse wood beyond, the Gentians make the floor a flagged pavement of sky. And this is only the beginning. For the road is rapidly nearing the level of the alp ; the forest dies away beneath us ; rare alder-scrub appears above ; old snow-patches lie dingy among the brushwood, and here and there have had to be cut away to make room for the road. The air has now the full divine resiliency and chill which belongs to the untrodden snow-fields.

Sad and dark are the naked alder-bushes among the snow, and no less austerely wintry in effect the dank brown earth from which the snow is only just receding. But the Soldanellas are springing everywhere, and their fringed violet bells are dancing merrily even down to the roadway itself. And on its lower side there is nothing now but a steep open declivity of short grass. Of short grass I say, but it is as much as you can do to tell that the grass is there at all, so overlaid it is with slabs of *Silene acaulis*, solid sheets of pink, amid the sheeted solid blue of *Gentiana verna* ; with golden dust everywhere of alpine Potentillas, and a rose-pink veil over the whole scene of *Primula farinosa*, thick dappled, too, with the dark purple stars of *Viola calcarata*. For the Pansy has already been beginning, peering unexpectedly out amid the brushwood, in many shades, from pure violet to white and butter-yellow. But it is not until you reach the alpine levels that the alpine pansy really comes upon the stage. And, when it does so, it could have little effect were it not for its overwhelming weight of numbers. For *Anemone alpina* comes on at the same moment. And what do we know of *Anemone alpina*; what had I ever known before of *Anemone alpina*?

Now we turn the shoulder of the hill and reach the pass, although the road still winds a little upwards, over stretches of this alpine grass which is nothing but the dim ground-work of a carpet more brilliant than any weaver ever wrought. And wherever there is a slope or hollow or bank, there the Alpine Anemone reigns supreme, among herbage which will in time grow longer than the short-cropped lawn where the Gentians and Silenes have their way. And though among mountain-plants we look for brilliancy of colour, we are never taught to expect any such oriental opulence as this of the great Alpine Anemone. It is in every stage of development, here ; on sunny banks from which the snow has long been melted, it has already shot up into fluffy bushes of nearly a yard high, each producing perhaps a dozen enormous flowers like water-lilies or tulips. White and gentle as milk are these flowers ; and their hearts are a tassel of golden fire ; and on the reverse they are stained with soft lilac, or bronze, or palest blue, on the silken down of their sepals. But close to where the snow still lies, the Anemones are only just shooting from the wet brown earth, and have the effect, but greatly multiplied, of golden-buttoned *Adonis amurensis* in a toy-garden of Japan. For here the foliage is only in embryo, tight masses of downy purple, from which are bursting huge round buds. They open with a stalk of two or three inches only, gradually revealing the pure snow of their lining, as the silken-lilac globe unfolds. In a very little while these also will shoot up on lengthening stems, until, above a yard-high mass, a yard across, of fern-like generous foliage, there will be a dozen resplendent bowls of the purest white.

To all the anemones one holds out the hands of affection. But there is not one of them more lovable than this royal great *A. alpina*. In our gardens, too, it thrives most mightily ; an old plant of mine carried fifty-eight blossoms this spring, and I was only vexed with it for producing so many that none of them could manage to be as large as if the plant had been content to put quality before quantity. Any deep loam, too, satisfies this vigorous friend. And an airy, sunny place. It germinates also with the most refreshing freedom ; though both my visits to the Mont Cenis were, of course, too early for the maturity of those wild *Struwelpeters* which are almost as beautiful in their season as the flowers themselves. And when I wrote again to enquire after them it was too late ; the high snow had descended, and all the *Struwelpeters* were flown.

But *Anemone alpina* is a fiend to collect. Let no mild maiden sally forth upon the mountains to get it, armed with her reticule and a penknife. Pickaxes and mattocks, to say nothing of dynamite itself, seem necessary before you can get to the end of its woody trunk. I have never got there yet ; and it is only when you have reached the end of the stock that the real roots begin. I have employed men for whole days upon the mountain, I have delved in the sweat of my brow for hours, and my manager has toiled on bended knees till the shadows grew long upon the slopes ; never yet, I think, have any of us really reached the end of an anemone's roots. Of course our labours resulted in a large quantity of healthy plants that have grown on without a qualm ; but even to get the anemone with so much of its stock as shall cheerfully emit new fibres is no task for babes or sucklings. Even the smallest pieces, apparent seedlings, send back a long thin thread of wood far into the bank ; and really, on the whole, I even think that the biggest clumps are the best to take. For you can at last, after trenching round them and pulling and pushing till you drip, haul them out in one solid lump ; and then they will divide up into a dozen or so black ligneous stocks, each one of which will grow on into a new plant. And again, sometimes, by mere fluke, one comes on a specimen which does not seem so ambitious as the others to twine its roots round the heart of the world, but makes a compact block.

I will not detain you here unduly on your knees before the anemone ; you shall have plenty more occasions for genuflection on the Mont Cenis. For now the road is meandering up the last inclines that lead to the summit of the pass, and there are marvels thick-set on either hand. At a turn of the way there is a new white speckling among the many colours of the turf ; it is *Ranunculus pyrenaeus* lying like the promise of a snowfall, and in the hollow thick as drifted snow. Then, yet another white, duller, greyer, distinct: *Ranunculus* (or *Callianthemum*) *rutaefolius.* Over the Alps in general this is rare, at least until you get into the southern ranges. But, where you do find it, there is usually an abundance of it. So, at this one shoulder above the road of the Mont Cenis, about half a square mile is covered with it ; and then you will not see much of the plant again, until you find it, more sparsely, where the Val Savine runs south from the Little Mont Cenis. It is, as I have said, rather a disappointment ; its glaucous, rue-like foliage very beautiful, it is true ; but the flowers not quite large enough for the leaves, not brilliant in the tone of their white, and with a green eye which diminishes their effulgence. But over all the springy turf they grow in vast profusion, and are even at their best where cultivation has spread a little manure over a fold in the hill-side, where the grass is apparently worth the mowing.

Now, from the Douane, the road runs swiftly down in wide loops towards the lake, between the infinite fine lawn of the alps on either hand. The great peaks loom one by one into sight, and the beauties of the Mont Cenis are unfolded. The run of two miles from the Douane to the Hotel de la Poste, is one delirious riot of revelation, alike in big things as in little. On either side of the road and up over all the grassy hills colour is slapped and spilt as on a child's palette—pink and azure and crimson and violet, gold and white and indigo. Climbing the steep acclivities of the distance goes a thick peppering of minute white spots ; and these are stretches of *Anemone alpina* ; among them, drifting here and there, as if blown by the wind into the hollows, like a fine film of white, which are the snowdrifts of *Ranunculus pyrenaeus.*

The Hotel de la Poste sits by the roadside ; at the back, in tier after tier, rise vast green downs towards the range of granite that towers overhead,—the Punta della Nunda. Beyond the Nunda, and behind the hotel, the wall of the range recedes, forming the glen of the Tavernettes, high above the lower alps, on the upmost fold of which lies the tiny Lac Clair, in the cul-de-sac formed by the Punta da Roncia, the awful northern precipice of Rochemelon, and the long arête of Mont Lamet. But the Lac Clair at my first visit was all under thick snow, and though I *did* succeed in getting *Campanula Allioni, C. cenisia, Viola cenisia,* and *Thlaspi rotundifolium* on the stone-slopes below, it was only in their earliest stages, when the very leaves themselves were scarcely discernable in the dead stumps of *Campanula Allioni.*

Looking across the road from the Hotel, one has the lovely lake lying below ; between us and it there intervenes a curious waste territory of grass and quartz. This is all honeycombed and pitted with young potholes, where *Corydalis solida* lives, and *Pulmonaria angustifolia ;* and in the depths of which the Holly Fern grows rank, amid boskets of *Hugueninia tanacetifolia,* and a dense undergrowth of *Viola biflora,* like a carpet of gold and green, The ridges and crests above these holes are spread with Dryas, and tiny *Salix serpyllifolia* lies in a green sheet over the surface, all gilded with fine gold-dust of its blossom. Then, wherever there is herbage upon the rippling slopes, are plastered slabs of *Gentiana verna,* among misty-pale blue clouds of *Globularia cordifolia* mingled with the many-coloured mountain Pansies, and enhanced by a profusion everywhere of yellow Potentillas, *verna* and *aurea* and *alpestris*. To say nothing of the richer, darker yellow which is *Alyssum alpestre,* or the clear citron of *Erysimum pumilum*. In successive raptures one slowly descends these slopes towards the lake ; and there the quartz tails away into lawns and laps of smooth short grass, which (and I speak plain words of fact) can hardly be discerned at all, except as the foundation to a carpet of *Viola calcarata,* in every shade, from pure white to the darkest violet, so thickly growing that the effect is that of a most dainty mosaic, in whose pattern, here and there, the trumpets of *Gentiana acaulis* strike a sombre note of indigo, and *Gentiana angulosa\** flares with a passionate azure, which, if any other hand had applied it, would, one thinks, have crashed against all the graded lilacs of the Pansies. But here, above the harmonizing green, not a bit of it. And the carpet is filled in, wherever space is left, by the pink powdering of *Primula farinosa,* and in the drier places above the water the Potentillas and *Geum montanum* glare among the others in the prodigality of their golden blossom.

So one stands on a little grassy headland, beside a little flowery bay, and looks out across the lake. Immediately opposite there is a dusky chine of boscage on the

---

\* I ought to have given this glory more notice. It belongs to Southerly ranges, and is rare. It is *verna,* pure and simple, but twice the size in all its parts, and with three times the vigour and robustness of *verna.* The calyx-angles are widened into broad wings, hence the name. It is perfectly easy to grow, and practically ever-flowering.

other side, and behind that, running up between the
hills, a wide and open valley of meadows, closed in the
furthest distance by a barrier of peaks. To right and
left of this tower stark mountains, whose snows are still
lying far down into the valley. The melting patches
have the strangest of shapes; one can see dragons and
giants, and intoxicated demons sprawling white over
the slopes ; there was one comfortable pussy whom we
watched from day to day, as she grew scraggier and
scraggier hourly, kittened at last, and then went off in
a precipitate decline. The grassy alps and downs away
across the lake are all filmed with a crumply saffron veil
over their banks and ripples and ridges. And that faint
glow means a hundred thousand million mountain pansies.

And how shall I paint the wonder of this without
yielding to enthusiasm ?

I cannot pretend to any catalogue of the wonders
that here wipe all spirit out of a gardener's heart, and
reduce him to the state of Sheba's Queen at her lowest.
Of course the high alpines were as yet fast asleep, or barely
stirring from their slumbers. But on the upper shingles
of the Punta della Nunda *Ranunculus glacialis*, on dusty
banks like the debris of a coal-mine, was opening its
golden eyes to the day. The leaves had scarcely
unfolded at all, nor the stems ; among the dust and
dirt there lay only those rich snow-white flowers so
cheerful and brilliant and lovable. For the Glacial
Buttercup is a plant that takes one's affection captive ;
indeed, for all the white high alpine buttercups I have
an affection that borders on dotage. They are in-

variably so beautiful, and on the whole so surprisingly easy to cultivate.

But it was an astonishment to me to see *R. glacialis* there on the shaly wind-swept arête of the Nunda. For as a rule one associates it only with the moist shingles round the mountain tarns at the very top of each high valley, immediately under the peaks themselves. Never before had I seen it on a sharp and exposed slope, where it could rely on no moisture except from the weather. A little higher yet, and *Geum reptans*, in vast, dead-looking masses, was just beginning to stir to fresh life among tumbled boulders of granite like the ruin of a Cyclopean palace ; the glossy bronze leaves of *Thlaspi* were discoverable ; exquisite *Petrocallis pyrenaica* was busy covering its dense green cushions with lilac stars, and *Gentiana brachyphylla* was turning its attention to buds ; I even found one tuft of *Androsace glacialis* that was free from snow. And over all the icebound rocks, falling from ledge to ledge until it made the cliffs like a stairway carpetted royally with crimson and purple, *Saxifraga oppositifolia* was falling in cataracts of glory.

Let us descend again over the grassy Alps. *Anemone alpina, Anemone alpina, Anemone alpina*, in magnificence perpetually astounding ; you find it snow-white, creamy, saffron, citron ; you find it with huge flowers, imbricated and perfect ; you find with its great sepals laciniate and feathered ; you find it with double and treble rows. There are rounded forms and many-rayed star-forms, and windmill-shaped splendours with sepals that do not fit. Some of them are blue outside, and some of them

are pink, and some of them are purple as a plum.   Who
is there that can dare to talk of *A. alpina sulfurea*, who
once has seen the type *alpina* in its splendour ?

Another thing remains to be noticed.   It is always said
that *A. alpina* is the calcareous plant, and *A. a. sulfurea*
that of the granites.   This is not so.   The Mont Cenis
comprises, indeed, a great variety of formations, granitic,
shales and quartz ;  yet among all these lifeless rocks there
is no limestone.   And yet *Anemone alpina*-type is the
reigning anemone.   And, among the snowy alpinas there
are, as I have said, forms of every intermediate colour,
ranging, though rarely, to the actual saffron yellow of *A. a.
sulfurea*.   And yet these yellow forms are not the true
*sulfurea*.   The fact is that there is either no real distinction at all between the two, or else a very solid and specific
distinction.   And a second fact, no less important, is that
differences of soil are held to be a good deal more important than they really are.   Prof. Bonnier's experiments
have shown conclusively the truth of what one had always
suspected, and what one's own gardening experiences
have proved again and again,—that it is almost impossible
to pronounce, of any plant, that it finally and absolutely
abhors one sort of soil and cleaves to another.   For we know
now that a species may be a granite-lover in three districts, and yet be found on limestone in a fourth (Edelweiss
is a notorious case in point) ;  while another, such as
*Androsace helvetica* proverbially associated with calcareous
rock, may ultimately be found thriving on igneous.*

* For this reason no reliance can be placed on rigid assignments of a
plant to one stratum or another.   The ascriptions in the Atlas de la Flore
Alpine, for instance, appear to my experience quite as often wrong as

As for these royal anemones, they have clearly no authoritative rule in the matter ; I will only add that while type alpina loves all formations alike, the sulphur variety, the real *A. a. sulfurea*, seems never to be seen off the granite in nature. And that, whereas one had believed them to be, like Mr. Pontifex's lobster, "as the angels, neither marrying nor giving in marriage," I now discover that they have sexual differences very often quite as marked as those of mere mortality. For you may find one flower that is a " perfect lady," without a sign of stamen or anther ; while a complete Romeo may be found next door ; tasselled with anthers and golden with pollen, but wholly lacking in carpels. He can fertilize Juliet, and cause her to conceive ; he can bear no children of his own ; nor can she cause children to be born of anyone else.

Now we come among *Ranunculus pyrenaeus*. I have often collected this alpine buttercup from its long, narrow, glaucous-blue leaves before. I shall never do so again. For this plant varies so indefinitely in beauty that it is not safe to collect it unless you can judge what form of bloom you are getting. Though all the blossoms, large and white, are splendid in their way, yet many thousands of them are poor and thin and starry, compared with the many other thousands that are large and round and fat. All over the steep short turf it waves on its six inch stems, and one may spend many happy hours there select-

---

right. Working the same plant in the same district too, Professor Burnat and I reach diametrically opposed conclusions as to the proclivities of *Saxifraga aeizoon*, which he calls a " calcicole preferént," while I rarely seem able to see it spontaneously happy anywhere but on the granite.

ing its best forms.  It grows here best on the steepest banks, and seems to be piled like snow in the hollow places of the hills.  So that, on a fine day, one must stand at the top, to look down into the innumerable white, golden-eyed faces lifted to the day ; while in time of rain or sleet you must stand below, for all the faces will be bowed in self-defence.

And oh, the best forms of *R. pyrenaeus !*  I do not mention those merely of eminent size or roundness, or those which have grown stalwart on plots of ancient fertilization.  But not only does the plant turn double, but it is even quite as beautiful thus.  Imagine two or three rows of petals, richly rounded, imbricated, enclosing the golden heart in their frilly cup.  It is like an exquisitely dainty semi-double white rose, after the Baby Rambler style,—and I call it accordingly *Rosa Bella.*  Then there is the other form, with more petals, arranged more loosely, like those of *Paeonia Moutan.*  In this form the carpels turn petaloid, and all you see among the tossed white foam of the flower are a few tinges of delicate pale green like those on a snowdrop.  This form is like a perfect double white Banksian rose ; it has a blank purity which I find it hard to describe.  And I have called it *Rosa Bianca.*  At present in my garden both *Rosa Bella* and *Rosa Bianca* are fast asleep beneath the frozen earth ; but I believe that they may both return in Spring, and abate nothing of their primitive loveliness.

In the gullies on either side of which the buttercups are snowiest, the snow itself is still lying.  But from the wet brown margin which is hourly widening, the flowers are shooting brilliantly. Delicate against the dank brown hover the fringed bells of *Soldanella alpina* ; and through the very snow-crust itself come piercing the long little bugles of *Crocus vernus*. *Crocus vernus albiflorus* is the correct name for this high alpine variety of the spring crocus ; but *albiflorus* it certainly is not, and you will find it hard to find any two flowers that are exactly alike. Some of them indeed are purely white, with rich golden stigma ; but many others are in varying shades of lilac, striped and flaked and feathered and margined, developing at last into a full violet. The one thing you may safely say is that in every one of its forms *Crocus vernus* is among the most lovely of all the children of the hills.

And anger clots the ink of my typewriter when I think of the contrast between these and the fatties that we complacently cultivate in our gardens ; only to be disdainfully pulled to pieces, it is true, by sparrows of an acuter artistic sense than our own, who cannot put up with those plump pantomine " principal boys " who pretend to represent the real fairies of the snow. Ah, for what price has *Crocus vernus* sold its birthright, and from the frail and delicate grace of its fluted fine chalices, developed into bumpers like the coarsest claret-glasses of a public-house ! Not that, in any circumstances, any crocus could achieve actual ugliness ; the innate good breeding of the race is too strong. But the pure line of the wild species stands far beyond any comparison with the pampered obesity that flops about in gardens.

Another bulb that sprouts with the crocus here is

*Bulbocodium vernum,*—to all intents and purposes a leafy Colchicum with ragged cups of rosy magenta. The flower-segments are strappy and dishevelled in effect, nor is the colour free from the forbidden shade ; yet, seen bursting from the sodden brown, the plant is a cheerful sight, and one lingers over it with pleasure. A little further down this same gully, filled with rocks and snow, we find, among Aeizoon saxifrages and Sempervivums only just attempting to make a move, that, above its uncurling masses of fine dark foliage running among the stones, the blue buds of *Anemone baldensis* are already lifting their silken heads. However, this we shall see again in fuller development, so need not linger now. Nor will I delay you with tattle about the priceless new pink Galium here discovered, which to me will always be known as *G. Tuckett-Browni*, for a cryptic but sufficient reason. This plant I neither sought nor saw. So now we hasten on downwards to the lower levels, and we come to the vast alpine swards again, —carpets of colour rolling away up and down into the distances as if thrown carelessly down for our approval over the counters of the Creator. What is the price asked for them ? A heavy one. The toleration of all the gloomy days when they are rolled up in the cellars of the world.

The alpine Pansy is here the dominant factor still,— violet, mauve, lilac, saffron, cream, butter-milk, white,— a range of shades and colours almost indefinite. Will it give us the same at home ? I am set to wonder this, because, although I have long had good big clumps of it in my garden, I was struck by my friend's suggestion that in cultivation one hardly ever sees or hears of it, although a plant so absurdly generous of such infinite beauties ought normally to be grown in every plot of ground a foot across. Can there, then, be something wrong about it, that one so seldom sees it cultivated ? Shy of growth it clearly is not ; but I must watch my plants, to see if, perhaps, they become grudging of their flowers in cultivation.* If this is not the case, then nothing can explain its rarity in gardens, except the obstinate blindness of the gardener to his best possibilities.

Pansies, then, are the groundwork of the pattern, in every shape and shade from white to richest purple ; but diversified with the interspersed slabs of *Gentiana verna* and *G. angulosa*, and wide mats of Globularia giving a softer and mistier tone of colour. Now and again the dark azure trumpets of *Gentiana acaulis* come in like deep notes of music in a lighter composition ; and Erysimum, Potentilla, Geum, Alyssum are crashing everywhere in a chorus of different yellows. But there is yet another yellow to hand ; for the smooth lawn is studded here and there with clusters of broken rock—natural gardens, so compact and portable that one longs to stub up one or two and bring them home just as they are. They are cleft and fractured and rotted into just the right lines ; and, wherever soil lodges, plants have made their home. Alyssum, mountain Senecio, these are all very well, but now is the triumph of *Androsace Vitaliana*; which the correct-minded call for the moment *Douglasia Vitaliana*, until it has again been put back among the *Androsaces*,

* March 24th. Every one of my plants is densely set with flower buds.

or again transferred to some other of the many names it has borne in its time, poor thing, whether *Aretia* or *Gregoria* or *Douglasia* or *Androsace*. It falls in sheets from every crevice here, and its yellow stands out from all the other yellows in a certain clear insistence that would be shrill if it were not so pale and pure. A sharp citron is the prevailing note of it, though I did not fail at last to discover a form that varied to a soft saffron. Each mat or wide tuffet of wiry, narrow-leaved shoots, produces hundreds upon hundreds of lovely little flowers like tiny nudiflorum-Jasmines, in such profusion that the leaves are hidden and the plant becomes a solid splash of colour on hill or rock. If only it would do the same at home. But I fear I must put it down as unsatisfactory. It does not bear collecting with any great willingness ; and, in cultivation, though by no means hard to grow, has not always, I think, much more inclination to repeat its alpine profuseness of blossom than has the parsimonious and peevish *A. glacialis*. But perhaps the comparison is severe.

*Androsace carnea*, which you will find peering pinkly among the grass round the foot of the rocks, is of a happier nature ; it is a narrow-leaved little clump of rosettes, rather *chétif* in appearance, which sends up, on stems that may be almost non-existent, and are seldom as much as six inches high, clusters of dainty little rosy Primula flowers, gathered in a lax head. And so at last, one drops down again into the domain of *Anemone alpina*, and through that zone again, to the richer meadow slopes below, where, on the brows, amid a dwarf fine scrub of *Rosa alpina, Anthericum Liliastrum* is coming into flower, and the big purple cups of *Anemone Halleri* passing towards seed. Water is flowing freely down in torrents from the melting snows ; just above the Pass itself there is even a little lake in a lap of the hills. Here all the banks are a mass of pansies and Pyrenaean buttercup. Islets and marge and rushy bogs are pink with *Primula farinosa* amid silver fluff of cotton-grass ; and at the end a level marsh of half a mile is solid with the bland citron of globe-flower, interwoven with the hot orange of marsh marigold ; composing together one sheet of colour, where not another tone is visible. Yet in a fortnight, they will both be gone utterly, and that whole tract be a frothing snowfield of *Ranunculus aconitifolius*. So, in the end, one may well weary of seeing ; we wander back again, and over successive downs of different blossom descend once more through the roses upon the Hotel de la Poste from behind. And so vast are those successive slopes that one has climbed to the *arête* of the Nunda, that though the hill at the back of the hotel looks nothing more than an insignificant hummock at first sight, one understands its size when one sees that a man half-way up it is nothing but an inconsiderable black speck, like a flea on the Marble Arch.

# CHAPTER III

### A LITTLE LATER

I HAD nearly a week amid the glories of the early alpine flora. But, in spite of my toilings on the stone-slopes under the Punta Roncia, I saw clearly that I had come far too soon for any profitable work among the high alpines. It was obvious that I must return in another three weeks or so. Also I was filled with curiosity to see what new profusion of beauty there might be at the end of July in the hay-meadows now so densely brilliant with alpine Anemones, Gentians, and all the spring treasures. However, my plans did not admit of any such return, and therefore I merely marked it down in my mind as one of the many million things which I hope to do some-day, if two or three million other things do not prevent me. But one plant there was that I felt I must attempt before leaving the Mont Cenis, despite the fact that it was the one plant most certain of all to be still under snow. But when you have learned of a sure and safe station for *Eritrichium nanum* it is not a few miles of snow that will deter the earnest-hearted.

I had had some difficulty in learning of this station, for the man who knew it refused to divulge the exact whereabouts. However, I merely had to apply to an even higher authority, and received all the information I wanted by return of post. In point of fact I do not think

my original non-informant need have been quite so scrupu-
lous, for really, Eritrichium, gorgeous and difficult and
local, is still extremely abundant where it does occur ;
if all the collectors in all the world with all their sacks,
combined to toil at the task for months and years, I do
not believe that they could strip even one range of the
alps of its Eritrichium. And that a fellow-collector
should refuse information seemed doubly hard. If wolf
is going to conceal the whereabouts of the sheep from
brother-wolf, wherewithal shall the wretched wolves be
fed ? However it made very little matter, as I say ; for
I easily got my information after all, and set out. I had
to set out, although the weather was ominous. For it was
my last day on the Mont Cenis ; away in the South the
Cottian Alps were clamouring for my coming. Accordingly I started through the greyness, unheeding the
warnings poured forth upon me by the landlord.

The way lay first down to the shores of the Lake, round
its upper end, and so along that gentle valley that I showed
you from the Nunda, flowing down from the Pass of the
Little Mont Cenis. (Be at peace, Mr. Tuckett-Brown,
if ever you read this passage ; I will not divulge the
dwelling of your *protégé*, even though I indicate some of
the steps on the way to it). The flowery meadows round
the lake are humped into banks and hollows of long lush
grass, among which *Anemone alpina* grows in bushes
and bowers. Innumerable other splendours there are
too, and the future hayfields are now a mosaic of colour
everywhere. And one also crosses wide stretches of
marsh-land round the north of the lake, where, over the

flat expanses, *Primula farinosa* lies like a rosy cloud. Among it there are wonderful forms of *Orchis latifolia*, —bronzy-leaved spotted-dogs far more darkly and densely spotted than any one sees at home. They are quite exotic in effect. One thinks of some Goodyera under a bell-glass in the stove. Then the path goes mounting again towards the broad valley up which our road is to lie.

Very gentle and pleasant is the walk, meandering mildly among meadows all a tapestry of flowers. There is one point on which I was anxious to satisfy myself. From the ridge of the Nunda we had commanded a complete view of this whole valley, and had been much struck by a certain broad field or plain half way up it. For this was a mere mass of white, as seen from the Nunda four or five miles away. Yet it was obvious that the whiteness could not be that of snow ; we puzzled over the problem, and argued. My friends' conclusion had been that lime or something must have been heavily laid down ; for my own part I hardly dared trust my own belief that the colour belonged to some abundant plant. Such profuseness was almost inconceivable. How can any flower produce, from four miles away, the effect of a sheet of white ? So that I drew near that plain in such anxiety, that day, that I had hardly eyes for the innumerable Gentians, Crocuses, Anemones, Androsaces with which the road is bordered, and which a week on the Mont Cenis had taught me to regard as quite common-place affairs. At last I reached it ; and that sheet of white was one unbroken mass of *Ranunculus pyrenaeus*. I had thought it was; I had never had the effrontery to proclaim my thought, even to myself. Yet there that wonderful buttercup stretched away across the levels, making the whole field look as if some giant housewife had stretched out one of her sheets to dry there.

But by this time the rain was driving down in steady lances, straight and solid as those in the Surrender of Breda. With bent head, like the buttercups, I hurried on my way, cursing my folly in having started, but resolute against the weakness of turning back. In a little I met the reward of bluffing the weather, for the rain rather grudgingly left off, and the day, though far from fine, began to be a trifle less obstinately odious. So I reached the Little Mont Cenis, and found more *Ranunculus rutaefolius* growing in the grass. And here, too, I found a new plant, and one of the first importance. For all this while I had been puzzling over the absence of Primulas. Of course *P. farinosa* is the invariable common-place of the alpine marshes throughout the ranges, but at this height, on them all, in every part, you usually find some other Primula in possession of the rocks and moorland. In the south it is *spectabilis* or *glaucescens*, in the Engadine *integrifolia*, in the Oberland that ordinary *viscosa* whose name has now been transferred back again to *latifolia*, leaving it as mere *hirsuta*.

And yet here, on the Mont Cenis, at the typical upper alpine level, and amid an unequalled display of the typical upper alpine flora, Primula stood so far entirely unrepresented. Then, just ahead of me, a bluff of rock blushed crimson, I ran towards it; *Primula pedemontana*. And

*P. pedemontana*, besides being a plant of very limited distribution, is one of remarkable beauty, too. It belongs regularly to that race of Alp-possessing Primulas which I was missing, filling the place of *hirsuta*, and in many ways not unlike it—though taller. There are several large flowers to the head, sometimes even ten or more, and these are of a brilliant gentle rose, with a clear white eye. The colour, of course, varies a great deal, and some of the special forms I collected that day were of a rich brilliancy. It now grows everywhere, from this point onwards, in the long cliffs and ledges of the rock, under the scrub that hangs here and there from the cliff-faces, and in the tussocky turf of the open moorland itself. Finally, if ever you are lucky enough to meet with *P. pedemontana*, you can always recognize it at a glance among its kindred. For the dark and dull green foliage, entire, or rarely toothed in regular little round jags, green and glabrous in effect, is edged with a definite hem of red-brown fur. This fine russet *bordering* (the felt covers, more scantily, the whole plant, stem and all) marks out *P. pedemontana* with absolute certainty from its brothers in the section—*P. cottia, P. hirsuta, P. villosa, P. oenensis* who never have this special contrast so conspicuously developed. The species is restricted to these Alps, and only a little further south, in the Cottians, is replaced by the even rarer *Primula cottia*.

At this point I lost my way. And perhaps it is better that you should lose it too. I wandered about for a long time amid tumbled boulders and a granitic chaos only lighted by the bunches of *Primula pedemontana* that glowed at me from the crannies. They had need to, too ; for the mist came down in a shroud of darkness, and had it not been for their illumination I might have foundered in the gloom. So ultimately I strayed upon the track again, and will leave you to discover whether it leads north, south, east or west, towards the Kirschenjoch where Eritrichium lives. In a little while the rain descended anew with steady passion, despite the fact that the wind was keen and fierce as a razor. In blank white night I hurried on, seeing nothing, and terrified at the fact that already broad patches of half-molten snow were beginning to block the path. I saw my prospects of reaching the pass reduced to a minimum. And of course this whole expedition was a silly affair. It is not at the end of June that you can attempt one of the high passes with the certainty of pleasure, or, indeed with any certainty at all except that of much snow and no plants. However, to the end of life one will always put one's trust in chance, and go on believing against all sense that one's own case will prove the unique exception to an unquestioned rule.

I plodded along, in an anguish that beggars words. There were no plants now, and nothing was visible but the swirling obscurities of the mist. Underground there was either snow or sodden black moorland from which the snow had only just receded. The rain had not quite decided in its mind whether it was going to be sleet or not ; and made up for the uncertainty by an added ferocity (like a bad-tempered person in a puzzle). I slipped and slithered blindly along through slush and over glazed wet rocks. Then there was a roar of waters in my ears; the veil of the cloud was torn; and I saw very far below me to my right the valley of a great river mapped out, and before me, very high up, the Kirschenjoch, clear against the sky behind, one smooth slope of snow, peppered here and there with boulders that looked black against the whiteness. The whole exploit was obviously hopeless; however, having come so far already I thought I might as well go on as much further as I could possibly get, on the faint millionth chance of finding something; instead of returning tame and inglorious back again, like the King of France and all his men. And so mercifully had the track mounted, by slow degrees, that it was not as if there were any question of arduous climbing. The way up to the Kirschenjoch was nothing but one gentle incline, whether over snow or not. Therefore I determined to continue, though the way was yet far. For now the weather seemed to lift a little, and I was encouraged by being allowed to resume connection with the lost world of visible things.

Away up in front of me stretched the glen, half-filled with snow, which became an unbroken sheet on the pass. On either side, in gaunt nakedness rose tumbled granitic slopes of black ruin. Down their dark cliffs little streams came roaring, and a roaring river now filled the glen where I was walking. I came at length upon some châlets, and then on the inevitable alpine plain where the cattle come and live in summer, while their attendants enjoy a *villegiatura* in the huts. No cows as yet, of course, nor people; the hovels might have been as long deserted as the horseshoe forts on Ingleborough.

The plain was blank and lifeless at first glance, until one saw that its whole expanse was covered with the Snow Crocus piercing universally amid red or yellow-green grass-spears just beginning to push ; but on such a day they were incapable of making any show. The Pyrenaean Buttercup lurked far down in the stage of tight purple bud ; one felt appalled at the exquisite temerity of a thing so frail as the Crocus, in thus daring to intrude on so in-hospitable a world. And the Primula was again hanging out in crimson rockets on the cliffs, so that one's way was cheered.

But now the snow became more insistent, covering more and more of the path, until, after leaving the plain, it very soon became a matter of all snow and no path. And I detest walking alone over snow. In company, lions are not more brazen than I on a snow-slope ; but, when crushed by the awful solitude of the mountains, I become the prey of ghostly terrors, and begin to suspect the snow of hiding from me the most dire surprises. Very delicately do I toddle over the plainest and most ordinary snow-beds, if I am by myself; with an idea that if I sneeze or cough unadvisedly they will probably open and let me through. So slowly did I now advance that it seems as if my progress must have taken hours. At last I could bear no more, and decided to exorcise my fears with food. Accordingly under some vast rocks, that sheltered me from the knife-edge of the wind, I rested awhile, and ate ; then, restored in courage, trumpeting defiance to the high hills and all the powers of the air, I tramped upon my way again. And now there was nothing

anywhere but snow; it was clear imbecility to expect
any plants, had it not been that from the virgin slope
emerged here and there those black boulders.  On these
I had already seen a few frost-bitten plants ;  and, knowing
the ways of Eritrichium, thought that if I could once
attain its level, it should go  hard with me but I might
perhaps find it colonizing one of these granite blocks.

I was now actually at the foot of the incline that led
up to what I felt must be the Pass itself.  Though I was a
little puzzled, for somewhere about here was due, by all
accounts, the Lago Fresco, a considerable piece of water.
Yet no considerable piece of water could I anywhere
discern, nor any inconsiderable one either.  It was one
unbroken whiteness ;  I was driven back on the conclusion
that the Lago Fresco must be lying *perdu* beneath a
solid sheet of ice, masked by snow.  And yet this seemed
odd, for so large a piece of water ;  nor, the slope being
so smooth and gentle and unbroken in its incline, did
I see any place flat enough for me to suppose that any
piece of water, big or little, could be hiding there.  So
I insisted on dismissing the problem, and told myself
I felt certain that I was on the final acclivity of the Pass.
In the meantime the clouds had again descended, the
wind was blowing more pitilessly than ever down the
snowy wastes of the Kirschenjoch, and the rain came
flogging through and through my bones.  In vain I
scanned those hideous boulders ;  nothing in them could
I see of any consequence.—*Primula marginata* was there,
indeed, looking as withered as I was feeling myself ;  but
it was a measled, half dead piece I found, hardly beginning

to recover from winter ; and otherwise there was nothing.
I cursed my folly in the whole expedition, and swore that
when I had reached a group of three big blocks about
ten yards further on I would positively not go one step
beyond them, whether I found them barren or no.
Through the blizzard I drearily toiled towards them.
Two of them were like frozen versions of Mrs. Hubbard's
cupboard. But the third was full of *Eritrichium nanum*.

Full—brimming, crowded with cosy clusters of
Eritrichium. I could hardly dare believe my eyes ; but
there is never any mistaking those silken rosettes of silver
fluff. It was Eritrichium this, all right, although it was only
just beginning to stir from its long sleep, and the sleet
stood out in dense jewel-work of diamond over its furry
cushions. And for a further tempering of the wind to
the shorn lamb (and some tempering of the wind was
necessary : I never felt so naked in my life, even the
flesh seemed to have been stripped from my bare bones,
and so did the black blasts blow through and through
me), that rock was rotten with ruin. I could easily lift
it away piecemeal in slabs, and quarry forth perfect plants
with two or three levering movements of the trowel,
and then a long pull that bodily removed a flake as big
as a paving stone. By this time I was so cold that sensation had wholly fled from my fingers, and to work
with them was like using so many chunks of wood.
However, with these lifeless implements I toiled and
tugged until I had a decent sufficiency of plants, without
sacrilegiously denuding that boulder. But, by the time
I had done with it, the unfortunate rock was certainly

in a sad state of *déshabille*. For I had pulled most
of it to pieces as if it had been so many layers of the
confection which is called Genoese Pastry, for the reason
that it is probably not Genoese, and certainly not pastry.
So then, almost sightless with cold, without feeling,
chattering in all my bones like castanets, and with the
wind going through my brain in so many blasts of aching
ice, I had to squat down and try to dry those wretched
fluffy plants, before I could dare to pack them in the tin.

However, the task was achieved at last: I turned and
ran, disregarding the surreptitious perils of the snow.
But at one point I had to make another stop.   For under
a boulder I suddenly saw something that gleamed like
living rubies in the greyness.  Through rain and storm, on
the black ground, against an iron background of rock,
*Saxifraga retusa* lay glowing like a dropped necklace of
red jewels.   And, often as I saw it later, throughout my
pilgrimage, and heartily as I worship it whenever I
do see it, I don't think I have ever more devotedly adored
it than at that grim moment, when I could have cried aloud
against the stars for causing me to stop in that Hell of
cold another instant.   It was a positive agony to have
to wait and quarry out those plants from the frozen earth ;
and a needless agony too, for, had I known it, *Saxifraga
retusa* was, as I say, to recur to me again and again in my
wanderings.   However, I could not know that, and bitter
experience has taught me that if ever you do omit to secure
a rare plant when you see it, you will never have a chance
of getting it again.

*Saxifraga retusa*, sweetest of its section, is, in habit,

like a wee *oppositifolia*, creeping flat along the ground in dense matted masses of shoots among the very highest alpine turf, packed close with tiny, leathery pairs of opposite leaves, of a deep and glossy green, and stems that stand erect three inches or so, carrying a head of small flowers, rather ragged in their petals, so that the effect produced is of a short and fluffy spike. The petals are of a bright rose ; stamens and other appurtenances of a truer crimson, so that the whole has a rich and startling brilliancy of effect. Add to this, that, against all reasonable expectations, *retusa* is much easier to deal with in ordinary cultivation than any other of its sections ; it is even better to grow (and even in my garden), than *oppositifolia* itself, fresh-gathered on Ingleborough. For it is a plant without fads, rooting in a solid clod, not asking for crevices or poor soil or contraptions, but perfectly happy running about in any cool rich ground, not parched or arid. It is a species of the Southern and the Western Alps, ranging from the Graians down through the Cottians, and along the high granitic ridges of the Maritimes. Although, with me, it makes no sort of fuss about soil, it appears by nature, so far as I have seen, only to tolerate the granite formations.

After this diversion, as the rain was growing steadier and the wind more bitter, I resolved that I would stop but once or twice again. And, in each case, perforce, to collect *Primula pedemontana*. For, considering the abundance of this, I had postponed my delvings among it till the return journey. Accordingly I sat for half an hour on a hummock which was red with it, and faithfully wrought at my task ; then continued again, collecting here and there, from ledge or boulder, always, I hope, with that respectful reasonableness and moderation which befits a collector. So at last, all was over, and I could set myself to a steady homeward swing. By this time it was pouring with a straight, passionless precision that meant uninterrupted business. As I strode homewards, looking neither to the right hand nor to the left, the rods of the rain smote down upon me densely, as if trying to punish me for the triumph I had achieved in their despite. It was but little I cared ; never in my life have I been colder or wetter ; but my spirits were warm as toast, and the powder in my heart was dry. I mocked at the storm-dragons, and towards the grey gloaming crawled back again up the steep ascent that leads to the Hotel de la Poste. I had to wring myself like a sponge on the doorstep ; the landlord was horrified at my condition, though rejoiced to hear I had discovered Eritrichium. I went at once to bed, and spent the next morning packing the " Roi des Alpes " amid sunshine of almost embittering brilliancy. In the afternoon I made my final farewell to the Mont Cenis, and went down to Susa, on my way to the Cottians.

" Final farewells," thought I.

But later on a friend came out to join me, and, after our explorations in the Maritimes, he declared himself so fired by my account of the Mont Cenis, that he insisted on going there immediately. This chimed exactly with my own desire to see the later summer Flora there ; so I made a point of discovering that we had time, and we duly returned to the Hotel de la Poste in the last days of July. The whole scene was changed beyond recognition ; Anemones and Buttercups had " hopped the twig of this life, as drummers, emperors, dustmen and generals all must "; cows had come up to the Alpine lawns and eaten them flat, until there was no longer a sign anywhere of Gentian or Pansy, nothing but short cropped grass over the downs and hillocks. Yet the unchanging miracle continued, and though all the actors were changed, the scene was no less gorgeously crowded than our own scene will continue when our own present " persona " has made its exit.

In the lush herbage of the hayfields around, where Anemones had been, there were now Campanulas in swathes and sheaves, *linifolia* like a giant violet Harebell, and *rhomboidalis* in luxuriant bending jungles, colouring all the fields from miles away. Among them stand up the golden suns of Arnica and Doronicum ; *Aster alpinus* scatters its purple cartwheels among the crimson cart-wheels of *Dianthus neglectus* wherever the grass is shorter, and *Linum alpinum* sheds over them the moonlight of its pale-blue stars. The flat fields to the South are a scarlet sea of Sainfoin ; on the northerly stone-dumps the white flowers of *Geranium rivulare* rise above bending pink radiations of *Dianthus sylvestris* ; and *Lilium martagon*, up or down, on slope or hollow, rings its ruddy carillon everywhere over the fields, as if in blessing ; and, on the slopes at the upper end of the Lake, which a month before had been all white buttercup and Alpine Anemone, there now lies an even denser snowdrift of *Anthericum*

*Liliastrum*, interspersed with the golden fluff of stalwart Hugueninia, and the cream and lilac fluff of *Thalictrum aquilegiaefolium*.

And on some of the slopes, even, the great snow-chalices of the Alpine Anemone are still lingering amid the lilies, rosier, and the harebells, bluer, than any I have seen anywhere else before or since. Though all the older glories of June are gone, too, from the grassy hummocks, the undergrowth of the herbage there also is now dazzling, with violet Polygala this time, and Alpine Clover ; and, instead of *Gentiana verna* we have *bavarica* in its sapphire splendour in the marshes by the lake, among a million stalwart spires of those *Orchis latifolia* whose spotted-dog leaves had been so impressive during the hey-day of *Primula farinosa*, now going back to rest.

Among the quartzy hollows in front of the Hotel the Dryas is a sheeted galaxy, the most glad-hearted and charming of plants ; over the ridges are all sorts of brilliant Onobrychis and Vetch and Oxytropis, with here and there a spark of *Dianthus neglectus*. *Campanula pusilla* occupies every slope of shingle, and hangs its showers of little blue-bells over the steep roadside banks, among Thymes and pink tapestries of *Saponaria ocymoeides* and wide purple sheets of the Alpine Calamint. Down in the ghylls *Senecio Doronicum* is in bloom ; and giving the lie to all I have said about it. For, in the Oberland it is an austere, refined and glorious plant. But here the foliage is laxer and coarser and not nearly so well-bred ; the whole plant has become a vulgarian, and the more abundant flowers are fat, and of an undistinguished yellow

no better than that of Arnica.  I dare not yet cope with
this question of *Senecio Doronicum* ; I have now seen so
many forms.  But not one of them could ever be called
precisely the same as the bald and weed-like plant which
bears the name of *Senecio Doronicum* in gardens, and
has much the same habit and flower as this Mont Cenis
form ; but the Mont Cenis plant, however coarse, grows
only in big clumps, and never runs about all over the
place, after the habit of the so-called garden *S. Doronicum*.
In the hollows, too, Hugueninia is now at its best, and very
beautiful.  It is a Crucifer, but attempts, with success,
to burke the damning fact.  It grows three or four feet
high ; its stems are clothed with magnificent ferny
foliage, its flowers are very small, but carried so densely
and in such splendid wide bunches that when they are
in full blow the effect is that of a rich broad mass of
soft gold.  It seems a lavish thriver, and I hope may
prove so in my garden, into which it had never before
entered, as I have a well-grounded distrust of *Cruciferae*,
especially when they grow large and stalwart.

But there are two new actors on the stage that require
special attention now.  The one is *Aquilegia alpina*,
which, down by the wooded southern end of the lake,
is now a glory of blue over the copsy ledges, and even in
and out among the meadow-flowers themselves.  Never yet
have I seen it so abundant ; but I could not resist a qualm
as to its form.  Memory is proverbially an excitable
thing ; and I have already tried to make all discount
mine in particular.  Yet I cannot but feel that the rarer
*A. alpina* of the Bernese Oberland and the Valais is a

trifle larger in flower, and solider in substance, and
more brilliant in the tone of its blue. This may be mere
imagination. Yet I saw the plant again in the Maritime
Alps ; and there it seemed to be exactly what I remembered the Oberland and Valaisanne plants to have
been ; whereas these blossoms on the Mont Cenis, though
they were of a beauty that impoverishes ordinary language, were yet rather floppy in texture, and, to *my* fancy,
just perhaps an eighth of a semi-tone flat in their blue.
However this may be, the whole stock of my collected
plants were brought from the Mont Cenis, so that I may
as well go on hoping for the best.

The other new actor is a greater rarity than the
Columbine. Down in certain shady gullies, close to
where the Columbine lives, but in places more densely
shady and filled with brushwood, may now be seen *Cortusa
Matthioli.* When I was here first the glen was half-filled
with snow, the alders were bare and black, and the
scene, in its wintry desolation, carried me straight away
back to the slopes of Nantai-san in March. It was hard
at first, then, to discover the fat green buds of Cortusa's
foliage, beginning to break up through the rich soil of
the copse. *Soldanella montana* was flickering its lovely
big bells in the dusk of the dark alders, but other sign
of life there was none, and the alders themselves made a
dingy tangle against the snow that lay grimy round their
innumerable stems. Now it has changed, and the wood
grown impenetrable with green lush life. *Cortusa* has
taken complete possession. Up and down among the
bushes (and nowhere else) are whole drifts of its large

soft leaves, like those of the wood Sanicle, but lax in their texture, and downy, and altogether reminiscent of the new *Primula Veitchi*, which, in spite of all my efforts I really do dislike. Nor are the flowers so wholly dissimilar, for *Cortusa* is a Primula in everything but name.

But Cortusa is far daintier and more lovable than the shrill and pushing *Primula Veitchi*, whose magenta squalls so deafened me, and made my garden so uninhabitable, that at last I carried the whole plant away on a trowel, as one carries a slug or other displeasant object, and plopped it out in the wild wood above Alice's Garden, there to thrive or not as it thought good ; and, anyhow, keep its squarkings to itself. *Cortusa Matthioli* carries, on a stem of eight inches or more, a bunch of blossoms, thin-stemmed, that hang down in the graceful way of a *Dodecatheon*, and give something of a *Dodecatheon's* effect. And true it is to say that they have a tinge of magenta ; but, please sir, it is a very little one, not clamorous or offensive. And, after all, everything depends on the way you wear your magenta, just as everything depends upon the way you wear your virtue. You may carry either with a modesty which disarms criticism ; or you may so placard and proclaim them that you become a loathing and a horror to all right-minded persons. And the Cortusa is mild and discreet ; it ends by being a gracious little plant, only asking of you to give it some shady copsy corner out of the way, where it will grow happily and strong among the other woodland plants, in the loose spongy decay of a century's dead leaves.

There remained after this, the high alpines and

*Eritrichium* for us to see. Accordingly we set off one day
for the Clear Lake beneath the Punta Roncia, which, on
my last visit, had been entirely under snow. The alps,
as we went, were now almost naked of flowers; tawny
cows were busy transforming them into milk. Here and
there, as one got higher, *Anemone vernalis* was passing
from its exquisite prime into its disreputable and dishonoured old age. I love the Lady of the Snow, and
have praised her with a warmth that I have been told is
in excess of her deserts. Yet her stemless great pearly
cups, all filmed outside with a silk of violet and golden-
russet iridescence, are lovely in the extreme when you
see them on the hills, although in gardens their size
diminishes, and their clear rainbow-splendours are
dimmed to something not far removed from dinginess.
But I do confess that I wish *Anemone vernalis* would
condescend to grow old with the self-confident frankness
of its sisters, instead of maintaining faded airs and
graces long after their time is over. Who was the woman
in " Denise "—Madame de Thauzette, of course—who
proposed to grow old beautifully, *comme les femmes du
dixhuitième siècle*. Well, that lesson has been laid
to heart by most of the alpine Anemones; they candidly
drop one set of beauties and adopt another no less
effective. But, at the time when *A. alpina* and *A.
Halleri* are magnificent towzle-heads of silver fluff,
*A. vernalis* is still trying to retain her youthful decora-
tions; and ends by looking like a raddled unreverend
dowager in a chestnut wig. She is the Mrs. Skewton of
the mountains.

When you reach the upper stone-slopes the flowers begin again. Here, where there was snow and little else before, it is still too early for the cows, therefore Primulas and Gentians have moved up here, and are as wonderful as they used to be down by the hotel in June. But there are richer marvels now to claim our attention, for all about among the stones are the narrow-leaved silky-grey tufts of *Campanula Allioni*, lavish of their purple flowers, like little Canterbury Bells, scattered close over the surface of the widely ramifying plant. But, shall I dare to confess it, I was a trifle disappointed with *Campanula Allioni* as seen on the Mont Cenis. It is a most august alpine, and I would not for the world say anything against its character " which well I know, afore her back or anywhere, is not to be impeaged " ; its flowers here *are* like Canterbury Bells, it is true : but like such very little Canterbury Bells—like such wizened parsimonious little Canterbury Bells.

And I do know forms, and I *have* seen forms, with bells of twice the size, and of the most fulminating imperial purple. Not to compare with those are these, lovely though they be in the contrast of their vinous-lilac with the greyish effect of the rosettes from which they spring. Only one special form did I find on the Mont Cenis, and this had flowers a good deal larger than usual, and of a soft pale lavender. I thought it very beautiful, and was pleased that my companion was by that time too tired of collecting *Allioni* to care for more than a few odds and ends of it. For *Campanula Allioni* is most vexing to collect ; it has a vast and trunk-like tap-root, and then a wide ramifying system of stolons, which are all supposed to die without benefit of clergy unless you manage to get the entire root complete. Of course this isn't true. Of course every stolon will make a plant if properly and carefully struck. But still one naturally desires to get as much of the tuft as one can. And the work is both tiring and disappointing, so vast is the root-stock of the Campanula, and through such rocky and impracticable ground do its lateral offshoots meander.

Yet a little above this we found, in a dry river-bed, our only flowering clumps of *Campanula cenisia*. For in the high stone slopes where it abounds we discovered, to our disappointment, that not even yet on the 31st of July, were the buds beginning to open. However, up above we got the plants, and lower down we saw the flowers. What more could heart of man desire? So I must place on record while the memory is in fresh flower, and before it has run too richly to seed, the full beauty of this little rare alpine Campanula, which has not always met with the praise that it deserves. It forms, if it can, a dense, wide, flat tuffet, made up of obtusely-oval, fringed leaves, of a clear bright green, arranged in neat rosettes. There is a tap-root, as in *Allioni*, but much slighter and more get-at-able. From the neck it emits lateral stolons, which ultimately strike out more or less independently for themselves ; and these often cover quite a large tract of ground, coming up unexpectedly among stones half a yard away from the main plant. For this reason the collector aims at finding

compact small clumps, growing in a bunch. Otherwise
the fine white threads of its rootage get tangled up, and
not the most dexterous comb in the world could get them
straight again. Close on the foliage, and carried each by
itself on a very short stem, appear the flowers in August,
so thickly produced as to hide the tuft. These flowers,
though small by comparison with those of *Allioni*, are
much larger than *Allioni's* by comparison with the
plant that bears them. They are rather shallow bells,
very deeply cleft into five segments, and their colour is
like that of no other alpine Campanula—a clear, pale,
rather hard blue, exquisitely brilliant, but softened
with a tinge of grey. They look straight up into the eye
of day, and a mass of them in full bloom is a thing to
remember. You can see no leaves. Though I have
often found *Campanula cenisia*, and though I had never
seen *Allioni* till this season, *cenisia* is really, I think, the
rarer of the two. *Allioni* has a smaller distribution, but
is found very abundantly within these limits : *cenisia*
has a wider range, but is a good deal more local. Through
all the Graian, Cottian and Maritime Alps *Allioni* abounds
on the granitic formations ; *cenisia* I have collected only
in the Bernese Oberland ; above Arolla (very sparingly),
and abundantly on the Mont Cenis, from which it takes
its name.

In cultivation, though *cenisia* seems also to prefer the
mica-schists and granitic formations, I have always
hitherto had more, and easier, success with this species
than with *Allioni*. However, both of them thrive very
freely now in my moraines, and indeed no other culture is

possible for *cenisia*, which is never found outside the highest shingles, whereas *Allioni*, which also abounds there, descends a great deal lower, and luxuriates in any rough slope, even in ordinary stony ground among grass on broken banks. As for *cenisia*, the frequency with which the collector is helped to get it up by finding it growing sandwiched between two flat slabs of stone, buried deep in the bank at an obtuse angle, indicates that by some such contrivance we could make it even more happy in our moraine-gardens than it is at present ; if need were.

Now, from these lower stone-slopes one scrambles up and up, over rough ground that later is one wide carpet of the Flannel-flower. But I should think myself dishonoured if I collected plants of Edelweiss. The thing is too common, and too facile, and too pretentious. Let it be. The plant is a snob. It pretends to be a high alpine, but the real high alpines will have none of it. It has to grow by itself in inferior places, too bone-dry for any well-bred people of the hills to condescend upon. Here the alien pretender prospers. There let it remain. I go upwards towards the peaks. And, on the next stone-slope begins another beauty which draws its name from the Mont Cenis. For, not only does one trample *Campanula Allioni* at every step, and *Campanula cenisia* fifty feet higher as well, but also the grey stones are lighted with the purple stars of *Viola cenisia*.

*Viola cenisia* is a true Pansy, and even more beautiful than *Viola calcarata*. It is a rare alpine of the western ranges, exclusively a moraine plant, occurring only at great elevations. I have seen it here and in the Oberland,

and I have always hitherto found it extremely difficult to cultivate, or even to collect. It runs about with exactly the same sort of root system as *Campanula cenisia*, sending up, more sparsely, its frail clusters of leaves here and there among the shingle. These leaves are narrowish, rolled backwards, slightly waved at their edges, clothed in a faint fine down that gives them a curious metallic tone of colour like iron. The abundant flowers are strangely beautiful, much rounder and more flattened in outline than those of *calcarata*, and in colour of a rich warm red lilac. But, what is more, they not only have a dear little eye of bright yellow, but on the lateral and lower petals there are usually a beard and whiskers, in one or two sharp lines of darkest purple, which give the flower an expression of waggish intelligence. So many of the Pansies have silly faces : the garden ones one often longs to slap, they look so stupid—like kitchen clocks ; even *Viola calcarata* has a face which is rather good than clever. But both *cenisia* and *valderia* are as sharp as needles. You can see they have a sense of humour.

After this, one has to clamber up and up, over stone-slopes more and more uncompromisingly naked and stony. Here, just passing over into seed, is my beloved *Iberidella rotundifolia*, which I would rather forfeit all subsequent editions of this work than call too often by the correct and hideous name of *Thlaspi* which it shares with so many dowdy little weeds. Here, too, in wide cushions of pale lilac, is that other dainty Crucifer, *Petrocallis pyrenaica*, now in such fulness of flower that one can no longer see the dense mats of fine fringy rosettelings, for the galaxy of pinky fragrant stars that lie so close upon them. Thank goodness, though *Petrocallis* grows here so freely on granitic stone-slopes, it is quite indifferent to soil, and thrives as heartily with me in open ground or in limestone moraine. Then there occurs *Ranunculus glacialis*, not as fine or brilliant here as I have seen it in the damper places where it is most usual ; and *Anemone baldensis*, throwing up its white Margueriteblossoms over the banks of detritus. And a brute to collect is *Anemone baldensis*, forming ramifying tangles of black woody fibres that never seem to stop long enough in one place to begin making anything that any decent plant would consider to be a root. And a brute, also, if I am to speak true words, have I always had reason to consider *Anemone baldensis* in cultivation. It is a very lovely plant, widely distributed in the stony region of the high Alps, and, to all appearances, of a most vigorous and thriving habit, that ought to make it prosper easily under any reasonable conditions. On the contrary, it is a real mimp, or I have found it so ; after innumerable experiments I have to chronicle precisely the same number of failures. *Anemone baldensis* has proved a great deal more impracticable with me than very many other high alpines of a far more limited distribution, and a far more miffy habit. And now that I have written this, probably next season will show me waving jungles of *A. baldensis* in some hopeless corner of my garden, where a few stray pieces may have been poked in despair, and forgotten.

We are on the very topmost of the ridges : before us a long snow-slope sweeps down to a gully of naked shingle.

And nowhere yet is there any sign of the Clear Lake. However, if one turns to look back, one loses thought of the Clear Lake in contemplating the manifold kingdoms of the earth unfolded to us from this high place. For in the process of climbing and collecting we have mounted very far indeed by now. Undiscoverable beneath us lie the lower Alps and the Lake of the Mont Cenis. One looks even over the mountain range that bars the Val d'Ambin, beyond the Little Mont Cenis, out and out into the tumbled ocean of the Dauphiné Alps. Our day was one of superb softnesses and colours ; pearly clouds and gentle iridescent distances. The remote snow was creamy and diaphanous, shadows came and went across the world, and the stretches of sky were serenely blue. The view was framed on the right by the peaks immediately above the Mont Cenis Lake, and on the left by the needles of the Dents d'Ambin. Beyond these we looked into the shimmering haze that tossed itself into the ripples and sunlit crests of Dauphiné. And full in the middle of the picture, very remote and clear, rose the three great peaks of the Aiguilles d'Arve.

The whole air was full of a majestic peace, leisurely and tranquil, warm with the little breezes of summer among the high hills. Clouds, white and innocuous, now and then came curling over the foreground of the picture, obliterating all the low-lands. Now and then their films would rise to where we were, close round the base of the huge red precipice, eddy about it gently upward, until, like a mist of oblivion, they caused the whole solid world to grow transparent and dissolve through ghostliness into nonentity ; then, in a little, russet shadows would pierce the greyness, ebb and flow as the vapours shifted ; gradually widen and grow into hard glimpses of precipice, until at length the veil would all ravel slowly and part again, floating away to nothingness above and below in wrack and wreath of vapour.   And always the vast sunlight slumbered over the earth : through thinning gauzes which turned it to silver, the constant illumination could still be felt.   Then silver dusk would become golden afternoon once more.   The guessed glory was revealed, and the Aiguilles d'Arve seemed tranquilly to glow and glitter with life in the farthest distances.   And, all down the long, long stony bank beneath us, *Gentiana brachyphylla* lay in tufts and sheets of heaven.

That last stretch of shingle proved very desolate. There seemed nothing there of any importance.   *Saxifraga biflora* is, to my thinking, a fat and coarse-looking affair compared with the other Porphyrions ;  I cannot collect it with any fervour ;  and it was not even abundant. As for *Iberidella*, which I wanted in seeding clumps, seeing that I seem at last to have awakened the world to its delicious beauty, it was sparse and rare.   Also I was vexed not to see the Lac Clair.   I had failed of the Lago Fresco ;  it was dreadful to suspect that all the lakes in the district were myths, like most of the mountains. And yet we had reached the last fold of the glen, immediately under the blank tremendous wall of the Punta Roncia.   In front on two sides of us were steep slopes of snow, and down behind lay only the way we had come, and the glory we had contemplated while munching our food. Therefore there was nowhere left for the Clear Lake to be. However I thought I might poke a little further ; my companion did not like the look of the snow-bank over which it was necessary to venture, and so I set off on my exploration alone, leaving him in the dismal hollow which was nothing but one smooth stretch of fine shingle, ruddy in colour and almost innocent of any signs of life. As for me, I crossed the stream on a bridge of snow, and ascended the slope until I reached its crest. And there, at my feet, down on its other side, lay the Clear Lake.

Such a clear lake ; a tiny little basin of water, like a silver shield forgotten up there among the hills. It was formed and held in by a ridge of grassy bank, and its upper shore was of rough stone, half hidden now by a snow-bed that ended only in the lake itself. Through the clean silence I could hear the tinkle of the melting drops as they fell into the pool. Now and then a crust of ice would break away and fall, with a small crystal sound. The Lake itself was clear as clear innocence, reflecting the sky in a pure sheet of blue. Amid the stones at its upper end *Iberidella* was unfolding its succulent bronzy-purple leaves, and, on the grassy bank, *Gentiana brachyphylla* was full of deep-blue pointed buds. On everything hung sunshine, and an infinite peace that seemed eternal. Across the ridge of grass one looked straight away to Dauphiné and the Aiguilles d'Arve. And here one felt the vast embalming stillness of the high mountains, that consecrated solitude which is more full of company than the densest crowd of men.

The only moments in life when one really ceases to be alone are these when one is engulfed in the loneliness of the hills; " their sound is but their stir; they speak in silences." And their talk is good.    Here one is a drop gone back to ocean ; freed from the illusion of a separate personality. The happiness of such rare moments is a thing imponderable and beyond expression.    And the comfort of these tiny instants is that they are really eternal.

Well, and why should I think it interests you to hear of what company I found by the Lac Clair ?    Very likely it doesn't.    Never mind ;    come along down again to the lower levels, and let us have another look at *Eritrichium*.    For my friend was determined to see " le Roi des Alpes," and pay his court :    so I again adventured the Kirschenjoch—though in circumstances very different, this second time.    For we had a day of unruffled beauty, warm and easy and charming.    It was as if the Kirschen joch were trying to be as pleasant as it had before been odious.    And then it was that I first realized the wondrous luck that had befallen me on that first visit.    For, having traversed the plain where the Crocuses had bloomed, and where we saw now no trace of them, their place being taken by myriads of *Ranunculus pyrenaeus*, with *Gentiana bavarica* down by the water-runnels, we came at length to my lunch-hut of boulders, and then to the slope leading up to what I had believed the Pass.    And yet there was no Lago Fresco.    There was no longer any snow, though, now, to hide it—only a roaring stream, coming over the rim of the pass :    and black rocks everywhere.    But still, and still——no

Lago Fresco, although there was nowhere left for it to hide.

So we went by on the other side from my Eritrichium-block, and continued up the slope, hoping to come on more, where one had been. And not another one did we find. All the blocks were as good as mine, and exactly like it, and populated with plants ; but in none of them was there a sign of *Eritrichium*. There was no more of the plant in all that district; through that blinding storm I had happened, by sheer fortune, to strike on the one boulder in which *Eritrichium* lived. I was the more devoutly thankful that I had left so much of it in situ ; and refrained from pointing out the favoured block to my companion. He, for his part, began to grow sceptical as we toiled up that arid slope. It was little that he had already been shown *Primula pedemontana*, long out of flower ; that he had seen *Ranunculus pyrenaeus* in its glory ; that we had even, down by the châlets, sighted pieces of the very rare *Saponaria lutea*.

But for this I cannot blame him. *Saponaria lutea*, low be it spoken, is a dowdy little thing. And, when you tell me that it is a most interesting speciality which is resticted to a few of these southerly granitic rocks, then I can only answer " so much the better." It is a low mat-plant, forming very wide masses, and producing cluster-heads of flowers which are of a pale straw-yellow, with blackish anthers. One of its most celebrated stations is the southern slope of the Mont Cenis : and I don't mean to damn the poor thing's character by saying it is positively ugly. No, by no means. Only that it

has not the remarkable beauty which one's dramatic
sense expects of a plant so rare.

At last we reached the summit of the slope. And the
whole mystery was explained. On the previous occasion
I had never reached the Pass at all. That slope which
I had taken for the Pass was merely a preliminary. *There*
lay the Pass itself, now, away in the distance, a mile
beyond, or rather less : and between us, large as life, lay
the mythical Lago Fresco, filling all the plain, until a
little hummock on its further side marked the summit of
the Col. And there, too, lo and behold, at once, in
splashes of lodged sky in the crevices of all the boulders
on our left, lay *Eritrichium nanum* in his fullest splendour.
He never wholly deserted us again, as we pursued our
way along the stony shores of the lake, where *Androsace
glacialis* was in such early stages, and so muddy with
silt, that one could hardly discern it ; and where, in the
wettest places, *Ranunculus glacialis* was just breaking
above ground in myriads upon myriads of dark metallic-
purple blobs among the rippling shingle. Nothing was
in flower here, even on the 1st of August. The Lake
itself was half-filled with ice, and on its shores *Gentiana
imbricata* (which is the high alpine form of *bavarica*,
even as *brachyphylla* is of *verna*, as I believe) was
barely beginning to send up its long buds above the tight
pale-green cushions of its fat and box-like foliage. But
at last the lake was ended, and we reached the rocks of
the actual pass. And here *Eritrichium* glowed and flashed
on the grey granite from every ledge and crevice. Nothing
else counted—not *Primula marginata* nor *P. viscosa*

(*latifolia*)—not even lovely *Saxifraga retusa* itself, that lay about in little mats of ruby crimson. One had hardly eyes for the view, and little more than a bare perception that even in the sunshine the wind was keen as a knife. One had to wander about from ridge to ridge, adoring the manifold wonders of the King of the Alps.

The King of the Alps, though, is a plant, I fancy, that varies. Always beautiful beyond the tongue or palette of man to express, he exists in some forms that are robuster than others. And a sure sign of this as I indicated earlier, is that his leaves should be solid in texture and oval-pointed in outline, as broad as you can get them. Plants of this complexion have a far stronger temperament than others, or at least such is my notion. I have collected *Eritrichium* on the Angstbord Pass, on the Kirschenjoch, on Piz Ot, on the Piz Languard, and the end of all my conclusions is that I have never again got a form quite so vigorous as that which hailed from the Angstbord Pass. From Languard, Ot, and the Kirschenjoch, the plants all have long thin leaves, very narrow ; and I suspect them, not I fear unjustly, of less robustness and resisting power than the more broad-leaved form from the Angstbord. But, of course, this may be merely my own vain imagination and fantasy, and the long-vanished Angstbord plants may have been just the same as all the others.

Let no one, anyhow, take me to mean that *Eritrichium* ever varies in its glory. The King of the Alps is always the King of the Alps, and his splendour varies by no jot or tittle, whether his leaves be broad and solid, or thin

and narrow.   There are few happinesses in  life like that
which comes from contemplating him on his native
grey rocks, in the regal splendour of his silver fur and
azure blossom.   So take we our  leave of him for this
book ;  we shall not see him again.   Come down to the
Mont Cenis once more, and prepare for departure : on
our homeward way discovering only an unusually
brilliant crimson form of *Saxifraga retusa*, and a *Primula
viscosa*, with flowers of a blue purple as imperial as those
of *P. glutinosa*.

Finally I want to remind you that this chapter is a
parenthesis and an anticipation.   This second visit to the
Mont Cenis comes only after our exhaustive wanderings
through the Cottians and Maritimes, on which your
patience, if it holds good, is now about to embark.

# CHAPTER IV.

## THE COTTIAN ALPS.

You are to forget all about *Eritrichium*, if you please, and see me departing for the first time from the Mont Cenis towards Turin. This was about the tenth day of July ; and, though I have given Mont Cenis the benefit of the doubt by classing it among the Graian Alps, I have to enter the caution here that it is on the last limit of the Graians, only separated from the Cottians by the deep gulf of the Dora Riparia.

From the plateau of the lake one descends in a series of hair-pin curves towards a lower level, and thence by further curves towards the valley of Susa, which lies so far below that it seems impossible that one should ever attain it. As one drops, the mountains on one's left, across the gulfs, tower higher and higher, as their full bulk is revealed. For the Mont Lamet and the Punta Roncia, which wall in the Clear Lake above the Mont Cenis, are but preparations and outlying bastions of the great mass which is Rochemelon, or Rocciamelone. The Rochemelon falls virtually sheer away to the Valley of Susa, and, therefore, so imposes its eleven thousand odd feet upon one's imagination that at one time it was held to be the King-peak of the range ; and, though it has now been deposed from that pre-eminence, it still remains dominant in one's memory.　So imposing is its revealed magnificence that one cannot wonder if people once over-estimated its actual height.　As advertisement is occasionally mistaken for merit among men, so conspicuousness is sometimes accepted as a substitute for genuine eminence among mountains ;　was not Ingleborough himself at one time taken for the highest hill in England, merely because he happens to be the most conspicuous and lonely ?

Rochemelon, rising straight heavenward as the road descends, gives you a synopsis of the alpine vegetation.　Above the valleys, long slopes and draperies of pine-forest.　Above these, châlets, and the beginning of the upper alpine pastures.　In sheets and folds of green, these now clothe the slopes and shoulders of the mass, and then the soil wears thin, herbage diminishes, ribs of rock begin to pierce.　A little higher yet, and there is only cliff and stone-slide ;　until the eye attains to the snow-clad crown of the peak itself.　For Rochemelon has, indeed, an unpromising name ;　one expects Melon Rock (though Melon Rock it isn't) to turn out an undistinguished affair, with a bulbous top.　But Rochemelon, in fact, towers in the most superb sweeps of severity towards a genuine peak.　It has the distinction, too, of being the first of all the high mountains to be ascended for its own sake.　It was a legendary seat of buried treasure in old days, and its name was Arx Romulea, from which most probably developed Rochemelon.　And a certain Bonifacius Rotarius, having escaped from Moslem hands in Palestine, made a vow to ascend the highest pinnacle of the Alps. Accordingly on the 1st of September, 1358, was made the earliest recorded mountain-climb for mountain-climbing's sake. Bonifacius achieved the Rochemelon ; a shrine was erected at its summit, and to this day it continues a place of pious pilgrimage.

But at last the stifling depths of Susa are attained. The change is so sudden, from the high air of the hills to the stuffiness of the valley, that whenever I have made the descent I have had both my ears filled with a painful drumming of blood. Susa is hot and insignificant ; with vineyards and a Roman archway. Here one takes train for Turin, and in a little while is passing under the needle-peak of San Michele, with a monastery on its point. San Michele is the watch-tower of the Alps over the vast sea of Lombardy. The train slides past it, out into the levels, and the mountains are left behind. In a little, though, one can look back and see the whole wall by which the plain of Lombardy is girt. Up in the distant north lies the main Pennine chain, and the grandeur of Monte Rosa. From this the Dora Baltea leads down into Lombardy. Then, behind us lies the Dora Riparia, down which we have come, coiling up among the Graians, with their long wall curving northward to join the Pennines. Across the south, very remote, runs a tumbling ruffle which is the range of the Maritimes ; and this, on the west, is connected with the Graians by the straight and not very interesting line of the Cottians. These form a serrated ripple of ridges, only broken by what seems to be a pointed cloud hovering above them in the middle. But that cloud is Monte Viso.

Well may this be called the Seen Mountain ; and well may it be the solitary peak which finds a place in the pages of the classics. (And how they must have disliked it, especially fat comfortable Horace !) For Monte Viso has, in extreme measure, that wild, proud austerity which the classics most dislike, and we most sedulously admire. I first saw it as the train flowed gently over the plain of Lombardy towards Turin. I looked back towards the Cottians, that lay low in a long purple line against a sunset that blazed with gold, and was filled with little clouds of rose and scarlet. Among these, then, and seeming more nearly akin to them than to the ragged ridges of earth below, there hovered that phantasmal pinnacle, far up in the west like a translucent amethyst. I knew that somewhere in that direction lived Monte Viso ; and that it was eminent. Yet the mountain was only a name for me, and for some time I could not believe that what I saw up there in the sky could really be mere soil and rock. However, as sunset drew on, the clouds floated away like glowing rags, and left the furnace of the west in unbroken clearness. And still that needle of amethyst hung solid in high heaven. I was forced to believe, and, in the believing, to recognize the Seen Mountain. Monte Viso belongs to the Cottian Alps much as Shakspere belonged to his family. They are a dim serration of dumps along his feet ; the peak rises so far above them that it seems unaware of their very existence. It will not even have art or part in the waters that spring from them. Alone, supreme, unnoticing, the Monte Viso dominates the whole Plain of Lombardy, and says Good-sister to

Monte Rosa herself far away there in the North across the level floor of the world. The peak turns an edge like a knife towards Turin ; it is even grander than the Matterhorn from Zermatt, inasmuch as it rises in a solitude so unrivalled and superb. Indeed, closely as it resembles the Matterhorn, Monte Viso has, to my mind, an almost serener majesty. The Matterhorn carries its splendour with a certain alloy of assertiveness, one feels it is not quite certain about its social position ; several of the giants in its " set " are its superiors ; most of them are its equals. But the Viso has never had to face the thought of a rival ; its sovereignty has always towered far beyond cavil, with the result that the peak now possesses the tranquil, affable and perfectly self-confident supremacy—unasserted because unquestioned,—of an archduchess in a tea-party of tobacconists' widows.

But it rules an arid and forbidding range. I do not greatly love the Cottian Alps, and " I will not deceive you, my sweet ; why should I ? " After the Mont Cenis they are a bathos. It was in the afternoon of the next day that I alighted from the railway at Torre Pellice, in the heart of the Cottians, and chartered a fly to drive me up the valley to the place which has the pleasant name of Bobby. This Pellice valley runs into the range parallel to that which takes one past Paesana to Crissolo, at the very foot of the Viso. And the Pellice valley is merely pretty and rich and hot. It meanders flatly, and is full of vineyards and chestnut forests. Above these rise blasted crags of black granite, that look lifeless and burnt ; they are riven and torn and tortured into folds and gullies and deep chines and ghylls. To the walker they will obviously give the maximum of labour with the minimum of result. It will be as much trouble to get up these as to reach the Clear Lake ; and without half the fun or half the reward. For these silly valleys run very low: instead of starting from six thousand feet, one will have to start from two at the most. And thus one's toil is trebled, for not only has one the doubled bother of the upward stodge, but one also has the further nuisance of ascending from hot levels wheie every step is equivalent to three in higher air. Therefore it was with forboding that I scanned those dark crags so high above me as I drove, and decided that I could not congratulate *Primula cottia* on its choice of residence.

I reached Bobby in the evening (the Italians call it Bobbio, and the French Bobi), and it was not till the afternoon of the next day that I set out to climb among the chines that lead to the peaks behind the village. The heat was torrid, and the rocks entirely granitic ; bald and brutal in line, rusty in colour and dull in display of flowers. However, while the general show is poor in the Cottian Alps, there are many special rarities peculiar to the range. It was not long before I came on the first. I had hardly asked my companion (the village school-master, and an enthusiastic botanist) whether and where we might hope to see *Campanula Elatines*, when that celebrated plant perked out at us from under a boulder, although we were still in the zone of the chestnut woods. And, from that moment, the Campanula went with us almost all the way. Like so many of its section, it is purely a saxatile plant, hugging the rocks, whether they be in sun or shade. On its own hills it seemed, perhaps, to have a faint preference for shade ; but then the Cottian valleys have a far more grilling heat than we can ever hope for ; and in our gardens it may be taken that *Campanula Elatines* insists on sun. It is not a difficult plant, on the whole, to grow ; though requiring cliffs of solid rock, and the minimum of surface moisture if it is to do well.

Add to which that slugs have a feverish craving for it. I have wheedled one plant into surviving in a shady hollow on my cliff, but the poor thing is for ever being eaten to the ground, and I cannot expect it to luxuriate under such attentions. *C. Elatines* is a curious, very beautiful species, haunting impenetrable crannies of rock, and especially rejoicing when the cliff, be it shady or sunny, so hangs that surface-moisture never visits the foliage with any excessive assiduity. These leaves, stalked, crenelate, broad, pointed, irregular as ivy, are clothed with a fine grey down that gives one no doubt as to the plant's hatred of moisture. The flower-stems run out in long branches that hug the rock with an almost muscular intention, like the boughs of that Cotoneaster which is sold as *C. pyrenaica.* They may reach eighteen inches at their finest development, perhaps, are branched, and thickly set with innumerable dark blue flowers, quite flat and starry in outline, with prominent stigma starting up in the centre. It has an alpine cousin, *C. elatinoeides ;* otherwise it belongs to a section which is most prominent round the Eastern Mediterranean. The type is *C.*

*garganica*, of Southern Italy ; the section may always be known by its wide open, flat, starry flowers ; all its representatives have a loathing of damp. The most familiar, perhaps, in gardens is that *C. isophylla*, which in cottage windows as in princely palaces (but rather more so), makes sheets of falling blue or white stars from hanging baskets, and which, in the whole world, is only found in a few hundred yards of limy conglomerate on the Capo di Noli between Oneglia and Savona.*

The mountain tracks, high above Bobby, become more and more confusing. I doubt if they are tracks at all. One descends into deep chines, only to crawl up out of them again ; the rate of progress is both tedious and slow ; one seems to spend an infinity of time and trouble in getting nowhere. Still the crags at the end of the " *combes* " (the same word as our " combes ") are as far above us as ever ; and on the rocks themselves there are few flowers to beguile the way. In a tumble of dark blocks there was indeed *Lychnis Flos-Jovis*, almost as beautiful in its big silky foliage as in the three or four great flowers of rosy pink that it carries on stems of ten inches or a foot. And over all the cliff that faced towards the sun there was *Lilium bulbiferum* in the most glorious abundance. On the most inaccessible ledges, in crannies where one would have thought no bulb could lodge, its chalices of orange stood up like wide flames of fire on the dark rocks. In the distance they were golden sparks of light springing on the precipices across the

---

* Even in November there are cushions of bright blue beauty, and I had the luck to find an albino after a bare five minutes under the cliff.

river, that ran below, down in the ghyll. But who can cope with the bulbs of *Lilium bulbiferum?* I leave such things as this to the professional collector. The labour is too great, for a result that is worth too little. For, after all, *Lilium bulbiferum* is a common plant that can easily and cheaply be bought in any quantity.

Otherwise, on these arid slopes and ridges, there was no show. There was a Dianthus making showers of rose, but the spring flowers were already gone, and the summer flowers not yet fully arrived to take their place. Nor are there many of them in any case. The mountain Flora holds its revel in June. But *Campanula Elatines* belongs to summer; and *Campanula Elatines* had not opened a single bud when I sweated up those rocky ribs in mid-July. But then, down by the path-side, a patch of greyness caught my eye. Had it not been for the situation, rather low, and quite accessible, in cracks of granite close to the track, I could have sworn at a glance that here was that impossible high-alpine, *Androsace imbricata*. And *Androsace imbricata* it was indeed; obviously the thing had seeded down there from some more normal situation higher up, in the sheer face of a precipice. But in any case, it here belies all claim to be a high-alpine; in these Southern Alps it seems to come quite low, down to three or four thousand feet, perhaps, although the centre of its distribution is always the higher rock at six or seven thousand. Whereas I do not fancy that the much easier, though still difficult, *A. helvetica* will ever be found below the mountain precipices close beneath the snows. *Helvetica*, perhaps, has not the

wide distribution of *imbricata*, but, as far as my own
experience goes, it certainly remains much more immut-
ably faithful to great elevations.   By this rule it should be
harder to grow than *imbricata* ;   yet, with me, exactly
the reverse is true.   Of course, I am on limestone—
beloved by *A. helvetica*—whereas *A. imbricata*, so far as
I have seen, is one of the few plants that are always and
absolutely calcifuge.   I have never seen it off the lifeless
formations.

It is interesting to note that these plants of the high
cliffs have often a marked tendency to descend as they
reach the southern limits of their range.   On the Monte
Moro above Saas, I doubt if you will see *A. imbricata*
under about seven or eight thousand feet ; on the Plan de
Bertol, and the Unteraar Glacier I know for a fact that
you won't ;   but in these southern ranges it descends
lower and lower, until it reaches what, to me, is its nadir,
here on the granite rocks behind Bobby, at a little more
than three thousand feet.   I freely collected it where I
found it, rejoicing in the chance, and ultimately, after
long search, discovered the original station from which
it had seeded down.   And here it was as impregnable as it
always is in its usual dwelling places.   It was growing
abundantly in a straight precipice of granite, from which
neither knife, tie-pin, trowel, nor stone-axe could avail
to dislodge it ;   effecting its foothold in crevices so tiny
that you could barely discern them, and there, in the
full glare of the sun on that pitiless cliff, expanding into
wide cushions of soft white wool.   Or rather, perhaps,
a light ashen grey is their tone ;   and, against the rufous

colour of the rock that Androsace made little hoary splashes, that at first sight were like those of a grey lichen that was also growing there. You may easily tell the plant's intense hatred for moisture by the way it thus clothes itself with so dense a fine pelt of hair that universal silver-whiteness is the result. Or you may approach the problem the other way, and see in that pelt the plant's precaution, to secure itself all possible humidity on the blazing rocks which it invariably haunts.*

For you will never find this particular Androsace except on cliffs that are absolutely dry themselves, and that face the whole fury of the sun from dawn to dusk ; and, even on these it is happiest under over-hanging ledges where the rain cannot fall upon its cushions. And when you realize what the sun's heat is like on these Southern Alps, especially when refracted from the burning walls of the granite, you will cease to wonder that *Androsace imbricata* is far more of an exile in our climate than its cousin, *A. helvetica*, which tolerates northern exposures with equanimity, wears a much less oppressive garment of wool, and has no objection at all to a good soaking in due reason. The two plants, however, are very close together ; one might almost think them different developments from a common original—the one having cultivated philosophy in a Shetland shawl on the

* A plant, like a human being, lives in a perpetual perspiration all day. This may not sound a pretty or poetic habit, but is a truth, which is better than prettiness or poetry. Accordingly, a plant has to take care, if it grows on high or dry places, not to sweat out more moisture than it can replace from the soil in which it grows. Therefore, high alpines take due precautions, most notably by putting on a thick Jaeger combination of down or wool, to prevent excessive or extravagant perspiration.

cool high limestone, and the other having malade-imaginated itself into a craze for sun-cures on the hottest granite, in a quilting of best Witney blankets.

But even the Androsace had passed out of flower. There were those lovely little cushions, built up of innumerable wee rosettes as grey as silver ; and on them abundantly were lying the brown relics of those pearly stars with rosy throat ; but of bloom remaining there was none. And I mounted at last upon my upward way again. And, in another five minutes I had come on my first specimen of the plant which stands, with *Saxifraga valdensis*, at the head of the rarities that alone justify the Cottian Alps in existing. *Primula cottia* is an outstanding species in the section of *P. hirsuta* (*viscosa*), and is restricted entirely to the granite ridges of the Cottian Alps, where it takes the place of *P. hirsuta* on the high rocks in the Oberland, just as *P. pedemontana* does in the Graians. But it has not quite the vigour of *pedemontana*, does not seem to grow into such masses, nor to be able to descend from the rocks as *pedemontana* can, to cope with the dwarf alpine herbage on the peaty ridges. *P. cottia*, as I saw it, adheres rigidly to the rocks, and forms clumps of three or four crowns. Its leaves are broadly oval, very feebly jagged, and dusky with a coarse dark down ; the flowers, which I did not see, are said to be of an unusually brilliant crimson-rose. Otherwise they are like those of *hirsuta* and *pedemontana*. It seemed to have a curious liking for the sunnier exposures on the cliffs, unlike the generality of its race ; though I found a number of plants whom this apparent preference had led into sad straits. For, on the hottest ledges, they were quite curled up and burnt brown by the heat.

And if I cannot give you more details as to the habits of this treasure, the blame must lie, if you please, with my companion. For while I lingered lovingly on these cliffs, trying to watch the little ways of *Primula cottia*, he scorned my labours from below; exclaiming " Des Primulas, vous en aurez plein les mains sur la Bocca Lorina ; ce n'est pas la peine de chercher là." Now, the Bocca Lorina is the station of *Saxifraga valdensis ;* therefore, when I heard that my Primulas were also to be garnered there by the armful, I ceased to quarry them laboriously from the rocks on which I was at that moment periclitating over grim slopes and gulches. And, when I got to the Bocca—but do not let us proticipate ; " our retrospection shall all be to the future."

So I descended towards Bobbio again, and saw nothing much of note on the way down, until we passed over a steep slope that was all spiry with the snowy delicate plumes of *Anthericum Liliago.* This is in the same line as *Liliastrum* (which, by the way, together with ugly great Asphodels, had been passing into seed on the ledges higher up), but smaller in all its parts, very graceful and dainty, intermediate between the rather ecclesiastical unction of *Liliastrum,* and the dishevelled cloudiness of *plumosum.* All three of these are easy and lovely ; I dare not start a preference. My companion on Mont Cenis, indeed, when I went back to it, damned *Anthericum Liliastrum,* because he said it had a senti-mental pietistic look, like a thing on a text. In this

accusation there is some truth.   St. Bruno's Lily might,
perhaps, be offensively angelic in its rather theatrical
meekness if you met it in a painting.   But you cannot
really vulgarise a flower, try as you may ; association
with conventional saints and sweetnesses may acidulate
one's idea of it, perhaps ; but one has only to see the
living thing again, awave on a wild hillside, to understand that such later notions vanish before the presence
of a beauty far older than the cheap tritenesses of
convention.   One has no right to let the flower suffer
from subsequent associations that one happens to
dislike.

Before I climbed the Bocca Lorina to collect *Saxifraga
valdensis* (sole reason of my coming into these Cottian
Alps) my kind friend the schoolmaster was anxious that
I should see some of the other rarities that abound in the
region.   He was even so kind as to give up a whole day
to accompany me.   We were to go up the long valley
which comes down from Mansoul, into that of the
Pellice, and is called the Combe dei Carbonari.   We were
to go as far as the little plain which closes its upper end ;
and thence, ascending at a slant along the mountains,
back again above it, attain finally to the high Col de
Barant,* under whose wooded chines, and in whose
gullies, abundantly occur *Aquilegia alpina, Anemone
narcissiflora* and the rare *Fritillaria delphinensis*, that
my friend was especially anxious to show me.

Accordingly, at break of day the next morning we set

* The final and penultimate letters appear both to be pronounced:
Baranntt.

out. It was a noble procession ; for there were not only I and the schoolmaster, but also a mule with which we meant to alleviate the labours of the earlier stodge, so as to leave our muscles fresh for the long oblique ascent to the Col de Barant ; there was also the mule's conductor, whose name was Daniel ; there was also a local squire, the friend of the schoolmaster. And there were Diane and Haro. To what species of dog Diane and Haro belonged I cannot say ; they were orange in colour, and of the greyhound persuasion, with reminiscences of the dachshund about their faces. Diane belonged to the squire, and Haro to the schoolmaster ; but they were friends, and pursued their quarry in common, with a common lack of success.

Through the clear greenish air of early morning we made our way up the Combe dei Carbonari. The valley is very beautiful, deep-sunk in forests of chestnut, with a pellucid torrent foaming down from the mountains at its head. Over rounded boulders of dark granite this roared and splashed ; and its colour was like beryls, of a pure marine blue. The mule-track mounted by its side, through the dense and dewy woodland. Here and there on the rocks that lay scattered, large as houses, among the tree-trunks or in opener places, were mats of *Sempervivum arachnoideum* in that transalpine form which has its rosettes so densely clothed in spider-webbing as to be white as wool. Indeed, on those black boulders it was white as snow itself that they gleamed. Here and there, too, by the roadside, the long arms of *Campanula Elatines* were hugging the stone, and from the

boulders sprang and swayed the copper-golden cups of
*Lilium bulbiferum*. As we mounted higher the daylight
grew harder, and the elfin mistinesses of the morning were
dispelled. We came into more open ground, and the
woodland diminished. Above and around us the chestnut
gave way to the pine, and the vegetation became more
alpine. Down by the river were tufts from time to time
of *Anthericum Liliastrum* in great magnificence ; and
now, on the sunny rocks and mountain-sides, the Lily
was flaming everywhere, like poppies in a cornfield. And
still the track went climbing and zigzagging upwards,
towards the mountains that looked so high above our
heads, and were really so little that they would hardly
have served as pedestals to the Clear Lake above the
Mont Cenis. This is what comes of starting from low
levels.

By the time the sun was up we found ourselves well
in the zone of the Alpine woodland. Rhododendrons
were all about in untidy tangles ; and it seemed as if the
snow had not long left them, so brown and sodden was
the earth. But of flowers there were very few, and
very few appeared, until we reached the final plain at
the end of the valley. This is called the Plan del Pis,
and is the invariable upmost pasture that one finds at
the head of all alpine valleys. It has a smooth sward,
and springs, and châlets for the summer dwelling of the
cowherds when they come up. At the other side of the
Plan begin, amid scattered pines, the long and sterile
slopes of tumbled granite that lead up to the crags of
Mansoul. Round the châlets dock and nettle grew

rank, and flowers were peppered over the smooth levels of grass. And this was to be the great display of the Cottian Alps. Alas, then, that I had come on from the Mont Cenis. Only the very richest districts would it be fair to visit after the Mont Cenis ; the wealth and the variety there are so pre-eminent. But here, the show was poor and the variety nothing wonderful. Present, indeed, were the obvious plants of the Southern Alps, and even, among the bushes, a little white Arabis that I suspect of having been the very rare *A. pedemontana* ; but of display there was none. The Gentians were few and feeble ; even the mountain Pansy only made isolated dots of colour. And on the Mont Cenis it hid the hills.

From this point, after we had fed, Daniel and the mule returned down the combe, while the rest of us began ascending the long path that winds upwards, far and farther above it, along the mountains that separate it from the valley of the Pellice. For some hour or so the track continues pleasantly ascending, with little more to make it in the way of bloom, than tufts of big white-flowered *Arenaria laricifolia*, and, when you get a little higher, clumps of *Gentiana verna*. But before you so climb, the rocks themselves contain one thing of interest. For here, in the veins of granite, is found pure asbestos. The schoolmaster climbed a slope to get me some ; and his friend told me that all the rock contained elements of it in a mixed condition. The real thing, when it was brought me, proved to be like brittle silk in dense skeins. It was very white, and glistered in the sun, and flaked

away, thread from thread, as you handled it. To the
feel it was light and unctuous ; they call it here the
Undefiled (ἀμιαντος, amiante). So one continues along
the ridge, perpetually mounting, until at last one reaches
the shoulder which hangs high above the Combe dei
Carbonari. Here there is a long, long slope, all clothed
with alder-scrub. And, for a little while, I had no
attention for the world, its prospects and cataclysms.
For that smooth incline was snowed over with the apple-
blossoms of *Anemone narcissiflora*. And *Anemone alpina*
still lurked in blossom among the bushes.

" On the Limestone Alps," says M. Correvon. I
have often seen this almost universal Anemone, but never
in such gorgeous beauty and abundance as here on the
granite. *Anemone narcissiflora* is certainly the kindliest
of its race—the kindliest, that is, of the mountaineering
section. For, while it is no less easy to grow than *A. alpina*,
it is infinitely easier to collect, and comes up so readily
in so neat a tuft of black fibres, that in half an hour one
may get a hundred or more. Also it grows in a finer and
more amenable turf than the dense meadow-ground
affected by *alpina*. Never was there a lovelier thing,
although it is not conspicuously like a Narcissus. It is
more like clustered apple-blossom, as I say. The whole
plant has a warm and endearing fluffiness ; the soft
leaves are palmate, and then deep-cut again into narrow
lobes ; and the silky stem bears a Marie Stuart frill
of three little folioles. Above this, in an umbel, appear
the flowers. They are carried in heads of from three to
eight, are about the size of a wood-anemone's, and in

colour of a creamy whiteness with a rose-red reverse that
is at its most brilliant in the bud-stage. They have a
golden eye of stamens, too, and they take one's enthusiasm
captive at once with their air of innocent heartiness there
in the wilderness. *Anemone narcissiflora* does not
attempt to rival the stalwart splendour of *A. alpina*,
but its homelier fascination is no less strong. It is a
strayed cousin, in Europe, from a section of the family
which makes its centre in the mountain-woods of Asia.
The Himalyan *A. polianthes* comes very near to it; and in
that same " genre," too, and no less valuable, is *Anemone
demissa*, newly introduced from the forests and uplands
of China. As for *Anemone alpina*, I need not notice the
plant again. Here it is, playing hide-and-seek among the
scrub; and here, still on the granite, it is still the snow-
white *A. alpina*. But on these Cottian Alps it is sparse
and a thing to notice, not the violent glory of the Mont
Cenis, beneath whose universal dominion one sinks
without comment.

We have to turn the corner, round this shoulder, and
continue climbing up towards the Col de Barant. I
lingered too long among my beloved Anemones. When
I turned to see the view there were dangers hurrying up
on the wings of the wind. But a wonderful sight it was.
We lay among the flowers and watched. From that
high point one looks straight out over the dark gulf of
the Combe dei Carbonari far below, to the naked granite
crags that rise in peak and pinnacle on the other side of
Bobbio in the main valley. To the right shoot rugged
ranges of granite again, and between these we have

stretched out beneath us the whole bed of the Pellice, and its junction with the stream of the Carbonari.    In this notch between the mountains we see it meandering down until it is lost in the sea of the Lombard Plain. And, of that Lombard Plain we here contemplate the calm ocean with as startled a feeling of wonder and awe as one experiences on first sight of the Cinhalese Jungle from Sigiri Rock or the platform at Dambûlla.    Nor was it the Plain in its ordinary mood that we saw.    To right and left, over the combes and naked ribs of blackness behind Bobbio, black snow-clouds were swiftly driving across the hills towards us.    The western sky was still clear and blue, but the clouds were racing over the zenith, and on those distant mountains snow was lodging white, and, between them and us, interposing a filmy veil of greyness as it fell.    So much for the mountain country. And the plain-lands out beyond lay under a solid pall of dense violet darkness, over which raced the clouds above us in a regular arch.    Under this vault we gazed into the indistinguishable obscurity of Lombardy, and only dim coppery gleams very far away shed any semblance of day through the livid blue night of storm in which all the Plain was buried.

We watched the wonder and majesty of the spectacle for some time, as an indemnity for the snow or rain that was shortly to chill us to the bone.    And in the end those showers never got to us at all, but were dissipated on their way.    So we continued at last, round the shoulder and up into the mountains again, getting every minute nearer and nearer to the rocky ridges so high above us still. This was a cool exposure, snow still lay, vegetation had only just begun. But amid the dinginess of the alder-scrub Soldanellas were hovering in thousands over the dark ground. *Saxifraga retusa* glowed like spilled wine in the most sodden turf, round rocks that were hardly emerging from the drifts ; and in the woodland, here and there, hung the lavish violet bells of *Primula viscosa*. And, as I am getting tired of putting after this name " latifolia " in brackets, perhaps you will henceforth be so kind as write it on the tablets of your brain, that *viscosa* in the old days meant the common rosy Primula which is so abundant on rocks and the highest heaths in the Oberland ; while this imperial plant was known as *graveolens* or *latifolia*. But in point of fact, the name *viscosa* belongs by right of priority to this plant ; therefore the ci-devant *graveolens* must now be recognized as the only true *viscosa* ; while the *viscosa* of former days must be contented with another of its names, and sink back into *P. hirsuta*. Let it then be clearly remembered, that I, whose ambition is correctness, shall always mean in future by *viscosa*, the violet-flowered Primula of the Southern Alps, instead of the little magenta-rosy plant which used to usurp the title. And this is the correct place, obviously, to make a certain quotation about the rose and its unalterable odour. But I will not do it.

After this the path goes higher and wilder ; the flowers get fewer and fewer. At last only an enormous alp of burnt grass separates us from the final ridge. It is a tedious ascent : most of the expected plants are there, but none of them fine in form or generous in quantity.

*Androsace vitaliana*—(I have paid my obol to correctness, and therefore, will cease to repeat that this is nowadays lumped with Douglasia and not with Androsace)—ought to be ashamed of itself here on the Cottian granites. For we know what it can do on the granites and quartzes of the Mont Cenis ; why then should it be so poor and moulting here ? It occurs in good quantity, indeed, but each plant is more draggle-tailed and wizzly than the last. Then one sees the remains of Snow-Crocus, of *Ranunculus pyrenaeus*, of other common objects of the highest alps. But there is nothing remarkable—except by way of omission. For, at this height, in this situation on these granites, all the northerly ranges would be thickly-dotted with *Anemone vernalis*, a plant practically inevitable on high downs like this. And here, though we hunted, all of us, far and wide, one sad and sickly specimen was all we could discover. This is a thing to note ; for, if I am right in my experience, it is not so often that you find the sphere of a high alpine so markedly diminishing as it gets further south ; unless its affinities are rather with the arctic ranges than the alpine. As is the case with *A. vernalis*.

Now we are on the ridge itself, and among the rocks there is only *Saxifraga oppositifolia*, and no *Eritrichium*, which I had fondly imagined I might find on these granites. And on the other side of the arête one looks down into deep gulfs—straight upon the valley of the Pellice, indeed, with Bobby lying like a toy five or six thousand feet beneath one's knees. The ridge which, on the side by which we have climbed it, rises in smooth

tilts of grass or rock, here breaks away in a succession of
jagged precipices, with chines and gullies between each.
When I hear that we have to descend into these combes
in order to see *Fritillaria delphinensis*, my enthusiasm
for that rare treasure markedly diminishes. In point
of fact it is very long since I ate ; and when the stomach
is void of food, it is not so easy for the heart to be stuffed
with courage. Until my inner alchemy has transmuted
some eggs and cherries and chickens into moral qualities,
those moral qualities will be found to have run out of
stock.

Accordingly, it was with burning inward wrath that I
descended those places, quite terrified, furious at being
terrified, still more furious at having to conceal my terror.
My grateful smile might well have blistered its victims,
as they helped me and my collecting-tin from cliff to
cliff. Very slowly I came ; the ground, besides being
abrupt, is also rotten ; the herbage is smooth as glass,
the brushwood brittle as lover's vows. And every time
I struck out a step for myself, that heavy tin would hitch
on a rock and swing off, and hit me in the small of the
back, and send me spinning into the arms of my protectors,
who thus, I felt with ragings, were confirmed in their
conviction that I was quite the most helpless thing ever
strayed unadvisedly from Brighton Esplanade. However,
at last I reached the slope at the foot of the cliffs without
misadventure, and we continued along a little goat-track
at their base. And at that point I struck. " Die I would,
if die I must," I announced with Dorothea von Stettin,
" But die on an empty stomach I positively would not."

Accordingly we sat and ate ; proper spirit flowed back into me in palpable warm waves.   In ten minutes I was dancing regardless here and there on those ridiculous inclines, and feeling that I could readily drive a motor upon them if need were.   Such is the combined strength of reinforcements from within, and stimulants from without.

For there are wonderful flowers in those chines ; *Aquilegia alpina*, though only in bud, was growing in bushes and jungles of luxuriant growth ; the Narcissus Anemone shone like little galaxies of fallen stars among the long grass of the slopes ;  and, from all those northerly-facing rocks, in deep moss and tussock, hung curtains of that Primula which you are to  remember is *viscosa*. *Primula viscosa* has a splendid beauty ; it forms vast woody stocks, and spreads into wide masses ;  the leaves are very long and large, and oval-pointed, loose in texture, and sticky with glands.   The tone of their green has a dusty note, thanks to these glands, and they narrow lengthily to where they join the trunk.   The flowers are not indeed very big for the robust size of the plants, but hang in close clusters from stalwart upstanding stems. And their colour is usually—for it varies to bluer or more vinous tones—a rich and brilliant purple.   It is an easy vigorous plant to grow, if you can give it firm rock into which to root ;  and, in the districts it affects, is very abundant at considerable altitudes.   It does not, as a rule, seem to descend so low as *marginata* does.

It is a species of the Southerly Alps, and I have never yet seen it off the granitic formations.   Indeed, I believe it to be genuinely calcifuge in nature. There are local forms of it : one is *cynoglossifolia,* which you will see inhabiting full soil in open places in the Engadine, where it forms broad masses in sunny ground; *latifolia* is but another ; and one is sorry that the old name of *graveolens* has passed away. For I used to think, indeed, that it was a libel on the plant ; but this year has discovered my error. The one disadvantage of *P. viscosa* is that it does stink : it stinks very markedly, with a rancid hircine odour. . . What's that ?—" A Primula by any other name would smell as——" Hush. And I refused to make the real quotation at you too ! And shame upon me too, and great wonderment, that I should call a nice gentleman like Brer *graveolens* " stinking Jim."

One can be very happy among the Combes de Barant. I have the pleasantest recollection of their sheltered copsiness and lushness of blossom down under the cliffs. Far below the ground falls away and away to lesser pinnacles of granite that soar above the fir trees. And all the bushes and open places are full of flowers ! Both the Anemones, *alpina* and *narcissiflora,* the budding Columbine, the Primula, *Tulipa celsiana,* and—at last— *Fritillaria delphinensis* itself. I have some respect for rare, interesting plants ; therefore I will only say of *Fritillaria delphinensis* that it is not of a beauty so outstandingly superior to the common *Meleagris* that one needs to climb so many arduous thousands of feet to see it. In fact, it is very like *Meleagris :* in fact, I almost think that *Meleagris* is the clearer in colour of the two. And now, having avenged my weariness, I will do justice.

And it was a great moment when I first saw the blackish-violet bell of the Fritillary nodding among the long grass and the Anemone, and the fading little golden Tulip. A wonderful thing it is, though whether I shall ever be able to grow it remains quite another matter. Among the vivid grasses it looks like a big blot of ink ; it has exactly the wide, pendent cup of *Meleagris*, exactly the habit, exactly the size of growth. But the flower, I rather fancy, is a trifle larger, and its colour of a more sombre claret. Otherwise it has the same chequers, the same weird and rather unholy fascination. There is quite a fair lot of it in the Combes de Barant ; but here its distribution is only beginning, and when you get down into the Maritime Alps it becomes abundant in suitable places (where also occurs the golden-yellow Fritillary which is called *Moggridgei*, and pronounced to be only a colour variation of *delphinensis*).

From the Combes we made our way out on to the ridge again, and then, over a vast slope of mountain, perfectly smooth and bare, set at a curious slant, not so steep as to be vexing, but quite steep enough to give one a feeling of being tilted up, we wandered down upon the charming little inn called the Chiabotta del Prá, which sits in a verdant plain of grass, starred with *Primula farinosa, Dianthus neglectus*, Gentians, and *Silene acaulis*. At its upper end the valley is closed by the stone slopes of Granéro, and that way lies the Pass of the Traversette, to Crissolo under the Viso, with the tunnel made at the summit by Louis II., Marquis of Saluzzo, in 1480 (he would probably have been father or grandfather to that

Dona Maria de Saluces, who was in waiting on Queen Katharine of Aragon, and became the mother of Katharine Willoughby de Eresby, afterwards the famous Protestant Duchess of Suffolk), aided by supplies from Louis XI. of France, as sovereign of Dauphiné across the Pass.

But all this country is full of bygone events. Does my faithful reader realize that these grilling ridges are the " alpine mountains cold," on which lay the bones of the slaughtered saints, when Milton drew the Lord's attention to the fact ? For these are the Valdensian Valleys, more famous now for their Saxifrage than for their faith. Yet the faith continues, though the bones have long since been all picked up. The Vaudois, since their return at the end of the seventeenth century, maintain the French language, and the Calvinistic communion, into which they allowed their own far older and more interesting heresy to be merged ; and are now found peacefully possessing the lands and the beliefs for which their fathers died. For England it is not unnatural that the Vaudois keep a special regard to this day. Each glen and waterfall as you descend from the Chiabotta down the long way to Bobbio, is hallowed by some story of martyrdom and massacre ; in those times, when non-intervention was not the fashion for the strong, it was England that stood by the weak to the best of her power. Puritanism in its great moments was not content to fight the tyranny of Popes in England alone ; English money and weight were freely given to the Vaudois, the mightiest voice in England nudged the deaf Gods on their behalf, and the Lord Protector proved not the Protector of England only.

And what remains of all this, in these hot valleys, where the vineyards sleep so peacefully under the sun ? The memory of high fervours, perhaps, and a seared horror of priests.  But these are mere ideas, and the lion lies down to-day with the grim wolf, who has ceased long since to devour with privy paw.  In other words, my schoolmaster told me that in his school at Bobbio, religion (so they call dogmatic hair-splittings) had ceased to be a matter of difficulty, Catholic as well as Protestant having approached the conclusion that goodness is undenominational, and education in wisdom not a matter of creeds or factions.  So peace reigns, and great Oliver's name still lives because of the stone embankment he had made to protect Bobbio from the incursions of the Pellice river ; and the fortalice up in the valley towards the Chiabotta only reminds me now that its name is Mirabouc, because in the neighbourhood of Mirabouc there is some floral rarity to be found.  And I believe that it is a dowdy little crucifer, probably *Braya alpina ;* not worth the finding ; or I should have searched for it.  Instead of which I swung unregarding down the gorge to Bobbio again, under banks all blossoming with Lychnis and golden Lily and *Anthericum Liliastrum* and *A. Liliago* and *Dianthus sylvestris* in a tangled riot of colour ; with the white wool-balls of *Sempervivum arachnoideum* lying thick on the stones, and the wiry long fringes of the Northern Spleenwort peering out between the crannies.

This Northern Spleenwort is extraordinarily abundant on the sunny granitic rocks, and in the stone walls makes towzled masses. It is the most distinct of ferns, by the fact that it is not like a fern at all. Its fronds are long, leathery, dark-green hairs, forked towards their end; they grow as wild as a wig, and the plant hybridises with the Wall-rue and produces *Asplenium germanicum*, which is exactly intermediate in appearance. At least, so they say; I positively dare to " hae my doots." For, is not the Wall-rue by marked inclination a plant of the cool limestone? And *A. septentrionale*, so far as my widish experience of it now takes me, is universally and by passionate preference, a plant of the hot granite. More than that, this year and last year, I repeatedly and abundantly found it in the granitic ranges; no less repeatedly (though much less abundantly, of course) did I discover its daughter, *A. germanicum*. *Never once*, in any neighbourhood where these were seen, could I discover a sign of *A. Ruta-muraria*. But, on the other hand, where *septentrionale* and its child were found, there, invariably, was also *A. Trichomanes*, in the most extravagant profusion, to say nothing of its green-stemmed sister, *A. viride*. What price, then, the suggestion that *A. Trichomanes* may prove, after all, to be the other parent of *A. germanicum*?

And now for the Bocca Lorina and *Saxifraga valdensis*. High, high, high, must we go for this, a great deal higher even than the Combes de Barant. For, unlike its nearest kindred in the race, the Silver Saxifrages of the Maritime Alps, *Saxifraga valdensis* is purely a high alpine, and

never of its own good will descends to valleys and rocks
of lesser elevation.   I had the station carefully described
to me before I set out from England in search of this
precious plant ; but though I made in my mind's eye a
faithful picture of the granite precipices on either side of
a gorge, yet I trembled as I set out, for well I know that
the realities of things have an awkward trick of not
corresponding at all with these mind's eye pictures that
we make.   However, I toiled upwards and upwards
towards the Bocca Lorina, which is the range on which
I was to find the Saxifrage.   I was desperate that day in
my resolves, as well I might be.   This Saxifrage, unknown
to our gardens (a pretender has always been sent you,
hitherto, under the name of *valdensis*), is entirely restricted
to a few localities high up in the Cottian Alps, on this
side or that of the frontier between France and Italy.
It has no near relations, until we come to *S. cochlearis ;*
and up to date it never seems to have formed any
alliances.   It sits alone on the half-dozen rocks or so which
are its only dwelling-place in the known world.   How
and why it developed there nobody knows ; everything
to do with its history and origin is " wropt in a mistry."

It is a long climb to the Pass.  But, as one gets higher
there are joys by the way.   From a grassy ledge *Linum
alpinum* hangs down in showers of bright celestial stars ;
*Primula viscosa*, which is abundant, but past its flower, on
all the rocks as you go, begins, when you get near the
ridge, to wag at you rich heads of purple.   And on other
rocks there is now *Primula marginata*.  This, again, is a
southerly species, and indeed, the race of Primula is far

more varied in the Southern than in the Northern ranges.
*P. marginata* we saw in the Graians, just beginning ;
here in the Cottians it is much more common ; in the
Maritimes, fifty miles further south, it is very common
indeed on the higher rocks.   And, if, out of all the race, I
had to choose one species alone to cultivate, I am not sure
that my choice would not fall on *P. marginata* (*P. Winteri*
having only just " come up, like thunder, out 'er China,
crost the bay ").

In the first place, it is quite indifferent as to soil ;
although I know it abounding on granite in the Cottians
and Maritimes, I know it also not a bit less prosperous
and abundant on the mountain-limestone above Saint
Martin Lantosque and San Dalmazzo de Tenda ; in the
second, while preferring shady exposures, it has no
prejudice against sunshine ; in the third place, it is a very
easy plant to cultivate,—by far, I think, the easiest of the
rock Primulas.   It will even thrive in the open border,
though it very soon tends to become leggy there, and
grow out of the ground on long rootstocks that one has
no notion how to deal with.   And this habit is easily
understood when once you have seen the plant *in situ.*
For it has a very peculiar habit ; it loves to fall far down
over the face of the cliffs in deep curtains, each rosette
springing at the end of a long, naked and almost woody
trunk, so that the whole mass makes a pendent sheet of
Primula.   These are the very shoots which come poking
out of earth if you plant the Primula in common ground ;
because they are annoyed at not being able to hang
down.   Therefore, I am now taking all my old marginatas,

and putting them at the lip of the ledges on the Cliff. Thence they will be able to fall forward and grow down, after the plant's normal, almost aerial, habit.  And there, if they thrive, they will be more beautiful than ever, on a rock so much more beautiful than their own.  If only you have eyes to note the idiosyncrasies and charms of different strata.

But the fact is that few people seem to have any adequate sense of the beauty of rock as mere rock. Without consideration of garniture or surroundings, rock itself can be one of the most beautiful things in all beautiful nature.  I would as soon chip and hack at a natural rock-face as I would try to quarry building blocks from the Lemnian Athena. Yet so many people seem blind to these possibilities of pleasure, and look on stone simply as a thing that gets in your way when you are making a path, or perhaps may be made useful as road-metal. They bash it down with hammers, and leave a venerable surface gashed and scarred and mangled beyond repair of nature; or they hew steps in it, of a raw and mathematical preciseness.  They have neither sight nor reverence ; yet gods as surely dwell in rock and cliff as in the oak or the glittering water.

Yet all stone has not the same mystery of holiness and beauty.  With my inevitable prejudice I find myself always going back longingly to the thought of this noble mountain-limestone of ours—the loveliest of formations that I know.  For, if it has not the rosy blush of the Jurassic, nor the rich glow and glory of Dolomite, yet its shades of colour, though gentler, are no less wonderful ;

and in form of individual block, it even surpasses either. See how it weathers and frets into the most fantastic shapes, how sometimes it keeps to stern and precipitous lines, unfriendly in their splendour ; or softens into *moutonné* shelves and declivities, on which velvety mosses lodge in lines and cushions ; or is often channelled smooth by rain, or washed into little ripples and ridges, or pierced and tunnelled into hollows and holes and rounded basins, where the moorland water lodges. And in colour how it varies infinitely : lilac-pink in summer haze, and grey in storm ; bone-white at times, and blue in winter, or darkening to black or violet in rain ; but always shaded and varied and graded in its tones, conveying in its successive moods the impression of its personality.

For, even if it be too mystic a thought for Jermyn Street, I can but feel that all the organic strata have more sympathy with the ways of the world than those grim primeval rocks that are congealed fire out of the time when no life yet was. Look at these sterile straight lines of the granite from which poor *Primula marginata* hangs on this Bocca Lorina—how stiff and pitiless and alien. This stone has never had any part in life ; life passes it by, receiving no companionship, and giving none. But, for those rocks that are built up of countless myriad myriad husks of existence, it seems as if the ghosts of their bygone component activities still linger in them, and make them one with the life that unceasingly flows on ; and friendly, and understanding, adapting themselves to the purposes of the world, instead of resisting stupidly, like the granites, and then gracelessly capitulating in ugly ruin. Compare the surrender ot a limestone mountain with the soulless collapse of a granitic. Take two: look round at gaunt Viso, now peering over the hills; it is nothing but a wreckage of sharp slabs and splinters, a mere tumble of desolation, when you draw near; and then compare this with the moulded and living loveliness of Croda Rossa, or the Drei Zinnen,—not a whit less splendid, though, than Viso, in the soaring upward rush of their peaks. Or, if you do not care to go so far, compare the noble lines of the Long Scar with the huddled gritstone masses under the Western face of Ingleborough, exactly like a rock-garden of the Victorian Era in their bald and chaotic barrenness.

In any case, whether or no you find anything more than mere fantasticalness in my thought, I can tell you that the people of the hills entirely share my view. For the granite mountains are as poor in their flora as the limestone and Dolomite ranges are rich. The plants are not at home or happy on the unsympathetic lifeless* formations. This is not, of course, to say that there are not many alpines and high alpines on the granite; there are even several very precious ones, which especially affect the granite. (But these are, for the most part, arrogant and exclusive species, that prefer to live by themselves.) I need only instance *Saxifraga florulenta*, *Androsace imbricata*, and that very *Saxifraga valdensis* to which we are now climbing. But the fact remains, that for general opulence and geniality of floral display you need never search the granitic mountains; they may give you here

---

* Hypozoic : not only " lifeless " but beneath reach of even the lowest, oldest, least living forms of life ; sterility absolute and unthinkable.

and there a rare plant ; but rare plants occur on the
limestone also : and there you will also have thrown in
the whole glory of the mountain flora in its richest
development. However, *Primula marginata* is quite
catholic in its views, and abounds with equal complacency
either on calcareous or granitic rock, generally asking,
though, to fall downwards in a cataract from a crevice.

Under such conditions, indeed, it would seem that it
goes on for ever. You will find whole sheets of it on the
way up to the Bocca Lorina, looking like compact mats
a yard across, until you dissect them and see that each
rosette springs from the end of a long separate trunk,
rooting at its base ; though young rosettes and old have
stems of such proportionate length that the effect of the
whole is that of one unbroken cushion. And now, after
all this, I have to add the crowning recommendation ;
for *Primula marginata* is very conspicuously beautiful,
even among the many conspicuous beauties of its family.
Very beautiful, in the first place, are the leaves, for these
are broadish, and rounded, of a leathery grey colour,
leathery in texture, and very sharply and boldly toothed
all round their edges. And that toothed edge is outlined
by a narrow clear line of golden-white powder, whose
effect, as of a silver hem, is quite startlingly beautiful
against the grey tone of the foliage. This powder even
persists down the trunk, and is dense on the buds of the
rosettes as they unfold. Then, as if this were not enough,
from the centre of the rosettes spring stems of three or
four inches, carrying each, in a loose head, a cluster of
from three to eight flowers. These are large and well-

opened, and of the most exquisite silvery lavender, which sometimes deepens towards purple, or lightens towards lilac, but always keeps blue as the dominant tone of the composition. In the centre of each blossom, too, the crystalline texture of its fabric is powdered with minutest pearl-like flecks of the powder, exactly as you see a denser powder in the blossom of *P. Auricula*. And somehow this gives the last touch of daintiness to the flowers ; the white dust stands out on the lavender ground like globules of rain on the surface of a pool.

I specially love and cherish *Primula marginata*. And well I may. For it was not long before I made a sad discovery on the Bocca Lorina. I had rather neglected and scamped *P. cottia* in the crags behind Bobbio, on the promise that I should have Primulas enough and to spare on the Bocca. And now, too late, do I discover that Primulas indeed I may have and to spare on the Bocca, but that they are all *P. marginata* and *P. viscosa*. *P. cottia* is nowhere to be seen, from top to bottom of the path (unless, indeed, at one point among scrub, I may have come upon a brace or so of rather miserable plants). In any case, whether it occurs here or not, the Bocca is as emphatically not the territory of *cottia* as it is that of the other two.

But by now I am high up, and the actual summit is in sight, though far above me still. Some way ahead of me are two russet coloured cliffs on either side of a precipitous gorge. They are not unlike the cliffs in my mind's eye-picture of *Saxifraga valdensis*. Over the top of the shoulder which I have just reached I make straight towards them, across rocky levels jewelled with Primula and *Gentiana verna*, Forget-me-not, and the pinky-lilac tussocks of *Petrocallis pyrenaica*. The place is one for careful going, too, for those cliffs, when you come to them, fall away down abrupt and slippery slopes to a great gulf below. I slithered cautiously about on the steep shales that lie at their feet.

These cliffs are of some micaceous schist, glittering with particles of light. They are very friable and rotten —all in pieces, crumbling away in flakes and slabs if you so much as blow upon them. I had not been playing round their base for five minutes, when I discovered that they were curtained, swathed and sheeted with *Campanula Allioni* in such abundance as I could never have believed. It was not till my downward journey, though, that I saw the plant in flower, on lower cliffs ; here it was all in bud, and never a cranny, never a ledge, that was not thick with the plant ; to say nothing of the dense mats of it that covered the shales beneath. It was a wonderful sight, but I had no eyes to notice it duly. My gaze, like concentrated gimlets, was piercing the upper courses of the rock for *Saxifraga valdensis*.

No loose end of attention could I spare for the Campanula, for the Primulas, Petrocallis, Achilleas, Artemisias and other treasures of that slope, not even for youngling plants of the rare thorny *Astragalus Tragacantha*, that here offered me a chance of securing good roots of this impracticable species, which, when developed, seems to send down its trunk for half a mile. If, in these moments, I stopped for any plant that looked convenient to gather, it was with reluctance and a grudging of the time and attention thus spent.  For by now my whole soul was twittering with a terror that I might not see *Saxifraga valdensis,* that I might even not have struck the right range of cliffs.  For no consideration would I ever lose this anguish which develops in the hunt for a plant ; nor need I justify it to anyone who knows the vastness of the hills, the limited range of rare plants, and the littleness of man.  It is a delicious pain, that fluttering which comes before the moment of achievement.  At least if the achievement duly follows after.  I was beginning that day to fear it might not ; to fear that only the dull ache of failure might be left me in the end.  I had quested fruitlessly along many yards of that hot cliff; and then, quite suddenly, I saw *Saxifraga valdensis.*

*Saxifraga valdensis* is the only plant of its kindred that haunts the granitic formations ; let that be remembered. It is also the only one of its kindred which ascends to great elevations: or rather dwells exclusively at great elevations—and it is remarkable in the further fact that it grows only in the most torrid places it can find, in cliffs as sunbaked as those affected by *Androsace imbricata.* Though many of the Silver Saxifrages tolerate sun, I know of none that demands, or even bears, quite the same grilling conditions as those in which alone you need think of finding *S. valdensis* on the Bocca Lorina.  I do not know, of course, its other stations ; but on this side of the Bocca it is extraordinarily local.  Off these particular rocks you will not, apparently, find it anywhere else—that is to say, it has a range of only a few hundred yards, if that. Small wonder that the plant is precious. In these particular rocks, however, it is very abundant, and their rottenness is such that clumps can, for the most part, be easily got. (If they are in solid rock, of course one does not attempt them ; it would be monstrous to run the risk of wasting a single crown.) But the plant seems practically never to seed down off its chosen rocks, and though I did ultimately find one lone little piece on a cliff far below in the valley, it was obviously a sad and sickly exile from its native heath.

And now for a description : *Saxifraga valdensis* is not related to the Silver Saxifrages of the Northerly ranges—*aeizoon, crustata* and so on ; its kindred are the pure-white-flowered Silvers of the Maritime alps—the two forms of *lingulata* and *S. cochlearis.* Indeed, so close is the relationship that it is a minor variety of *cochlearis* which through all these years has been passing in our gardens for *valdensis.* And, to a rough glance, the two plants are much alike ; a second glance teaches you that there can never be any reason to confuse the two. *Cochlearis minor* and *valdensis* both form tight masses of minute silver grey rosettes, and, beyond that first resemblance there is little real similarity. The leaves of *cochlearis* are fatter, shorter, broader at the tips, arranged in a much looser rosette, in a much looser mat of rosettes. They tend to stand apart from each other, so that if you lay your palm across a clump you will feel a number of stiff little points. So much for *cochlearis minor,* then ; before I leave the plant I will just add that M.

Correvon has added a new confusion to the already sufficient confusion of the race. For some of you may have been interested in a fresh Saxifrage which appeared two years ago under the name of *Probynii*. I know that I was ; and puzzled vainly over its provenance, and how it developed specific rank. It seemed to me an old acquaintance. And now I find that an old friend, indeed, it is—mere *Saxifraga cochlearis minor*—which my good friend of Geneva has launched upon a zealous world under the name of Sir Dighton Probyn, in whose garden at Windsor he happened to see it specially luxuriant.

Quite different from this in essentials is *Saxifraga valdensis*. It forms, on its native rocks, the hardest, smoothest, tightest domes I have ever seen, except among the tiny Kabschia Saxifrages. The leaves are narrower and a trifle longer than those of the little *cochlearis*, they are of a darker grey-green, with more definite blobs of chalk in the dentation round their edge ; they are not so thick through, do not broaden so markedly towards their tips, do not stand erect or apart, but, on the contrary, lie unrolled so flat and close that if you lay your hand on a clump of *valdensis* you will feel only a smooth hard surface under your palm. The flowers I cannot yet describe ; that day on the Bocca the spikes were only emerging from the rosettes ; and on the homeward journey they mouldered off. All I saw was the little unfolding croziers, densely set with ruby-coloured glandular hairs ; I believe that the large, pure white flowers are carried in smaller numbers than in those of any form of *cochlearis*. But, in nature, *valdensis* is far more

generous of flower spikes than any variety of *cochlearis :*
it is as lavish as any Aeizoon. At the same time,
though *valdensis* holds unquestionable specific rank,
there can be no doubt, I think, that it has an old
ancestral relationship with *cochlearis ;* as, indeed, I
think, has *cochlearis* in its turn, with the lingulatas.
With regard to cultivation, I have found no difficulty
whatever yet, either in sun or shade, with *S. valdensis.*
It answers readily, it seems, to the conditions that suit
any other Silver of the *cochlearis*-kindred, but sits in the
sun with an especial happiness, worthy of that Queen
Anne, who by dint of doing so succeeded in becoming
" as fair as a lily, as brown as a bun." As for *cochlearis
minor,* we have all grown that triumphantly for so many
years that we need say no more about it here.

These cliffs of the Saxifrage, however, do not mark
the summits of the Bocca. These rise yet another five
hundred feet or so, over a sward of Gentians, where the
buds of *Dianthus neglectus* are perking up in their myriads
towards a grand display in about a fortnight. At
present, though, they are only a promise. But I collected
a certain number, because I was told that here the
prevalent forms were fine-flowered and dwarf in growth.
We shall see. And now—the top of the Bocca at last !
How I always long to look over the other side ; and when
I succeed in doing so how disappointingly it usually
resembles this one. However that desire to see over
on to " the other side " is, I suppose, one of humanity's
most salutary instincts, alluring always to incessant
effort—the parent of science and religion and spiritual-

ism and every other form of energy. On the other side of the Bocca, then, I discovered stone slopes half hidden in snow, and more snow beyond, and distant peaks of bare stone, and a grey sky, and an icy wind. Looking back I saw Viso towering over all the lower ranges ; seen from the side he is less knife-edged—or rather you see the blade broadside, instead of edge on, as the ridge shoots up to its culminating peak. However the mountain is always unquestioned king of the range ; behind him, like a queen on his pillion, rises the lesser splendour of the Visolotto. And all the ranges are a wilderness of dead granite, dark under a darkening sky.

Ah, how the wind whistled and whirled across the snows. In a very few moments I was too cold for any but a perfunctory search. However, I discovered *Campanula stenocodon* just beginning to shoot from the stone-slope; but as I hope to show you this in flower, I will not linger here among the blasts on the Bocca. The other object of my hunt I did not find. I bore the failure calmly, having got the far more important *Saxifraga valdensis.* For the plant I missed can never be anything but a gardener's curiosity, an extremely difficult species, high-alpine, restricted to a few stone-shingles and mountain marshes in the Cottian Alps. This is not to say that *Gentiana Rostani* is not of rich beauty. I grow it still. It survives in my wet moraine, and flowered this year. It has a rough intermediacy between *verna* and *bavarica*, is notable for erect shoots, thinly clad in very pointed, narrow, oval leaves (in pairs, alternately facing this way and that) of a bright pale green, rather thick in texture, and incurving to the stem. The long-throated, starry flowers are nearer to *verna* than to *bavarica*, but they are of an even clearer, sharper Cambridge blue in colour. It has, on the other hand, much more of *bavarica's* habits and preferences—indeed, I rather fancy it replaces *bavarica* in the high places of the Cottian Alps. It is never found at any but great elevations ; there is only a very little of it here on the Bocca, in a small marsh about two hundred yards down, which at the time of my visit was still under snow. Its more favoured stations are higher yet, in the stone-slides under Paravas, and here and there throughout the district round the Viso; always in the dampish places affected by the high-alpine Gentians that take after *bavarica*.

No wonder if such a plant be always likely to prove even more difficult and exacting than most of the exacting difficult little Gentians from the upmost screes and moraines. I shall keep it with joy as long as it condescends to stay; but it is not a thing which one wishes to collect in any quantity, seeing the uncertain tenure of its life. Nor will customers ever come tumbling over each other to have borders of it. Without a pang I desisted from a pallid search, and descended again from the Bocca to Bobbio, feeling, each time my heavy tin came bumping against my back, that with a stock of the real *Saxifraga valdensis* I could laugh at lesser lacks. The Cottian Alps had fully justified their existence.

# CHAPTER V.

## THE BACK DOOR OF THE MARITIMES.

For into the Maritime Alps I was determined to penetrate, not by the main entrance, which is the Col de Tenda, but, like the hireling who is no true shepherd, over one of the high passes up in the centre of the range. I was afraid my publisher, like he of "The Wrong Box," might prove averse from the expense of a map; therefore it is that I saw fit to delay you now and then with an attempt to explain to you in words where it was I went, and how I got there. Well, as I have said, the Cottian Alps come down, as it were, in a straight wall, until the Maritimes cross them at right angles, stretching away to east and west. Exactly at their juncture the Vermenagna valley runs due south into the Maritimes: at its head rises the Col de Tenda, climbing straight over a notch between Marguareis and the Rocca del Abisso; and so on, down the gorges, past San Dalmazzo among its chestnut-groves, to Ventimiglia on the Mediterranean. But as San Dalmazzo sits at the head of this Southern valley, so, some fifteen miles west, another similar valley runs down from the Alps to the sea, and has at its head Saint Martin Lantosque, but no carriage way, only a mule track, leading over to the north side of the range again, by the Pass of the Fenestra. And, so tumbled and wild are the

mountains that intervene between these two deep-chan-
nelled water-courses, that though, as the enviable crow
can fly, only so few miles intervene between Saint Martin
and Saint Dalmas, yet it is easier for those who are not
crows to reach the one from the other by traversing all three
sides of a square, instead of briefly cutting along the
fourth side,—in other words, from either place to go all
the way down the river-bed to the Mediterranean, all
the way along the coast between Nice and Ventimiglia,
and then again all the way up the other valley to its
head.

And my problem was how best to reach Saint Martin
Lantosque from Bobby (it is nowadays called,
indeed, Saint Martin Vésubie, for no reason known to
man ; but what right-minded person will ever be able
thus to dishonour the name-place of *Saxifraga lantoscana ?*). Saint Martin had old memories for me, that
made it the centre of my pilgrimage. You cannot visit
the Maritime Alps without paying a call on *Saxifraga
lantoscana ;* to say nothing of the fact that high up
behind St. Martin the ancient King of all Saxifrages
keeps his lonely court. Obviously one might have crossed
straight over the Col de Tenda ; done the district round
San Dalmazzo first, and then come on, down the valley
of the Roja, along the sea-board, and up the valley of
the Vésubie to Saint Martin. But this would leave one
stranded, with no easy alternatives for our luggage but
to go back the same way;—and, anyhow, in an unfavourable position for the next step in my proposed journey.
Therefore I cast about in my mind for another way.

And it so happens, that where Borgo San Dalmazzo (nothing to do with San Dalmazzo de Tenda on the other side of the Col, which, for purposes of euphony I sometimes call by its French name of Saint Dalmas de Tende) lurks in the corner of the Lombard Plain, at the junction of the Cottian and the Maritime Alps, there not only flows down the Vermenagna Valley from the Col de Tenda in the south, but there also runs up due west the long course of the Gesso river, which is born in the flanks of Argentera, the king-peak of the Maritimes, rising in the heart of the range. And under the shadow of Argentera lies the famous and luxurious bathing-establishment of Valdieri, and round Valdieri lives *Viola valderia ;* and across the mountains to right and left of Argentera there run two or three high passes all leading over into the Valley of the Boréon on the southern side, where there is a charming little inn by a waterfall, and whence you descend easily in two hours or so upon Saint Martin Lantosque. And on all these passes, on the rigid granite, lives *Saxifraga florulenta.* Accordingly I decided that it should be from Valdieri that I would get to Saint Martin ; exploring the northern side of the range before passing over on to the Mediterranean slope.

I had a crowded day getting to Valdieri from Bobby. My first excitement was that, when I reached the station at Torre Pellice, I found my *Saxifraga valdensis* sitting undespatched on the platform in its tin. For some red-tapish reason they refused to send it. I struggled and wrought in vain against their refusals. And the train was now anxious to be off. Then, just as despair was gripping me, I heard voices at my back ; and after many centuries, reaped the reward of England's kindness to the Vaudois. For a minister of their faith was bidding farewell to an English Bible-woman behind me. I leaped upon him with choice phrases ; he remembered ancient benefits, and so energetically interposed with the officials on my behalf, that *Saxifraga valdensis* was registered and sent off in half the time it takes me to write this history. Then, piling gratitude upon his head, I jumped into the train, and, as it moved out of Torre Pellice, meditated, with sighs of relief, that the Lord Protector and the mighty-mouthed inventor of harmonies could not be said to have wholly lived in vain.

The train glides down the Pellice Valley, and goes finally to sleep at Pinerolo, on the edge of the Plain. Or rather, it is here that one alights, and steps into an odd little steam tram, which conveys you due south, at the side of the dead straight high roads leading along under the hills, from Pinerolo through Saluzzo to Cuneo, the metropolis of that corner of the Plain, where the Cottians meet the Maritimes. Another eight miles or so, to the south-east, and the Plain ends at Borgo San Dalmazzo, in the last nook at the intersection of the ranges. I had for my journey a glorious day, with air as clear as water. As one passes under the foot-hills of the Cottians, Viso dominates the earth at every step. All the lesser masses, Mansoul, Granéro, Paravas, huddle along his knees ; and the mountains rise so abruptly from the plain that each combe and chine above Crissolo or Bobby is clear to view. I can see right up into all the

Combes de Barant, and note the microscopic shadows
which are the gullies where I went so gingerly. How
august and high it looks ; can it be possible that I ever
ascended thither unaided by wings ?  And how clearly
defined in that crystal light : I can watch that shoulder
where I lay and saw the whole Plain embedded in violet
gloom.  I can see that it is filmed with scrub; with fancy's
eye it is almost possible to see the Anemone shining in
snowdrifts from afar.  But gradually the puffing tram
swallows the distances ;  at each bend begins another
straight level stretch of many miles.  Gradually Viso,
and the Combes de Barant, and all the Cottians slide
imperceptibly northward, and are left ; gradually the dim
billows of the Maritimes draw nearer and take shape, and
become solid mountains in the golden light of the afternoon.

It was at evening that we snorted up into Cuneo
and came to rest.  Cuneo is a big bald place, with arcaded
streets and a Bishop whose name is Andrew.  More
than that I do not know of Cuneo, nor desire to know.
Three times in one year have I visited the place ; each
time I have disliked it.  But on that first arrival I did not
know the doom in store for me ; therefore I approached
Cuneo with an open heart, ready with warm feelings
for any town that lay under the shadow of the Maritime
Alps.  One's likings and loves are proverbially im-
probable ;  there are many mountains and many ranges
of greater beauty and conspicuousness than the Maritime
Alps, yet there are none that I think of with greater
affection, nor with such a *serrement de coeur*.  Their

lines are rather huddled, their peaks of no wonderful
prominence, the main formation of the group granitic;
but the very memory of the Maritime Alps moves me more
than actual sight of many another more eminent range.
Perhaps it is the beauty of their names ; perhaps it is
thought of the strange ancient plant that has chosen
them for its last dwelling-place on earth ; in any case I
would gladly make Ortler and Jungfrau into footstools
for Marguareis and Argentera. And, therefore, in the
thought that I was arriving in the hills I most love, some
of my tenderness flowed over upon the abandoned
fortress-city of Cuneo, lying on its wide hillock at the corner
of the Plain, with its walls converted into leafy promenades.
It lay very peaceful in the glamour of red sunset.  I
thought it a pathetic place ; until my troubles began.

For, be it known, from Cuneo one has to take another
tram, at the other side of the town, across what is left
of the Plain, to Borgo San Dalmazzo ; and thence, by
carriage, up the eighteen or twenty miles of the Gesso
Valley to the Baths of Valdieri.  Therefore, on alighting,
I demanded a porter to carry my luggage across Cuneo
to the starting-point of the other tram.  And they
allotted me the local idiot.  And the local idiot seemed
to have no idea in his head except to understudy the
Wandering Jew.  For he ambled incurably up and
down and round and about the walls of Cuneo, until it
became quite clear that he had no notion where he
meant to go.  When I protested he bobbled at me
unintelligibly.  I followed in wrath at his heels, as he
led me hither and thither.  I was helpless.  I ask you,

what is one to do when one's guide is an idiot, who merely bobbles at one ? There is no use in appealing to the passers-by, for not even they can make the idiot understand. At last, when it seemed to me that I had completed the same circuit about six times, I determined to end these cycles of purgatory. Accordingly I seized my bag, shouted farewells at the idiot, and poured pence in his unwashed palm. If it were not for the quotation, too, I should be able to tell you the truth, which was that I weakly gave him a lavish franc, to be rid of him. He then departed, still bobbling, and I was left, *planté là*, with my bag, in the midst of that desolating town, with sunset drawing on, with about twenty-eight miles of journey still before me—up a mountain valley—and no idea how I was going to achieve them.

I found a hostelry at last, and enquired of trams and means. They were extortionate and hostile poeple. I discovered that the last tram to Borgo San Dalmazzo had just started, from just round the corner. My only chance now, of getting to the Baths that night, was to charter a carriage and drive the whole distance. Even so it was plain that I could not hope to arrive before midnight. The landlord, also, demanded great prices, and was cold about the entire programme. I gathered that it was yet early in the season (the snow having lain for so long that year), that the road was arduous and difficult, besides being in bad repair after the storms of winter. However, I clung to the information in my guide-book, that the Baths of Valdieri were always open from the third of July to the third of September. Therefore, this being the tenth of July, it was quite obvious that there must be people there already ; and that, where these had been able to arrive in their carriages, I also should be able to arrive in mine. Accordingly I insisted on a chariot's being found, and in the end consented to pay large sums for the hire of a small and ricketty victoria which just held me, beside the driver. Anything in life would have been better than to stay in that horrid pot-house ; to say nothing of the fact that even if I had, next morning would have confronted me with exactly the same problem, the same extortions, the same wurra-wurra. So I went out (having eaten nothing for many hours, and seeing no prospect of eating anything for many hours more,—until, indeed, I should arrive at the luscious fleshpots of the Baths), and purchased cherries from an old woman at a fruit-stall. Not understanding her dialect, I timidly proffered two halfpence, to see what would happen. She promptly compiled me such a pyramid of cherries that I shrank before it in affright. And then she added red currants as a sort of discount or *pourboire.* However, I reflected on the length of my drive, and decided to take all she offered. Laden with my purchase I climbed into the victoria, and we lumbered out of Cuneo.

Never shall I forget the paralysing dullness of those first seven or eight miles to Borgo San Dalmazzo. The road was perfectly straight, and as flat as a Bishop's biography ; we crawled along it at a snail's pace. I know of no combination so crushing, so annihilating, as that inflicted by a straight flat road (without a motor).

Nothing ever seems to come any nearer ; every effort to be useless and ineffectual. I offered the driver cherries to stimulate him ; but he contemned them. It was in the last moment of twilight that we ultimately drove into Borgo San Dalmazzo, through its narrow little street, and out again up the valley of the Gesso. Away to our left, ghostly-white in the gloaming, curled the broad road that runs south over the Col de Tenda. After that the night closed in, and I saw nothing more ; only the vast darkness of the mountains hanging over us. But a friend of mine, who subsequently came up the Gesso valley by day, tells me that there is a limy cliff not far from the Borgo, on which you may see a great Saxifrage, that must certainly be *lingulata Bellardi*. Not for me such sights. We toiled and crawled up a road that became increasingly more difficult and dilapidated. My driver was conversational, and I applied to him to confirm my own anticipations of the comforts we should find when at last we did arrive. He was not encouraging, however ; to magnify his backsheesh he dilated on the horrors of the way, and maintained that we should not arrive till many hours after midnight. I then understood him to say that there would be no one in the place. This, of course, was nonsense, as the hotel always opens on the third of July ; and still we imperceptibly advanced through the blackness.

Suddenly the fireflies appeared. I could not believe, when first I saw them. Dancing specks of light flickered here and there. It was uncanny. But, in a little while they were everywhere, restless phantasmal sparks of green flame in every bush. They courted each other,

soared and hovered, made lacy lines and patterns of
light as they pursued each other in a saraband over the
sapphire background of the night, or floated steadily
against the pitchy blackness of tree and bush. I had not
thought there could be in Europe any show so wonderful
as the illumination I saw one night in the Jungle of Ceylon,
as I drove over the soundless sand from Polonnarua, and
through avenues all outlined and lit by galaxies of
shifting fire. But here, less prodigal in their display,
indeed, and less lavish in their multitude, I do not think
that the European fireflies were any less bright than their
kinsmen away in Asia. They went with us now up the
mountain valley, almost to our destination. We passed
on slowly, at a crawl, past little villages—Sant, Anna,
Valdieri, past a lighted hunting lodge where the King of
Italy was lying in wait for the chamois, past a wide opening
in the mountains in our left, where the pass goes over,
through Entraque, up to the Madonna della Fenestra,
and so down into France and Saint Martin Lantosque.
It was all silence, a blank monotony ; one was too tired
to think or talk. Very far ahead there hung a triangle
of green gloom, which showed us the sky at the end of the
valley, between the enclosing ranges.

Soon the road became a stone-slope. Banks of snow
lay close upon it, and the surface was worn into holes,
and strewn thickly with blocks and boulders. We had
to halve our pace, and jerk heavily upwards over the
rocks as best we might, confiding in luck rather than
anything else. The snow-patches just gave us ghostly
light enough to see the surrounding desolation, and the

ruin of the roadway. I found it almost impossible to believe that Bath-patients—dyspeptic Countesses, and arthritic Italian generals of large size—had already come up this ravine since the third of July. No repairs had yet been made to the highway; the stone-falls of winter from the slopes overhead on the right were still lying undisturbed. It was now long after midnight. At last we were over what seemed the worst piece, and entered a gorge of solid night, where nothing was visible any more. Dense forested mountain-sides rose straight up on either side; below in its ice-bound gully brawled the Gesso river; the darkness was like jet. The inverted triangle of sky now hung nearer to us, or rather the ranges whose contrasting obscurity created it by their contrast were now more actual in the foreground as we drew closer. Then, down at the blackest heart of the blackness I began to feel, half-doubting, something like a dim blur of a darkness less intense; something like the reminiscence of a long-dead and ghostly luminosity. You had to look away from it, before you could be sure it was there. In the very depth of the gorge it glimmered, barely discernible, a thing you were conscious of, rather than a thing you perceived. And the guide was conscious of it, too. He waved his whip and told me that these were the Baths of Valdieri.

Through a deathly stillness we drove across a bridge and up to the front of the hotel. I could discern an arcaded frontage, and a mass of masonry like a mountain. One could only see a yard or so. What one divined from this was almost terrible in its immensity. And still no

light, no sound anywhere, no sign of life. It was
wonderful and ghastly to stand there in the midnight,
outside that closed barrack in the heart of the mountains.
It was so wonderful that one almost forgot one's anguish.
But where was the cheerful illumination, where the warm
welcome, where the wide-open doors, letting out a flood
of light? I dismounted, realizing that everybody must have
gone to bed. I climbed broad flights of stone steps, into
an open empty hall. It was a pillared colonnade like
a Pharaoh's Palace, with arches carried indefinitely
far above our heads, on columns vast as those of a
Cathedral. We wandered up and down the dim
expanse, shouting into the silence. The flame of the
carriage lamp wavered among the blacknesses, and showed
us to each other like pismires roving on the floor of
cavernous night itself. And still nothing happened.
On and on I wandered, down the arcade, to where I
thought I saw a glimmer: nothing. At the back the
arcade led to a staircase, where a gigantic clock ticked
awfully. But still no sign of life. The driver wandered
away at last, to try and find some living creature, perhaps,
in the caretaker's cottage. I was left alone in that weird
catacomb, crushed by the sense of its black immensity.
The Gesso river roared outside in the darkness, deep down
in its bed, and the ticks of the giant clock reverberated
with a hollow sound through the empty world. Otherwise I might have been sitting lone in the ruins of great
Babylon. And that ticking only emphasised the
solitude; the echoing of my footsteps on the stone-flags
was disturbing and terrible.

In the end my driver roused a sleepy porter from his
rest. He came with a light, and ran upstairs to rouse
more people. In a little while down came the secretary
of the establishment, frightened and pale, attended by
minor officials. He met me with an eye of dismay, and
told me that the hotel was not open at all ; that not only
were there no patients in residence, but that there was no
food, no bedding, no accommodation—nothing. However,
in the extremities of despair despair itself is banished.
I protested that it was well past midnight, and that one
couldn't turn out even the proverbial dog to sleep in the
bed of the Gesso river. Furthermore, that where they
themselves were finding food and lodgement, there,
obviously, must there be sufficient lodgement and food
for me also. For some time we wrestled together in that
hall, while the torch-bearers waited round us. Ultimately
he was convinced, though less by my eloquence than by
the fact that I proved to be the incarnate destination of
a bale of letters that lay waiting in the office.

A room was opened, bedding produced from cupboards,
bread and meat and wine prepared for a hunger that was
almost too extreme to appreciate them. And so, amid
a whirl of compliments and protestations and apologies,
I ate my dinner, and paid off my driver, and sank into a
log-like rest. It appeared that the season had been so
late that year, and the snow had lain so long, that the
hotel did not mean to open until the fifteenth of July,
instead of the third. Hence these anguishes. From
which I suffered more than my landlords ; for they, when
once they had recovered from the shock of my arrival,

decided to make the best of the matter. Accordingly, though I had no attentions, and slunk about unregarded among the caretakers who were peppered like tiny dots up and down the uncarpetted wilderness of the corridors; and though I meekly subsisted, in a corner, on the bread and cheese, the rough red wine, and the cold meat that nourished *them*, I found, in the end, that this hospitality was rated higher than any I have yet enjoyed in the hills, and that I was called upon for terms that I should consider quite adequate at Nice.

All the next day it rained without ceasing. I could see nothing, except that at the back of the hotel soared into the clouds a bank of dripping beech-forest. I wrote letters, and wandered up and down the vast desolations, into vacant ball-rooms, and along passages so wide that two carriages could have raced in them abreast, and had a good long race at that, well worth the watching. But on the morrow it was cloudless. I sallied forth betimes to explore. The Baths of Valdieri, celebrated from time immemorial, sit immediately at the foot of the Argentera, the highest point of the Maritime Alps, which rises in tier after tier of granitic crags, straight behind the hotel itself. And at this point other valleys come down into that of the Gesso, so that the Baths have no lack of expeditions.

All these glens lead up to passes over the mountains into France. Beyond the hotel penetrates the Val Valletta, under the western wall of the Argentera, till at its head it splits into the two Passes of the Ciriegia and the Mercantour, on either side of the Cima Mercantour,

from whose point you look down, on the southern side, to
the glen of the Boréon above Saint Martin Lantosque.  On
the other side of the Argentera, steeply climbs behind
the Hotel the Val Lourousa up towards the Gelas di
Lourousa, and the Col del Chiapous, under the eastern
cliffs of the peak.   And, immediately opposite the Hotel,
across the Gesso, flows down the wide and lovely Valasco
valley, embosked in forest, which ultimately leads to
a wall of mountains, where the glens curl round, and lead
up passes parallel with the Ciriegia, far above the Val
Valletta.   It was in the Valasco Valley that I determined to make my first voyage of exploration, because
this also is given as a habitat of *Saxifraga florulenta*,
though whereabouts the treasure might be seen I did not
then realize, peering up with a cricked neck at the mass
of granite that rises across the stream to the left of the
valley, and shoots up sheer through forests of laburnum
to the pine-zone, and thence again goes soaring in a
naked jag of rock—one huge cone-shaped mountain,
composed everywhere of rocky little shelves that are in
reality formidable cliffs.

I had been told that within half an hour of the hotel
the Flora of the Valasco Valley was rich and beautiful.
This is more than true ; in ten minutes even the laziest
may be revelling in a show of flowers generously sufficient
for all whose ambitions do not soar to the population
of the highest peaks—" the austere little people of the
hills," to whom my own allegiance remains always so
constant.   Just across the stream there is a stony waste
which is all aglow with crimson mats of *Saponaria*

*ocymoeides*, with woolly Sempervivums innumerable, and a lovely Achillea like white Marguerites. Here and there among them rise the soft blue suns of the perennial Alpine Lettuce, which comes perking among the stones, being always at its happiest in the poorest, hottest and most pebbly ground. A little higher and you see Aeizoon Saxifrages among the rocks, and occasionally strayed broad masses of *Primula viscosa ;* the shelving cliffs that rise up and up on the right are copsy with Laburnum in showers of gold, and among these is the lovely *Rosa ferruginea,** with its foliage of copper and steely-blue, contrasting so ingeniously with its big flowers of soft pink. Then, on the open ledges, gleam the gorgeous cups of *Lilium bulbiferum*, among the seed-spikes of the Asphodel. There are Columbines too, and *Aster alpinus* abounds with its golden-eyed cart-wheels of purple, amid the sprayed rosy stars of *Dianthus sylvestris.* In the long grass at their feet you will still find Asphodel in flower, and the two Anthericums, and Veratrum, handsome and ominous. *Biscutella* showers out and about its loose heads of pale gold, *Nasturtium pyrenaicum* does the same on a smaller scale and in a richer tone, and *Tulipa celsiana*, among the long-spiked Orchises and the pink pokers of Polygonum, is just closing the last of its little golden goblets. Where the ground is more stony, silky-grey *Lychnis Flos-Jovis* is opening its big carmine flowers everywhere, and the Parsley fern is sprouting in bushes among the dark rocks.

* An obscure species, whose name may ultimately have to be abolished. Let us say, then, *Rosa glauca*.

A little higher yet, and a splash of purple among the
slide of big boulders distracts your attention from
*Achillea Herba-rota* on a rock. Here you have the
celebrity of the place ; for this is *Viola valderia.* Now
I do not know the nature of *Viola valderia* ; the description I have already given of *cenisia* exactly describes
*valderia* also. Except for two significant differences :
*valderia* is found only at lower elevations than *cenisia* ;
it is much rarer, being confined, if the name is right, entirely
to this district ; and, instead of being stoloniferous, and
running about with many minor rooting branches until
it forms a colony two or three feet across, poking up
between the stones, after the lavish habit of *Viola cenisia,*
*Viola valderia* makes only one compact tuft, on a single
tap-root, which never sends out runners. In other words,
it is identical with all descriptions of the species called
*Viola alpina,* which I have never yet collected, from the
Eastern Alps, where it is supposed to have its only
dwelling. And more than this, Prof. Burnat declares
that *Viola alpina* is nothing but a synonym of this *Viola
valderia.** Into such profundities I will not plunge.
*Valderia,* anyhow, is a brilliant and beautiful little
mountain pansy, twin-brother to *cenisia,* except in its
habit, and in its love of lower elevations.

It ought, on these counts, to be much easier in
cultivation. I cannot talk yet of this with any certainty ;
Our boxes from Valdieri met with such delays in transit

---

* But Correvon's plate of *Viola alpina,* in the " Atlas de la Flore Alpine,"
represents a densely tufted plant quite unlike *valderia,* and with different
flowers, nearer to *calcarata* than to *cenisia.*

that I am not at this moment sure whether *valderia* recovered from its journey. But these mountain-pansies have all, it seems, a little something miffish in their nature, no matter how robustly they may bloom and thrive on the sunny slopes of their native hills. I have already raised the question of even *calcarata*, the robustest of them all (and my mark of interrogation was not obliterated by the fact that there are now immense wide tufts of it in my gardens—until this spring began to promise me as rich a show of flower as they give on their own Alps). *Cenisia* I would almost go so far as to declare impossible, and of *heterophylla* from the Southern Alps I have not a much more cheerful tale to tell. And, now that I have written this, I know these lines will have a far more favourable effect on my mountain-pansies than years of the most sedulous culture—next summer will certainly swathe my garden in the purples of *calcarata*, and raise me up a whole blooming boscage of *cenisia*, *heterophylla* and *valderia*. To kill a plant, you need only write in the *Gardener's Chronicle* that it is thriving ; insert an obituary notice of it, and the thing, no matter how moribund, will immediately bush out and prosper like a Pelargonium.

So I hope I am adopting a wise treatment for the alpine violets. They have all a radiant loveliness which is very captivating. They are the most personal of flowers, and their little witty faces always twinkle with shrewdness. *Valderia* is among the most humorous of the family; *calcarata*, perhaps, with all its beauty, has not quite so keen a sense of fun. *Valderia*, I am sure, has something of Christina of Denmark, Dowager of Milan —and well she may, for here at Valdieri, on the northern slope of the hills, we are not so far from Tortona, along the same side of the range, but further east, out in the Plain, where Christina had her dower-palace, lived out her closing years, and died, in a place hallowed no less by the more tragic ending of one of the last shadow-emperors who had a show of reigning in the west.    For in Tortona was beheaded the well-meaning Majorinus.

The companion, indeed, who joined me at Valdieri after two days, felt more enthusiasm for *Viola valderia* than for any other mountain-pansy ; and this, although I showed him in succession *calcarata, cenisia, heterophylla,* insisting, like a showman, on their respective beauties: yet nothing could wean his affection from their first fine raptures over *valderia.*    This, I believe, must have been because *valderia* came on him with the shock of novelty, and all the others merely repeated the effect.    For, as I say, *valderia* is twin to *cenisia ;* if you go crazy over the one you cannot contrive to keep more sane when you see the other.    But my friend remained beyond reach of conversion.    I think he even undervalued, subsequently, a Viola more brilliant and august and exquisite than even these.    But that is the tale of a future day.

The Valasco valley mounts steeply, after you have passed the stone-slope of the Viola.    Along the track are dotted splendid old firs.    And across the river, brawling below, they stand in a steep forest, up and up on the flanks of the mountain opposite.    At last they tail off and grow rare in the uppermost gullies ; and after that the granite is bare and sheer. Those gullies, immeasurably far above one's head, are probably, as I now know, the haunt of *Saxifraga florulenta*. If Ball's citation of the plant from this valley be justified, as, indeed, there is no reason why it should not be, seeing our close neighbourhood to Argentera, and the universality, here, of the granite that *florulenta* insists upon. One can only go slowly, at this point, so incessantly must one stop to look back at the unfolding ranges behind the hotel. Below one's feet drops away the valley up which one has come, and, on the other side of the glen of Valdieri that cuts across it below, there climbs a steep beechen forest to the point at which the pines in their turn take possession ; and high above these, and perpetually higher at every step, unroll the splendours of the Argentera—gaunt spars and precipices and pinnacles of naked granite, sweeps and stretches and long slides of snow and ice, towering to the tremendous summit of the mountain, nearly eleven thousand feet above the sea. And on those inhospitable black cliffs, in those grim gullies, there also, even up to the famous couloir under the peak on its northern face, dwells the oldest and loneliest of Saxifrages.

Another one lives here in the Valasco Valley, and pervades all the granitic glens of the Maritime Alps, rising high, too, on the bare stone-shingles. If you descend here, and cross the stream, and make your difficult way over forested deep mossy ground, full of *Astrantia minor* and *Atragene alpina*, you will come at last on *Saxifraga pedemontana* in masses, in a tumble of moss-bound granite blocks. But *S. pedemontana* shall not

detain me long ; it is a rare plant, indeed, and almost
unknown in cultivation.   But it is a Mossy—although a
very handsome Mossy.   Its greatest beauty, to my
thinking, lies in its foliage.   It has very thick, succulent-
looking leaves, rounded in outline, and slit into two or
three overlapping rounded lobes, which are vandyked
at their hem with rounded regular jags.   Their colour is
of an abrupt and splendid clear green, even in the depth
of winter.   They are more brilliant than even those of
*Wallacei*, though smaller ; much more opulent and fat in
general effect.   For *Wallacei* is the species which *pedemontana* has the hard luck to compete against, or perhaps,
the " bragian boldness."   For in the matter of blossom
*Wallacei* wins easily, and, indeed, it is clearly presumptuous, one feels, of *pedemontana* thus to challenge the
magnificent sovereign of the Mossies.   The tall, branching
stems of *pedemontana* are well and gracefully furnished,
certainly, with flowers of quite as pure a white as those of
*Wallacei*, but their size is not proportionate to the ampli-
tude of the foliage, and their outline is a little narrow, as
compared with the generous expansion of *Wallacei's*
snowy cups.   However, making allowances for this,
*pedemontana* remains a species of outstanding beauty and
interest.   It is only not equal to the very best, and, if
we ignored everything but the very best, what would
our lives and our gardens be like ?   Pure *pedemontana* is
restricted entirely, I believe, to this district, and seems
to insist in nature upon granitic formations.   However,
in the garden it appears perfectly amenable, and is
thriving handsomely on the Cliff.

Continuing to mount on the right of the stream, one arrives ultimately at the inevitable little grassy plain, which is walled in by an amphitheatre of bare mountains. In the middle of this plain there sits one of the royal hunting lodges—the funniest little object, like a one-storeyed castle made of cardboard, with cardboard turrets at each corner, and the whole thing painted in stripes of red and green, or whatever may be the regal colours of Italy. To this palace does Italian majesty resort when in pursuit of chamois over the neighbouring peaks. And, thanks to this propensity of Italian majesty, all the mountains are seamed with admirable paths, which come in very handy for the less distinguished explorer. Up one of these now leads the way, sharp to the left, and up and up, and still up, until even the pine-trees diminish, and at last there was nothing but a wilderness of red granite, flaked here and there with increasingly numerous stretches of snow. And a line of telegraph poles straggled up it, inappropriately leading one on. There were no flowers of interest. Gentians and *Viola calcarata* had been dotted about at the beginning of the climb, but soon died away, and nothing took their place. Where Rhododendrons lay dark and rank above the snow-field that filled a gully, there gleamed, it is true, a few blooms of *Anemone alpina*, and here, at last, it was *A. a. sulfurea*. But poor at that. Otherwise one tramped for ever upwards through desolation unrelieved ; and the earth with all its mountains slid gradually down beneath one's feet.

For now one was almost on a level with the peak that

towers so stupendous over the Baths; the naked mountains around seemed no higher than one's self by this time; in the intense and sunlit clearness of the air the silence and the barrenness of that stony world were almost frightening. I continued up that rocky hollow, and at last there was nothing before me anywhere but snow. In front rose a pass, pure white. I debated whether I should attempt it or not. The telegraph poles, startlingly black against the snow, encouraged me by climbing all the way up the Col, and presumably all the way down the other side. They were heartening guides; where they could go, and where they found it worth their while to persevere, it would clearly be possible and profitable for me to persevere also. In the end, then, I decided to continue. Beyond doubt, also, I was by now in the zone of *Saxifraga florulenta*, and it should go hard with me, but I must see it on the cliffs to either side of the pass.* I launched out upon the blazing slopes of snow, putting my handkerchief over my eyes to avoid that deadly conjunctivitis which you can catch in a few minutes from exposure to sunlit snow in the rarefied air of the high alps. The snow was good going when you were on it; but here and there big boulders emerged, or ribs of large shingle, and round the edges of these the snow was melting very insidiously, for, if one went unadvisedly, one's foot plunked through most disconcertingly, all of a sudden, into

* Burnat quotes it, on his own authority, from the Mercantour, the Ciriegia, the Fremamorta, the Mte. Matto opposite the Argentera, on the N. side of the Gesso Valley from the Baths: and on J. Ball's (who also quotes Mte. Matto) more vaguely, as "near the Baths." Ball himself gives the Valasco Valley as a locality for it.

dark depths. This might merely produce annoyance ;
or, if one were going too quickly, might rick one's ankle,
or sprain it, or break it ; and in utter solitude, at such
heights, such a disablement might well prove fatal. So
that, take it all in all, I had no pleasure in the actual
ascent of the slope. I think that had it not been for the
deliciousness of the air, and the glory of sunlight, I
might even have desisted and gone back. But the air
was full of a clear and crystal tranquillity ; little cool
breezes hovered ; and the sun was flooding the mountain-
world with pure light. So, thanks to the inspiriting
radiance of it all, I plod, plod, plodded up that endless
slope without flagging, and, where stones emerged,
jumped gingerly from one to the other, hoping for a good
event.

I reached the pass, to be met by keen blasts of cold.
Down on the other side there was a small lake, masked
in snow and ice. The snow was still lying everywhere,
and only on one southerly exposure was there a single
open piece of scree. Towards this, I need hardly say
that I immediately stumbled ; after long traverses,
arrived ; and there, for the first time, set eyes on *Thlaspi
limosellaefolium* unfolding its pink flower-heads almost
unnoticeable among the russet flakes of granite. By
that time, however, I was so cross with the non-produc-
tiveness of the Valasco Valley in its upper reaches, that
it was all I could manage to collect a few plants of this,
and I will not show you the delightful treasure until I can
do so in richer display and from a smoother heart.
Up and down among those shingles and snows I slid and

sought.  I got up to the big cliff that overhangs the
lake, and worked down along its base.  For here, if anywhere in the range, I ought to be finding *florulenta*.  And
there was no sign of it.  There were purple clusters of
*Primula viscosa*, there was a white Arabis in flower,
there was *Anemone alpina sulfurea* growing as a crevice-
plant among the rocks, in situations such as I had never
before imagined it would tolerate.  Otherwise there was
emptiness.  I resolved that I would just make the circuit
of the lake below, explore the granite ridge on its further
side, and then return, whether I found anything or
nothing.

And it was still nothing.  At last, satisfied that the
quest was hopeless, I determined to indemnify myself
with the view.  And this, indeed, was well worth the
toil.  From the little Lac de Portette one looks straight
away over tumbled downs and ridges of bare granite-
shingle to the Passes of Basse de Druos and Fremamorta
(where the telegraph poles go), carrying one up over into
France and down upon Saint Etienne de Tinée.  For,
all along the south, between you and France, not more
than two miles away, lies unfolded before you the whole
grim barrier of the Maritime Alps, in their fullest and
most forbidding splendour.  Round the corner to the left
stands Argentera ; and the ridge goes sweeping thence
along the head of the Valletta Valley, to the Cima
Mercantour, and so on, to these mountain masses beyond
the Lac de Portette.  It is all crag and snow-field, white
stretches broken by jags and pinnacles of dark rock—a
panorama of stern hostility and magnificence.  From

the ridge that holds up the lake one looks almost straight
below upon the Val Valletta. It lies so deep down that it
seems tiny. One can see its whole course, nearly, though
its beginnings, away by the Baths, are masked by the
granite mountain which stands on our left. And at its
upper extremity one can see how the Val Valletta ends.
For at its head surges up to Heaven the Cima Mercantour ;
on either side of this is a depression in the stark wall
that closes the career of the Valletta so abruptly. That
to the left is the Col Mercantour, and that on the right
is the Ciriegia Pass, by which it is my intention, when I
leave Valdieri, to climb over into the valley above Saint
Martin.

And it was with terror and awe that I inspected the
Cherry-tree Pass that day. (Why Cherry-tree ?) For
it loomed very high and awful against the distant horizon ;
and rose like a blank cliff, in tier above tier, from the
valley that crawled so humbly down at its feet. But,
more than that, and infinitely worse ; almost the whole
of the pass was an unbroken sheet of snow, except for
a dim strip of darkness near the top that looked like a
shingle-slope. That snow lay in its unsunned hollows
throughout the year, I very well knew, but that the
entire Pass should still be under snow in the middle of
July was a catastrophe unheard of. What was the good
of questing there for *Viola nummulariaefolia*, which was
one of my main reasons for desiring to cross the
Ciriegia ? And there was yet a further consideration.
For my luckless companion was due to arrive the
next day, and had already forewarned me that he

had no " head," and was terrified of hills and snow. And, on his second day in the Alps, I was proposing to lug his inexperience over that tedious and probably appalling Pass !

For, bad as it might look on its northern face, I knew that the Ciriegia was much worse on its southern, falling away into France with a dramatic precipitance that would certainly prove trying to the nerves of all concerned in the descent.    I sat on the ridge above the Lake and wondered what diplomacy I should adopt with my victim.    For, if I could not succeed in getting him over there, I should per- force have to change my elaborate and cherished plan, and spend much money in pursuing an entirely altered route, going down the Gesso Valley again to Cuneo, and over the Col de Tenda to San Dalmazzo, in a way that would make the whole pilgrimage to Valdieri simply so much dead waste of time and resources.    I decided ultimately that, in the first place, I would charter a guide, to hold tremulous hands, and put trembling feet in their appointed slots, and, generally, inspire confidence ;  and that, in the second, I would myself paint the perils of that Pass before- hand in colours so lurid that when  he  got there my com- panion should be agreeably disappointed by finding the thing as simple as A B C in comparison with the dangers he had anticipated.    It is always good policy to bank a greater deposit of heroism than you will ever have occasion to draw a cheque for.    On these conclusions, then, I rose up and made my laborious way down the snow-slopes again into the Valasco Valley, and so back once more to the Baths.

The next day my companion arrived, and I duly spent the hours in making him gibber over the prospect of the Ciriegia. In the intervals of doing this we explored the floral wealth close round the Baths. For here, in damp places, you will find a plant of some rarity which is called *Tozzia alpina*. It is not only rare, but also ugly, a dowdy Scrophulariaceous thing, with microscopic yellow flowers. No more of it. There is also *Cardamine asarifolia*, likewise in wet places. But this, on the other hand, tends to be rather coarse and unworthy. A third local product is *Potentilla valderia*, which is abundant in the stony ground below the road as you approach the hotel from below. This, as I grow it, is a small neat plant, with three-lobed leaves of the loveliest silver colouring. But, in its native haunts it grows large and ample, sending up to the height of two feet and more, from a bush of leafage, its corymbs of flowers, which were only in bud when I was at Valdieri, but which I have reason to believe, show too much of the green calyx between the too-narrow white petals of the flower, to make any effect worthy of its port and silvery splendour. In my own garden it has so far spared me this disillusionment by refusing to flower at all.

The last and most important speciality of the Baths is *Ulva labyrinthiformis*. But, in case you should unanimously write at once to the Craven Nursery for this rare plant, I will hastily add that it is a cryptogam which grows in the hot sulphur waters and covers the whole hillside where they trickle in a curtain of thick rubber-like brown jelly, inexpressibly revolting to see, or smell, or handle. This precious plant is cut off in strips, and laid upon old ulcers and scars and wounds ; and these it heals at once, perfectly : *experti crede*. I tried it on my own thumbs, off which the mountains had chipped slabs. A precious vegetable it is. There is never too much of it at the Baths, where it is in incessant request among the bath-guests. Accordingly it has to be propagated, to keep the supply renewed. They throw out broad slips of plank on the slope, or very shallow long wooden troughs. Over these a certain amount of water runs, and with the water develops the Ulva. So that, in a little while, the wood is hidden beneath a dense coat of that transparent, warm, elastic jelly.

The Baths have their season in August, and then are crowded ; only by the nobility of Savoy, however. No English traveller appears to have even heard of them. And yet no more delightful place of sojourn could possibly be imagined—if you do not have to undergo the Ulva. The situation is of unusual delightfulness—deep in a wooded narrow gorge, with the Gesso roaring beneath, under mossy cliffs that are curtained with *Primula marginata*. On all sides of you shoot up noble mountains, with, for the most part, practicable hunting-paths leading up their flanks ; and, for a rare advantage, three or four mountain valleys converge at this point, so that there is practically no limit to your choice of expeditions ; while, within five minutes of the hotel, as I have said, if you weary of sylvan shade among the beeches, you may be out on ground that is carpeted with a dozen different sorts of brilliant flowers. As for the hotel itself, daylight stripped it of none of the majesty conferred by night. It is an enormous block of stone, like a Roman Palazzo, so titanic in its conception and execution that the sight of such a thing always seems a miracle, so far from human habitation, up there among the woods all by itself in a wild glen between the hills.

# CHAPTER VI.

## THE ANCIENT KING.

THE Val Valletta runs long and flat and dull into the heart of the ranges behind the Baths of Valdieri. One resents this the worse, that if it chose to climb a little more definitely, it would save one a certain amount of the rigid ascent one has at last to make, in order to get up the barrier of mountains at its head. It was early morning when my companion and I set out for the Ciriegia Pass. It was not quite such early morning as I had meant it to be, for final packings and fusses are apt to consume more time than one anticipates. But the Valletta Valley still lay cold in the blue shadows as we trudged along its level stretches, seeing nothing of any moment. And at its head we had a full prospect of the Ciriegia all the time. And that Ciriegia rose to the sky, like a sheer white wall, with sheer walls of rock beneath. It seemed to shut out the Heavens as we advanced. I could feel the spirits of my companion growing bluer at every step, like the shadows in the valley. At intervals he moaned, contemplating stark death ahead of him up there in the sky.

The mountains drew nearer and nearer, more and more imminent. No track nor way of ascent could I see on the Ciriegia. It was straight stones, and then straight snow. I grew desperate in the thought that well might

a new comer, fresh from England, quail before such
forbidding prospects ; and still more desperate in the
absolute necessity of fighting down those qualms and
lugging him safely across. My voice assumed a hot
heartiness as I encouraged my victim, and smeared him
with preliminary compliments on the excellence of his
walking powers.

He accepted these propitiations in a gloomy silence,
and was not even cheered when I happened incidentally
to mention a true fact—namely, that from straight in
front the meekest of inclines presents inevitably the
aspect of a sheer wall. And so, indeed, we found it, of
course. We crossed a little plain at the end of the
valley, and then began to mount briskly over the stone-
slopes on the right. It was as dull as dull ; but as easy as
despair. There were no plants of any value ; all the
slope was sodden with the snow that had only just
departed from it. Up we toiled in silence, and up and
up and up, until we came into the domain of the lowest
snow-patches, squashy beds of slush, that slunk ashamed
among the stones. And ever, as we went, the climb above
our heads looked higher and more blank. Until, in the
end, my companion's aspirations gave out ; his pent
feelings boiled over, and he wailed, " I cannot do it."

I felt red murder in my veins at this, and realised
none the less that now was the supreme necessity for
diplomacies. My voice assumed an awful blandness as
I deprecated premature givings-up, assured him that no
climb was ever one tenth as hard or steep as it looked from
below, pointed out the tedious alternative before us, if

he carried out this intention of defection, and finally insisted, with a hilarity that I was far from feeling, that he was clearly too heroic and agile a mountaineer to be perturbed by such trumpery trudges as these. I turned upon him a face to which smiles were rigidly affixed as if by pins, determined to carry the situation through as far as it could be made to go, by force of resolute glossiness. And my sweetness so far prevailed that he did not sit down then and there, nor go home. In despair he continued, without answer, to ascend that slide of stones.

It *is* a dreary stone-slide, that,—composed of bald red granite blocks, too large to admit of any shingle-flora ; and disheartening to walk on, even with the track. This, indeed, was in ill repair after the winter, and was still slippery with melting snow. It appeared that we were the first non-native mortals that season to dare the altitudes of the Ciriegia. Now there were a few sodden ferns beginning to push, and *Saxifraga pedemontana* sat in gloomy lumps among the darkness. I threw glee into my tones, and pointed these out to my victim with much the same violent joviality that the surgeons had a way of in my childhood, when they used to show me fluffy chenille monkeys, in order to make me undergo an operation peacefully. Thus did I beguile the toil, until we came over the first ridge, and fairly embarked on the snow-fields that now, without interruption, covered all the way up to the Pass. And I need not say that the going was of the easiest possible. Even if a blind, lame, and drunken lunatic had managed to fall down on those inclines, he could not conceivably have rolled more than

two yards, no matter how imbecile and inebriated. The
snow rose up in long steep bank after long steep bank ;
but the foothold was good almost to excess. For under
the sun the surface was growing slushy. We realized anew
the advantage of that early start on which the guides try
to insist when any snow-expedition is in question.

As violent death was found to be no longer imminent
or even possible, my companion came to life again, and
began to utter words. I caused him to look down upon
the snow-slopes he had dared, and despise them. Seeing
that he as yet refused to do this, I adopted another tack,
and showed him their awfulness, in order to insist on his
own prowess in surmounting them—a prowess that must
needs make child's play of any further difficulty we might
meet (for I remembered the southern face that was yet to
come). This answered better ; so well, indeed, that in a
little while he was even beginning to look down the long
inclines in a superior manner. Having got my victim so
far, I felt at ease. I knew he would confront any horror
rather than go back down that snow-mountain alone.
He was definitely committed.

So, with heart secure, I trudged upwards, zigzagging
in successive footholds up each long bank ; and paused,
at intervals, to watch the unfoldings that were going on
in the distances behind us. The sun was high by now,
and there were clouds occurring here and there. Down
below, in the twilight, lay the Val Valletta. But only its
beginnings near the hotel. So steep had been the climb
that its head was hidden from us by the slope up which
we had come. And then, on either side, loomed the gaunt

splendours with which we were rapidly coming to deal on
equal terms. Clearly could I see the little ridge above
the Lac de Portette, from which I had first appreciated
the terrors of the Ciriegia. Mountains flowed away
beyond, in range after range towards the Cottian Alps.
On the right, straight above the creek where lay the
Baths, shot up, in wooded bank above craggy wooded
bank, in ridge above rock-ridge, to naked peak after
naked peak, the whole snow-clad glory of the Argentera;
from which, towards us in a sweep, came rushing the
linked chain of the Maritime Alps, ending over our heads
in the pinnacles of Mercantour, and beginning again on
the other side of that shallow white depression high
ahead of us, which was the Ciriegia Pass.

Much more monotonous than Piccadilly, that Pass was
a more formidable tramp. We had, on that thirteenth
of July, about three solid hours of snow-walking, on
sludgy snow at that ; up successive slopes, each steeper
than the last, that none of them seemed to get us any
higher, through a new one was perpetually being disclosed
in front of the one we had just surmounted. However, our
spirits mounted as steadily as our feet ; and with much
more apparent result. We both began to feel that we
were really achieving something ; we grew pleased with
ourselves, and consequently approved of the world at
large. But there still remained the question as to whether
*Viola nummulariaefolia* would prove to still be in bed
under a coverlet of snow. For, though I had heard of it
throughout the high granites of the range, I knew that
it was certainly recorded, among many other records,

from stone-slopes on the right of the Ciriegia near the summit of the Pass. Therefore I was in hopes that we might make our first acquaintance with it there.

And, amid the unbroken snows that I had seen from the Lac de Portette clothing all the Pass, I had, as I say, discerned one or two dark strips near the Col which gave promise that, here and there, a southerly-facing stone-slope at the top of the Pass might, perhaps, turn out to be already clear of snow. And at last our tramping that day brought us in sight, after many false promises, of the actual Pass itself. My hope was justified. There on the right lay a long bank of shingle open to the light of the sun, still dank and clogged indeed with melting cold, but yet capable already of revealing life. Towards this accordingly, diverging from the track made by earlier footfalls, we plunged into a snowy hollow, and up over a snowy slope, until we came out on the rough banks of our desire.

On that high slide, eight thousand four hundred feet above the Mediterranean, life as a matter of fact was but very sparingly revealed. Ten days before, and the coverlet of snow must have been unbroken : the shingle was still dark and dripping with moisture ; dark and dripping, though, here and there dim buds of vegetation were pushing. And, if meditation were permitted, I would here add that nothing in the world is more august a " miracle " than the awakening of these stone-beds, far up on the necks of the mountains. The piercing of young life through so dank a desolation is something tremendous to watch ; the minuteness of it all, and the undeviable determination. Here was a dead jostle of sodden shingle, on it lay the sodden brown wraiths of last year's plants ; yet already out of death was emerging life, at ten days' notice, like a politician's brand-new Constitution, but more efficacious and perennial. Down in each skeleton rosette lurked a core of young verdure, and among the stones were rising everywhere wet little dark-green leaves, hurrying up to lighten in the sun. *Saxifraga retusa* soon leapt to view ; *Thlaspi limosellaefolium* was even in bloom, and there was abundance of the inevitable alpine crucifer, *Hutchinsia brevicaulis*, which is equivalent to *H. alpina* of the less granitic moraines. But where was *Viola nummulariaefolia* ?

We poked and peered and routled among such growths as we could discern. Soon we came on the *pousses* of *Campanula stenocodon*, spearing freely through the shingle. Other minor matters met our view—problems and ambiguities. I fixed my attention on a plant that was coming up with tiny dark-green leaves, rounded, heart shaped, whose stems had a ramifying habit among the stone, appearing here and there. It was obviously a Violet. I spotted this at once, of course, for *Viola nummulariaefolia*, and cried aloud in joy. And then my companion grubbed up a piece of it, and lo, it carried a pod that was no less obviously that of some little crucifer. Not only disappointment, but discredit was my lot. The search continued, more and more fierce. Never had either of us set eyes before on *Viola nummulariaefolia* in the living leaf, so how were we to know the plant if we found it, seeing that here there could be no hope of a flower (I do not count the mouldered, miserable tags that are all I have ever received from collectors, by way of *Viola nummulariaefolia* ; moribund and mangled fragments give no guide to the appearance of a plant in its natural health and character)? But gradually my spirits revived as I began to see that there was absolutely nothing else on that slope *but* my discovery, which *could* answer to *Viola nummulariaefolia.* Those leaves I had seen could not possibly after all, belong to any other plant than a Violet ; and there could be no other Violet at such an elevation than *V. nummulariae-folia.* This process of exclusion, combined with the infallible Ball's reference, put my back to the wall and restored my confidence, until at last I boldly confronted my companion: "I do not believe that was really a crucifer at all," I said. " Take out the clump and look at it again." He did, and we found that the cruciferous pod belonged, not to the plant itself, but to a stray fragment of *Hutchinsia* that had got entangled in it. But we found more than that. The plant itself was carrying old seed capsules ; and those capsules were those of a Violet. *Viola nummulariaefolia* had been discovered and unmasked.

We stopped and collected, but I will not give you the Violet's portrait, nor that of the Thlaspi, until we have found them both in the full radiance of their bloom. And while we sat there the clouds came swirling up at us out of France, hiding the Mediterranean and all the earth, enveloping the ridge in a white tide of darkness. We thought well to continue on our way. And now I felt that we were approaching the crisis ; in another minute we should be looking down that terrible southern slope of the Ciriegia. It was in silence that we cut across the top of the stone-slide, under bare pinnacles across which the gloom was floating in swift wreaths and eddies ; and came gradually down on to the notch of the actual Pass itself. We looked over on to the southern side. For now we were indeed on the coping of the wall of France.

The Ciriegia drops straight away ; the angle is like the side of a house. Clouds prevented us from seeing the gulfs below, which was a mercy ; but what we did see was sufficient to make me thankful that we had already come so high and far as to put going back again out of the question. For that raking slope was many feet deep in solid snow ; quite easy to descend, of course, and quite safe so long as one kept one's head and one's feet (as one always does if it is really necessary that one should ; for accidents never happen on places where one is afraid), but undenyingly daunting to look down upon— and none the less daunting for the cloud-wracks that came surging up it, and billowing round our feet, like solidified breaths from some cold hell beneath, that brought with them a charnel-house chill. All the world, what we could see of it in fleeting glimpses through the spume, was dark, and grey, and cold. The awe of a mountain mist in grim places is calculated to sink into the marrow of one's bones.

Fortunately, out of extremity is borne endurance. My companion, who had not liked the beginnings of the

Pass, now faced its abrupt obverse with a stoical calm. He said little, but it was clear that he was determined to do or die ; even though he felt death to be the more probable alternative. I was able to tell him that the test was short, if sharp ; otherwise heartenings were unnecessary, and, therefore, out of place. To encourage people in doing what they have made up their minds to do, is not only to waste one's own breath, but also to irritate their pride, by suggesting that it needs reinforcement. We sat accordingly in silence in the pallid gloom of the ridge, and ate lunch to fortify ourselves, while the guide carried our bales and boxes down to a place of safety below. Little bright Gentians were blue in the rocks of that *arête*, but I saw no sign of *Eritrichium*. Yet, just opposite, overhead, rose up the peak of Mercantour, on which the King of the Alps is known to have his royal seat ; the summit is only twenty or thirty minutes climb from the Pass, and if the day had been clear I should certainly have gone up, seeing that we had time enough and to spare. But in so thick a mist it would have been tedious work. Having so stormily attended one *levée* already of His Majesty, I thought it unnecessary to dare death, and incur fatigue, by pressing for a second.

At last the guide was dimly seen returning through the clouds at our feet. My companion rose up like the armed and iron maidenhood of Antigone, going out ἄκλαυτος ἄφιλος ἀνυμέναιος to her death. Although I am bound to say he made less noise about it than that rather grim and forbidding young person, that Suffragette born out of due time, in an era when forcible feeding was not invented.

He gave his hand to the guide, who planted his feet for him in the proper holes : and so they proceeded down that slope, beneath the red granite cliffs of Mercantour. They went with majestic slowness. I followed after in their track, confident in the guide's strong arm. I had need to be, for how difficult it is for a beginner to realise the fatalness of clutching the inner bank. To keep perfectly upright is really the one way of safety.

But the lesson is hard to learn. My companion never attempted to learn it. There he was, descending the Ciriegia, with a drop of unknown death below, over as steep an incline of snow as I have known, and as soon as the guide released him, he went leaning inwards all the way, crouched down, clutching the snow-bank with his right hand. The least slip, the least yielding of the snow-clod on which his downstretched left foot was resting the whole weight of his body without support, and he *must* have gone. Nothing could have saved him. He was spending all his defensive forces and muscles on the inner side, where no danger was, and leaving himself without refuge or protection on the only side whence any danger could threaten. His stick was useless to him, and even added peril, for he had that also fixed below him, and carrying his weight ; whereas, whenever due attention is necessary, the more experienced mountaineer will always plunge his stick in the bank, above and behind him as he descends, and thus goes upright in the dignity of that erect poise which is the peculiar prerogative of man.

These are weighty teachings. Let me not be thought to hold up any methods of my own to imitation ; nor to be of mountaineering tread unjustly vain, " and the nice conduct of a —pointed cane." I am merely quoting general rules ; so far as my own practice goes, if I avoid the grosser errors now (supposing that I do), it is only that I have suffered from them through so many seasons, that at last sheer instinct has eradicated them. Years alone, and no wisdom of mine, have given me a surer foot among the hills and a serener heart. Alas, that this hill-craft is but an acquired characteristic, then, and cannot be transmitted to my descendants. The blow is softened to me by the fact that I have not got any. (This to reassure the many people who write and tell me they are certain that I am unmarried, from the tone of my writings—Dear dear Sophia of my heart, would you then so clearly transpire through my works, supposing you had heard me with a kindlier ear ?)

In any case, I followed slowly down into the mist, down and down and down. The snow-bank was like the steepest of ladders. So violent was the drop and so deep the snow, that, standing in one foothold, it was difficult to set one's foot clear into the next. The slope got in one's way. But, however slowly one may go, the mountains always seem to soar up like birds as one descends. In five minutes the Pass seemed as high above me as my own ideals. As to the Mercantour, it had shot up to the stature of Heaven ; its blank red wall on my left ran aloft into infinity, until it grew dim and was lost in the white vapour. No plants on this drear frontage ; nothing. Grey obscurity enveloped all the slope, swirling and shifting, lightening and darkening. And now the sharp zigzags of the track brought me up against the buttress of Mercantour. For an instant the mist dissolved into a pearly shade. And in that momentary rending of the veil I found myself looking straight into the face of *Saxifraga florulenta.*

For a moment I could not believe my eyes ; for another moment I felt convinced, insanely, that some botanist must have put the rosette there as a practical joke. So monstrously apposite was its appearance at just that point. Then, when my reason had ceased rocking on its seat, I rent the welkin with a cry of triumph. Down below, my companion, not unnaturally, gave a jumping start that nearly sent him headlong. However, learning in that cry its cause, he readily forgave its effects. We stood together with our feet in half a yard of snow, and in awe-stricken silence contemplated for the first time the Ancient King of his race, the most wonderful plant in all the ranges of the Alps.

It was an imperial moment, tremendous, breathless. There are not so very many people living who have set eyes on *Saxifraga florulenta* among its native cliffs. It has not long been known to man. We have not yet kept the centenary of its epiphany ; for it was revealed to us by Molinari about 1820. In 1824 the plant was duly named, described and figured by Moretti ; and after that, for so many years lost sight of, that at last the tale of a great red-spired Saxifrage haunting only the highest granitic precipices of the Maritime Alps came to be looked on as a myth. Botanists rambled the lower ridges and found no sign of the reported treasure. *Saxifraga florulenta* passed, like Saint Ursula, out of the belief of rational people. Its very name was usurped. And then, after many seasons, it was rediscovered in 1840, on the Fenestra, by an ignorant English tourist. Ever since that day, to see *Saxifraga florulenta* at home is the Garter of a botanist's ambition. Nor is that ambition lightly achieved. The range of *Saxifraga florulenta* on earth is entirely limited to the loftiest couloirs, gullies and cliffs, in the main granitic mass of the Maritime Alps, from Enchastraye in the West to the Valmasca Valley in the East of the range.*

It is, as I have said, probably the oldest of its family, and represents a development of Saxifraga different from any we now know. It stands alone, and there is no other extant Saxifrage that in the least resembles it; whereas all the rest have recognizable twins or cousins in the clan, three-styled *florulenta* hugs its drear precipices in a splendid isolation, and resolutely refuses the kinship of lesser Saxifrages from lower down.

If this be so, you will ask me why I am thus openly revealing to you its dwelling-places under their own names, instead of clothing them in cunning pseudonyms. My reasons for discarding that course (which I admit I had

---

* A cycle of myths and legends has gathered round *Saxifraga florulenta*. In especial Ardoino's whole account of it is a mere cento of collected errors, in which few details, if any, are to be trusted. In case his mis-statements beget or perpetuate a false tradition in others, as they have already done, for instance, in the case of Hugh Macmillan, here are the facts : discovered by Molinari, 1820 ; named and figured by Moretti, 1824, then lost ; rediscovered and figured, Bremond and Barla, 1840 ; Reuter and Boissier, 1852 ; after this repeatedly by Lacaita, Boissier, Reuter, Cesati, Lisa, Burnat, etc. ; flowered at Valleyres in the Jardin Boissier, June 16th, 1876. In 1898 I saw a specimen from the Fenestra figured by Mrs. S. de Wesselow, at Cannes.

contemplated) are these. In the first place, the haunts of *Saxifraga florulenta* are very high, very remote, very expensive, tedious and difficult to come at ; in the second, even when you have got into its mountains, and toiled up to its levels, the cracks, gullies, cliffs and chines where it dwells are not smooth places where the inexperienced will be glad to tread ; in the third place, the plant itself clings to them with such determination that it is the fruit of much experience and care to pluck its immense rosettes undamaged out of the microscopic vertical cracks into which they root so firmly and so far ; and, finally, those rocks themselves are solid and hard as everlasting doom.

Therefore, in such grim high places I do not fear, for that grim and thorny treasure, any danger from the trowel of the itinerant spinster, or the casual tourist. I have no scruple, then in naming the Ciriegia, the Rovinette, the Fenestra, the Valmasca, to my readers in general. Most of them will neither have the time nor the resolution to go there ; few, if they did, would have the will to dare the blank wall of Mercantour and the Cima Rosaura : and of those few, even fewer would be able successfully to rend asunder the solid cliffs and draw thence their pearl. And, with regard to the professional collector, I am hardly less at ease. Distance, height, difficulty of access combine to protect the plant from *his* ravages also. But, above all, *Saxifraga florulenta* will never be an ordinary garden-plant. It will never be " worth his while." It will never, probably, prove the meek and amenable glory of the millionaire's cement-built " rock-garden " ; and therefore it will never pay the nurseryman to go out and ravish those rocks, even if his respectable feet could support him there. For the gardens of the curious there must always be a few specimens kept in cultivation ; but *Saxifraga florulenta* refuses, so far, to shake hands with civilization, and leaves the decoration of our rocks to the no less rare, but more humane species from lower down. And, finally, if *I* were to be devious about the stations of the plant, the would-be collector need only turn up any standard book of botany, to find every one of its localities clearly set forth.

As for us, that day, time ceased out of our consciousness ; we never noticed clearing clouds, or dizzying cliffs. We belonged entirely to the great Saxifrage. And my companion, who had suffered tremors and descended the side of the cliff so gingerly, now went skipping and leaping heedlessly on to pinnacles and across gulfs that might have made a goat feel sick in its stomach. It is true that when I drew his attention to this development, he remembered to answer in wan tones that I had no notion " how he hated it " ; the fact remains that on a mountain side, among the plants you want, terrors vanish clean out of mind, until your tin is full and you have time to call them back again.

All over the Southern cliffs of the Pass, up the sides of Mercantour, the Ancient King is abundant. One hoisted oneself onward from rosette to further rosette, in ever-increasing passion of delight, clinging, regardless, to any knob or wrinkle of the rough granite, and mounting incessantly until the track was suddenly seen to be lying hundreds of unheeded feet below. But the plant was very difficult to collect on these crags; the rock was densely hard, and the crevices immovable. I shall show it you in finer form, and discourse upon it yet again at large when I have led you into the high stony wilderness of the Rovinette. And now I will faithfully paint you the King and his habits, that you may know him once and for all, if ever you are so fortunate as to set eyes on him.

*Saxifraga florulenta* forms one single rosette of almost uncanny splendour : its leaves are of a deep and refulgent green, without any trace of silver or down. They are quite smooth, very long and stiff and narrow, but gradually narrowing further to their base, sharply ciliated at their edge, and running to a point so hard and spinous that the plant is as prickly to handle as a holly.

The shape of the rosette gives clear warning of the plant's habits; the leaves lie close and hard upon each other, forming a solid imbricated disk; but that disk is always, in well-developed specimens, curved inwards, like an irritated sea-anemone's. Thus, you will see, as the plant stares straight out at you from the faces of the rock, that incurving formation is specially adapted to keep rain from lodging in the heart of the glossy cup; whereas the other big-rosette Saxifrages, *longifolia, altissima*, and *Cotyledon,* all splay out their leaves flat and backwards against their rock, so as to get the full advantage of any moisture there may be about. *Florulenta,* on the other hand, only begins to curl backward when the last and most glorious moment of its life approaches.

For after a sufficient number of years have passed, the rosette ultimately feels itself strong enough to flower. Up from its heart comes a stout glandular spike which develops into a stocky spire, of some eight or ten inches, very thickly set with nodding flowers of a purple rose, most wonderful to see. The topmost flower, as in the Aeizoons, is usually of monstrous size, and has, often, five styles and fifteen stamens. The leading flowers on the lateral shoots generally have three styles, though not invariably. It is only the weaker collateral blooms on the branches which are content to follow the common fashion of the family, by only possessing two. And, after this display of magnificence, the plant, having seeded, invariably dies, like Anne Boleyn, *sans nul rêmède*. *Saxifraga florulenta* never proliferates or throws offsets. When you find a plant with half a dozen crowns, these are either the result of a mutilated spike, or else a cluster of symbiotic seedlings. But the King Saxifrage has been libelled in its name. From my intimate acquaintance with it at home this summer, I can see that it is not " slow to flower," not a bit of it. What it wants to do, on the contrary, is to grow on as quickly as it possibly can, so that it may flower and die in about five seasons from its first germination. Unfortunately it throws its seeds all over the place, and they seem to sprout with extreme liberality, in every sort of unlikely corner. Many of these, then, like the seed in the Parable, fall upon ground so stony that they can make but little headway—say, in a chink too narrow, or in unfavourable soil.

But the gallant plant will not, for all that, give up the

struggle. Despite its faddiness and the difficulties of
its culture it has a constitution of remarkable vigour.
So that ill-suited seedlings continue for scores of years
in their place, holding their ground against untoward
conditions, but making no progress ; every season
trying anew to get up flowering strength, and never
succeeding. And this brave habit it is that originally
earned the plant its ominous name. It was called slow-
flowering merely because unhappy specimens lingered
long in pots without ever showing signs of bloom. Even
the hills are dotted with unhappy specimens, hopeless of
flower, while as for specimens in cultivation, they always
were unhappy. Ultimately, too, the resources of such
an ill-placed rosette are exhausted. It lives on in its
cranny to an immense age, perpetually hanging fire, and
developing at last a deep dense cone of dead foliage round
a central axis that develops long and fat, until it is like a
carrot ; on the top of this sits a dwindling tuft of leaves.
So, in the end the plant gives up the struggle and dies
flowerless. One is for ever seeing such ineffectual corpses
on the ledges, looking like sodden tufts off a black poodle's
tail.

But the more fortunate pieces than can do as the
essential nature of the plant desires, grow gleefully on as
fast as they can, until, in two or three years they are wide
rosettes of lucent green. As last year's growth never
falls, you can easily see the age of any given plant by the
size and thickness of the sere *substratum ;* and flowering
specimens always have beneath them only so very thin a
layer of dead foliage, so rapidly dwindling as it approaches

the neck, that you can see how fast the thing has developed in a few seasons, from the first little crown of thorny spines, into the great glossy disk from which the spike is springing. I must have seen many thousand plants of *florulenta* ; never once did I see an old plant flowering ; all the stems were being sent up by vigorous young plants that had been able to grow merrily without check or starvation, from the first moment of their sprouting. Either this Saxifrage hurries on rapidly, then, to its glorious consummation, if it can ; or else, if it cannot, it heroically protracts a long and barren life which proves abortive in the end. If a plant cannot get up steam enough to flower in four or five years, it will hardly be able to do so at all. It is obviously, that is to say, a robust species, requiring the most generous conditions of culture.

In nature, too, you can also gather the robustness of the plant by its good humour as to soils. I have found it in rich humus, I have found it in silt, in turfy sods, in rich yellow loam, and in disintegrating dust of the moraine. And in all these different soils it was hale and brilliant and hearty. Nor does it in nature seem to be anxious about aspect. On those gaunt cliffs, indeed, it seems most to enjoy the steep and rather shady gullies that shoot up out of reach of the last pines, towards the peaks above ; but it is not by any means confined to northerly exposures, and, though it avoids the thoroughly sun-baked rock-fronts, it is quite happy to have full warmth of daylight for a good many hours out of the twelve. But what the plant absolutely must and will have, in all conditions, is a vertical position. Never, never will it grow with its face flat up to the elements. Even when you find it in moraine, or out in the open moorland, it will always be lying squeezed closely on its side, twinking and winking at you with its rich green eye as you toil up the slope of rock below.

Moisture in the ground it smiles at. I have even found it in crannies of a cliff over whose face the water was trickling ; but against all moisture from on high it shuts up its face as tightly as it can. And another thing : whether on turf or moraine, whether in damp ground or dry, you will never see the plant otherwise than cramped close between slabs of granite. Never does it seem too closely squashed for its comfort ; so long as there is root-room in the cliff behind, a rosette eight inches in expanse will be perfectly happy screwed up in the recesses of a cranny a quarter of an inch wide. And it also shows its essential good-temper and will-to-live, by the readiness with which it seems to germinate ; for seed appears to spring wherever seed falls, whether on detritus or moss, or among grass and weeds at the foot of the precipice. What becomes of such afterwards is, of course, only the business of each individual seedling ; the point is that the seed should germinate so freely.

But, indeed, the whole plant is a mystery. How, whence, and why it came upon these rocks only in the world ; why it should be so robust in many ways, and so delicate in others. Why its beauty stands so far away from that of any other Saxifrage. Most mysterious of all its problems is that of those glossy leaves. They are as hard and spiny as a juniper's, glittering, impenetrable, indestructible. They have neither felt nor down, nor any other danger sign. They are as bald and stalwart as any leaves one has ever known ; and yet, in reality, they are more delicate than any. They are as delicate as the petals of a Camellia ; bruise a leaf, break a leaf, crush a leaf, the plant thus insulted will soon give you news of its feelings on the point. The wounded leaf goes brown, and then black, like a broken Camellia petal. It dies hideously, and you will be very fortunate if the whole rosette does not follow suit. The same fate befalls you if a drop more rain than the plant thinks permissible ever lingers for a moment too long in that green shining basin. You can see, then, where the difficulty arises in cultivating a plant which otherwise wants to be so vigorous and hearty, only asking to be encouraged in the most robustious growth. All these years I have gone on yearly losing plants in pots, because the pots stood flat on the ground, and the rosettes lay flat on the pot, and received all the rain that happened to be going. Now, having studied what the plant most hates and requires, I have had to put all my florulentas on their sides.

These points being successfully attended to, *Saxifraga florulenta* is by no means reluctant to thrive. Well-treated, it is even content to renounce its love for granite ; the old plant on my Cliff is as happy as most that you will see on the Ciriegia or the Fenestra. And no less happy and vigorous there are the collected pieces of last season ; one, even, which had apparently gone off black to death, is pushing a point of new green from its heart—thereby proving the truth of my contention as to the real essential vigour of the plant's constitution. But you can understand from all this, how dire are the dangers you undergo in collecting it. For, in the first place, it roots back tight and far into the narrowest crannies of a cliff whose crevices not a crowbar could split, as a rule, nor widen ; in all negotiations you have to respect its foliage as you respect the honour of Cæsar's wife. For, if you even touch it unadvisedly the plant says " hands off," and pricks you severely ; if you continue undaunted and grasp it firmly, on the nettle principle, the plant may give no sign of indignation at the moment, but, as soon as you have got it home, and paid the postage and the bill for pots, it will inform you clearly that you have hurt the feelings of its leaves, and that they are not prepared to stand any such nonsense. " Do not try no impogician," says the Saxifrage, " for I will not abear it." And, accordingly, within a week of being laboriously potted, the whole batch will turn black and die.

But, even supposing you have made a crevice loose, and got out the plant untouched ; or have held it by the neck and slowly wheedled it forth entire from the crack, by waggling it to and fro with slow regular movements, pulling towards you all the time ; even then, I say, you are not safe. You have yet to pack it and despatch it : and those imperturbable-looking solid rosettes are more intolerant of surface moisture than even *Eritrichium* himself. You have to wipe and polish *Saxifraga florulenta* as if each rosette were a mirror ; you have to make elaborately certain that the whole face of the plant

is perfectly dry. Otherwise those leaves will moulder
and mildew more certainly that even such downies as
the high Androsaces, although they have neither fluff
nor felt, nor anything apparent to mildew with. And
then, after this is finished, you must so carefully lay the
plants in their box, and so carefully compress them,
that not a leaf is bruised or broken, while at the same
time the mass is wedged firm and tight. Do I make
it plain that *Saxifraga florulenta* is not a species that
smiles upon the casual and careless collector ? And yet,
I repeat, the thing only asks to grow rapidly on with you
in rich soil, so long as you respect its foliage, and take due
care that its face is dry.

When you have got it home, indeed, the plant
always presents the most irate and despondent appearance, it is true. No pains can prevent the rosettes from
getting squeezed and towzled in their tin. And the plant
resents this. A month after potting your florulentas
will be looking the most miserable of sulky objects—their
hard and glossy leaves, so firm and orderly, now turned
limp and dull and dishevelled as an unkempt wig. They
flop about over all the place ; many of them are turning
brown and rotten ; there is no more prick in any of them.
But do not despair. The plant, you will have gathered,
has normally a habit of keeping its old leaves ; they form
a deepening cushion of deadness under the green rosette
of the season's growth round the increasing carrot of the
stock, instead of decaying away or being shed, like the
discarded foliage of other plants. Therefore it is no ill
sign in autumn that the outer leaves of your plants should

be going dark and dead. It is their way. As soon as
the shock of removal has been surmounted the green
heart of the tuft will be throwing up fresh ones ; the
process is being continued, it seems, through autumn and
winter, so that the persevering rosette may be ready to
do its best when spring returns. And note that it is
always a good sign when your plant's leaves grow glossy
and emerald and prickly ; for this Saxifrage is like the
mirror of the fairy-tale : when its lustre is dimmed, and
its thorniness turns limp and flaccid, then danger is near.
And woe betide you, though, if it be the inmost heart of
the plant from which begins to spread the black death ;
for *Saxifraga florulenta* lives only from its heart, and has
no lateral resources. The first sign of blackness in the
centre of the rosette means that you will soon be in
mourning for the Saxifrage. And one should mourn in
purple for a splendour so imperial. For, of all the plants
I have ever known, this august and lonely glory is by far
the most sensational to discover. The King of the Alps
himself shrinks into a mere little lovely high-alpine forget-
me-not.

Of what avail is it then, for me now to try and
appreciate the other treasures that occurred to us among
the Saxifrage in the southern face of the Ciriegia and the
Mercantour ? As Kings and Popes sink out of sight,
obscure, at the coronation of Napoleon, so do even
*Thlaspi limosellaefolium* and *Viola nummulariaefolia*
dwindle almost into plebeians beside the royalty of the
King Saxifrage. Yet both of these were here in flower ;
and, as for *Androsace imbricata*, it was as little accounted

of as silver in the days of King Solomon, when at last we came upon it outlining invisible crannies with its cushions of greyness, that were still snowed-under with their little white stars. White, indeed, I call them, for courtesy; because they are usually so described; but in reality (unless it was that the neighbouring snow-field injured them by contrast) they were of a curious yellow, that was even a little unclean in effect, and reminiscent of the Infanta Isabella's linen. And rather squinny too, in shape and size, though in number like the stars of Heaven.

And, then, amid our huntings, we were suddenly aware that we had come down, unnoticing, from the southern wall of the Ciriegia, and were fast descending, over slopes, to a wide snow-field, stretching away below. And the clouds were scattering, the air grew clear, we looked out over the tops of many intervening ranges, towards the Mediterranean.

# CHAPTER VII

## OVER THE WALL OF FRANCE.

FRANCE lies deep down below us, indeed; we are as flies hanging on its wall. Beneath us runs the Valley of the Boréon, in such a depth that it can hardly be discerned; but the eye roams over an ocean of tumbled ridges decreasing towards the sea. And the Valley of the Boréon is geographically in France, as indeed is every step of this present journey downwards, although the Douanes and the final territorial distinctions do not occur until you are half-way on your descent from the Boréon-Cascade to Saint Martin Lantosque. But a notable change there is already, as soon as one begins to come down from the crest of the Ciriegia. For, whereas on the northern side, in the shadow of the peaks, there was universal snow and desolation, and vegetation rare and scattered when at last it leaps to life, as soon as you have come over the pass and on to the southern slope, life begins to unfold heartily, the illumined cliffs grow rich, and snow is as rare here as blossom in the northern rocks. A little lower still, and, at the levels which, above the Val Valletta, gave us nothing but bare, dank, and sterile stones, we shall shortly see a riot of the mountain flowers.

But at present we are crossing the wide snowfield that lies immediately under the southern face of the Ciriegia.

And here, all over that pure expanse, lie scattered relics of the great Saxifrage. For those plants of *florulenta* that struggle on for years in an unpropitious cranny, and can never be anything but barren stocks, as barren as Mary and Elizabeth, Queens—these, I say, die at last at their post, heroic in their persistent futility to the end. So there, on the ledges they lie dead, towzled black tufts of rottenness. And there, too, lean or lie the successful stalwarts that have succeeded in flowering and scattering their seed; and, in success, have turned to dead, stiff skeletons. Then winter descends upon the corpses, the storms and long snows of winter, and the wild winds of the Alps. And the dead bodies of the Saxifrage are blown down, washed down from their deathbeds, upon the snowfields that lie beneath the cliffs. And here, at every step, we were passing sodden black poodle-tufts of *Saxifraga florulenta*, or sere seed-spikes, emptied of their germs, that lay still or rolled a little here and there, across the frozen surfaces of the snow. Then, when we had traversed that expanse of white, we came down under a further range of cliffs beneath, and here too, in the crannies, the Saxifrage abounded still, with *Androsace imbricata* in more sunny places, and *Saxifraga retusa* actually growing round its eldest sister's roots. And *Draba tomentosa* was busy trying to get itself mistaken for the Androsace.

Below these rocks again there was the lap of fallen blocks that always fills the upmost end of each high alpine glen before it begins to descend towards the main valley so far below. And here the most notable thing that I call to mind was *Senecio Doronicum*. For this was a

brilliant plant, yet different from the brilliant *S. Doronicum*
of the Oberland, no less than from the large coarse
*S. Doronicum* of the Mont Cenis.   The Ciriegia plant
had rather flimsy leaves of a clear darkish green, wholly
devoid of white felt on its lower side; had a tufted habit,
had noble flowers of a refulgent golden yellow.  (The Mont
Cenis plant cultivates a more clustered habit, as I told
you, has a certain amount of tomentum, is larger, coarser,
flappier in every way, with flowers of a paler and much
less royal yellow.)   Whereas the Oberland plant is an
even finer gentleman yet ; never growing in more than
two or three crowns together, and most often in isolation ;
with leaves like waxed leather, stiff and solid, of a blue
iron-grey in colour, and silver-white beneath with felt.
With a scantier felt are clothed the stems, and the flowers
are of a very deep old gold, that verges upon imperial
orange.

Senecio Doronicum* did not seem frequent on the
Ciriegia.   We only came on a few tufts of it among stones
that were otherwise rather disappointingly barren.   Thus
we climbed the last ridge of the stone bank, and began
descending the sunbaked slope that drops steeply towards
the Valley of the Boréon.   And suddenly all the world
was gay. *Myosotis rupicola*, *Viola calcarata*, golden
Geums, brooms and sunroses were everywhere ; *Gentiana
acaulis* lay lavishly about, and among its scattered great
goblets on the ground, rose up incandescent rose-crimson
spikes of the sweet little Nigritella hybrid.   And here
*Gentiana acaulis* was splendid too in its clear blues ; for the
first time in my eyes, for my lines hitherto had always been

cast in districts where *G. acaulis* is addicted to slaty and dowdy shades ; or, if ever I have visited places where it grows beautiful, such as the Engadine, it has been at a moment when the cerulean trumpets have all been withered wisps of deadness. Therefore in the hot sunshine of this slope I lingered long in contemplation of its grandeur ; revelling, too, in the beauty and ineffable fragrance of that lovely Nigritella, most charming of the mountain Orchids.

After the incline in the sunlight, our track runs down into the woodland. This is scant scrub at first, grows taller and denser as one goes ; until, having traversed the zone of larch, one enters that of the Scotch Fir, which seems the main staple of these lower mountain forests, with here and there a plant of the uncinate *Pinus montana*. In the lowest reaches there was nothing, of course, in the forest of Scotch, except golden flowered little brooms, and *Saxifraga aeizoon* in the more open patches, where there was rock. But in the larch wood up above, the trees, being still in their very earliest stages, were only just beginning to cast a lacy shadow over grassy glades that were all a carpet of flowers. For here the Spurred Pansy was nearly as brilliant as on the Mont Cenis, here *Gentiana acaulis* more beautiful and abundant than I have ever seen it, like dropped trumpets of azure in every direction, and among them stood spikes of Orchis, pink and purple, and pale straw-yellow. And other yellows, too, were there in abundance, the profuse yellows of the Alps ; and, among the stones of the track as it descended, *Viola valderia* condescended to occur in places uncontaminated by the presence of *Viola calcarata*. The glades were threaded with clear little streams, that meandered silent among the grasses and the Gentians ; one could not step for the flowers that dotted every foot of sward ; the light came filtering through the boughs above, in a dappled filigree pattern on the ground.

Thus we came down into the silent dark forest of Scotch fir : and down, and down, until at last, mapped out beneath our feet, among the serried trunks, we saw the Boréon Valley and the little hotel. So here we deserted the path, which curls and twists ; and slithered straight towards the lower levels, until we came out into luscious hay-meadows full of Campanula and Astrantia and Saint Bruno's Lily. In five more minutes we had gained the Hotel Boréon-Cascade.

The Boréon Valley runs down from the high stone slopes between the Argentera and the Cima di Gelas. As soon as it has fallen from the alpine barrens, it is a deep forested glen, which curves throughout its length, until at last it converges with many other mountain valleys, at Saint Martin Lantosque, the head of the Vésubie. At about half-way it is joined, at a right angle, by the Val de Salèses, and near this junction, upon which descends abruptly the path of the Ciriegia Pass, sits the Hotel of the Waterfall. A charming little hotel it is too, simple and quiet and clean, only about an hour or two's drive up from St. Martin. Hither, in summer, many people come a-pleasuring, and they could not choose a pleasanter place. For the Boréon River, which has hitherto flowed placidly down the glen, here sees fit to indulge in the caper that gives the inn its name. Or, to put it differently, and remove all blame from the river, the valley is blocked by a huge barricade of hill, so that just below the hotel, the ground falls stiffly away in a drop of three or four hundred feet ; whereas, above and below this barrier, it descends in a gradual and decent gradient. Therefore over this impediment falls roaring the Boréon river, making a waterfall that shoots out, in clouds of spray, into a rocky cauldron away below, in a gorge for ever wet with spume, where rainbows float under one's feet against precipices of darkness illumined here and there by emerald moss and ferns and jewelled with shafts of sunlight down there in the gloom where their walls are for ever clad in the diamonds of the powdered water. One stands upon a wooden bridge across the neck of the chasm, and cranes over upon the roaring depths. And just beyond the bridge rises a big bulk of rock, the head of the precipice down which falls the cascade. From the sheer face of this stand out tall pines of tortured outline, as delicately proportioned and placed as any detail in a Japanese garden. The whole scene composes into a picture so perfect that not a leaf or twig could you profitably alter ; no, not even a single spike of the Aeizoon Saxifrages that spray and shower their creamy whiteness over all the rocks, to the very rim of the cataract itself.

But even this is not enough. For, over the head of that big cliff above the waterfull there comes, smooth and silent, another body of water gliding down over the roots of the pine trees, and dropping plumb into the shattering

spout of the main river. Thus the Boréon Cascade consists
of two, the upper and the lower streams, that blend about
halfway in their course. But the upper stream is wholly
different from the brawling whiteness of the lower one.
It slides sheer and calm down into the foaming mass
beneath it, like a sheet of smooth glass falling into another
of broken glass. And thus together, in a roar of splendour,
they plunge into the misty profundities of the gorge, and
the bridge and the rocks and all the hill vibrate with the
intensity of their unresting magnificence.

Never rest the waters, and never rest the weary either.
But for a moment, before we begin our long excursion
up and up out of the Boréon Valley, into the slow curling
glen of the Rovinette, let us dawdle among the treasures
that live within five minutes of the Hotel Boréon-Cascade.
For that rock over which comes gliding the stream of glass
is not only clothed with Sempervivums and *Saxifraga
aeizoon,* but its shadier ledges are plumy with the silver
showers of my beloved *Astrantia minor* ; and sheeted
with *Primula marginata* ; and set in a carpet of *Arnica
montana.* Here and there are Orange Lilies, and in the
long grass wide white plumes of Polygonum like cloud
solidified.

And, if you wander, even slippered, up into the wood
behind, you will find the world hidden by Oakfern, and
the special Boréon-form of *Saxifraga cuneifolia* making
neat carpets and patterns over the deep moss. You will
see the golden eyes of *Viola biflora* peering at you from the
shadowy places ; and you will see Spotted-Dog Lung-
worts in the most fantastic variety. *Pulmonaria*

*angustifolia* one knows in Dorset woods ; *Pulmonaria officinalis*, dowdy and diseased-looking, one knows in cottage gardens ; and one knows the azure glory of *Pulmonaria arvernensis*. But this variety of *officinalis* (if this it be) was quite unexpected by me, and miles remote in its leafage, from the *P. angustifolia* that haunted the hollows in front of the Hotel de la Poste on the Mont Cenis. There are no flowers here, though, so of them I cannot speak. It is the leaves that are so wonderful. They are very broad, and they are varied and spotted in a manner so excessive as to remind one of those horrible variegated leaves of Anthurium that fill the hot-houses of the rich. On their hispid dark ground of greyish green some of them are spotted, others splashed or flaked or patterned with a livid white which looks as if their surface had been blasted with vitriol ; in one form, even, almost all the leaf was white, with only a narrow rim of normal colouring round the edge. And these monstrosities have a beauty and a wonder, though the beauty be morbid, and the wonder merely an agapeness that such apparently artificial developments should here be thriving in the unsophisticated wilds.

Now gird we up our loins for the stony elevations once more. Up along the stream of Salêses and thence again up the winding valley of the Rovinette, towards its source. This is a big expedition, let me warn you ; it takes all day, and to enjoy its full savour one should start at six, on pain of having, in the end, to hurry home, as was my fate. For the sun, alas, is always high in heavens before my limbs are thawed for walking. The preliminary

walk is long and dull and hot.   All the first part of the
way meanders slowly through dense and stuffy spruce
forest ;  to right and left the woodland rises in an unbroken wall.   However, as the valley of Salêses leads
off into that of the Rovinette, open spaces at last begin
to occur ;  above tower the massive barriers of mountain
which separate these valleys from the ranges of Our Lady
of The Window, leading up from Saint Martin, over the
Col de Fenestra, down upon Entraque, and so to Valdieri
in the Gesso Valley.   On another side rises no less steep
the lower walls of pine, above which tower the Ciriegia
and the Mercantour.   But the valley lies so low, and the
woodland rises so sheer, that of the peaks above we can
get no hint as we go.   It is not easy to divine the vast
scale of these ranges, until one sees that the pine trees
are only minute fur on the slope of Armella, to our right,
where they dwindle upwards among little scars of rock
that are really precipices.   So the way continues, curling
towards the left.   Then, on the ridge beyond Armella,
I recognise the pine-clad gullies into which I climbed,
some ten years since, on a dull October day, for my first
acquaintance with *Saxifraga florulenta*.   For now, in all
the rocky ledges and ridges and ghylls above the pines on
either side, up to the Col de la Rovinette beyond the
head of the stream (not to be confused with the Col delle
Rovine, at the top of the Boréon), the most ancient of
Saxifrages freely holds its own.

The way becomes gradually more open ;  but remains
as dull as ever.   We are always on the granite in this
district, and the result is a woeful sameness in the flora.

The reigning Saxifrage is *aeizoon*, flowers are few and poor. We were both of us bored and wearied with the first two hours of the Salêses glen, and then of the Rovinette. And the more depressed that it had been painted for us as the most brilliant floral centre in the range. True that we saw, on a grass slope three miles away, long snowdrifts that proved to be *Anthericum Liliastrum* ; true that in the black boulders under which we passed, the Orange Lily was flaring to heaven ; true, even, that *Viola valderia* greeted us from the stones of the pathways. But the walk remained arduous and dull ; nor, though we were getting higher, did the wood sufficiently diminish to give us any view. But in the rare glimpses we did at last see something noble ahead—a something that caused hope to spring again in our hearts, and put fresh spirit in our feet.

I have said that, as a rule, the high points of the Maritime Alps impress one rather with their volume than with their isolated magnificence. But the Rocca del Abisso makes one exception to this rule ; and a no less brilliant exception is made by the peak that dominates the stone-slopes of the upmost Rovinette. For this is the glorious and famous peak of the Cima Rosaura. As you ascend the valley, still curving to the left, you gradually begin to see the open stone country unfolding before you at the head of the glen. The mountain world reveals itself in peaks and crags far above the shingle-slopes that slide away beneath their lowest cliffs. And then, as you go, the stark pinnacle of the Rosaura takes charge of the whole scene. Like a curse that huge needle goes shrieking up into the sky on the right. It stands quite alone, looming over the Col de la Rovinette, with its stone-slides filling the end ofthe glen with desolation ; it is naked as truth ; it is of russet and grey in colour ; it has the terrifying beauty only possessed by bare and lonely mountain peaks. And its finger allures one's hope towards the screes at its feet. Not only do the pine trees by the path diminish as one continues upwards, but, in the presence of that pinnacle one becomes less conscious of them. One's feet go more springingly over the track, and the loose stones do not seem nearly so loose as they did.

At the upmost cow-pens the valley curves finally towards the left ; across the stream a second track diverges here, leading over many ridges down again deep into the Boréon Valley, and so, once more, after a long ascent, over a depression between two long shingle beds descending from the crags, to the range of Our Lady of the Window. The Window itself is made by the convergence of two splinters of granite in one of the highest peaks. Down below, at the head of the valley, immediately under the peaks, are the Hospice and Chapel of Our Lady. Thus one can gain these by a side pass from the Boréon, without going down to Saint Martin, and up the regular mule-track of the Col. But not the Col and not the Hospice, and not the Window, and not Our Lady are the essential celebrities of the Fenestra. But, in 1840, on the cliffs high up behind the Sanctuary, was redis-covered, by that nameless English wanderer, the long-lost and half discredited *Saxifraga florulenta*. He had met Brémond and Barla, experienced collectors, at the Hospice.

At the day's end they gathered once more to compare their respective quarry. Out of the boxes of the botanists came specimens of ordinary interest ; in the ignorant amateur's, among a mass of weeds, lay the mythical glory of *Saxifraga florulenta* ; and its finder had had no idea what marvel it was that he had met with on the desolation of those dark cliffs. To this day it will often happen that travellers or pilgrims coming over the pass will bring down to the chapel, in wonder, a spike thickset with hanging great rosy bells of blossom. Less often, perhaps, than in former days ; for I am told that above the Sanctuary the plant is not so frequent now ; you have to diverge to remoter and more perilous cliffs. Long life, then, and unvisited peace to the oldest of Saxifrages, to the capital ground of whose dominion we are now rapidly approaching. Though the grim plant would not thank us for such a wish; preferring, as I have told you, a short life and a merry one, to any mere length of un-profitable days.

Beyond the cow-pens of Valmellina, the glen of the Rovinette rises quickly towards the uplands. But still it continues uninteresting ; one first has to surmount long alpine ridges of short grass, set with Gentian and hybrid Nigritellas, glowing rosy. After that there is a dip, and one then has to climb a steep gully of pine and rhododendron. But, after that last arduous stodge, one comes out into the upmost valley. And this is a lovely little plain of grass as green as emerald, ridged round by hummocks and downs, where Alpine Clover and Gentians and Geums are flowering. Its upper end is closed by a

blank amphitheatre of precipices; to right and left
stone-slopes descend in a wild desolation from other
cliffs; and on the right, along the side of the stream,
one can climb over big fallen boulders, up the track
which leads to the highest level of all, where the Rovinette
rises amid stone and snow, and the path continues, under
the Rosaura, over the Pass.   For not even yet are we at
the high-alpine level.   The little plain is a delusion and
a fraud; it is beautiful exceedingly; many little streams,
clear as diamond, meander over its surface, and their
margins are splashed with the azure of *Gentiana verna*.
But there is nothing else, and it is even a disappointment
that the Gentian should be mere *verna* so high up.   The
first time we mounted the Rovinette Valley we were,
accordingly, so disappointed by the time we had traversed
the plain, that we very nearly desisted from further exploration, and went home again.   Fortunately one always
has an instinct to attain the last and highest point
attainable; also, if one has ever collected in the hills,
one has learnt that another five minutes of climbing often
mean the difference between floral poverty and all the
outpoured wealth of the shingles.   Accordingly, though
with sulkiness, I set myself to mount the slope of fallen
blocks that comes down from above, beside the waterfall
of the Rovinette, where it splits up among them into the
many little streamlets of the plain.   It was a steep and
dull bank; until it became jewelled with innumerable
trumpets of *Gentiana acaulis* in every shade of blue.   So
I rallied my forces, and soon surmounted the final ridge.
My companion, however, preferred to remain below.

And now, to my joy, I really did find myself at the end of everything. Here was the actual source of the Rovinette, and, beyond, there was only stone and shingle and crag extending upwards in magnificent dreariness to the Col, and closed in on either hand by pinnacles of granite. Immediately before me lay a tiny little lake, mother of the river, clear and blue as a beryl. It slept among black boulders of granite so big that they made islets and promontories and peaks. The water dodged amid them into coves and creeks and inlets. One was for ever finding pellucid depths lying unsuspected in the dark shadows, as one leapt from block to block. And then there was also a snowfield, equally unsuspected until you found it lurking round the bases of the boulders ; and often there was more still water sleeping close by, uncannily quiet and transparent. I was making for the nearest stone-slope. This struck me from afar as promising. It lay in fullest sunshine, and ran down from high cliffs that belonged to Rosaura, straight above my head. Accordingly I plunged across the tumble of boulders, alternately leaping from one rock to another, or climbing laboriously up and down where this was not possible. Long before I had achieved that toilsome hundred yards or so I felt that the little lake indulged rather too freely in pools and snowbeds and blocks of stones as big as houses. And this desolation was on too big a scale to admit of plants. But at last I made the final leap on to solid open ground ; and here was my stone-slope underneath my feet.

And I was justified of all my hopes. Here were flowers lying like patches of jewels over the whole scree ;

here were tufts of azure Myosotis, here *Thlaspi limosellae-folium* was even passing over ; here Achilleas and Artemisias were showing promise, and *Saxifraga pede-montana* beginning to flower. And here, above all, began the first loveliness of *Viola nummulariaefolia.* Now, at last, you shall have the opportunity of joining me on your knees before the charm of the tiny Queen-violet of the Maritime Alps. For I believe that *Viola nummulariae-folia* is yet another of the treasures that are only to be seen in this particular range among all the multitudinous ranges of the earth ; and, even here, it is never found below the highest alpine levels, and never found except on the granitic formations. It seems purely and exclusively a plant of the shingles, in fact ; although it occasionally stretches a point up here, and is to be seen among herbage —just below the crest of the Ciriegia, for instance, and at the head of the Rovinette even on patches of the stone-slope where grass, in many years, has at last been able to effect successful lodgment. But the Viola, all the time, insists on abundance of stone ; and, for our own gardens, it must always be looked upon simply and solely as a moraine plant.

It is a difficult thing to collect. It forms one tap-root, with a number of other rooted stolons, after the habit of *Campanula cenisia ;* but the shingle in which it grows is so very much coarser than the shales beloved of *cenisia,* that the labour of getting perfect roots is trebled. One has to lift out block by block, and very often there is a vulgar great tussock of grass that conceals the issues. Far down and all about go the Violet's wandering root-

threads, peering here and there, and shooting up growth
where you least expect it, half a yard away. It is a
labour of much patience to collect all these wandering
lambs that belong to the central sheep. When you have
garnered them, they behave like other lambs, and get so
tangled up together that there is no unravelling the
flock. But, once collected, I do not believe that any
difficulty need be found about the cultivation of *Viola
nummulariaefolia* in the moraine. If it were miffy or
mimpish it would not tolerate the intrusions of coarse
grasses in its own domain. M. Correvon says it is
" *rebelle* " to his culture, but I am not sure if he has
ever given it a fair chance. For in the past I myself
have several times achieved mere failure with *Viola nummulariaefolia*, and now, having seen the plant at home,
I clearly see where lay the whole cause of that failure.
For the plant resents having its roots needlessly hacked
and mangled. The lateral stolons, if torn from their
parent, want very tender care if they are to be made to
root successfully. But collectors, economical people, have
naturally tried to make their plants of Viola go further
than they fairly could. In other words, what they have
sent out to their customers, for high prices, have only
been poor little lateral threads, reft away rootless from
their parent, and without any real hope of striking out for
themselves.

Therefore the Violet has failed far more often in
cultivation than *Campanula cenisia* or *C. Allioni ;* and
this, simply because the plant is so very much rarer than
either of these that the collector thinks he must needs

split up his Violets pitilessly in order to make a better profit ; whereas the Campanulas, which are quite as intolerant of being hacked to pieces, and quite as reluctant to root from mangled offshoots, he can afford to send out in a more or less perfect state. At least, I took a vast deal of pains this year with the Violet (one always collects for oneself infinitely better than anyone else ever can), I pursued its fibres to their uttermost end, I broke off no stolons, either there, or when they got home ; and I sought, as far as I could, for the younger and compacter plants, whose roots it was easier to keep tidy. And, up to this present moment I have had my reward. Whatever they may see fit to do next season,* not one of my Violets looked back, suffered, or was in any way peevish, from the first moment of their arrival in England. Even in the open moraine they seemed to have established themselves by the end of September ; and, though they are nearly all of them gone to bed now underground, I have every hope that they will come up as green and fresh again next year as *Campanula cenisia*, which never seems to go to bed in my garden at all.

Now for the picture of what M. Correvon calls so misleadingly, " la Pensée bleue." For *Viola nummulariae- folia* is not a Pansy but a Violet. And, of all the mountain violets, Queen. It is a very low-growing high-alpine, clinging to the ground, and perking freely about with shoots that are clad in tiny round leaves, bright green and shining, heart-shaped, and clearly recognisable as a

---

\* " Next season " has now come, and so, very vigorously, has *Viola nummulariaefolia* also.

Viola's, even when first you see them sprouting in flowerless tufts among the moraine. Its root system I have
already painted in lively tones; one plant will cover
quite a tract of ground in time; and a yard or more of
flowers, breaking everywhere from among boulders or
grassy tussocks, will be found by the harried collector
all to be springing from one main root, though each little
tuft or leaf and flower may seem to have sufficient fibres
of its own, away at the end of the long white root-thread
which ramifies down between the loose barren rocks
until it has found feeding-room in the soil beneath. These
frail roots, remember, are of no profit. They are
plausible, though; they enourage you in the hope that
they will grow, but grow they will not, with any readiness,
unless the plant still has the continued support from the
main tap.

And the flowers. These are very freely produced,
and on very short stems. They are pure violets, not of
any large size, rather rounded and flattened in outline.
Their first golden quality is their abundance; but it is
their colour that sets them so far above those of most
others of their race. For they are of a wonderful clear
and cool pale lavender that does verge toward a lilac-blue,
though blue is not an epithet one could ever give them:
their nuance is far too subtle and apart to be thus labelled.
And then, on that lovely ground, the little violets are
pencilled most exquisitely with fine lines of purple. But
really, I despair of rendering in words the precise shade
of *Viola nummulariaefolia ;* you are to imagine a colour
much softer, much clearer, much richer, but no less definite,

than that of the periwinkle ; and then, on this, those streaks of a purple so dark that by contrast it looks black. It is a dear, queer, little freakish face that this Violet shows so abundantly to the day.

After the Viola it almost seems a bathos to talk of even *Thlaspi limosellaefolium*. And yet this plant has a beauty not only conspicuous in its own race, but conspicuous also among all the plants of the rock-garden. It is, in a word, the Maritime Alp *remplaçant* of the dearly beloved *Iberidella rotundifolia*, which it costs me a new pang each time, to call by the ugly and dishonouring name of *Thlaspi*. In habit they are the same, tufted plants of the highest moraines, running down into the bank with one long tap-root, to seek their sustenance. But, whereas the leaves of *rotundifolium* are fat, waxy and fleshy, of a livid iron or bronzy colouring, lying usually close in a tight, flat tuft, those of *limosellaefolium* are narrower, much lengthier, almost spoon-shaped, quite ordinary in texture, and of a bright, ordinary green. The weed called Lamb's Salad has a strong general likeness to them.    They do not lie close to the ground in the same way as *T. rotundifolium's*, but tend to stand more independently.    The flattened flower-heads of *rotundifolium* are of a rich lilac-lavender ; those of its cousin are of a warmer and lighter rose-lilac.    I dare not set up any preference of my own, nor can any new friend shake my loyalty to the *Iberidella* of my salad days.    But certainly *limosellaefolium* must take at least equal rank in one's affections.    My companion, unbiassed by old friendship, so worshipped *limosellaefolium* that when at last I showed

him the other, he merely pished at it, and no reproofs
could make him do otherwise. I have to admit that
*Iberidella* was not there in quite its finest form ; and
that the new beauty certainly is, in all ways, really the
finer, better thing.

But the fact is that both these plants have a rare
winsomeness ; their comfortable cosy habit, their
abundant heads of blossom, close packed together in
those barren places : the delicate brightness of their
colour against the grey stones amid which they huddle :
and, last of all, the keen deliciousness of their fragrance,
combine to earn them in one's heart a very select place.
And they are Crucifers too, so that their beauty has a
double merit ; for they are violating all the family
traditions of dowdy ugliness. And one associates them
too, with such glorious days of bright clear air, in the
topmost stone-slides of the desolate places. They never
descend, and can never have any contaminating association, therefore with commoner flowers from the lower
levels. They are both of them supremely well-bred—a
reversion to the time before their now vulgar clan condescended to become more or less useful weeds, and
purveyors of gross green food to humanity.

Add to all this, they are both of them perfectly easy
to grow. Indeed, of the two, I actually find that
*limosellaefolium* is, if possible, the easier. Although it
is confined to the topmost moraines of the Maritime
Alps, while its cousin roams all the other ranges freely,
*limosellaefolium* seems to be a trifle freer in habit, to
run more readily into larger tufts, and to be even more

prodigal in the way of blossom. And it gives yet another sign of superior affability. Never, never, so far as all my experience goes, will you find *Thlaspi rotundifolium* anywhere except in the shingle of the high screes ; but *Thlaspi limosellaefolium* is more adaptable, and occasionally occurs in crevices of the cliffs, although it does not seem to tolerate the invasions of grass so cheerfully as *Viola nummulariaefolia*. Indeed, it does not tolerate such invasion at all. On the scree you will only see it where the stone is naked. The reason is not far to seek : the Violet has a thousand ramifying rootlets, and a scattered habit ; it can laugh at the toughness of a tussock. Whereas the *Thlaspi* has a dense habit, and only one main root to rely on, so that to be smothered up in grass is fatal to its comfort. But, as I say, unlike its cousin of the northern ranges, it is quite happy as a rock plant, if it can have a crevice to itself. And, on the southern cliffs of the Ciriegia you will see it hanging out in pinky masses from the dark rock.

So much then, for the presiding deities of that slope at the foot of the Rosaura. Having done them due homage I mounted further, towards a precipice that impended over a snow-bed, higher up. One climbs and climbs ; down beneath, in the hollow made by that cirque of naked mountains all round the head of the Rovinette, lies the little blue lake among the black boulders ; snow patches are here and there. Straight overhead, now, quite close at hand, soars the pointing finger of the peak. I reached the snow slope, and climbed across its rampart, to where, between snow and rock, there was a deep gully.

The snow had melted away along by the cliff's foot, leaving a dank hollow, as high as a man. Down into this I dropped, and stood to scan the rock above me. And there, in this late season, and this retarded spot, *Primula viscosa, nêe latifolia,* is still hanging out its dense clusters of rich purple ; while, a little lower in the crevices, sway and swing at the end of their trunks, the flower-stems and the lilac-blue blossoms of *P. marginata.* Then, a little higher up, *Anemone alpina sulfurea* is bearing small blooms as a crevice plant ; and with it, as a crevice plant also, for the first time of seeing in my life, I was astonished to find *Anemone narcissiflora.* And then again, higher yet, look up into the blank face of the cliff ? There once more, in the vertical impracticable crannies, shine dotted the lustrous, thorny disks of the royal and ancient Saxifrage.

For now we are in the very metropolis of *Saxifraga florulenta.* Nor, on these rocks, his chosen seat, does the Saxifrage seem to trouble at all about aspect. True, that you will not find him on the very hottest of the cliffs, but on all the others he generously prospers, no matter what their exposure may be. On either side of every gully, on ledge or slope, those rich rosettes are everywhere to be seen clustering. And never does one weary of seeing *Saxifraga florulenta ;* no plant I know gives quite the same effect of opulence and sombre splendour. In those ghylls I must have seen thousands of plants, and I repeat, for the cultivator's benefit, that never once was a flower-spike being thrown up by old and toilworn specimens, but always by insolent, strapping young rosettes that had had the luck of being able to grow on as quickly as the nature of the plant desires.

I still climbed. Here there were sparse pines, and banks of dripping Rhododendron. And still, on either side of the gully, but preferring the cooler exposure, the Saxifrage had tucked itself into every available place. I found big plants of it huddled together ; I found clusters and colonies ; I found three splendid disks like so many targets, all of a row down a vertical cranny. The effect of their spiny glossiness was as of some great sea-creatures clinging to their rock in the deep twilights of ocean. Then there were babies in the crannies, and babies at the foot of each rock, thriving equally, apparently, whether they were in moss, or in silty detritus, or tangled up, actually, among the roots of the scrubby Rhododendrons.

One had to scramble and sweat over abysses and up cliffs and on to perilous smooth slopes. The three giants anyhow (seeing that there was so much of it on that cliff) I determined I would have ; and it was a mighty wrestle I had to undergo before I got them. They were high above my head on their ledge ; it was impossible to see them from below ; only by straddling across the depths from a huge boulder could I even get within poking distance. And, as soon as I had done this, the boulder made a strong effort to hurl me down the precipitous slope of rocks. It gave a lurch and toppled ; I had to leap aside as if rehearsing for the part of a chamois,— never the one for which my age and configuration best fit me. So, after this, when the echoes of that falling boulder had died away far below, I had to swarm the cliff

with my unaided eyelashes ; I was dripping with ardour
by the time I succeeded in effecting any lodgment.
However at last I was near enough and moderately firm
enough, to begin poking. With my pointed stick I wedged
and prodded and pleaded and wrought, with all my other
muscles meanwhile toiling overtime to keep me in position.
In the end the riven rocks began to give, although the
nose of my stick remained permanently out of joint as a
consequence of its energies that day. And in the end I
prised out those three giants with perfect rootage, dropped
exhausted off the cliff-face like an ant from the side of a
bath ; and, after having lain for some time panting
among the Rhododendrons, continued on my upward
way.

I was oblivious, now, of altitudes and time and weather ;
it was simply a question of exploring that gully to its last
point, to where it lost itself in the expanse of the upmost
fells. And the Saxifrage still abounded ; but only in the
gully itself, never on more open ground. There were
stretches, too, of rock that seemed able to exist without
it ; and then again, after a barren fifty feet, you would
come once more on ledges seamed and lined with young
rosettes. I had left the pines far down behind ; the
Rovinette lay mapped out, tiny, at my feet ; across intervening ranges I could see Mercantour and the peaks of
the bare ranges that form a theatre at the head of the
Boréon valley ; I topped the long slope, and came at last
on to the bare expanse of the mountain moorland. Here
the Saxifrage markedly diminished ; probably because
the rocks themselves diminished, and scant herbage

began to take their place.  I have no doubt that if one went higher again to the cliffs of the mountains themselves that rise above the moor, one would soon come on renewed abundance of it.  The elevation, here, cannot possibly be more than eight thousand feet, even if it be as much or nearly as much ; one cannot pretend that the Saxifrage would naturally shrink from such a paltry height.  However by now I was well up in the clouds ; all the moorland was in a pale gloom, and cloud-wreaths swept white across the darkness of its surface.  And, over the whole expanse stood up, in a ghostly brilliance, the golden little chalices of *Tulipa australis*.  This delicate beauty is closely akin to *sylvestris* and *suaveolens*, but much neater and dwarfer.  It is a real alpine Tulip ; we have already seen it, and called it *celsiana*, at Valdieri and in the Combes de Barant ; but I purposely reserved comment until we should have seen it in full force on the highest fells above the Rovinette.  For, in these gaunt places, the sudden apparition of a dwarf brilliant-yellow Tulip emerging in myriads from the dark moorland is positively startling ; to find a thing so bright, at altitudes so forbidding, is sufficiently surprising ; to say nothing of the effect, in that darkling pallor of the clouds, of those golden cuplings standing up so bold through the grey twilight.

The Saxifrage still hugged the gully, but, before descending I thought I might as well explore the rocks to right and left ; and sure enough, I found the thing at last out on the open moorland.  Of course, even there it was in close cover, tightly wedged on its side, between granite slabs that no might of man could part ; but still it was something to have found the Saxifrage in a rather unusual dwelling-place. And it was on a cliff just below that I collected a plant of no fewer than seven rosettes, each with a flower-spike pushing. But five minutes later I glimpsed a treasure which wiped even this from my mind. For upon a rock above my head there shone an enormous rosette, from which was spouting a spike which promised to be at least a yard high. It was only beginning to unfold, like all the rest, but its fatness and vigour were quite pre-eminent, even if, by taking thought, my memory may perhaps have added a fragment of a cubit to its stature. But, alas, it grew on a little range of cliff overhanging a ghyll ; and though the rocks were full of fine rosettes, ready to hand, that special one, king of them all, was ungettable from every point. Of the others I might take a small toll at my will ; but that Emperor grew on the furthest, lowest edge of a little overhanging rim of rock, in just such a position that neither from above nor from below could one crawl, jump, climb, depend, or otherwise get near enough even to poke at it with the stick. I hung lovingly over, I leapt up frantically from beneath ; I made a dozen efforts, remembering Bruce and the spider ; each time I got a little nearer, and never near enough ; each time I walked away in a stern despair, resolving to struggle no more ; and each time I came back again, as if lured by a magnet, for " just one more try." And every effort was in vain. My heart bled, as I foresaw the crowds that would gather round that King-spike if ever I could

make it look its best in Vincent Square; the thought
of vain glory drove me, as it has driven many million
millions of other fools before me, to repeated forlorn
hopes, each more forlorn and limb-imperilling than the
last.

For my experience is that if one tries these dangers
often enough, they diminish at every attempt, until
ultimately one achieves one's purpose. " Despair of
nothing that you would attain ; Unwearied diligence your
point will gain," is not an encouragement addressed to
Mrs. Allen alone ; I Dracula-ed about, perspiring, over
the cliff, until at last it was borne in upon me, that without
greater and more certain danger than I liked incurring
all alone up there on the mountains, the winning of
that spike was quite impossible. I desisted accordingly
from the battle ; and how thankful I now am to think I
did so. For I could never have succeeded in getting
the treasure home undamaged and unbruised ; the other
flowering spikes I collected unanimously mouldered
off fruitless on arrival. My companion and I had con-
cocted pink dreams of how we were going to exhibit the
plants in full bloom within a few weeks of their unpacking.
But we did not then recognise the morbid fragility of those
solid hard leaves ; nor the plant's resentment if any of
them be broken or crushed. So now I rejoice to think of
that huge spike left triumphant on its ledge: *Ave Cæsar,
moriturus, Augustus ;* by now it has flowered and lies
gloriously dead in achieving of its duty and destiny ; the
skeleton stands black on its ledge, or has been blown
into the gully below ; and from all the crannies, with

the arrival of Spring, will be germinating the children it
has left to fill its place.

By this time the clouds were drifting thickly at this
height ; only a few feet lower down and all the hillside
lay clear, though dark under the shadow of their pall ;
time was drawing late, too ; I could guess that now we
should have to hurry dully back the way we came, instead
of, as I had hoped, climbing the intervening ridges, and so
home again down the upper reaches of the Boréon valley.
I descended hastily another gully ; still finding the Saxifrage here and there ; as well as a certain amount of
*Androsace imbricata*. One comes down, in the end,
by some riven crags of granite above the little lake. And
here, too, is the Saxifrage, though sparingly. I crossed
among the blocks, for one more look at that sunny
stone-slope at the foot of Rosaura. And for some time
I lingered idle there in the sunlight to get warm again,
among the tufts of *Thlaspi* huddling pink among the slabs.
Until suddenly I saw something that made me catch
my breath, and rub my eyes. I was looking up the bank ;
surely—*what* was that peering out at me from under
a stone ? What ? What ?

ἆρ ἔστιν : ἆρ οὐκ ἔστιν ; ἢ γνώμη πλανᾷ ; καὶ φημὶ καπόφημι κοὐκ ἔχω τί φῶ.

But no, though I might affirm, and deny, and wander in
my wits, and not know what to say, it was not sister
Ismene in a Thessalian bonnet, it was *Saxifraga florulenta*—
royal plant of the cliffs, here thriving quite as happily in
the dust of a stone-slide. Descending that incline, one
had had no chance of seeing it ; for it grew only wedged
in beneath rocks, with its disk staring straight out in

such a way that as one came up from below its glossy dark face caught your eye at once. I found there six plants in all, seedlings evidently from the rocks above ; they were vigorous rosettes, too, though unable to grow on quite so quickly in that sandy rubble as they would have liked. There was a good deal of dead foliage under their rosettes. But still they were healthy enough, a miracle to see in such a place. And a fit ending to that very long, but glorious day, in the remote high valley of the Rovinette.

# CHAPTER VIII.

## THE COURT AND GENEALOGY OF THE SILVER KINGS.

OF the many treasures I had been told to expect in the
Upper Rovinette valley only one defrauded my expectation. Nor did it really do this, either ; for, as soon as I
realized that the whole of that valley was granite I understood that there was no use hunting there for *Saxifraga
lingulata* ; I soon concluded that when M. Correvon named
it as one of the jewels of the Col de la Rovinette, it can
only have been by a *lapsus calami*,—for *pedemontana*,
which there duly abounds. And this turns out to have
been the case. There is no use in hunting the Silver
Kings of the Maritime Alps anywhere except on the
Jurassic limestone farther down and farther east. The
same rule applies to the flora throughout the no less
granitic valley of the Boréon. For this, also, we had in
duty bound, to explore, though after the riches of the
Rovinette we could not hope that it would yield us much.
Nor did it. But the expedition is easy, and can be
undertaken after lunch. The granite never fails, though ;
and the flora therefore is dull ; the same must be said also
of the Lower Boréon, which one traverses on one's way
down from the Inn to St. Martin Vesubie. The descent
from the Cascade takes two hours and more ; largely
because the road, though " carriageable," as the Italians

have it, does not aim at being luxurious also, but is to all intents and purposes, a very stony and bumpy mule track.

From the Cascade one first winds down the steep hillside in a succession of corkscrew curls, and after that continues along the uneventful curve of the valley round towards Saint Martin. It is a steady descent from the wooded levels of the waterfall, towards the lower forests. The ground is everywhere granitic; there are dwarf brooms and golden papilionaceae; but otherwise nothing of any great interest to see as you go. About half-way down you come to the actual frontier, where soldiers, outside a little shanty, watch against the introduction of things forbidden from over the wall of the Ciriegia. After this, we are definitely in France. And France continues astonishingly like the Italy we have just left—the same trees and shrubs and grasses; the same rocks and ranges; there is nothing to tell us that we have crossed a mythical line, which, for all its illusoriness, has been written deep in blood and tears of men. The surface of the world is one; the absurdity of such evanescent distinctions strikes us anew each time we cross such an invisible hypothesis as this, where one land ends and another begins, and there is nothing to show for it, and the unbroken earth continues just the same as before.

Frontiers may impress themselves when you find grey fortresses guarding a pass; one may be taken in by the bull-dog ferocity of Franzensfeste, or the Gates of Verona; but here among the uncivilized hills, the mockery of such delimitations leaps to sight. But, if it be insignificant,

the frontier of France, all along the Maritime Alps, makes
up by being supremely inconvenient. It plays hide and
seek with you ; you are for ever coming upon it at unexpected corners. It dodges in and out among the ranges,
and ultimately leads you such a dance in the Roja Valley,
that, between Ventimiglia and San Dalmazzo you go into
France, and have a Douane, you then go on into Italy a
few miles further, and have another ; before very long
France crosses your journey again with a third ; and Italy
begins once more (and finally) with a fourth, about a
hundred yards short of San Dalmazzo itself. The reason
for this trouble, lies, like the reason of all other troubles,
in the desires of men. But the men, in this case, were
kings. For it happens that the kings of Italy already
possessed the hunting rights on the northern side of the
range ; accordingly, at the time of the cession of Savoy
to France, Victor Emmanuel insisted, and Napoleon
III. consented that, under the new territorial arrange-
ments, the kings of Italy should also possess the mountain
valleys on the southern slope of the range, so that the
whole district might be their hunting-park. Consequently,
to the confusion of the frontier, which is now one of the
most intricate in the world, like a design for lace, Italy
possesses all the geographically French glens that run
from the Mediterranean slope up into the high alps,—
Mollières, Ciastiglione, Rovinette, Boréon, Fenestra and
Gordolasca. The substantial result of these diplomacies
is that the traveller is reduced to madness by the incessant
occurrence of a Customs House wherever it seems least
likely that a Customs House should be.

All the alps are out of sight now ; below us, down over slope after slope of hay, lies Saint Martin Vésubie among its villas.  The prospect opens up into the mountains on the right, and at last, to our left, we begin to see the valley of the Fenestra, which runs parallel to that of the Boréon up to the Hospice and Pass of Our Lady of the Window.  In all the hayfields hang the bells of *Campanula persicifolia* in every shade of porcelain-blue ; and the vegetation changes very rapidly from that of the pine-zone to the chestnut-hidden luxuriance of the southern river-courses that face the sun, and decline towards the Mediterranean.  And here, at the head of the Vésubie, at the top of the main valley, with other mountain glens ramifying up from it to right and left to the Alpine passes, sits Saint Martin, on a little hillock at the junction of the Vésubie with the torrents that come brawling down all round from the high snows of the Boréon, the Balloure and the Fenestra.

And it is, to me, little less than a miracle that this delightful small place so rarely sees an English visitor. It has a charm and a sweetness altogether its own.  There is abundance too of excellent hotels, cheap and clean and pleasant ; while around are villas hidden among gardens and tall trees.  There is a beautiful old murky nucleus, also, of ancient houses, well away from the hotels, and yet quite obliterating them in the general prospect of Saint Martin ; there is a " Place " with clipped planes, where the polite inhabitants take their walks at evening and scan the fashions, and then eat dinner in one of the arboured restaurants that run along its upper side ; while from the railing along its lower side, you look straight up to the head of the valley, where the grim mass of the Balloure blocks the sky. There, they say, the ghosts of the murdered knights of the Temple hold revel over its cliffs and peak ; all this district is haunted with tales of the Order, and its agony ; the last refuge of the knights, and their last stand, was attempted in the gaunt fastnesses of these hills. And a heavy massacre was made of them on the Balloure—so says legend.

And there is no lack of flowers either round St. Martin ; those who are wise enough to come up here in June report the whole country one sheeted blaze of blossom ; and in the hayfields the towering vermilion of *Lilium pomponium* emerges from a solid sky of *Myosotis alpestris*. Saint Martin, in fact, is the pleasure-town of those who dwell by the Mediterranean ; hence the abundance and excellence of its accommodation ; all the permanent residents of Nice have a summer Villa, or take lodgings, up here, and make the place their refuge from the solstitial heats of the coast, which is no longer bearable, even to a native, in July. But, to the foreigner this pleasant corner of the earth, easy to get at, cheap and beautiful and close to the most wonderful flowers in the Southern Alps, remains as little known as Holy Lhasa.

Its season opens at once too early and too late for his convenience. The residential life of Saint Martin does not begin until the floral life of Saint Martin is at its first height ; that is to say, about the middle or end of May. By which time the foreigners have all fled home from the increasing heat of the Mediterranean coast ; and the full season here is in July, by which time the travelling Englishman has not begun to think about packing his boxes again for his summer holiday. When the time does arrive for his annual exodus, July is gone and August beginning ; and by then the high Northern Alps are more clearly indicated for his needs ; these southern valleys, in August, are too tropical. Saint Martin itself, though some three thousand feet above the sea, is peculiarly grilling in its sheltered *cul-de-sac*, and much more trying to the heat-hater than San Dalmazzo, which sits a thousand feet lower, but in a perpetual delicious little draught, at the foot of the Col de Tenda. And yet, if some brave soul could ever manage to break the chains of custom sufficiently to come abroad or stay abroad, in May or June, I heartily recommend him to visit this St. Martin, and I guarantee that its charm and pleasantness, and the beauty of its flowers, will cause him fairly to " gasp and stretch his eyes " as if he had had been listening to the mendacities of Matilda.

In mid-July the meadow-glories were gone. But ten minutes walk, round the head of the valley, and over the stone bridge that spans the Vesubie, takes you into the shadow of the limestone ranges opposite, across the river, where the heart of the gardener begins to open out again like a Palestine Rose. Not until one has got into realms calcareous again does one fully realize how one has fainted and dried up under the long dominion of the granite. After all I have said, I need hardly disclaim ingratitude or lack of devotion to the Princes of the granite, and to their Ancient King. But the lands he governs are a

dreary waste ; a rubble of ugliness, the abomination of
desolation spoken of by Daniel the prophet. It is only
here, on the kindly canvas of the limestone, that Nature
begins to apply her effects at ease. No more isolated dying
species, gaunt in the intensity of their determination
to live on against all untoward circumstances ; here, on
organic rock, built up of bygone lives, the life of to-day
is happy and at ease ; the plants stretch themselves out,
and fall into that comfortable mood best described as
*deboutonné*.

The first thing to appear, hanging from the hewn
stone cliff to the right of the roadway, as it curls round
at the head of the valley, is that special beauty *Campanula
macrorhiza*. *C. macrorhiza* is yet another of the species
that belong to the Maritime Alps ; it is predominantly
a limestone plant, extremely abundant in cliffs and walls,
from the level of Saint Martin, almost down to that of
the Mediterranean itself. But it has not nearly so much
in common with the Mediterranean Campanulas as has
*C. Elatines* from so much further north in the Cottian
Alps. It has nothing to do with the Garganica-section,
that is to say ; but is much more closely akin to our own
*rotundifolia*. It justifies its name by forming a vast
and fleshy root-stock, running back into the minutest
crannies of the cliff. In this habit, of course, it follows
*Elatines* and *isophylla* ; but the precaution is one that
is inevitable for any Campanula that chooses to grow in
dry and grilling rocks. Yet *C. macrorhiza* appears even
happier on shadier exposures ; thence it throws out tufts
of glossy leaves, toothed, rounded, roughly kidney-shaped,

quite devoid of fluff and any objection to rain. From these tufts spray out and downwards a sheaf of very fine, branching stems, that, in their time, clothe all the rocks in a loose cloud of blossom. The flowers are closely related to those of the Harebell ; they are much more numerous, a trifle smaller, rather shallower and more widely open in the bell, and of a warmer shade of lilac-mauve. The seed capsule stands erect, instead of nodding as in *rotundifolia*. The flowering season knows practically no limits ; early July is its hey-day ; but it must be a dark hour of autumn and winter that shall not give you a few showers of blossom along a cliff of *Campanula macrorhiza*. The rocks descending from Turbia are said to be blue with it, even in the deadest hours of January. Nor does this amiable quality fail it in cultivation. The plant is not only of the utmost good nature in the garden, but it continues to bloom there in all its characteristic abundance, as long as our winter frosts will let it. Not only that, but it grows from the smallest fragment, which is an added recommendation in a plant that has an enormous root-mass, and specially affects the solid rock.

Another minute, and the vinous blues of the Campanula are supplemented by the golden sprayings of *Hypericum Coris*. And *Hypericum Coris* is universal now ; it is in the rocks, it is on the sloping banks, it is abundant even in the sandy gutters by the wayside ; and it seems positively unseemly that so rare, precious and high-priced a plant should there be growing in such brazen prodigality. That *Hypericum Coris* should play at being a wayside-weed, is really like the Emperor Nero, supplementing the purple of empire with the laurels of the actor. It is not either decent or dignified. However, there ends any syllable of reproach that anyone can level at this most exquisite of plants. And, please, sir, a very little one ; and one on the right side. *Hypericum Coris* is the treasure of its race ; among the brightest jewels that the rock-garden can have. It grows here and there and everywhere, both at home and abroad, in any sort of sandy silt ; but nothing comes amiss to it, neither loam nor peat nor moraine ; you can call it indestructible.

Along by the Venanson road it is riotous in roadside gritty mud, no less than on open places of the rubbly banks to the sight, where in stony scree it forms wide tufts of colour ; and indeed, in companionship with *Linum salsoloeides*, makes one united carpet of gold and silver jewels. The plant grows into a dense, very low tuft, about an inch high, of many little shoots, clothed in wiry narrow leaves like some wee pine or juniper, but of a bright grey-green. Up above these, springing sideways this way and that, to the height of six or eight inches, shoot the wiry flower-stems. These also are scantily clothed with the same linear leaves, and are so freely and graciously branched that each spike is a loose fountain of flower. And those innumerable flowers are stars of the brightest pale clear gold, beautiful in shape, beautiful in their size, beautiful alike in their colour, number and habit. Furthermore, the plant is affable even in its rooting-habit, forming so neat and compact a tuft of fibres in its native silt, that, in favourable circumstances, you can pluck up the whole clump, perfect, without the intervention of the trowel.

It is of universal abundance in these districts, and seems especially fond of rubbly, sandy places. But it thrives no less in the crevices of the cliffs ; and appears to have sworn blood-brotherhood with *Campanula macrorhiza* ; for, in the rocks where you find the one well established, you will rarely fail to find the other also. Which means that the Hypericum, besides being indifferent as to soil and situation, is quite indifferent also as to whether it grows in sun or shade. But, whereas the Campanula seems to have a faint leaning to the shady sides of rocks, the Hypericum seems to have as much inclination, and no more, to sunnier slopes ; yet the two often meet and prosper together in complete happiness, on sunny rock or shady. Down the valley of the Vésubie they go with you to the very edge of the Mediterranean ; the Hypericum I have seen myself in November (no longer in flower, of course) by the roadsides descending from Turbia ; and then again they both go with you all the way up the Roja Valley, and are abundant together even on the hottest exposures of the rocky slope above Tenda.

But on the warmer banks the Hypericum, as I say, has another comrade, as faithful as is the Campanula on the cliffs. This is that loveliest of Flaxes, *Linum salsoloeides*. This has very much the same habit as the Hypericum, but is much laxer in growth. It makes fewer shoots, and longer shoots, clothed in a longer fur of wiry, pinelike foliage. The flowers, not so many, on frailer, floppier, branched stems, are much larger,

and singularly beautiful. They are wide cup-shaped
stars, reminiscent, almost, of some small convolvulus ;
and their colour is of a delightful white, faultless and
pure, not in the least creamy, and yet mysteriously warm
in its tone. There is a shell-like glow at the heart of
the blossom, and outside it, which gives one the effect
of a pearl's iridescence. Sometimes you find bigger
flowered forms than others, and sometimes more compact
forms than others, but all are lovely ; I especially cherish
a creeping dwarf, which runs closely down over the faces
of the rock, before breaking into its galaxy of bloom.
*Linum salsoloeides* gives us a welcome surprise—one of
the many surprises, good or evil, that are always diversi-
fying the path of the gardener. For this is a typical
Mediterranean plant, confined to the hottest of Mediterranean slopes, where it revels in the most torrid heat. It
actually comes down to the level of the sea itself. And
yet this plant of blazing, bone-dry banks, proves, as a rule,
quite hardy and prosperous in the damp conditions of
English cultivation. Why this should be so I cannot
tell ; sufficient for me to chronicle the fact with joy and
gratitude. It is more hardy and trustworthy, indeed,
than the Gentian-blue *Linum austriacum*, which grows
some thousands of feet higher, on the grassy ridges of the
Southern Alps, where it replaces *Linum alpinum* of the
Graians and Cottians.

So continue we our way along the Venanson road.
All the gutters are golden with Hypericum, and where
there is an open sunny bank, the Linum joins it in a
riot of loveliness. High overhead rise wooded slopes

towards grey crags of limestone up above ; and soon
their lowest bastions are impending over the roadway
itself.   Do not let us look at these yet awhile ; for here
begins the reign of a treasure so illustrious that to me
anything else afterwards would be a bathos.   Therefore
let us trudge along this pleasant road a little further,
rejoicing in the easiness and beauty of it.   For this road
is Paradise to the tired collector ; here he is able to gather
half-a-dozen first-class rarities almost without stirring
from the highway.   I, who have always longed ana
toiled to find a mountain crowded with rarities, yet with
a good carriage-drive all the way up it, have met my
nearest approximation to that ideal on the Venanson
road.

The highway rounds the hill and turns the corner
at last, into full sunlight, where, on the banks, Hypericum
and Linum redouble their glories among the purple
bushes of wild lavender, and all the odorous grey
vegetation of the Mediterranean slopes.   Above this there
are white rocks of limestone, half-clothed in a dense and
dwarfish beechen copse, for us to explore.   It is exactly
like certain tracts of our own scar-limestone, this ;
except that it is curtained in strange Sempervivums.
And then, from a niche in the rock, blazes violently out
at you the vermilion of *Lilium pomponium.   Lilium
pomponium* is a rare plant, peculiar to the Provençal Alps.
It has nothing to do with the stinking yellow horror which
nurserymen will always send you under the name of
*pomponium,* and which is really *L. pyrenaicum.*   (May
dogs devour its hateful bulbs !)   The true *Lilium pom-*

*ponium* belongs to that family of scarlet lilies which occupies hot places round the eastern half of the Mediterranean basin, ranging up to the Siberian Steppes, and comprises, besides *pomponium, tenuifolium, Heldreichi, carniolicum* and the well-beloved old *chalcedonicum* of cottage gardens. The range of *pomponium* begins low down, on rocks above Bordighera, and reaches up to Saint Martin and Saint Dalmazzo. It is said to be abundant in the meadows of Saint Martin, but there, of course, the herbage had all been cut, and the Lily had completely passed. I considered myself very fortunate thus to come so unexpectedly on these lingering blooms of a plant which I had known to occur in the district, but had had no hope of happening upon in flower so late in the season.

On that hot shoulder of limestone *Lilium pomponium* was quite frequent ; it grew sometimes in stony open pans of ground, but was at its best when sprouting from among low scrub, in richer soil, on some warm ledge. Here it was sending up stalks from two to three feet high, well clothed in those narrowish pale green leaves, which stand up along the stem, and have a dim line of silveriness round their edge ; and here it was hanging out on each stalk, at wide distances, from three to five of those large Turk's cap blossoms, which are glossy as your dining room table, of thick waxy texture, and of the most flagrant pure sealing-wax scarlet that ever rejoiced your eyes in an appropriate place. In the stonier open slopes the growth of the whole plant was much smaller, and it restricted its efforts to a pair of flowers at the most ; and,

I daresay that down in the meadows it may show more richness of development than in the best places up here, and an even greater generosity in blossom. Of its culture I have, as yet, nothing to tell, except that it is a plant quite at home on the hot limestone. I see no reason to suppose that, either in requirements or in constitution, it differs at all from *Lilium chalcedonicum* to which it is so closely related. Its flowers, perhaps, appeared a little smaller in proportion to its growth than are those of *chalcedonicum* ; but all these red Turk's caps are of the same race ; and comparisons by memory are not only odious but treacherous.

And now, exhausted with the splendours and the glare of the Venanson Road, we may retrace our steps to where the limestone rocks come down and hang over the roadway, on our left, as we return towards Saint Martin. And here, always in the cool shadowy side, if it wants to be happy, you begin to see, even at the highway's edge, that most precious plant, from which I should like to say that Saint Martin was fortunate enough to take its old name. Unluckily, the case is the other way round ; *Saxifraga lantoscana* was named after the place, and not the place after the plant. None the less, this should inspire every true gardener with an ambition to go on pilgrimage to a town which is illustrious enough to have given its name to so illustrious a Saxifrage.

Let *Saxifraga lantoscana* now take the stage effectively, in a new paragraph. It is all over these limestone rocks, up and up towards the peaks and cliffs overhead. But you will never find it frequent, or at its best, except

on the side turned away from the sun. It has a rigid
preference for the shadier rocks, and on these it makes
wide cushions and mats, which get wider and massier
as you climb higher, through the steep and tangled
copsewood, towards the ranges of grey rock above. On
every ledge hang out its great cushions of silver-grey;
these are seeding everywhere too with profuseness; each
small cranny or wad of moss below has its seedling or
young plant (even so is this beautiful treasure seeding
already on the shady rocks of the Cliff at Ingleborough,
which so closely resemble its native cliffs opposite Saint
Martin). It hardly seems to vary at all in habit; to
nothing like the same extent as *cochlearis* or *aeizoon*.
The only variations I saw were one that seemed large in
foliage and profuse in spike, and another, drawn-out,
etiolate and spider-like, because it happened to be growing
under a bush. For in the upmost reaches of the rock, it
becomes so abundant as even to be found among scrub
at the rim of lower ledges; higher up, it depends in
masses nearly a yard across, among chains of *Primula
marginata*, which seems quite indifferent as to whether
it be on limestone or on granite, and shows itself as
brilliant here as it was at Valdieri, with a willingness
that would certainly not be imitated by the more bigoted
*P. viscosa*. Also there was an acaulis-Gentian of the
*Clusii* persuasion, occurring in and out among all these;
with, I doubt not, many another delight peppered in
between, in its time. By mid-July of course there was
not a flower to be seen anywhere on these cliffs, neither of
Saxifrage nor anything else; I could judge, though, that

*lantoscana* is not nearly so floriferous in a wild state as it fortunately is at home. A cushion, half-a-yard across, will only be responsible for a couple of flower-spikes ; whereas, in our gardens, a piece of that size, if we attained it, would produce at least ten or a dozen.

And now begins a controversy, which I really cannot spare you. In the name of holy truth I beseech your patience. If I can, I will not only plant you a new treasure in your gardens, but will also root out the noxious weed of error. I will give you back *Saxifraga lantoscana*, and I will add you the best of all *Saxifraga lingulata*-forms, the greatest and grandest of the white-flowered Silver Saxifrages ; and this means making *amende honorable* to *lantoscana* for the long error of years. I had even dared to deny its existence. This is what I said of the plant in my first book ; " After years of confusion and unhappiness I have come to the conclusion that there is no such thing as *Saxifraga lantoscana*, or *Saxifraga lantoscana superba*. These are frequently offered in catalogues, and they are all forms, simply varietal forms, of *S. lingulata*. You will find them all, passing from one to another, in a batch of *lingulata* as you collect it, going up to Saint Martin Vésubie. . ." Now, the one drawback to these statements is that it is not type-lingulata you collect going up to St. Martin ; it is pure lantoscana-form all the way. " *Lingulata* " is a mere *façon de parler :* the Bellardi-form *only* occurs round the Col de Tenda ; the lantoscana-form is *entirely* restricted to the neighbourhood of the Var and the Vésubie. At the same time, my remark was, and is, technically correct ;

confusion still reigns among the Silver Saxifrages of the Maritime Alps, botanists are at war, much ink flows incessantly over much paper on the point. Even *Saxifraga florulenta*, oldest and most unmistakable of all its race, is still chronicled by the Kew hand-list as a variety of *S. lingulata*. After which it only remains for Kew, either to produce a new hand-list (as I believe, is intended), or else to make *S. longifolia* into a variety of *S. burseriana*.

My remark, I say, is technically correct. Prof. Burnat, the greatest living authority on the Flora of the Maritime Alps, divides the splendid " *Saxifraga lingulata* " into many varieties ; two of which belong to this range (there are others in Sicily, two in the Abruzzi : *S. lingulata australis*; and *S. lingulata catalaunica*, in Spain), and one of these he calls *S. lingulata a Bellardi* (of Sternberg) ; this is the Tenda Saxifrage ; the other is *lingulata β. lantoscana* (of Engler), of the Vésubie. Now let us consider, then, the affinities and divergencies of the three Silver Kings.

Let me begin with an attempted picture of *lantoscana*, rarest of the three, though abundant as a weed on its chosen rocks. And when everything is said and done, I shall maintain that *lantoscana* deserves by now to be held by the gardener, at all events, to stand on its own feet as a separate species in a triad ;— yes, though I be led a Martha to the stakes for it, with all my own volumes bound about my neck. To the botanist, though, it must remain bracketed with *Bellardi* as another local development from one archetype, not yet to be finally differentiated.

*S. lingulata lantoscana*, in the first place, is peculiar to northerly, cool, and shady exposures, unlike both the others. Here it forms very large and rather loose masses of rosettes. These rosettes are irregular in outline, as their leaves appear to be of unequal length. The leaves tend to splay upwards, outwards and backwards ; they are narrow, but swell suddenly to broadness at their point ; they also recurve sharply at the tip, and their whole tendency is to curl down at their edge. They are of a succulent consistency, yet not quite to the pitch of fatness, and have not the conspicuous central groove of *S. lingulata Bellardi*. Their essential and unvarying distinction, to my mind, is their colour scheme, for they are of a peculiar, very characteristic yellowish blue-green grey, filmed with silveriness ; and, round their edges runs a solid brilliant line, or broad hem, of silver-white.* The flowers are carried more or less one-sided on their stems ; the spike may be a foot high, it bends and bows beneath the weight of countless big flowers, brilliantly pure white in colour, most gloriously beautiful, and most gracefully borne. And the spikes, stems, and calyces are slightly glandular, in about a third part of the plants noticed ; this is very important. So much for *Saxifraga lingulata β lantoscana*.

Now let us have a look at *Saxifraga cochlearis*. This

---

* Boissier and Reuter distinguish *lantoscana* as being " of a less grey-green than *Bellardi*, verging on brown, with leaves shorter and more convex, the lower ones much longer, and not drawn out to a sharp or gradual point, lacking the furrow, and with a thinner margin of silver." Engler merely : as being shorter and less drawn out in the leaf, and with a thinner margin. (As to the margin I differ completely, as above.) Burnat admits the very distinct apparent differences, but adds that there are many intermediate forms. So there are, but whatever one may feel about individuals, there is no confusing a boxful of one plant with a neighbouring boxful of the other.

is a very much smaller plant, but of the same massed habit. It haunts, for preference, the sunnier limestone rocks in the Roja Valley (though it wanders along the Mediterranean coast, I believe, as far as Portofino), tolerates any amount of sun-heat, and has no partiality for high elevations. But here, too, you have the same leaf-scheme. The leaves of *cochlearis* are far smaller, thicker and fatter than those of *lantoscana* ; its rosettes are perfectly regular in appearance, and the whole plant is of a silvery blue-grey with powdered chalk in every pore. But you have the same swelling at the leaf's end, though much condensed ; so abrupt is the swelling in this case, that the effect is that of a round leaf like that of a sundew's, at the end of a narrow stalk. This is what has earned the plant its name—*Saxifraga cochlearis*—the Spoon Saxifrage. And the flower-stems and calyces are *invariably* more or less glandular, especially at the base of the spike.

Now *Saxifraga cochlearis*, unlike either *S. l. Bellardi* or *lantoscana*, varies indefinitely. In the hottest places it sometimes even becomes so condensed and minute as to develop the form which has so long been plausibly sent out by English nurserymen to do duty for *S. valdensis* (Correvon's new *S. Probynii*). In normal circumstances, no plant could be more distinct in appearance from either *Bellardi* or *lantoscana*. But appearances are not to be trusted, neither with plants nor people. And *Saxifraga cochlearis* occasionally condescends into shady gorges and sunless gullies ; in other words into the very places which *S. lantoscana* insists upon possessing in the valley of the Vésubie. (In one such you shall presently see it, below Saorgio.) And, where it does this, *S. cochlearis* does not flag or dwindle or decline, as *lantoscana* dwindles in the sun ; on the contrary, it waxes very fine and fat, and thrives exceedingly.

And, in the course of doing this, it gets obviously nearer and nearer and nearer to *S. lantoscana*. The habit becomes large, the foliage pale, the degree of swelling at the leaves' ends varies, the chalkiness diminishes, until ultimately you have the yellowish grey-green that distinguishes *lantoscana*. Finally *cochlearis* comes actually to shake hands of brotherhood with *lantoscana*, (and thus, through *lantoscana*, with great *S. l. Bellardi*). From all its stations I have now a very large series ; in this there is an indefinite amount of variation ; but it is very significant to me, that where *cochlearis* affects such situations as are invariably demanded by *lantoscana*, there is approximates most markedly to *lantoscana ;* indeed I have among my plants of *cochlearis* from the Saorgio gorge, one which is so unmistakably pure-bred *lantoscana* itself that I have no choice but to believe that a label must have been misplaced in the potting. Whereas it is only on the hot and sun-baked exposures which *lantoscana* would rather die than haunt, that *cochlearis* really takes on the grey colouring and closely-matted minuteness of habit that give it specific rank. And here, in case these suggestions are universally condemned as heresies, I will cover my own enormities by reminding you that when first he found *cochlearis* in the herbarium of Charpentier, even Reichenbach himself leapt so far off the track of possibility as to think it a hybrid of *lingulata,* and—*cuneifolia !* *

Now these polemics draw to an end as we approach Tenda, and make our bow to *Saxifraga lingulata a Bellardi.* As *cochlearis* is smaller than *lingulata lantoscana,* so *lingulata Bellardi* is larger. It haunts the cliffs of Jurassic limestone, from 3,500 to 5,000 feet, and seems indifferent as to whether it has a sunny or a shady exposure. One may detect in it, perhaps, a *faint* preference for cooler slopes and ledges, but this is not so marked as to prevent it making some of its most magnificent masses on sunny precipices. Its masses are enormous. I have found them so large that it has been all I could do to embrace one with both arms outstretched. It forms, too, a long, black, and woody rootstock, much more definite than anything usually produced by *lantoscana* or *cochlearis.* These, besides their main root, hold to the ground by minor fibres from the different rosettes, so as to come away from their ledge in a well-rooted wad ; but though each separate rosette of *S. ling. Bellardi* strikes with perfect ease, there is no collecting wild plants as one collects the compactly rooted tufts of the others. *Sax. ling. Bellardi* makes no minor roots, though a few fibres may blindly wander about in the mass itself ; you simply have to break away the whole cushion from the black trunk that runs

---

* I shall not be burned for heresy in this. Engler has actually treated *cochlearis* as a variety, only, of *lingulata.* Boissier could not wholly agree to this, though freely admitting the varietal status of *lantoscana.* Burnat himself is only unwilling to accept Engler's treatment of *cochlearis* because he himself has never succeeded in finding any intermediate forms between *cochlearis* and *lingulata.* I suggest that the missing link is *lantoscana,* approximating in turns to both the others.

deep into the hillside; then divide it all up into individual rosettes, and each one of these will root for you freely.

The rosettes of *Bellardi* are much larger than those of *lantoscana;* they are very much more towzled and untidy. They form wider, denser tangles, more closely pressed together. Their leaves are about twice the length of *lantoscana's*, perfectly narrow, arranged quite irregularly round their axis. Though they sometimes splay about on the ground, their much more usual tendency is to rise up and stand out in every direction, like a dishevelled head of hair. Imagine an *aeizoon paradoxa*, multiplied by three and then electrified until all its foliage rises on end; that will give you a faint picture of *Bellardi*. The leaves are substantially the same in design as those of *cochlearis* and *lantoscana;* yet wholly different in effect. The swelling at their tip, though present, is much slighter and more gradual than in *lantoscana*, very much more so than in *cochlearis*. Their texture is thinner, solider, more leathery; they are not so sharply rolled back as those of *lantoscana*, are drawn out by a long sharpish point, and have a noticeable central furrow; their edge is marked with a very regular dentation of silver dots, and their colouring is of a very dark grey-green, quite distinct from the yellowish-glaucous note of *lantoscana*, or the powdered whiteness of *cochlearis*. (The central furrow is most apparent in *lantoscana* when its leaves are young, at which time also they have a rich lucent green, almost as deep as those of *Sax. ling. Bellardi*.) The flower spikes are more freely produced than those

of either *cochlearis* or *lantoscana* ; otherwise they are
similar in design, though at least twice the size of even
*lantoscana's*. But they are *never* glandular in any part ;
only three specimens of *S. l. Bellardi*, out of all those
examined, could show a few glands on the calyx. The
whole stem is invariably naked and smooth.

As for the flowers, they are the same in scheme, just
as the arrangement of them on the stem is much the same,
in all three species. They are produced in enormous
snowy plumes, arching upwards and outwards with a
glory unrivalled in the whole race. *Saxifraga lingulata
Bellardi*, which, until last summer was wholly unknown
to the English cultivator, is going to be the most brilliant
and precious of all the Saxifrages. It is magnificent in
size, lavish in flower, robust in growth, dazzlingly pure
in colour, and exquisite in the airy grace of its waving
white fountains of blossom. As you see it streaming
from the Tenda cliffs in pennons of immaculate purity,
it simply makes your heart jump open and shut, like
Mrs. Caudle's when she saw a rose ; so M. Correvon has
recorded. As for me, I was too late for anything but the
splendid grey and silver jungles of its foliage. I can clearly
see that it clean wipes out *Saxifraga longifolia* from the
gardener's list. *Longifolia*, royal though it is, has a
dumpy, stolid spike, and a yellowish tone in its flowers.
And, above all, having produced those spikes, *longifolia*
dies as irremediably as *florulenta*. Whereas *S. l. Bellardi*
(and, indeed, all forms of *lingulata*), not a bit less in size,
carries its spires of blossom with the most regal grace,
and their opulent arching sheaves are of the most perfect

and refulgent white. And then, having produced you one such spike, *Bellardi* does not die, like the weaker vessel. Not at all, it continues yearly adding to the number of its rosettes, and producing its flower-spikes with growing generosity, until at last you will have a dozen or so, all waving this way and that, from the central mass of grey-and-silver a yard across. Add to this, that *Bellardi* is of a happier temper, too, under cultivation, than *longifolia* : does not undergo the attack of any disease, and asks of you nothing but a good ledge (of limestone in nature, though I do not see that it makes any trouble in the garden), open to wind and weather, either in full sun, or facing towards the north and west. But. while *S. ling. lantoscana* is practically unvarying, always distinct, and never leaves the Vésubie neighbourhood, *S. ling. Bellardi*, on the Tenda cliffs, *does* vary, and varies so clearly in the direction of *S. lantoscana*, that in Burnat's own station, my second exploration yielded me, among a thousand pure *Bellardi*, one plant that was to all intents and purposes as much pure *lantoscana* as if it had hailed from the gorge below St. Martin. Add to which that young seedlings of these two forms are absolutely undistinguishable.

A last word, on the moral characters of these beauties, to make sure that they are fit acquaintances. They do not so far, seem to contract any alliances with each other (at least I have seen none). But they all have a curious tendency to matrimonial entanglements with the Aeizoons. It is a *mésalliance* to which I wonder they should condescend. However, one beautiful thing at least has resulted, if the attribution be true. For Sündermann has sent out, under the name of *S. Burnati*, a plant which claims to be a child of *aeizoon* and *cochlearis*. This makes humped domes of fine, long silvery leaves, and has flowers which are as white as those of *cochlearis*—a lovely thing. And in my garden there are now many seedlings coming on, that show clearly in their leaves the influence of one or other of the Silvers of the Maritime Alps either of *cochlearis* or *lantoscana*—for great *S. l. Bellardi* has not long enough been in my possession to begin letting its fancy lightly turn to thoughts of love.

In nature it is *lantoscana* whose character indeed lies most liable to "impeagement." In the gorge of the river going down to Vésubie I collected, many years ago, large quantities of it. And among these (and among these only) have turned up several plants which are, at least, open to suspicion. Their rosettes are more regular, their leaves rather more sharply pointed, their contrasting beauties of silver and deep blue-grey rather more marked, than that in type *lantoscana* ; and their flowers, besides being carried on stiff spikes, unlike *lantoscana's* usual waving grace, are smaller than they should be, and tainted with that stodgy greenish-yellow which occurs among the Aeizoons, and never, by any chance, among the true-bred silvers of the Maritime Alps, whose colour is always of the purest snow-white. Therefore in these plants I suspect the blood of *aeizoon*; although, so far as I know, there was no *aeizoon* at hand in that place. Indeed, *aeizoon* seemed to me inexplicably rare, at least on all the limestone formations here, despite the fact that at home, on limestone or on anything else, it prospers and spreads so abundantly.

Then again, on the Col de Pesio, I came upon another kindred rosette, but longer and sharper, with the same stocky spike, and the same dowdy flower ; here *aeizoon* had obviously wedded *Bellardi* ; the alliance was the less in doubt that *aeizoon* was plentiful on those rocks, together with *Bellardi*; although, of course, in the ordinary way of nature, *lingulata* has passed well out of flower before *aeizoon* thinks of opening. And, finally, I must add a note of warning ; from M. Correvon's own garden— (though he himself well knows and prizes the genuine *lantoscana*)—there has proceeded in time past, by mistake of some underling, a " *Saxifraga lantoscana* " which has no relationship or affinity with true *lantoscana*, which has not even a drop of *lantoscana's* blood, but is nothing more or less than a mongrel *aeizoon*-hybrid, closely akin to *S. Churchilli*. And I am told that Sündermann also sends out a plant which is not *lantoscana*, under that noble name. Well, my own pieces at least are above suspicion, all gathered with ease and joy on the only rocks in the world where *lantoscana* dwells, and where no other Saxifrage can show its face.

So come we back again to Saint Martin, laden with our treasures ; and you, probably, wishing that no Silver Saxifrage had ever been heard of. And yet, in the getting clear of error there lies a joy which makes the process worth its pains. I cannot feel that your patience, if you have had it, can go lacking its reward. And, anyhow,

there is no more bother before you ; the way lies clear for
pure pleasure in seeing of these Saxifrages, when you have
reached the Roja Valley. This you might perhaps do,
arduously, over a high pass—the one up by the head of
the Boréon, in point of fact, by which, after much toiling
for a whole day, from before dawn till after dusk, you
might ultimately drag your sore feet down the Miniera
Valley and into San Dalmazzo. But the collector must
never stray too far from civilization ; otherwise his
harvest soon gets far too large for him to carry. He has
to be within reach of a place from which he can disburden
himself of it from time to time. And all this I say to cover
the fact that we mean to drive extravagantly down
the Vésubie Valley in a hired carriage ; and thence by
train to Nice, and on to Ventimiglia, and thence, in the
same sybaritic luxury of a one-horse shay, all the way
up again to San Dalmazzo de Tenda. And this, although
from St. Martin, down along by the highway side, there
runs to Vésubie twice or thrice a day, just such another
little toy railway as brought me from Pinerolo. But
this was too dull a method of progress for our views.

The drive from Saint Martin goes gently down the
long valley, and takes four hours or so. Below the village,
and for some way further, the Canterbury Bell towers
splendid in spires of purple on the banks, and here and
there are the misted pale-blue suns of *Catananche bicolor*,
with their dark violet eyes. Then follow fertile vales,
where, I remember that years ago, in autumn, the
Colchicum was abundant, though there now is nothing in
flower. After these, however, the road enters the Gorge

of the Vésubie, which is a deep cañon, several miles in length, between cliffs of white limestone so close and so high that daylight is always muffled in the gully that runs between them. They sometimes seem almost to meet overhead, and from their walls reverberate awfully the screeches of the little train, which is always meeting or overtaking one at the least propitious corners. They are hung, too, with cushions of a little Potentilla, possibly *Saxifraga*, which annoys one by looking as if it ought to be something so much more precious than it really is. It hangs dotted up and up the sheer faces, like myriads of dead bats or swallows' nests. I do not know that a swallow's nest is particularly like a dead bat; but there are points, if you are charitably inclined towards simile, in which a tuft of Potentilla might be like a dead bat, and others, again, in which it might be quite as like a swallow's nest.

But do not carp. For here, at a wider turn in the road, *Saxifraga lantoscana* once more takes possession. In beds and cushions and sheets and masses, at this particular bay of the road, it seems to clothe every suitable inch of space from top to bottom of that precipice. In flower-time the cliff must look like a drying-ground of the fairies, so thickly hung would it be with waving flags of white. It was here that, in days gone by, I collected my first lot of the Saxifrage, amongst which turned up those suspicious pieces such as I never found a sign of this season among the myriads that clothe the limestones opposite Saint Martin. From the cliff's foot slides away an extraordinary slope of rock. flowing down to the road in an unbroken level tilt, like the side of some Egyptian palace, upset but undamaged. Over all that incline, so steep as to be slippery and uncanny and even perilous, there are lines and tussocks and colonies of the Saxifrage ; actually to the road's edge it descends, and it was from the road's edge that I gathered it, in five minutes, those many years ago, by clutching the nearest tuffets I saw until my arms were full. But beyond that, the Saxifrage ranges up the whole slope, and thence again all the way up the whole precipice, where it has the added advantage of being quite impregnable. Mark this place well, for it is in a gorge exactly similar, and on rocks the same, that we shall ultimately see *Saxifraga cochlearis* most closely approximating to *S. lantoscana.*

After the road emerges from the Gorge there is nothing more to see in mid-July. For now we are down on the burnt levels of the Mediterranean, the herbage is ashen-grey by nature, no less than ashen-grey with dust ; only a rare little bloom here and there of some pink Rock rose, or the fluffy prettiness of *Coris monspeliensis* (which I shall not honour with further notice, seeing that it stands confessed a biennial), remain to remind you that ever there was such a thing as a flower in those grilling regions —which are yet within so easy a distance of the high snows and their riches.

# CHAPTER IX.

## THE GATE OF THE SOUTH.

THE Mediterranean Riviera in mid-summer is exactly the same as the Mediterranean Riviera in mid-winter. The same sharp and arid glare, the same harsh colouring, the same impression of a violently painted scene on cardboard, all hard outlines and rigid definitions. The only moment of the year when that landscape seems to take to itself a soul, is in the middle days of autumn ; when something not unlike a decent wistfulness possesses it, the colour softens, and the distances melt in gentler tones than at any more high-spirited point of the season. In the climax of summer not even the dust exceeds the measure of dust during fine weather in winter ; and, though all is baked dry, there is hardly any alteration in the general picture, since this coast is the special domain of evergreens and succulents, aloes, agaves, cacti, and other such unchanging vegetable growths. Only flattery could give the name of " green thing" to the inconsolable grey sadness of the olive, much less to such a tree as the eucalyptus, which wears, year in year out, without any cleanly shift of garment, the same dingy leaden drapery, like an everlasting mackintosh cape, concealing horrors. So that the pleasure towns of the coast lie embedded in much the same unalterable verdure through the heats of July as in the depths of winter. Nor do they themselves wear any different appearance. They are crowded, as ever ; they are like London out of the season, when there is "positively no one in town,"— except incalculable thousands of busy people running about enjoying themselves this way and that.

My description, at least, applies to Nice, when at last our journey landed us there a little after mid-day, with an hour or so to wait before the train took us on to Ventimiglia. True, that the shops were many of them shut ; but then there were very nearly as many open, even though the day of our arrival was Sunday ; true that there were no alien women driving about in ambitious hats ; but then there were very nearly as many natives as there ever are foreigners. And perhaps more, indeed ; for during the reign of the alien, the native seems to retire to his cave like a coney, and be no more seen, until the clamorous horde has retreated again. The streets were very cheerful in the heat ; up and down in the shade of the trees that line them went trotting Sunday crowds of people ; people, of course, who are the " positively *nobody* in town;" for the high commercial nobility of Nice is away up in the hills now, taking mountain air in its Villas at Saint Martin Vésubie.

Lucky to have so pleasant a place so near at hand. We had started about seven from Saint Martin ; by eleven or so we had reached the point where the Valley of the Vésubie (and the toy-train line) ends, at a little village of the same name, by the junction of the Vésubie with the Var, where occurs a station of the Nice-Puget-Theniers

Railway. One endures a wait here, either on a grilling little platform, or in the verandah of a nasty little inn. For contemplation one has the bed of the Var, in summer a wilderness of stones a mile across or so ; and beyond it rise sluggishly the lower foothills of the Maritime Alps, which are no longer alps, and not yet really maritime, mere wooded peaks and ridges tailing away down towards the coast. And, from Vésubie little more than an hour brings you into Nice.

Having lounged and lunched we proceeded forward from Nice. One by one, like beads on a chain, we threaded the pleasure-cities of the Mediterranean. They were all of them technically asleep and shuttered ; they all of them seemed, in reality, to be quite wide awake. The only sign of any dead season was the scaffolding round the Casino at Monte Carlo, which was being painted anew ; and a notice to the effect that it would be fatal to put your head out of the window between Mentone and Garavan, because of temporary erections inside the tunnel. The day was without cloud ; the coast lay gasping in all the jejune glory of its heyday. So we passed along, and under the hill of lovely Mortola, most lovely of Riviera gardens and best of botanical collections too, until the moment came for us to alight at Ventimiglia. Ventimiglia, that hell of the traveller in the height of the crowded season, where he has to wait for hours at the Douane, embowered in boxes, is a very different place in the depth of slack summer. A sleepy warm desolation possesses it ; the railway officials lounge delightfully, there is everywhere a relaxation of tension ; and under

the high arcades of the Douane, our two small portman-
teaux looked quite ashamed to be taking up the attention
of so solemn a sanctuary ; and sat together on the vacant
bench, looking like a pair of love-birds alone in Saint
Paul's.

We found that the official diligence for the Col de
Tenda had already started ; and that the next did not
intend to make a move till after midnight. Accordingly,
as the hour was about three, we decided on the extrava-
gance of a fly. We laboriously selected one with a horse
of comely appearance ; at least my companion said that
it had a comely appearance, but I suspect his choice to
have been biassed by the fact that on the box sat a little
black dog the size of a rat. However this may be, we
mounted up, and duly started on the next stage of our
pilgrimage. The horse belied its appearance, and proved
slower than a romantic drama in five acts ; with the
result that I did not sufficiently appreciate the beauties
of the Roja Valley, until, later in the year, when, whirling
up and down from Mortola in a motor, I was left free to
enjoy the scenery, instead of drearily wondering all the
time, when, if ever, we should reach a bend in the road
that always seemed a mile away, no matter how long the
intervals you left between each look. Few experiences
are more killing to the sense of enjoyment than straight
stretches of level highway, under the stupefying sun of
afternoon. Especially when these stretches, in reality,
are sloping uphill persistently, but without any of the
excitement of a real ascent : so that your driver considers
it necessary to keep his horse at a funereal walk the whole

time, restraining it firmly whenever it shows any light-hearted inclination to trot.

Now, of course, we are once more on one of the historic highways of the earth, for the first time since we left the Mont Cenis. From the most ancient period of man the Col de Tenda has been the Gate of the South. At the head of the view from Ventimiglia, over a notch in the ranges, towers up the cone of Monte Bego; and Monte Bego, thus clearly sovereign of the country, has been a god since the days of *Homo Grimaldii*. And, since first that *Homo* came and went, other races of men have so occupied this valley that the road must be thick in the dust of many generations, and is still to be traversed by all wheeled traffic that wishes to get from the Mediterranean coast to Turin and the Plain of Lombardy. At this moment, as, no doubt, for centuries uncounted, the Col de Tenda is a fortress of such importance that the railway and the high-road are not allowed to approach it, but are made meekly to wriggle under the mountain by tunnels two miles and more in length. Thus, situated as it is on a highway crowded with motors and traffic, Saint Dalmazzo is better known than Saint Martin, sitting up at the end of a mere *cul-de-sac*, more than thirty miles from any railway, and with nothing beyond it but mountains impassable to all except pedestrians and mules. " Better," indeed, is not saying much ; absurdly few are the people who know San Dalmazzo. Nor do its own compatriots frequent the place as they frequent Saint Martin. However, this neglect may soon be cured. Not long will Saint Dalmazzo lack the amenities of a railway ; the

line already runs from Cuneo on the northern side of the
range, through the tunnel beneath the Pass, to Vievola,
immediately at its southern foot. And the work is
diligently continuing ; by now the viaducts and lines are
being laid down between Vievola and Tenda. Then will
come the turn of San Dalmazzo, and the railway will
ultimately coil down to Ventimiglia, thus forming
a direct route between Turin and the Western Riviera.

In the meantime, the missing link is made good by
excellent public motor-services, that in summer run
several times a day from Ventimiglia, through San
Dalmazzo up to Vievola, in connection with the trains
starting northwards through the tunnel. And they also
run from Nice, over the Sospello pass, joining the main
Tenda road at Breil. But choose, if you can, the motor
from Ventimiglia ; for this whirls upwards at a decent
pace, indeed, yet with a reasonable regard for safety at
corners ; whereas the motor from Nice considers nothing
but speed, and roars round the most curling corners like
a streak of lightning on two wheels, no matter how thick
may be the roadway in dust or unctuous mud. You can
see it rock and sway with Jehu-ness, as it rushes at you
up the road ; in two seconds it has grown from a speck
to an elephant ; a crashing earthquake goes by ; in another
instant, before you have regained breath, or wiped your
eyes clear of dust or mud, the elephant has become a
speck once more.

So much for the possibilities of travel. Now bring
back your sympathies to contemplate this particular
journey of ours up the Roja Valley in a one-horse shay,

with an unsociable little black dog on the box. Very slowly goes the road from Ventimiglia up the lower courses of the Roja ; stretch after flat stretch succeeds each the other, with the inevitability of Amuraths. (I don't know who they were, but they proverbially succeeded each other, so it is all right). At last the gorge begins to make up its mind that it is going to be a gorge ; it narrows, winds among cliffs ; bright green-blue water swirls along red volcanic rocks.

And here, over the river bed, and the shingle and the cliffs above the Roja, the Oleanders are blooming in a waving jungle of deep green foliage, densely crowned with their glory of rich rosy roses. Behold, in amazement, this nurseling of greenhouses waxing splendid and impressive as the tale of a fisherman's prowess, in the pebbliest of rubble in a river-bed, and on the faces of bare sun-baked cliffs. There is one point, where the Roja makes a curve out of a cañon : you see the dark rock behind, the green diamonds of the river rippling in shadow ; behind a wooded mountain rises, all of granite shelves, with half a foot of cultivable soil laboriously banked up between each, almost to the very top ; and the foreground, whether in sun or shadow, is one blaze of Oleanders in the shingle, stalwart stocky bushes of deepest green, snowed under, as it were, by a drifted fall of huge roses, beneath the weight of which they wave and bow in the breezes that come down the ghyll.

After this the gorge never changes its mind again about being a gorge ; you climb steadily up it—in a very gentle but incessant climb, so gradual that until

you come down it again you cannot realise that it is a
climb at all. The glen takes long bends this way and
that, circumventing the barriers of mountain that always
seem to be blocking its course. Every time we thought
our carriage really had ascended a little, the road was
sure to dip, and undo all our progress again. For though
we are now advancing towards one of the most famous
alpine passes, the Col de Tenda rises high and abruptly
from comparatively low elevations. The Roja river
flows leisurely down from the range in which it takes its
rise ; or rather, in the course of years, it has worn itself
so deep a channel that its fall is no longer violent or
rapid. We crawled along above its bed that afternoon ;
and afternoon gave place to evening ; through the
twilight we passed, as in a dream, beautiful little ancient
town after town perched high on its pinnacle above the
Roja river ; little towns that had there perched and
lived, probably, from time immemorial ; had been
barbarian once, and then Imperial Roman, relapsed to
the invaders in the disintegration of the Empire, and then
once more come back to the old allegiance for the last
time, in that ruinous burst of energy which reclaimed
Liguria for Justinian and Theodora—only to lose it again,
and for ever, in the exhaustion that followed so inevitably
on the passing of those triumphant but expensive
Eternities. So, at last, dark night is born in the bed
of the Roja river, and its blue shadows steadily mount
high and higher up towards the mountain-ridges, where
the sun still lingers red on the bright green pine-scrub.
The first two Douanes are passed in the gloaming, and,

as we crawled under the vast amphitheatre on whose crest lies Saorgio, the twinkling lamps up on the mountain showed that night had fairly settled down. It was verging on dawn before we drove into sleeping San Dalmazzo.

But at this point I will desert the carriage, and bring you in a motor, by day, from Mortola to San Dalmazzo. The excursion, thus performed, takes about two hours and a half. I invite you to it, because I want to show you Saorgio and the gorge beneath. For the road here takes a sudden bend in the gully under the hill. As well it may, because it seems to be running straight into a cirque of impassable limestone cliffs that rise so high as to shut out half the daylight. And, all along the crest of that frontage, looking down upon the road at its foot, huddles and scrambles on the ridge the noble ancient town of Saorgio. Seen from beneath it looks like a picture in a fairy-tale book; a thing unbelievable, perched so far above the world, so obviously ungetatable. It is only when the road has wriggled through a deep ghyll and come round to its third Douane at Breil, that you come upon a branch road that coils round, up and up the limestone cliffs at the back, until it can climb over into Saorgio from behind.

But not less notable than Saorgio is the gorge below it. Here you come, for the first time in this valley, upon a solid stretch of limestone. And here at once, you have the result of limestone. Down the rocks and over the ledges hang cascades of *Saxifraga cochlearis*. But the situation is of the shadiest. There is one rather wider point where a certain amount of sunshine can be enjoyed, but, for the most part, that deep glen is filled with coolness and moisture and perpetual shadow. The situation is exactly the same as that preferred by *Saxifraga lantoscana*. And it is here, as I promised you, that you shall see *Saxifraga cochlearis* doing all it can to make up for the absence of its elder sister. It imitates *Saxifraga lantoscana*, that is to say, to the utmost of its power. It is no longer close and small in the rosette, as it prefers to be ; it becomes large and pale and diffuse and spatulate, develops into that form which has been called *cochlearis major* in gardens, and ultimately even approaches to the very distinct colouring and shape of *S. lantoscana*. But the two species do not grade into each other nowadays; *lantoscana* exclusively occupies the Valley of the Vésubie, while *cochlearis* is sole tenant of the Roja. It is at this point below Saorgio, though, that the highway sees most of it; and here it is splendid and abundant, as is *lantoscana* at that similar bend of the road which occurs half-way down the gorge of the Vésubie. One has no doubt that they could both of them be found abundantly also on the higher reaches of these limestone rocks ; though nowhere else.

At Breil the Sospello road comes down over a pass to the left, and the whole valley widens for a space. If you go up to Tenda in autumn, you will have the marvel of *Rhus Cotinus* before you. As soon as you have left the Mediterranean levels, the reign of the Sumach begins. Thenceforth, wherever the hill-sides are stony and fairly open, the Sumach is dotted lavishly ; while higher up, over the limy rocks, there is nothing else at all in the way of a bush.  Accordingly, in autumn, the hills for miles and miles in front of you, are as if thickly dabbled and splashed with bright, fresh blood ; and the upmost screes and shoulders are one glaring stream or sheet of scarlet ; of pure scarlet, dazzling to behold.  Driving up one day at the end of October, I saw a gully of shingle far away ahead of me, high up between two bare peaks ; and that grey cascade had what looked like a broad and regular hem on either side of refulgent blood.  When I went up a month later, the glow had faded like the roseate hues of early dawn ; the mass of colour still remained there, but it had gone dead and stale, like a sanguine cloud at sunset when the radiance is passed.

Between Breil and the next village, which is called Fontan (for we are in France again), Ball says that you may find that very rare plant *Ballota spinosa*.  I don't advise you to.  It is an ugly dowdy, and its calyx-lobes are protracted into ferocious thorns.  It is a plant of hot and arid places ; hence these precautions against the hunger and thirst of any animal that may pass by.  You can even see it in the torrid cliffs immediately above Ventimiglia, as you first drive out along the Tenda Road.  After Fontan the valley flows uneventfully for a mile or two, at the foot of grey rock-walls.  It is wide and sunny and fertile here.  But then it suddenly grows strict again, and enters a long and very narrow gorge, between towering cliffs which are no longer of limestone, but of the darkest porphyry.  All the vegetation changes as if at the touch of a fairy's wand.  The rock itself is like rusty-black

velvet. It has the look of something seared with fire.
The whole ghyll, some miles in length, is congealed Hell.
And on the blackened ledges and rock-faces, the plants
are white. For here you still see the silver foliage of
*Cineraria maritima*, which has taken a flying leap up
from the Mediterranean levels ; and on all the boulders
and shelves, the trans-alpine form of *Sempervivum arachnoideum* lies like mats of cotton-wool, pure as snow against
the blasted darkness of the rock.

When you have done with the burned cliffs, you come
out again into more open ground, where limestone resumes
possession. At a turning of the road you have your
fourth Douane, and are now in Italy once and for all.
And just round the corner, where the main valley widens,
and two minor valleys run down into it at right angles
from either side, lies San Dalmazzo de Tenda.

And San Dalmazzo de Tenda, even more easily got
at than Saint Martin Vêsubie, is not less delightful.
Perhaps one might actually call it more delightful. There
is no town here of any kind, just one straggling little open
street of a village ; one charming hotel, conspicuous alike
for comfort and cheapness ; a very few villas, and a re-
established convent, which was used for an hotel after the
Dissolution, until it was again granted to some exiled French
nuns, and now adds a convenience to the place by having
a tower with a clock in it that strikes. Thickly round San
Dalmazzo and up the neighbouring slopes rise forests of
chestnut ; we are too high for the olive, but the vine
still prospers on the sunny banks. The village lies above
a wide sweep of the Roja river. (I need hardly say

that this is pronounced " Roya, " need I ?   I should not
so frequently find occasion to talk of the Roja river if it
were pronounced " Roger "), in an open elbow of the
glen.   Down upon San Dalmazzo from behind, steeply
between pine-clad ranges of granite, descends the Valley
of the Miniera de Tenda, up which you can wander into
the high heart of the Maritimes, either following the
main glen, or diverging (as I shall make you do, and as
you may wish I hadn't) along its right-hand branch, which
becomes the Casterino Valley, and then the Valmasca
Valley, and ultimately brings you to the foot of Monte
Bego's sacred peak, deified by a race now forgotten, which
filled the rocks around its base with barbaric carvings,
never to be deciphered by the historian.

Cool, then, blow the mountain breezes down the
Casterino Valley upon cosy little San Dalmazzo in its
chestnut woods ;  and there they meet with other cooling
breezes that blow from Briga in the opposite valley that
opens up in front of San Dalmazzo, on the other side of
the Roja, running eastwards towards the Ligurian
Apennines, and the southerly foothills of Marguareis.
So that San Dalmazzo, at two thousand feet above the
sea, is never hot in summer, and never cold in winter.
Even in mid-December the snow cannot lie here ;  and in
mid-July the delicious heat is perpetually tempered by
gentle draughts from the glens of Briga or the Miniera.
The mountains immediately at hand are of no terrifying
height ;  there is no snow anywhere about ;  the cliffs
rise up in tier above tier through a thin garment of pines ;
and, to see the royal peaks you must needs make a long

pilgrimage up the Miniera valley. And, of these lesser ranges, some of them are limestone, and some of them are granite ; so that you have the prospect of a double Flora.

The especial deity of this district is *Primula Allioni*, rarest and most precious of its race. Not a thousand miles away from Tenda you will see it. I will lead you to a place I will not name. Indeed, I do not know that it has a name at all ; in any case I will not too curiously expound its direction. I will only say that so far as I have seen and known *Primula Allioni*, there is no use in hoping for this, any more than for any other sensible plant, except on the limestone. Ascend with me a certain very rough slope of stone and earth that leads up to a calcareous cliff in full view of the sun. In the face of this, from below, we think we have spied certain cavities in the rock face ; and, knowing the peculiarities of Allioni's Primula, for these cavities we passionately make. The lower slope is clothed in *Hypericum Coris*, Rockrose, Scabious, *Campanula macrorhiza*, Catananche, Lavender, and many another odorous Mediterranean herb. Then, as soon as you have reached the first beginnings of the cliff, you will find three rarities ; nay, four, occurring ready to your hand. Here, running along in the tiniest crevices is *Moehringia sedoeides*,* making masses and turfs of bright green foliage, narrow but succulent-looking, to earn its name, and with white stars of four-petalled

* Rare *Moehringias* are special in the Maritime Alps; *sedoeides* is the only one I saw, but there are two others, much more precious, *dasyphylla* round St. Martin, and *papulosa* near Tenda.

flowers scattered loosely over each tuffet ; then there is delicate *Micromeria Piperella*, a charming small labiate, sprouting in clumps from the live rock ; from the sheer walls drop cushions of *Potentilla Saxifraga*, whose white blossom has long passed over ; and *Passerina dioica* hugs the cliff with its fine-leaved branches—a funny Saxatile shrub, like something Japanese. I say nothing of *Saxifraga cochlearis* already beginning to appear.

Now we are above the preliminary rough slope, following the line of the cliff upwards at its foot. In the first pecked cavity there is nothing ; in the second, still nothing. However, this rock has been described to me as a " véritable Eldorado" yielding *Potentilla Saxifraga* and the Moehringia, no less than the Primula. Therefore, having found two of these, the third can hardly be far away. Up a steep scramble, I saw another little grotto ; towards this I scaled the grass ledges, while my companion pursued a milder course below, not liking the look of the climb. And, as soon as I got there, *Primula Allioni* was seen hanging in sheets and curtains from the interior walls of that cave. After that fateful moment, too, we found the plant incessantly, over the whole of the cliff from top to bottom. When I descended from the grotto I met with my companion plucking it on the rock-wall below. Every here and there came tracks of rock that were inexplicably barren of it, but if one continued again another ten yards or so, one was certain to find the plant once more ; and, where it occurred at all, it occurred in the most lavish abundance. Finally I can report *Primula Allioni* as growing even round at the base of the precipice, in open cliff exposed to full wind and weather, unprotected in any way, and bare to the sun practically from dawn to dusk.

Let no one adventure lightly, though, on the pursuit of *Primula Allioni.* Forewarned, we were forearmed, with stone-chisels and a big hammer apiece. For whether in cavity or open cliff, *Primula Allioni* inhabits only the tightest, tiniest crevices of limestone rock as hard and sound as iron. You rarely or never find any rotten stratum ; you rarely or never find the Primula except in the hardest faces of a hard range. And the roots run back, too, into the inmost recesses of the mountain—fat white threads they are, rushing hither and thither through the flaws of the strata in pursuit of nourishment, where you would say that no nourishment could possibly be found. A tuft an inch high will have root-threads of a yard in length sometimes. Therefore you have to go to work with due reverence and caution in collecting *Primula Allioni ;* choose your rock and your crevice with circumspection ; wield hammer and chisel with the utmost delicacy, lest you merely squeeze off the head of the Primula in any indiscreet wedging out of the slab from below.

The ideal is a downwards-running crevice, into which you can drive your chisels from above, so that a whole piece splits and falls, leaving the Primula's roots exposed along the upper surface, in all their hungry entirety. Once, also, I found whole colonies of seedlings on a cliff of rather loose conglomerate ; and occasionally you will find young plants, sometimes even big old tufts, that have seeded down off the rock-faces into beds of sandy silt at their base, from which you can lift the whole thing, complete to its uttermost fibre, almost without a touch of the trowel.   The fact remains ; neither from its own habit, nor from the steep cliffs where it dwells, is *Primula Allioni* a plant for the amateur collector.   It is true that when I made my second visit to those cliffs I had only my faithful trowel to help me, and yet got quite as rich a harvest as before with hammer and chisel ; but this involved search and labour more than usual, and a practice in using the trowel on solid rock, acquired laboriously through many years.

Nor would any ordinary trowel be of avail.   It must be the long thin fern-trowel, of which I have such abundant experience.   Nor shall anything shake my allegiance to this simple, but perfect, tool, which levers down vast slabs of rock with the utmost ease, and really puts one beyond need of hammers, except for *Androsace imbricata* and *Daphne rupestris*.   A fellow-collector once tried to put its nose out of joint ; he must needs think he could improve on my model, and appeared one day with an implement like a young harpoon.   It was about three feet long, was more difficult and burdensome than a baby, had no proper balance, and proved to be almost entirely useless except in simple turf ; and even there a small trowel did the work quite as well, though with less fuss.   However, the harpoon was useful for threatening intrusive children.   You pretended to hurl it at them ; they immediately dissolved in tears and dismal screams.

*Primula Allioni* is a species entirely restricted to the eastern limestones of the Maritime Alps. Its nearest cousin is *P. tyrolensis* of the Dolomites ; but this, though close in blood, is very far removed in appearance from *Allioni*. It is smaller and much rounder in the leaf ; greener, and not so viscous ; and never seems to develop into the cushion-like masses formed by *Allioni*. This is a highly specialised plant. It only occurs at low elevations, and is so tolerant of warmth that no place seems too hot for it. You often find it sharing a dry cavity with the Maidenhair Fern. But it has assumed a crank. It usually prefers, if it can, to hang from the roof and walls of shallow limestone caverns, in such places as can never be directly visited either by sun or rain. And these remain its favoured spots, where it makes its finest growth ; although you will also, as I say, see it thriving in condensed tufts, quite happily, on the open limestone cliff. In point of fact, all things considered, it is a remarkably good-natured plant ; very remarkably so indeed, when you consider its rarity and its peculiar habit. Even though the plants you collect may, despite your efforts, be mutilated by the time you have got them out of the rock, they will none the less start rooting again with vigour, as soon as you have got them home.

But in view of its arid situations, in order to preserve its own moisture and capture any more that may be about, the plant has had to take special precautions against drought ; and the result is that this grotto-haunting species of the solid precipices has become so sticky all over with glandular exudations that after touching it you feel as if you had been playing with glue. And every grain of dust and dirt adheres to those leaves as if cemented there by the Romans. This stickiness, too, incidentally makes the plant troublesome to pack ; for the gummy mass has a great tendency, unless you are very careful, to ferment and mildew *en route*, especially if sent in the summer heats. The pieces, however, make a fine recovery if well treated.

*Primula Allioni* forms a tuft or close rosette of these sticky leaves ; they are oval, rounded, broadening from a narrower base, and as a rule, quite smooth, or very feebly toothed, at their edge ; and they have a silvery-grey sheen shed over the dark green surface by their glue-glands, countless as the stars. And they never drop ; the leaves of each year die away into dry flaps of membrane ; in the course of years there is a long trunk, thickly clothed from top to bottom with these withered sticky tabs, and carrying the rosette of the current season at the end. An old plant will consist of forty or fifty such trunks, all contemporaneous, and so forming what looks like one unbroken cushion more than a yard across. If you attack it you will find embryo roots preparing to strike out, from the end of each long bough ; and every one of these will make a thriving plant. You can pull out half-a-dozen or so from any given mass, and do no harm to the rest. The buds are protruded one to six at a time, at the side of the rosette, so that the stem can go on lengthening from year to year regardless. And you will find, on an aged plant, dead withered capsules far down on the trunk, that may have been contemporary with George III.

The flowers begin appearing in winter, and continue up to their full display in May and June; they are very large, and freely produced, of a soft rose with a clear white eye. So very beautiful they are, that I must give them a special note. By the end of March, alike in garden or on the cliff, my little collected pieces are busily emitting fantastically large flowers of a seraphic bland pink, pearly-eyed. In cultivation, *Allioni* is not nearly so difficult as one would think, although demanding care. Like many plants of special requirements, it is otherwise of a fundamental amiability; unlike certain other species which have no definite ascertainable wishes, and yet remain incurably peevish. Nor have I seen reason to believe that *P. Allioni's* special wishes are so exacting as one would fear. I doubt even if it has any; it certainly seems indifferent here to rain. But in the first place, I do believe *Primula Allioni* insists on having calcareous rock, or calcareous rubble. And then any uncomfortable niche, with root-room (and perhaps under a ledge), will set it going as if wound up : I find that my own plants in the cliff seem quite indifferent as to whether they are planted in overhanging nooks, or on the open rock-face itself, exposed to all weathers ; every one of them alike is continuing to thrive and grow and unfold. And there they get no sun until the afternoon (some of them never) ; and the winds sweep icy down from the North, and on most of them the incessant Ingleborough deluges descend without mitigation.

But the Primula is not the only treasure on these rocks of Tenda. For now, on almost every stone, lie blue-grey mats of *Saxifraga cochlearis*, much tighter, smaller and bluer in these open places than it was in the deep gorge beneath Saorgio. And on the slope itself, among the Lavender, stand the beautiful cups of *Linum viscosum*. This is a tall, herbaceous plant, its stems thickly clothed in pointed broad leaves, gummy to the touch. It rises about a foot or eighteen inches, and each stem produces several large solid flowers of a rich lilac rose, which occasionally varies to a lilac-mauve. In the garden it grows with perfect ease, and is far too seldom seen.

Then, on a bank, in long grass among the Mountain Pine, I found a single plant of *Lilium pomponium*, passing out of flower. No doubt that there are others on that hill-side ; but this was the only bloom remaining, and I was surprised to see it so far up in the hills. Hardly had I recovered from this shock than another confronted me. For weeks, whenever my companion had been ecstatic over anything, I had duly put him in his place by remarking, " Ah, but wait till you have seen *Aquilegia alpina.*" And now, lo, and behold it—a few final flowers, fading and shabby ! And I was staggered with horror at the sight. Surely the alpine Columbine must terribly have grown in my memory, or else terribly shrunk in fact. For this thing here was a poor, measly little affair, by comparison with the enormous sapphire stars that I remembered or invented. And then my rocking reason sat firm again on its throne. I realised that this was not *Aquilegia alpina* at all, but the last fadings of *Aquilegia Reuteri.*

*Aquilegia Reuteri*, in point of fact, is yet another of the special glories that distinguish the Maritime Alps above the other European ranges. If you want to see it in character you must ascend the Valley of the Miniera de Tenda. And the Valley of the Miniera, besides being granitic, is very long and very steep and very hot and very dull.* We were told that it took two hours of easy sauntering to reach La Maddalena, up in that divergence of the Miniera which leads to the right, and is called the Val Casterino ; and we found that it took three and a half hours of solid stodging. I draw a veil over the feelings with which we viewed our informant, and the Miniera generally. Nor did our welcome at La Maddalena quite correspond with our heat and our weariness, our hunger and our thirst. Not to put too fine a point upon it, our hosts were scantly pleased to have two total strangers dropping in on domestic bliss " *en villégiature* " among the wild mountains. They eyed us with frigidity as we climbed over the garden-railing, and indicated that tea might be obtained, perhaps ; but that the meal was over, and the fire gone out, and the bottom of the kettle fallen through. And, pray, what would *you* say, then, or I, or any other normal person, if we retired into the remotest Alps for solitude, and then saw two strange figures toiling up into our garden, armed with trowels and collecting tins ?

But there are bright spots in even the Valley of the

* I've been severely rebuked for saying this, and, of course, it isn't true. But it was true to me, the day I mounted the Miniera. What closer approximation to truth can you expect ?

Miniera. And the brightest of all is a slope quite blue with *Aquilegia Reuteri*. This occurs just at the divergence of the side track towards La Maddalena, and a little way short of the silver mine in the main valley, from which it takes its name. Here, on a bank of very stony, grassy rubble, the Columbine abounded in rich profusion of blossom, and just below, in the gravel bank, by the path, *Campanula stenocodon* was in flower. And Reuter's Columbine is certainly a glorious and lovely thing, when one sees it doing its best. You may take it, roughly speaking, as a diminished version of *A. alpina*, but this gives only a quite inadequate description of a plant which, though it does not rival the Alpine Columbine in size or splendour, yet strikes out a line of its own in the way of colour. For the blue of *Reuteri's* big flowers is even softer, paler and clearer than that of *alpina's*. At twilight, among the coarse grasses on that grey slope, the balancing innumerable blooms seemed to glow like a pure blue fire. They have a quality of effulgence denied to the solid sapphires of the Alpine Columbine ; their intense, clear radiance shines from afar. Among the abundant flowers I also found a portent that I have never before seen among the wild mountain Columbines—namely, a perfectly double form—*monstrum horrendum*, obese and dreadful. Of the plant's culture I can say nothing yet. I can only say definitely that it is an evil beast to collect, for the ground it chooses is chunky with big blocks of stone, amid which its trunk goes meandering down to an unknown depth before it begins to think of sending out root-fibres. Even baby plants are as difficult to acquire as happiness.

Your best chance is to pry away some overhanging sod above the path, on the chance that if it be large enough you will find among the sifted *débris* a few young seedlings with more or less perfect roots. In cultivation I think *A. Reuteri* is so far entirely unknown and ungrown.

The Campanula is of a different spirit. We have already seen it beginning to shoot from the highest shingles on the Bocca Lorina and the Ciriegia. It is a plant of the upper stone-shingles, and, if it were not so amiable, I should be surprised to find it here, so low down and accessible. It makes, it is true, a long thin tap-root, and but few frail laterals ; yet, after the Columbine, almost anything would be easy to collect ; and therefore one approaches the Campanula with double joy. This is the first time we have been privileged to see it in bloom. It is a rare plant, and even rarer in cultivation. Let us observe it. *Campanula stenocodon* has almost the habit of the Harebell—delicate and straggling, thin and wiry, with very narrow, dark, smooth leaves. The flowers, which are carried as in the *rotundifolia* section, are of a deep violet blue ; their shape is the peculiarity that gives the plant its name. For they are formed like a long narrow trumpet, quite distinct from those of any other Campanula one knows. I see no reason to doubt that it will prove quite easy of cultivation in the moraine. I might have spoken with even more confidence ; only a plant labelled *stenocodon*, that was put into my new moraine this spring, sprouted up into an immense clump of what seems something like ordinary *linifolia*. So that I am to suppose the plant was mistaken in the potting ;

unless I am driven back on the far more awful, and indeed incredible notion, that *stenocodon* is merely a high alpine variant of *linifolia* or *rotundifolia*, and reverts to type, after the horrible habit of *C. Scheuchzeri*.

One ought to know more of the Miniera Valley. Perhaps some day I may return there, when the bottom has been restored to the kettle. For the wide glade of La Maddalena is beautiful. The boulders are sheeted with *Primula marginata*, and bushy with *Dianthus sylvestris*. High over the head of the valley loom the grisly precipices, the snow-fields, and the naked peak of the Rocca del Abisso. Round to the left at the foot of this goes curling the Casterino Valley, and becomes the Val Valmasca, leading towards holy Monte Bego, and the Lakes of Marvels, and the rock-carvings which are the " Marvels," that give the lakes their name. On Monte Bego the King of the Alps again holds his court ; and the Val Valmasca is sacred to an even auguster plant than *Eritrichium*. For those gaunt granites mark the extreme easterly limit of *Saxifraga florulenta*.

The upper pine-woods over La Maddalena are full of Fritillaries, purple and golden, *Moggridgei* and *delphinensis*, and above these, like stretches of bluebell in one of our own woods, floats dense down the copsy distances the azure haze of *Aquilegia alpina*. We saw a great bowlful of it at La Maddalena; the sight made one apologise on one's knees for ever having thought for an instant that *A. Reuteri* could even be a form of a glory so royal. Then again, in the meadows, grows *Linum salsoloeides*. In the stone slopes among the woodland just above San Dalmazzo, there is abundance of the rare and interesting, but not overwhelming, *Geranium macrorhizon*. In the scrub rise up strange tall Campanulas, and the orange fires of *Lilium bulbiferum* glow from the grassy glades and the black rocks that rise among them here and there. And in the chestnut groves themselves by San Dalmazzo you will find dainty pink *Cephalanthera rubra*, which ought to be " *rosea*," and is the especial pride of one lone wood (I believe) in Gloucestershire. For the rest I can credibly report that *Viola nummulariaefolia* closes its reign in the upmost moraines above the Miniera Valley, and that there also occurs *Campanula Allioni*, and occasionally assumes huge-flowered, dark violet forms which are as the sun to the moon of its ordinary rather pallid little bells. This is no fancy of mine ; I have seen this marvel : " *Vu ; ce que vous appelez vu ; de ces yeux vu.*"

The Briga Valley, on the opposite side of the Roja, sets up on an entirely different principle to that of the Miniera. It is, I think, calcareous from end to end, with the exception of a granitic outcrop at the beginning ; and is said by Ball to bristle with rare species. He uses the more dignified word " abound," it is true, but the impression left on one's hopes is that every rock is showered over with priceless Saxifrages and Campanulas. This fact adds to my irritation in having nothing of moment to chronicle from the Briga Valley. It is a delightful stroll of a mile and a half up from San Dalmazzo, it is true ; and the hostelry is charming, embowered in gardens and arbours where you sit out to take the little

breeze of summer that so rarely fails.  But we toiled up
an immense vine-clad slope just opposite, in full sun, only
to find on those limestone cliffs nothing that we had not
abundantly collected before.

Very possibly the rarities may bristle, after the
exasperating way they have, on the side of the valley which
we did not visit, namely that which faces north.  We
descended, empty, from that precipice, re-crossed the
river, and went up the little dry stream-bed which comes
down into the main Briga Valley behind the village, and
is called, I think, the Rio Secco ; but it may be the Rio
Freddo.  Assuredly on the *lucus a non lucendo* principle,
if so ; nothing less " freddo " could well be imagined,
in the grilling heat of that afternoon.  Whereas Secco it
certainly was ; as dry as any bone, and all the grey
shingle of the vanished streamlet hidden by flowering
miles of lavender.

And in this valley *Saxifraga cochlearis* lives.  On every
rock, whether in shade or in hottest sun, there are mats
and vallances of *Saxifraga cochlearis*.  I collected many
different leaf-forms ; for the flowers were long over.
However, as the flowers vary almost as indefinitely as the
leaves, in their roundness, splendour, and purity of colour,
I nurse the hope, based on previous experience, that even
as thin, cheap-looking leaves mean as a rule poor starry
flowers, leaves that are fat and well liking will produce
me solid snowy cups of blossom on those gracious rose-red
stems that bend and waver so beautifully.  And here,
too, one can see how it is that *Saxifraga cochlearis* is such
a treasure in gardens ; it is the thriftiest and easiest and

most jovial of its easy jovial race. It does not care a hang whether it is growing in torrid sunshine or in dark shade ; in the one case it will hump itself up, screw its foliage tight, and settle down in a neat hard mass to enjoy a roasting ; in the other it will spread itself, and get large, and make up its mind to revel in the cool shade. Nor does it care what rock it has ; in nature it remains, like all the Silvers of the Maritime Alps, faithful to the Jurassic limestone ; but in our gardens it will thank you kindly for anything you choose to give it. A sandstone rock at Kew has a more richly flowered plant of *cochlearis* than any I came on in its native hills. For, as a culminating recommendation, *cochlearis*, following the lead of *S. l. Bellardi* and *lantoscana*, is a great deal freer with its flowers in cultivation than in a wild state. And, after all this, how dare I accuse the Briga Valley of barrenness ? Does it not show how the Maritime Alps corrupt the soul of a collector with their unparalleled largesse, that after only ten days among their treasures he is so *blasé* as to count a day lost and sterile if it " only " yield him one such first-class rarity and dear friend as *Saxifraga cochlearis* ?

However, as we get nearer and nearer to the Gate of the South, the harvest gets still richer and richer. Not yet have we set eyes on the King-Silver of the Maritime Alps. We must climb a little nearer to the Pass. The road continues winding upwards in a gorge from San Dalmazzo, coiling this way and that in sharp turnings, until the valley opens out, and you see before you, in a broad bay, the town of Tenda, lying on a hill, at the foot of the ancient citadel.   All around are large mountains, many of them grassy and bare ;   immediately behind and above the town rise three or four huge naked pinnacles of limestone, blazing red and grey in the pitiless sunshine.

Tenda is a lovely place.   I have not sampled the hotel, but am told it is very comfortable ;   and, indeed, from what I saw of it, lunching there one day, I should judge the favourable report a true one.   In early summer it would well repay one to make head-quarters at Tenda, for the exploring of the neighbouring ridges and valleys. And Tenda, too, is a time-worn and tear-stained place. It has the charm of a town that has at least " walked on " in the unending drama of history.   It is quite little, very old and peaceful, lying on the slope of its hill, at the foot of the higher slope that leads up to the crags above. But there have been heart-burnings over Tenda ;   and ambitions have circled dark round the gate-keeper of the Pass.   Look at the wrecked citadel above the town ; there, among a wilderness of stones, rises the lone jag of masonry which is all remaining of the Castle.   And here (says Ball's " Alpine Guide ") in her own citadel, looking out over her own town, the last sovereign lady of the Alps, Beatrice Lascaris, Countess of Tenda and Duchess of Milan, was strangled by order of her husband, the Duke Filippo Maria Visconti.   He had married her to get possession of her dower—the city and the County and the Pass.   She was older than he ; and, as soon as he had got the goods he no longer cared about the lady.   He trumped up an accusation that was known, even at the time, to be forged, and had his marriage ended with a bowstring.

And, if the County remained in his possession after this unrighteous deed, then it has yet a further interest for us English. Seeing that thus it might once have had an Englishwoman for mistress. There are but few places in Europe over which Mary Tudor was not at one time Queen, Countess or Duchess. Tenda is not among them ; blended in the duchy of Milan, it should add yet another to the weight of crowns that brought so much glory and so small profit to that weary little red-haired head. It is seldom, indeed, that the plant-collector in Europe can escape the ubiquitous royalty of Queen Mary ; as Duchess of Milan it is she who allows him to pluck her Saxifrages from the cliffs of Tenda : as Countess of Tyrol she watches him hammering out *Daphne rupestris* : as Queen of Naples and Jerusalem she has a vested right of guardianship over *Iris Lortetii* and *Lithospermum rosmarinifolium* : as Queen of Spain she is the sovereign lady of *Erinacea pungens* : and to the Queen of Sicily I am quite happy to leave her monopoly of ugly little *Antirrhinum siculum.*

Enough of this. I wonder if my historical musings bore my readers as much as they bored my companion of this year ?* (Surely I may plead, at least, that they are rare ?) He suffered in silent patience, though. Well I got to know the blank look that came into his face, when some oddment of remembered history cropped up in my mind

---

* Especially as Tenda, of course, reverted to the Lascarids after the dissolution of the Visconti Duchy of Milan, so that Mary was never Countess of Tenda after all.

at the sight of some place we visited; and was instantly proclaimed by a tongue too rashly confident that everybody shares my own passion for ancient associations of tragedy or romance. I cannot think that anywhere blooms *Saxifraga Bellardi* quite so white as where some murdered Duchess of Milan may have bled; whereas, to many a right minded person, a primrose by the river's brim, Good hope and profit brings to him: And it brings nothing more.

However, I here scored my one success with the Countess Beatrice. Of all my historical odds and ends she alone contrived to rouse an answer in the mind of my companion. He was stirred to signs of consciousness; and twice, on the way up the rocks, he paused, of his own accord, to tell me that it made him quite sad to think of " Pore-pore-Margaret " (for so he humorously termed her). In memory of that triumph I feel rewarded, and will spare you any more such annotations. And you needn't be too prompt, either, to shed droppings of warm tears on those stones of Tenda. For, after all, Baedeker gives the lie to Ball, by telling you that the Duchess Beatrice met her end, not here, but in some castle near Milan, in the Lombard Plain. And Queen Mary, like Queen Anne, is dead.

However, let us take it that Tenda has anyhow seen tragedies; and be done with it. Other hearts must often have broken in Tenda, and other necks also, many a time, though they were not weighted with the crown of Milan, nor circled with a line of scarlet. So let us climb up through the old town, by a street that carries the sad

name of Beatrice Lascaris. At last, leaving the cemetery
below, you come out on the level of that ill-starred castle
at the summit of the hillock, dominating the town and the
wide valley stretched out below in the sun. Sun, too,
lies fierce on the steep slope that mounts above the castle,
towards the crags now so close overhead. Over all the
banks are aromatic grey herbs, lavender and sage and
southernwoods. The red earth seems to breathe a hot
fragrance as one follows up the track. One draws nearer
and nearer to the cliffs as one climbs : then, for some hours
continues along their feet, until at last we abandon the
path to mount a long and very steep incline of rotten
limestone, towards a high and serrated ridge. The going
here, though safe in reality, was daunting, perhaps, to one
unaccustomed. Or it may have been that " pore-pore-
Margaret " was taking her reprisals. In any case my
companion failed to appreciate the beauties of that climb,
and wandered off upon lower tracks, with the result that I
monopolised that blazing day's harvest.

For it was not long before the goal of the pilgrimage
hove in sight. For there, high up on a shelf of a torrid rock,
were masses of a wiry-haired Saxifrage that could only be
*lingulata a Bellardi*. These were quite impregnable, of
course. However, I continued climbing up what was now a
precipitous and shallow gully of rotten limestone. Because,
where there are ancestor-plants on a cliff, you may usually
reckon on finding young descendants at the foot. And,
sure enough, in another moment there they were—not in
quantity, indeed, nor of any size, but still unmistakable
with the long, thin leaves, towzled and wild in design—

so distinct from *lingulata* β *lantoscana ;* not only in their doubled size, and in their fine-drawn tenuity of leathery, spidery leaves, but also in that clear beading of silver spots round their rims, which is quite different from the broad uniform hem of silver into which the chalkpits develop round the leaves of *lantoscana,* so much fatter and shorter and more rounded and recurved. But at the same time I was puzzled ; for here among the true *Bellardi* there were several plants of a form which seemed to swell more definitely at the point of the foliage, and to have that foliage shorter and broader than the type. This form was almost pure *S. ling. lantoscana* of the Vésubie. And I had happed by luck on one of the stations from which Burnat records, among perfect type-*Bellardi*, the occurrence, very rarely, of intermediate forms, which at last merge into perfect type-*lantoscana*. Not everywhere does *Bellardi* thus grade off ; while *lantoscana*, in its own home never seems to return this compliment by grading into *Bellardi*. And the tiny seedlings of *Bellardi* on these rocks above Tenda were absolutely indistinguishable from young seedlings of *lantoscana* opposite Saint Martin. And yet the two develop into such wholly different splendours. Even so, of two con- temporaneous babies, like as two peas, the one will turn into Klytaemnestra, and the other into divine Helen. Finally, as I say, I did get one plant which seems at present to be as true-bred *lantoscana* as if it had been born by the Vésubie.

I scrambled in solitude among those collapsing shelves, heeding nothing of the difficulties that stung me at every turn. For be it known that these precious Silver Saxifrages on their cliffs (and *Primula Allioni* also), are hedged about with a bodyguard of the most spiteful little Junipers you ever regretted running across. Not only do they prick you with an equal ferocity, whether you sit on them unadvisedly, as often happens on a precipitous declivity, or try to wander through them, or lay a rash hand on the nearest bush for support : but their injuries have a venom which leaves a red, tingling spot wherever they pierce. In number and size these guardian angels were not, indeed, so conspicuous here as on the cliff of *Primula Allioni,* but they were all the more deadly, because one did not notice them, but tried to climb up by some meek little tussock, which, when clutched, turned out to be a vegetable hedgehog lying in wait for you there between two boulders.

However, in a few moments more, I was beyond reach of these troubles, as I sprawled along the faces of that rock. (For now the gully had climbed so far up into the cleft between two jags that the whole ground lay in the shadow of the one that towered on my right.) In the sunshine that flogged the opposite cliff there still loomed down at me, no less unattainably remote than ever, those masses of *Saxifraga Bellardi.* But now they were no more regarded. There let them stay, and enjoy their grey-and-green old age. Down below is another treasure, no less valuable, and even more exciting to my sentiments. For *lingulata Bellardi* is a new friend ; whereas it is now many years since first I saw *Saxifraga diapensioeides* in the old days of Backhouse, at York, and fell then and there in love with its neat, hard denseness, the compact minuteness of its charm. Ever since that time I have tried and tried again to make the plant return my passion, or at all events requite me with a certain amount of regard. But always with, at the best, only such a pale success as amounted to parliamentary failure.

And now I see the reason : I had persistently given *Saxifraga diapensioeides* what it didn't like. And, however devotedly you may love the dear gazelles of your fancy, no matter what they be, whether children or plants, if you go on giving them what they don't want, even with the best of motherly motives, you will never succeed in winning their affection in return. For, whereas passion is an uncalculated largesse given by the divine insanity of our souls, affection is more nearly the emotional currency with which one pays money down for goods duly delivered. However this may be, the fact remains that I had always looked on *Saxifraga diapensioeides* as a lover of rock-chinks in the very fullest sunlight ; and treated it as such. And here it now is growing only on the coolest of exposures.

In the shady slope to the right of that gully the Saxifrage was abundant, spreading and seeding profusely in the black humus that lodged between the slabs and layers of a very rotten white limestone, exactly like the rotten flags of the scar-limestone under Ingleborough. Even among the moss, and on the lower side of coarse grass tuffets, it was prospering in complete happiness ; and on the sunlit side of the gully there was not a trace of it. Young plants were coming in battalions to take the place of their parents ; and these were wide flat tussocks, often eight or ten inches across. Of course the flowers were over ; but I do not think that *diapensioeides* ever varies,* although if pressed under a stone or in some such unnatural position, the form of its foliage may elongate, until it comes to look almost like a tinier version of tiny *valdensis*.

These crags, indeed, are near those from which Maw mistakenly chronicled the real *valdensis*, that rare beauty which you have already visited in the Cottian Alps, and found insisting on granite rocks in the sunniest of positions. There is, of course, none of the real *valdensis* on these limestones ; but I did not even succeed in finding any of that minute form of *cochlearis* which is almost certainly the source of Maw's mistake—that same *cochlearis minor*, indeed, from the Caïros valley, which has for so long usurped the name of *valdensis* in our gardens, and which then became *cochlearis minor* in a spasm of honesty, until M. Correvon came along and turned it into *S. Probynii* as a reward. But it is curious how *cochlearis* seems to hug the low valleys. One has a notion that the Silver Saxifrages are all alpines, if not high alpines. Yet these hot Maritime ranges are their paradise, and they cling to the lower rocks even here ; while *cochlearis* hardly seems to stir very much above the neighbourhood of the river-beds—certainly never appears to luxuriate in the more mountainous situations.

---

* Except to that lovely citron-yellow form, which for so many foolish years has been going about the world under the absurd name of *S. aretioeides primulina*.

But it is not *valdensis* that is really twin-brother to *diapensioeides*. For this you have to range the far south-eastern alps until you are lucky enough to come upon *Saxifraga tombeanensis*, which holds the median position between *diapensioeides* and *Vandelli*, though closer to *Vandelli*. It is interesting to notice, how, in the whole race, each beauty seems to duplicate itself. Many species of Saxifraga are apparent twins—*cochlearis minor* and *valdensis* ; *burseriana* and the thicker-spined, harder *Vandelli* of the Bergamasque Alps ; *Bellardi* and *lantoscana* ; *tombeanensis* and this lovely *diapensioeides*. Only primeval *florulenta* is without any twin, or even any third cousin, anywhere in the race.

*Saxifraga diapensioeides* belongs to the section of the Kabschias, and of that section is the smallest, hardest, neatest, most charming and compact. The silver-grey leaves are very wee, blunted and compressed, and very tightly serried in wee rosettes. The whole plant forms a hard flat mass, often half a foot across, and not half an inch high. So beautiful are those silver scabs on the rock, that I quail at the irreverence of comparing their feel to that of some wrinkled and warted skin of an aged toad. Yet there is no other comparison that rouses in my mind anything like the living, pulsing, but cold-blooded sensation of those hard, yet elastic masses among the stones. They do not prick or yield to the touch ; but you feel a thousand knobs of dull, blunt points, that give you exactly the sensation of a firm, corrugated hide. And then up come the glandular little flower stems about three inches high, each carrying, in a short loose spike, from two to four very large white flowers, perfectly pure and beautiful and snowy.

And, now that I have seen the Saxifrage growing, I believe that this book may be justified to you of your labours. For sight does often give a key to cultivation ; and, now, since I have watched this plant *in situ*, and noted what it likes, and treated all my own plants accordingly, I find that this Saxifrage, long reported as one of the miffiest, is, in reality, going to prove one of the best-tempered in the garden. How often, alas, does it happen, that a plant earns itself a bad name by pining persistently, under methods of culture which are repugnant to its very soul, and which five minutes acquaintance with it at home would put right ; unveiling, at the same time, the natural energy and good will of a species that has long appeared to be the worst of miffs and mimps. Give *Saxifraga diapensioeides* rich dark vegetable soil, in between two slabs of rock that *must* be calcareous, and in a situation where the sun will not strike upon it violently, and I pledge myself that you will have no further trouble from it, but much joy.

And, for a final word of recommendation and encouragement, I will add that this treasure allows itself to be collected and packed without turning a leaf. This is always a sign that a plant wants to do well in culture, if you give it what it likes. Things difficult to grow are ill to collect, as a rule, and certainly are ill travellers. But of this Saxifrage, though many and many were the pieces I sent home, both in the torrid summer when their dis-soiled roots were bone-dry, and late in autumn when they were wadded with wet, not one of them failed to take hold of their new conditions even more promptly and completely than *Bellardi* and *lantoscana*—and of these I have no complaint to make in the matter, I can assure you. *Saxifraga diapensioeides* is a rare plant, and not easy to come by. It occurs, but only sporadically, in such limestone cliffs as these, in the main Pennines, the Western and the Southern Alps ; getting, like so many rare alpines, much more diffused as it comes down from the north, where the south side of the Valais, I think, is its farthest point, yielding it only here and there.

For years I had hunted *Saxifraga diapensioeides*, and hunted quite in vain, on places wholly ill-suited to its requirements. These cliffs, then, are marked in my memory with a stone even whiter than themselves. I scrambled about for happy hours, over the shelving lips of the abyss—winding backwards, that is, above the gully, along the shady ledges of the right-hand peak, among mats of *diapensioeides*, interspersed with here and there a piece of *Bellardi*. Then I returned, and climbed to the notch in the ridge that separates the two jags of limestone, at the top of the couloir. Here there were other marvels, which almost seemed a bathos after the Saxifrages. For, although I had foreknown that I ought to find these on the ranges up above the Tenda cliffs, I had never quite dared hope, being a cautious hoper, that I really should. Mountains are big, and collectors little ; there are long odds against one's hitting on the one place where a given rarity occurs. Therefore, in my triumph, I looked with lack lustre eyes on *Asperula hexaphylla*, which is only found in this neighbourhood, on a little Iberis which I believe to be the similarly restricted *I. garrexiana;* and on that precious ' *Phyteuma Balbisii* which replaces *comosum* in the crevices of the Maritime Alps. A lot the Phyteuma cared. The other two I dutifully collected, but the Phyteuma told me very plainly that it didn't matter whether I looked at it or not, I wasn't going to have it, anyhow. For, like *comosum*, it grows only in the solid rock ; there was no rottenness anywhere where it occurred. I had neither hammer nor chisels that day. Accordingly I desisted from vain toil, and slung myself over the notch, on to the other side.

My feet slithered down upon a stony slope in full sunshine. Away below there were mountain-pines, and far away beneath these again in the distance, stood, like little nine-pins, the peaks of crag that had looked so gigantic from Tenda under their feet : and then, deep down beyond these again, lay mapped out the broiling valleys of the Roja, running up towards the Col de Tenda. Big coarse grasses were in sheets and tussocks over that long stone-slope ; but among them, were sheets and tussocks no less big of *Saxifraga Bellardi*. In the cliffs themselves there was still a certain amount of *diapensioeides*, but this side was as clearly the kingdom of *Bellardi* as the other had been of *diapensioeides*. And, on this bank the sun lay full from its rising, until about two in the afternoon ; from that hour onwards it would fall into the gully across the notch. Compare, then, the preferences of the two plants in the matter. I have already expatiated to you on the wonders of *Saxifraga lingulata α. Bellardi*, so that here you need do no more than rejoice with me, and glorify the good earth, for these huge masses of it, lying in dark wiry tangles among the grasses and on the stones. In half ten minutes you might have packed a washing-basket full, and not the slightest difference made to the luxuriant lavishness of that slope. There are big old plants, and big young plants ; some have leaves more finely wire-drawn than others, or swelling to a rather broader point at their tips. Not one of these begins to think about admitting any Christian-naming cousinship with the half-sized *lantoscana* of the Vésubie valley away in the west. In other words, the *lantoscana*-form is only found here on the shadier side of the ridge—that is to say, in a typical *lantoscana* situation. Of course the flower-spikes lay sere and finished here and there by the cushions that had borne them : but *Bellardi* is certainly freer in bloom when at home, than either *cochlearis* or *lantoscana*. On that ridge it was of limited distribution, too : one day in autumn, I climbed a good deal higher on that side, across slopes exactly similar to this, without finding more than a few pieces of the Saxifrage, and these pieces lodged in crevices of the cliff itself. And on our first visit that blazing summer day, my companion, wandering patiently on up at the foot of the cliffs down on the other slope, whence I had climbed over, never once set eyes on either *diapensioeides* or *Bellardi*. Lower down the range, too, it again diminished, I found : but on that one strip of stony grass, perhaps a hundred yards across, it was as abundant and flourishing and bushy as even the groundsel in the Yorkshire Garden.

On the rocks themselves, among the cool moss, was
abundance, also, of *Primula marginata.* Among it I was
astonished to see a certain amount of *Saxifraga aeizoon :*
very little, but still the plant was there. This puzzled me,
until I remembered that from the other side of the notch,
across a profound gorge right down in the valley I had
noticed dark porphyry rock ; presumably the Saxifrage
had seeded over from its chosen haunts, and was now
moderately happy on these alien formations. For I do
not know what may be the experience of other collectors ;
but in the course of my travellings it has always seemed to
me remarkable that *Saxifraga aeizoon,* which, in gardens, is
the weed of the family, in all its forms, and takes especially
to limestone as a duckling to water, should, in nature,
so far as my experience goes, so tend to eschew calcareous
rocks and cling to the sandstones, quartzes and granites.
In the Southern Alps, both Eastern and Western, you are
apparently almost safe from *Saxifraga aeizoon,* as long
as you are on the limestone : you are no less safe to see
*Saxifraga aeizoon,* and *Saxifraga aeizoon* only, the
instant you get on to the lower granites. In the Dolomites
too, you find *crustata* everywhere, but you rarely set eyes
on *aeizoon* until you come to granitic outcrops, like that
below Puflatsch on your way up to the Frommerhaus
from Bad Ratzes under the Schlern. In the Graians,
the Cottians, and the Oberland, the same rule holds good,
so far as I have found ; except that above the Gemmi,
there are waving slopes of *aeizoon* which the rule of the
place would make one think are on calcareous ground,
unless one is to correct one's memory by the proved

proclivities of the plant, and hold that they are really a
granitic outcrop after all, above the white limestone of
the pass.    However, if you want to see more of it in the
Maritimes you must descend at last with me from this
delectable ridge above Tenda and say farewell to the
Southern face of the chain.    And I must add also, in
defiance of my small experience, that Burnat says of
*aeizoon* in these ranges, that "*il semble être un calcicole
préférent.*"    (It also inhabits limestone in the Dolomites.)

Up from Tenda winds the road of the Roja, almost
entirely treeless now and open, through various gorges
and tortuous defiles, past cliffs which in the spring,
according to M. Correvon, are an undulating whiteness
with the plumes of *Saxifraga Bellardi ;* until at last you
take a few steep turns upward, and reach the present
terminus of the railway at Vievola.    Straight above you
hangs blankly the Gate of the South, that vast wall of
mountain over which climbs the Col de Tenda.    The railway takes a humbler course.    Hardly a minute elapses
after leaving Vievola, before you are plunged in the darkness of the Tenda tunnel.    When you emerge at length,
the alpine wall towers behind you, and your way runs
northward, down into the plain of Lombardy at Cuneo.
Gone are the seaward valleys, and gone the sunshine of
the Mediterranean : the vegetation is not pine-scrub and
juniper and lavender any longer.    It is beech and birch
and oak and other northerly things deciduous.    In late
autumn I again approached the Col de Tenda, and approached it this time by motor, on the highway from
the Plain.    The day was sinking, with clouds lying low ;

the hour was darkening towards twilight as we span up the Vermenagna Valley. The hilltops vanished into a floor of cloud ; only now and again, remote above us up in the sky, there glimmered against the gathering greyness the whiter greyness of snow, among iron-coloured ridges. And, on either side, the pinnacles and banks of the mountains were all one smouldering fire of beech-scrub, flaming huskily upwards until they passed abruptly into that pale haze. Here and there were little ruined fortalices, looming black as night in the gloom, on beech-clothed peaks that stood out like teeth from the slopes.

And somehow the dimly fiery glow of that russet colouring, the level mist, the straight acclivity of the hills in varied folds and chines, with every now and then a prominent tree or boulder or castled eminence, all made a picture that exactly recalled some upland gorge in Japan, towards the sad ending of autumn. But there :— one of the woes of travel is that the world is always found to be much the same wherever you may go ; trees still grow with their roots downwards and grass is green. One is perpetually being reminded of old things, instead of startled by new : one finds Westmorland in high Ceylon, and Nantai-san takes on the name of Vermenagna, and stretches of Korea drop down into the heart of Cumberland. Nature is too fond of repeating her effects ; so much repetition as she indulges in would be fatal to any literary reputation, were it only that of a writer of penny novelettes.

However, a thing beautiful is always a thing beautiful, no matter how often you see it, nor in places how diverse.

And I will always take off my hat to Japan, wherever I
may find it.   But anyhow, I am proticipating ; for the
present occasion is summer, and we have just emerged
from the tunnel, in our train, and slid gently down into
Limone at the northern foot of the Pass.   There is nothing
very beautiful about Limone, except its name and situation, unless you also except a bust of George Meredith
in the Market-place, who, if I remember right, spouts
water off a pedestal, and certainly calls himself Saint
Peter.   But Limone has lovely expeditions :  turn back
towards the Pass ;  then, on your right, run various deep
valleys, climbing into stony ravines up at the foot of the
Rocca del Abisso.   On your left there opens a similar
valley, wide and level, blocked by a barrier of mountain
—a spur running out at right angles to the range.   And
this, from Limone, looks almost impregnably high (though
its ridge be mainly grass), ending, as it does, overhead, in
the huge white limestone mass of Marguareis.   By that
grassy ridge climbs the Col de Pesio, which traverses a
saddle on the top, and then drops deep, deep, deep, into
another valley under the north-eastern face of Marguareis,
and descends to where sits the rambling old monastery of
the Certosa de Pesio ;  which is now, by all accounts, the
loveliest and most pleasant hotel in the Alps, easy of access
from Cuneo and Mondovi, commanding, from amid its
ancient chestnut woods, one of the finest views that
Europe has to show.

This is not an advertisement.   I have never been to
the Certosa, nor is the Manager my aunt.   But I saw
fit to give you inklings of where the way leads which we

are now to pursue, At first the track winds up that almost flat Armellina valley from Limone—a cobbled mule-track, hemmed in by a wall that is bushy with *Asplenium*. Then we turn to the left and enter a rocky gorge. And here both in sun and shade, on cool rocks and torrid, there is an equal abundance of the King-Silver Saxifrage. Indeed I think that here there were even larger masses of it than on the cliffs beyond the Tenda crags. And it was here that I collected the only real variety I found. This was a plant which seemed to be nearly double the size of even the usual magnificent type, and to be doubly profuse with flower-spikes taller and ampler. After emerging from the gorge, one comes abruptly up against a bulky spur, standing off at right angles from the ridge so high above us. Up and up and up one toils over shoulder after shoulder, of bastion after bastion. Although Limone lies already at three thousand feet, and the pass cannot well be more than six at the most, we both, I think, felt that day's toil more severe than any other we encountered, before or after. No doubt the fountain of fatigue was in ourselves. Often a perfectly easy stodge will crush one's endurance ; while, another day, some really arduous climb will give one nothing but bracing and gloriousness of spirit. Well, so we laboured up that steep and interminable bank for ever and for ever and for ever ; and, up in the sky on our right the wall of the main ridge never seemed to get any lower or any nearer. But at last we saw above us the final shoulder of the spur ; put out a spurt, gained it, and dropped, panting, to appreciate the world.

It is a wonderful world to appreciate, too, for the mountains are unfolding before us, high and far, alike to the north and the south ; and behind us, as we lie, the spur of the hill goes steadily up to support the ridge, like some titanic buttress.    And to the right the bulk of Marguareis seems to swell like a thing in a nightmare ; and across the Col de Tenda which divides them, the splendid peak of the Rocca del Abisso shoots up from its pedestal of mountains, crags, and snowfields.    But all this shall you see, with spirits discharged, when you descend again, and here take your farewell of the Maritime Alps.    At present let us lie and pant, pillowed on sweet herbs, in a bed of short fine grass, patterned over with *Dianthus neglectus*.

For this is the first time that our travels have brought us into any fullness of the Untidy Pink.    On either side of the shoulder drops away the slope into a close brushwood away beneath.    Below that stand out little teeth of rock that are really crags, and down beneath these again, lie obscure worm-tracks which are the valleys of roaring rivers, flowing down on either hand into that of the Vermenagna, the swallower of them all.    The air is radiant and warm, filled with the scented silences of the Alps.    All over the sward, in open places and lurking among copse, are peppered red, in a wild confusion, the flowers of the Dianthus.    We are drawing near to the as yet unharvested meadow of the uplands ; and the Dianthus, among the golden Arnicas, is the flower that first begins to greet us.    We stand on it, walk on it, lie on it ; impossible to do otherwise, for half the turf is nothing but those cushions of finest lawn-like foliage, from which, on stems two or three inches high (or more among the bushes), spring lonely the huge rose-red flowers, round, delicately jagged at the edges of the petals, and lacquered on their underside with a clean coat of nankeen yellow. When first you see the Untidy Pink in fact (and why " untidy" the Lord of botanists alone knows)—it fairly takes your breath away ; it is so paradoxically neat, so profuse in blossom, so imperious in the splendour of its colouring. It has a long tap-root, with a few thready laterals; makes one dense and serried tuft of grass, and flowers amazingly : a species peculiar to the southerly ranges, the Dauphiné, the Graians, Cottians and Maritimes. And in cultivation it asks only for deep light loam in an open sunny place, and, as far as my experience goes, no persuasions will induce it to tolerate the jejune conditions of moraine, which seem so well to harmonise with the views of *Dianthus alpinus* and the others.

But even finer things were to follow. For now it was time to continue our upward way, from shoulder to further higher shoulder of the buttress. And here the grass was yet unmown ; indeed, you could hardly have seen to mow it, so dense was the glow of flower beneath which it lay hidden. On either side of us fell away the interminable " glacis " of the slope. We toiled up along the grassy *arête*, until we came on peasants actually scything little patches of hay on a hill-side, where no decent English haymaker would think of being able to keep his foothold. And all those slopes were aglow, as if with a thousand tones of living light. There was *Dianthus neglectus*,

tawny, and rosy, and crimson ; Arnica, pale Bearded
Harebell, Orchises in untold multitude, and SaintBruno's
Lily throwing up its pure spikes like some self-conscious
saint amid a ballet of worldlings in orange and carmine
and sapphire. Then, looking down the southern side,
I saw a new picture, rich and beautiful as one of
Flemwell's. For that long bank was one sheet of nothing
but Arnica blossoms, golden as the sun ; but above these
stood up, in close array, a no less rich profusion of narrow
Orchis spikes, in every shade of pink, lilac and purple—
the tapering, exquisitely-scented tails of *Gymnadenia
odoratissima*. And that contrast, of royal purple and
royal gold—of aspiring lances shooting up from a firmament
of rayed suns, was almost too perfect for one to believe
that it could be the unaided work of nature. One can
safely say, anyhow, that no planned effect in the garden
of a Rothschild could thus leap to such a pitch of easy
perfection.

Up this *arête*, so beautiful that it delayed one anew
at every dozen steps, the slope laboured on until it reached
the foot of the main ridge. And this still looked as if it
were growing taller every minute. However, we set
ourselves to breast it. And suddenly the flowers left off,
so that we could labour undiverted. They thus left off
because we had come on to the granite rock. Under a
barren cliff of this we mounted, until one more pull brought
us out, beneath a bluff of limestone, on to the stretch of
down that is the saddle of the Col de Pesio. Over this
meander wide levels, with here and there a little beck
flowing among Rhododendrons in a hollow, between

banks on which the Spring Gentian is still lingering. But all that lawn was eaten or mown, and flowerless. We wandered across the expanse, until we could look down into the Pesio Valley on the other side. So far below does it lie that we could only see where it began in the uppermost pines. From here, though, looking out towards the east, we had a grand view of the Apennines that hem in the Pesio at its head. For the gaunt inhospitable white mass of Marguareis falls away on this side in the most splendid series of precipices, and beyond there stretches a vast desolation of limestone, between Marguareis and the crests and ridges of Montgioje.

All that apparent wilderness is profitable ground, though. For there once more begins the reign of the well-beloved white high-alpine Buttercups. Not once, have you noticed, in places never so suitable and lofty, have we seen a sign of any mountain Ranunculus— neither *parnassifolius*, *glacialis*, *crenatus*, *Traunfellneri*, *Seguieri* nor *alpestris*. For most of them seem to prefer the limestone. Anyhow, it is not until you get high limestone, on Marguareis and Montgioje, that *alpestris* and *glacialis* begin to " occur." *Alpestris*, indeed, is abundant among the rocks of this range on their northern side ; but *glacialis*, apparently, is among the few high alpines whose distribution diminishes instead of increasing, as you get further south. For it is only reported to occur " here and there, in the Alps east of Tenda." Which, considering that the Alps east of Tenda, beginning with Marguareis, belong to the Ligurian Apennines, amounts to saying that neither *alpestris* nor *glacialis* is to be

found in the Maritime Alps at all. Marguareis, too,
possesses another very illustrious mountain Buttercup ;
for here, I believe, is the only district where *Ranunculus
aconitifolius* lets his fancy stray towards his relations.
Here he has wooed and won *R. pyrenaeus.* The result is
*Ranunculus lacerus*, a unique hybrid, resembling its mother,
but a little taller, and with divided leaves. Of this
species I will say no more, because I did not succeed in
setting eyes on it. *Ranunculus pyrenaeus* is certainly
as matrimonial as Henry the Eighth, though : in the far
Western Maritimes it weds *Seguieri* and produces *R.
Yvesii ; R. Luizeti* and *R. Flahaultii* are also its children
by *R. parnassifolius.*

We returned from the Pass to that limestone bluff on
the edge above Limone ; and there we quarried *Saxifraga
caesia*, until a dark storm came driving at us across from
the Rocca del Abisso. Blue-black night swallowed up
the peaks, and soon engulfed the valley beneath. Columns
of gloom sank into its depths, and swept across the
brilliant distance of mountain behind. They seemed to
move without motion, very slowly. There was a furious
wind by now, yet the veils of the storm never wavered
in their smooth and imperceptible advance. Then it
was on us ; in squalling furies of hail that hurt like whips.
We took cover among the Saxifrages on the rock, and
beguiled time by plucking up some pieces from ancient
tufts of *Primula marginata* that were there growing like
any ordinary full-soil plant. So, in a short while, the
roar of the hail grew less, and the weight of darkness
lessened. Out of the black purple, spears and shafts of

light began to advance across the undiscoverable valleys down below in the murk, with the same steady motion of the hail-sweeps before. These were now passing up towards the north, and every moment the south was glowing sunnier, while the plain of Turin grew veiled with a moving mist of waters. More and more the clouds broke up ; as through a film the uttermost mountains were beginning to dawn and glitter through the greyness, until at length the Rocca seemed to cut the darkness suddenly into shreds ; the storm dragons swirled this side and that ; the peaks stood out above the chaos of vapours, and then, in a little, all the range was clear. As soon as the hail was over we descended down that rocky slope, on to other bluffs where not only was *Saxifraga caesia* abundant, but also both *lingulata Bellardi* and *aeizoon.* And it was here that I found (and left behind) an ugly, dowdy-flowered hybrid, that was not quite good enough for *aeizoon*, and not nearly good enough for *Bellardi.*

By now the air was pure ; the afternoon was full of broken clouds and tenderest colours ; the long wild range lay lucent before us, in soft tones of amethyst and sapphire under racing clouds across the wet blue, from where the Rocca del Abisso towers over the Col de Tenda, away through all the ruffle of peaks and passes, to far-off Argentera, glittering with its snowfields ; and then, up to the right, rippling in the middle of the full Cottians, the whole shrill splendour of the Viso—the great ridge and peak seen sidelong—leapt up to answer the presumptuous Rocca with a regal shout of supremacy.

Valleys and plains and peoples lay somewhere away below all this, like beetles in the basement.   The world was full of mountains, and of mountains only.   And so, in the radiance of that afternoon, let us take farewell of the Maritime Alps, ranging out before us at their loveliest, in the moistened golden air, to say good-bye.

# CHAPTER X.

## ROCCA LONGA.

IT was in the early chilly morning that we rose up and went away from Limone. Extreme and bitter was our penury, for we had abundance of bank-notes and yet no money. I had to chaffer for tickets with the official at the station. It proved, by successive enquiries, made in tones that grew more and more abject, that even second class fares were beyond our means. My humble request sank to a third. The presiding power laughed much. That foreigners should travel by any class except the first is always a marvel to the native ; and when he handed me out two little common-looking tickets, it was with an ironical bow, and the comment that here were the " biglietti " of our Grand-ducal Lordships. And, accordingly, in a packed compartment, like a cattle-truck, largely populated with fleas, did our Grand-Ducal Lordships descend from Limone down the beautiful Vermenagna Valley to Cuneo. And here our troubles ended. We were at last restored, like the Vicar of Wakefield's daughter, to " affluence and innocence," though not without so much preliminary anxiety and wurra-wurra, that I began to think it might be necessary to invoke the aid of the Bishop, whose name, if you will remember, is Andrew.

After breakfast we set off again from Cuneo for Turin. It was still early bright morning, the brilliance of the sun was young and fresh, as the train went puffing over the levels of the Plain. Behind us the Maritimes sank gradually, and grew dim in the heat. Viso soared more and more threateningly as we drew level with the knife-edge face that he turns towards Turin. The railway carries you further out in the flat than does the tram, so that you get a more panoramic view of the range. And the day, too, was clearer than my first. For you could see the foaming snows of the Graians up in the north, and far beyond these, across to the right, appeared little points and masses and ridges of roseate snow, the mass of Monte Rosa,—the Weisshorn, the Dent Blanche : a tiny jag peering over the shoulder of the line that ran from Monte Rosa was the Matterhorn. So we reached Turin, and, after a Carltonian lunch started forward for our second visit to the Mont Cenis, which has already shown you the King of the Alps in his glory. And thence again, in due time we set off once more across the earth, for Rocca Longa and *Daphne rupestris*.

At first the journey was a nightmare, though. We had done well on the Mont Cenis, and each of us had despatched four large square biscuit boxes packed full with treasures (including the King, not to mention also some *Saxifraga Bellardi*, which there had been no means or time to send off from Limone). These boxes had duly gone down from the Mont Cenis to Susa, and thence, we were told, had safely embarked for England. What, then, was our horror when we descended to Susa ourselves, to find those eight precious packages still standing in the Post Office. There were difficulties, it seemed— for the first and only time in all my experience. It was the more maddening, that so many parcels of mine had already been sent off from here without a word of protest, in earlier summer. However, there was clearly no help for it now but to lug the things along with us to Turin, and there see them unquestionably registered for departure with our own eyes. Accordingly we lugged them. There was no one else to help, in the sun-baked empty little street of Susa. Have you ever lugged four very large and very heavy square biscuit-boxes for a quarter of a mile ? Until you have done so, you can have no notion how many corners a square box manages to have, nor how sharp they are. However, we got them all, and our luggage, into the train, and the train set off. Halfway to Turin we had a change ; out they had to come, one after another. It seemed as if the procession would never end. They stood piled on the platform like a pyramid, looking like bricks from a child-giant's building box. When the express came in, it proved to be both full and impatient. One by one those boxes had to be handed up into the carriage, and somehow disposed of amia the feet of its patient occupants. These were as good as gold, and much kinder. They lent a hand to our labour. But their eyes grew wider and wider as biscuit-box succeeded biscuit-box in an unrelenting string : they thought us quite mad. We, meanwhile were crushed to the earth with shame, and red as Monte Rosa in the sunset. We hated those eight boxes passionately, and felt apologetic even for our own existence. The one bright spot on our black horizon was the prospect of being finally rid of the whole nuisance at Turin.

However, when we reached Turin, and had handed those interminable boxes one by one again out on to the the platform, we found that there was not a minute to spare for despatching them. The train for Basilea was on the actual point of departure, so that we had to turn and run for it. To run for it, I say, and with all those boxes. By now we moved as if in a bad dream ; it appeared that those boxes were going to cling to us to the end of our days. We began to feel like Vanderdecken, or the Wandering Jew. However, there was now no time to meditate comparisons ; the procession moved in precipitate state down the platform of Turin, through wondering crowds. Eight porters advanced, in single file, each carrying a biscuit-box. We followed in the rear with our own baggage. The *cortège* must have had an imposing and even oriental look to the spectators ; it was like a picture of the Queen of Sheba going to see Solomon, with propitiatory presents. On the platform we made one convulsive effort to get the boxes sent ; but were soon forced to abandon our last hope, by the multiplicity of documents that came clamouring for our signatures, while the train continued squealing to be away.

It was after midnight when two blighted beings, crushed now into meekness by the tyranny of the biscuit-boxes, crawled out of the station at Basilea. With one accord we fell upon the hall-porter, and insisted that he should despatch the confounded things next morning, without saying another word to us about them on any account. We were almost too desperate to care whether he discharged the commission or not. We were due to start again about five the next morning, so that it was impossible for us in any case to register them ourselves before departure ; and really we felt that death would be preferable to another day in their company ; to say nothing of the fact that after fermenting thus long in the tropical heats of Lombardy, there could be no reasonable doubt that both *Eritrichium* and *Bellardi* were by now an indistinguishable jam of rottenness. At break of dawn, accordingly, we fled from Basilea, refusing to give another thought to the boxes, and finding quite sufficient solace in the exquisite sense of freedom that fell upon us like balm, in the release from those haunting horrors. And the hall-porter might have done anything he liked with them, for all we cared. However, at our next address he sent us on their receipts with perfect faithfulness, and, in the fullness of time, every one of those boxes arrived at its destination, having seen, like Odysseus, the cities and the ways of many men. And of their contents, not one leaf had suffered : *Eritrichium* and *Bellardi* and all the other treasures arrived in quite as sound a state of health as anything despatched in other boxes that did not have so adventurous a career.

From Castellar you go up to Rocca Longa. And Rocca Longa is the most ungetatable point in a remote and ungetatable district; there is no accommodation that could be called civilised : there are no railways within many a mile ; Rocca Longa itself rises from the midst of so big a boss of mountains, that there is no point from which you can even see it. Or, rather, there is one point, and one point only ; where the deep gorge of the Valbonne drops at last into the main Val d'Arlet ; there, right away up in the sky between the cliffs do you get, as you pass, just one glimpse of the white limestone cone which is the actual summit of Rocca Longa. From the vine-clad Osteria of Castellar, however, there is nothing to be guessed of it ; only vast green mountains all round, unclimbably high, precipitous with great bluffs, and every-where clothed with pines. But Castellar is a pleasant little place: it lounges over the slope of the hill, where the Val d'Arlet with its stream runs down at an angle, to lose itself in the wide bed of the Ronca River. With an open view, then, stretching before it down the broad Varronca, and with fragrant vineyards embedding it all round, Castellar lies taking the sun—a serried mass of dark-brown roofs made broad and flat against the heat of summer, and richly coloured with age, all huddling over a hill with a huge russet cliff rising straight behind it.

It is in the green chills of dawn that one sets out from Castellar for Rocca Longa. The air is cold and solemn, to fit the solemnity of the occasion ; for you are sallying forth now on a good solid climb of six hours or so, to pay your respects to a plant which is among the rarest and most beautiful in the world. Not only that, but the most impregnably seated ; more than that, the most remote and difficult to see. " Non cuivis homini contingit adire Rupestrim." For a few hundred yards one follows the level road running south from Castellar, then a track diverges, and begins steadily climbing the enormous mountain on your left. All the rock of the district is calcareous : and here there are screes that might be lying under Robin Proctor or the Long Scar, so exact is their resemblance to the screes of the mountain-limestone.

And here, everywhere among the chips, are perking the rosy flowers of *Cyclamen europaeum*. Some say, indeed, that this little plant is a different form ; but anyhow it stands so far as *europaeum*. And loveable and lovely beyond telling, wherever you may see it, whether abundantly, in fullest sunshine of the open scree, or, less commonly, peering from dewy grass at the edge of some bush or copse. My typewriter, which is an opinionated machine, will always insist on calling them " Cyvalmes," otherwise I should certainly have talked of Cyclamens more freely than I have. For in all the garden there are no plants that more completely take my heart. They are so invariably, so indefatigably beautiful ; their whole personality so winning and sweet. Exquisite they are when their pink blooms come fluttering up like little butterflies among the stones and herbage ; but not a bit less beautiful are they when only their leaves are above ground. Such wonderful leaves, too, rounded and violet-like in *europaeum*, ivy-shaped in *hederae-folium* ; but always blotched and flaked with patterns of white upon their dark surface of grey-green, whose underside is of a deep red-purple like their stems. *Hederaefolium* has the bolder form, and the finer variation ; but *europaeum* does not lag far behind. They both send up their butterflies in autumn, though *europaeum* is already doing so in July, and, perhaps, does not continue so late as the other. I love them both with such passion that I am always doing myself discredit in other people's gardens, incurring unpopularity and scorn. For the wealthy and learned convey me round among their rarities, and are filled with indignation when I break away from my dutiful raptures over some ugly elm-like shrub, exceedingly new, which bears no beauty, but produces rubber, in order to throw myself on my knees before a clump of *Cyclamen hederaefolium* profusely blooming amid its leaves, in coarse grass at the foot of a tree. " Oh, *that*," they say, in tones of scorn, " that grows everywhere ! "

Yes, the dear treasures, they do grow everywhere, and thence draw yet a further merit, besides that of their loveliness both in leaf and blossom. They like leaf-soil, and all the Cyclamens seem heartily to appreciate lime (though I doubt if they insist on it) ; they will grow in open ground and shady ; and, where they really like you, will spread broadcast on their own account over your whole sward or woodland. Even in paths of gravel and stone they will be happy. The finest pieces of *hederaefolium* that I have seen were in a blazing-hot garden path, sprouting so thickly from the semel that you could see nothing but a carpet of bright pink or snowy-white a foot across. They are all of them southerners, of course,* and their centre of distribution is the Mediter-

---

* *Europaeum* comes up into the Swiss Alps, and is on sale at the flower stalls of Interlaken. And there are some English woods here and there which it has so immemorially occupied that its claim to rank as a native has sometimes been admitted.

ranean basin. Therefore they would revel in a warmer climate than mine. Yet even here they are all beginning to do well (they take a good time to establish, I think). I speak only here of the main beauties nearest home, *europaeum* and *hederaefolium;* but I also take delight in *cilicicum, africanum, ibericum, Atkinsi,* and the most exquisite *libanoticum.* So that of this precious *europeaum* here on the copsy hills and in the hottest stone-slopes round Castellar, I will only add that it is pre-eminent also in the possession of the sweetest imaginable fragrance.

In the gloom of stormy daybreak the path mounts rapidly. Dense darkness covered the hills across the valley of the Ronca ; all that we ever saw that day of the alpine sunrise was a livid bronze that ultimately tinged their masses of cold blue. The worst of weather threatened ; vast snowfields up in the north gleamed lurid for a while amid the shifting volumes of storm, and then were finally shrouded from view as the clouds settled lower and lower. However, there was no help for it but to continue. One does not come all the way to Castellar, to be beaten back from the Rocca by rain or hail. Besides, the weather is generally open to a bluff ; the worst of clouds, if firmly confronted, very often turns, like the devil, and flees from you. And there is always the chance here, that the tempests will pass away to the greater ranges in the north. This in the end proved to be the reward of our pertinacity ; for, as we mounted, the lowering darkness grew lighter and lighter ; the banks of gloom began to shift clearly northward ; and at last the day was fully on us, open and grey, but without imminence of wet.

All that hill lies in shadow through the morning ; this is the reason why one chooses this side, by which to ascend to the Rocca, so as to come down again in the afternoon, through the glen of the Val Riario into the Valbonne, which will then be in the shade, while this slope would be in full sun by that time. The ascent is extraordinarily long and high ; yet seems achieved with extraordinary rapidity. The fact is that I have made it before ;—ask me not the story of that first ascent ;— " Infandum, regina, jubes renovare dolorem." In that former attempt on the Daphne, I was ignominiously baffled by cloud within a hundred yards of it, on the very topmost ridge itself. Let us say no more, but hastily turn our attention to the rocks of limestone beneath which the track is now ascending.

For not only are there here beginning Primulas of different and interesting sorts, but also there is abundance of *Phyteuma comosum*. Now this is a rare treasure, not to be collected but with hammer and chisel ; for it inhabits only the smallest crevices of the hardest mountain limestone. To the limestone it is firmly faithful, and is a species restricted to the southern ranges. In the Dolomites it is especially notable : on a cliff behind Cortina you will see it in rock more hard than iron, making wide masses. The plant forms a huge, fat and waxy yellow rootstock, which pours and moulds itself deep into soil-less crannies, drawing nourishment from the lime ; from the cliff-face, no crevice being visible at all, hang the tufts of foliage. This is of a very dark, livid leaden green, almost black in general effect ; the basal leaves are stalked, broad, irregular, roughly ivy-shaped, pointed and jagged. Sometimes they are almost grey with a fine down, but normally are quite smooth and glossy. The flowers come up in dense heads, on stems of two or three inches. They are wonderful and weird, a bunch of long, dark blue tubes, like elongated, twisted Chianti-bottles, from each of which protrudes a stigma like an immense fine feeler whisking about this way and that. Contrary to reasonable expectation, *Phyteuma comosum* is not only very good natured about growing on and striking fresh root from a mutilated stump, but it is also very easy-going with regard to ordinary conditions of culture in the rock-garden—easy-going, that is, for a plant which has every right, by all appearances, to be so difficult and exacting. A good chink or crevice, with deep good soil, will suit it well. The one drawback, as I have said before, is that slugs adore it with so notorious a passion. So notoriously, indeed, that when, right up on the Ciriegia, close to eternal snow, my companion found a big fat black slug perambulating the cliff, he had much reason on his side in announcing that this must be a sign that *Phyteuma comosum* was near.

Having collected a few convenient plants of this by smashing away the rock, we continued on our way. The track was loose and stony, most awkward to walk on ; but all around there were so many plants that one hardly noticed the climb. Indeed, it is well that the Rocca should be so remote and hard to get at ; for the whole range is prodigiously rich in rare plants. As we went, there shone orange lilies, and *Genista radiata* spidery

amid the scrub ; but now we were getting almost too high
for the noble leaves of the Christmas Rose which abounds
in every bush and in all the stony grass at the very roadsides round Castellar, and must be a snowy glory in winter
and early spring.   Soon after this one emerges above
the first range of cliffs which had looked so stupendous
from the village, and comes out of the copse upon a
smooth shoulder of mown grass where there are châlets.
On the other side of this the track goes mounting stiffly
again, through more copse, towards yet another hitherto
unsuspected wall of precipice, over which, be sure, will be
found to loom another and yet another after that ; so
that you never seem to get to any definite top at all.
This is the disheartening part of these Alps, their lack of
finality.   You are always finding one more wall of cliff
above the one you have just laboriously surmounted in the
fond hope that it was really the last.   So we go zigzagging
up now, under more rock, until the path through the
thick brushwood gives a little holiday by meandering
along a shoulder, where there are a few limestone bluffs
to be profitably explored.

For here there is not only abundance of the Phyteuma
tufts, fairly easy to persuade out of their crannies with a
hammer (for the cleavages of the limestone lie in convenient
lines), but also there are a certain amount of young seedling
plants in the moss and silt beneath the rocks.   And these
babies are not only easy to take, but one acquires merit
by doing so.   For they would inevitably go under in the
battle for life if one left them ; never by any chance, anywhere, have I found a full-grown plant of *Phyteuma*

except in the solid rock. Removal is the only chance these strayed infants have of survival. And then there are Primulas : there are handsome tussocks of *spectabilis*, which we shall see yet finer higher up : there is a broadleaved, downy and soft-textured plant that is kin to *Auricula*, and which, until it reveals itself a novelty, I shall call *P. Aur. Obristii*\* : and there is *Auricula* itself in that noble *albo-marginata*-form which is so splendid on the Cliff at Ingleborough, and whose proper name is *P. Auricula Bauhini*. This has all the huge robustness of *Auricula*, but the leaves have a brilliant line of white powder round their edge, which lavishly overflows, as a fine dust, onto the surface of the leaf itself. The dusty-grey flower stems are stalwart, and rise to eight inches or so, carrying more than a dozen gorgeous blossoms, very fragrant, of a royal golden yellow.

The plant belongs to the southern ranges, and is different as chalk from cheese from the few-flowered, balder *Auricula* of the northern limestones. For calcareous the species always is in its likings, whether plain or silvered. You will find wide sheets of it on the southern cliffs of the Rocca, and even far down below in the Val d'Arlet, at a point where the diligence stops long enough on your way down to Savinanza for you to rush up, and poke off a few tufts from a rock on which it is making star-fishes of grey and white. All this warm district is indeed, the main country of the Primulas. Their race is one which prefers the southern to the northern hills; even as *Anemone vernalis* and *Ranunculus*

---

\* *P. Similis* (Stein) ; *P. Balbisii* (Beck).

*glacialis* abruptly diminish and grow rare as you get south, so, as you get north, quickly lessen the number and the variety of the Primulas you will find ; until, in the Oberland, besides *Auricula*, and the universal *farinosa*, you will only find *hirsuta* in possession. But here, in these sunny lands, all the hills and valleys join in a riot of Primula, and the rarest of the race combine to make the chorus more illustrious.

On these rocks there was a happening. For, as my companion was plucking trunks of Primula from their nook, a little dormouse walked straight out of them, and sat on his hand, and blinked at him with expressionless eyes like beads. We were overjoyed, and received the visitor with sweet words. To none of these did it pay any attention. Ultimately my companion put it in his pocket for future reference. I entered cautions against this step, being afraid that the mouse might get squeezed against a rock in the excitement and difficulty of climbing after *Daphne rupestris*. However, mouse's finder seemed properly impressed with the peril, and a sense of responsibility. He walked forward as carefully as if he had been carrying roc's eggs for the Sultan of Babylon. Mouse, however, behind his silence, concealed wisdom and much strength of mind and will. For, when at last we sat down to administer milk and air to the captive, it was discovered that without saying a word, he had inconspicuously vanished into his native wilds again.

Now the path was really drawing near, through thinning woodland, to the shoulder of the huge mountain range which had blocked out the sky from Castellar. In the silt of the track-side there were a few pieces of *Saxifraga mutata*, and, just where the path turns over the actual shoulder, a mass of weathered boulders, on which were growing *Primula Auricula* and *Saxifraga aeizoon*. From the shoulder itself, which was a down of short grass, with a few pine trees, and here and there a rosy flower of *Cephalanthera rubra* unexpectedly appearing, we had a clear prospect right over the Varronca, where the Ronca river swells again and again into little bright blue lakes that lay motionless like patches of sky that morning, deep down between the tumbled pale-green ranges of the hills. On the other side, away into the northern distance, rolled other high ranges. Beyond these, and higher still in the north, all the snowfields lay buried in violet storm. From this prospect we turned away sharp to the left, up over the ridge. Here we entered on a pass of meadow-grass, diversified with big rocks, and bushy with dwarf beech. Among these were tufts of the larger Hellebore, and on the rocks little hovering flowers. It was so perfect a fairy-glade that one expected every moment to see its occupants come forth and dance. And this was the summit of that first pass.

And then suddenly, for the first time, we set eyes on Rocca Longa. And Rocca Longa struck us with terror as we gazed; for it seemed twenty miles away at the least, an enormous, enormously distant range of limestone, misty-blue against the risen sun, jagging up in ridge after ridge, to the highest summit, which also happened to be the most remote. Yet ours had been, perhaps, quite the nearest way to the Rocca. Thus securely defended is the Daphne, on a range that rises right from the very centre of a mountain pedestal, wholly devoid of roads or any means of access ; besides being well cut off from any known corner of the earth. However, we justly attributed our momentary depression to lack of food, and advanced to where there is a dairy-farm on the Col, and innumerable cows, there to purchase milk, and drink it to the accompaniment of our own eggs and bread and chocolate. It was a lovely halting-spot—when you got away from the trampled muck of the cows and pigs.

For we were up now, in the cleared air of morning, fresh and sparkling with cool breezes, yet warm with the first virgin rays of the sun. Away before us, over an amphitheatre of meadow and valley, ranged the long mass of the Rocca, and now we could see that its extreme remoteness had been the result of atmospheric effect. For, standing against the sun, its whole bulk was in flat soft tones, devoid of relief or salient detail. Far and high though it undoubtedly was, it was neither quite so high nor nearly so far as it had looked at first sight. Up behind us as we sat there rose also a wonderful hill, precipitous and peaked, with rose-pink pinnacles sticking out all over it ; and pine-scrub in the gullies. It bristled with points like a hedgehog, and was even more densely spiky than those puddings which are adorned with almonds stuck in on end ; a fashion adopted from the style of rock-gardening favoured in the fifties.

Reluctantly we stirred from our rest, and renewed our journey towards the remote Rocca. But now, as the sun rose, relief and shadows were being quickly mapped out upon its slopes, and the distances diminished. The way led round, under the rampart of soil that upholds this high valley. There were curious bare pans of black silt to cross; otherwise grass and scattered coppice, composed of charming little isolated beech trees, dwarfed and Japanesed by wind and weather, which one longed to carry off bodily, but that one felt certain they would revert and grow big as soon as they had surroundings more sympathetic. A final pull up among Rhododendrons, and we were fairly embarked on the last climb. And by now the day was wholly fair and fine. It was with dancing spirits that we strode along the track, rising gradually at every step, towards the goal. At length it reached the foot of the ridge, and then began briskly to mount, though at an easy slant, round each successive buttress of the towering calcareous wall which is Rocca Longa.

The going was over a certain amount of loose white limestone, with limestone cliffs becoming bigger and more imposing as one drew towards the upper bulwarks of the ridge. But principally there was a small low scrub of Rhododendron and such-like, growing in black peaty humus. Shadow lay still cool on this face of the mountain, and all the little bushes and blades and flowers were thickly jewelled with dew. Then, on the stonier ground, *Saxifraga caesia* began to occur, and soon became more and more frequent. Its lovely little flat blue-and-silver tuffets of tiny rosettes were almost hidden now by the big white flowers hovering above on wiry frail stems of three or four inches. I mean no disrespect either to flower or tuffet, when I say that its appearance here was a disappointment. For on this mountain once dwelt the more lovelier and far rarer *S. tombeanensis*, which some German collector, however, is said to have utterly exterminated. (And even thus may his own offspring be exterminated also, and his race wiped out !) For a fine exquisite beauty is *S. caesia*, indeed ; we all know it, and we all grow it ; so I need say no more of that universal jewel, which is only, I think, a trifle less hail-fellow-well-met, than the even more minute *squarrosa* of the Dolomites. *Tombeanensis*, though, is yet easier and heartier than *squarrosa ;* and, in appearance, close to the neat cosy beauty of *diapensioeides* : but it is a very rare plant of the high limestones, restricted usually to a few cliffs in the Southern Alps of Tyrol and Lombardy. It takes its name from the Cima Tombea, far away in southern Austria, which is also, curiously enough, said to be another of the very few stations for *Daphne rupestris*. The two rarities seem to hunt in couples.

Despairing, then, of *Saxifraga tombeanensis*, we tramped on over the increasing luxuriance of *S. caesia*. And the wide world widened away before us, in shallow tones of lilac and green and pale clear blue to the uttermost distance, and the high snows peered at us from among the cloudbanks up in the north. From the shade of that hill-side, it was as if we looked out through a film of deep water, so cool and solemn was the air. But then, as we walked, we were brought up short by a sudden flare of crimson on our right, among the pallid blossoms of Rhododendron. And it is *Silene Elizabethae*. It was well, indeed that I did not warn you beforehand in detail of the many treasures I expected to show you on the Rocca ; for if I had, you would have insisted on bringing a sack, and we should never have got here at all.

Queen Elizabeth's *Silene* does not occur in hot shale-slides, then, as reported ; Queen Elizabeth's *Silene* occurs in very stony places, on the coolest exposures of the northerly-facing mountain-limestone. Here the slope is sparsely clad, and its surface is a rocky rubble ; and here, accordingly, occur the bright tufts of the *Silene*. It forms one immensely long tap-root, that wanders far down among the gravel, but usually grows in ground so loose that patience can easily extract it, while the plant is also quite capable of striking readily, should you only succeed in getting half the main carrot, or even less. At its end there emerges, close on the ground, a splendid rosette of long narrow leaves, pointed and glossy, brilliantly green : from this come forth a couple or so of rather dark and downy flower-stems, which rise languidly, like a swan's neck, some four inches from the ground, though their own length may actually be seven or eight. And these bear one, two, or three flowers, which are of enormous size, with ragged flopping petals of rosy-crimson. It is a glorious plant to see, glowing at you here and there among the dull and common-place pinks of the Alpenrose. Henceforth it goes with us all the way up the ridge, where-ever the ground be tolerably bare and stony : while, down on this northern side, by the shingly bed of the Riario river, it has seeded all over the place in the gravel, and is as easy to extract as promises at election-time. But apparently it avoids the warm exposure on the south of the Rocca, and remains exclusively devoted, so far as I could see, to the white limestone. And *Silene Elizabethae* is a treasure in the garden, where it will grow quite happily without trouble, in any decent conditions, and where its outstanding splendour at once prevents you from being so ungrateful as to remark that faint alloy of magenta which lurks in its crimsons, as in the crimsons of every other alpine *Silene*. And, above all, it positively revels here, for ever, in the moraine. My companion actually dared, forsooth, to hint that it looked biennial. Biennial, indeed! *Silene Elizabethae* is as perennial as love or folly. Have no fear of it on that account.

In the excitement of perpetually coming on fresh flowers of the *Silene*, like some draggled carnation, sitting tight in the stones beside the path, we made short work of the remaining pinnacles of that ridge, over whose buttresses we had successively to climb. Near the top began small signs of a certain very precious buttercup, and there were flowering tufts of *Rhodothamnus* actually between the blocks of the track itself. This, however, we did not pause to collect. We foresaw that all our time would be needed for our main quest ; and besides, we hoped to find the *Rhodothamnus* again, when we should have more leisure. We ought to have known better than this, and were well served in the end. But true it was that that day was already monopolised ; we had neither hours nor muscles to spare. We topped the ridge, then, disregarding *Rhodothamnus*, and came out suddenly into the full sunshine of its southern face.

All the southern face of Rocca Longa is a succession of

warm grass downs, with ups and dips, falling away in tiers towards the lower levels. At least, one calls it a grass down, but the turf is mainly composed of a Primula for which you will rarely pay less than eighteenpence a plant in England—and then never get the true thing after all. We have already sighted *Primula spectabilis*, but now that we have come out on many miles of sunny lawn there are nothing but sheets of its matted tufts (interspersed by tufts of *Gentiana Clusii*, and starred with the blue flowers of *Linum austriacum*), it is time to have a word about the plant. This is, in reality, a rare species, restricted to the Lombard Alps. It belongs to the cousinship of *glaucescens* (which is usually the plant sold under its name), *Wulfeniana*, *Clusiana*, and the other leather-leaved lawn-makers of the southern ranges. It makes large tufts, that grow in densely clustered masses of rosettes. The leaves are big and very broad and oval, curling back at their tip till it looks as if they really had no point at all ; and their edges are quite entire, that is to say, without any jags or dentation. They are much softer and less leathery than those of its nearest relations ; but also have, if you look closely, that same fine line of whitish membrane running round their rim, that you see so clearly in *glaucescens*. They are very closely dotted with microscopic glands or pores, which makes them both look and feel like rather rough green skin, besides giving their colour a dullish dusted note. The flower-stems come up in May, are purplish, and rise to four inches or so, producing from three to five (or more) huge and brilliantly lovely flowers of a rich warm rose. *Primula specta-*

*bilis* deserves its name ; nor does it belie the appearance of good nature that it has, thus rioting massively in the turf ; for I do not find there is any difficulty about its culture, in any good open place, in a good hearty loam. You will notice that it is not a rock species, and does not ask for the fussments preferred by *viscosa, pedemontana, marginata* and *cottia*—although with such advantages it will also do well.

We wandered very gleefully along that turf. What it must be like in flower time, I dare not even begin to imagine. When we saw it, of course, in the first week of August, there were none of the Gentians or Primulas or other spring flowers remaining. Only the Bearded Bell stood stiffly up here and there, hanging out one solitary flower, from the dwarfed stem it assumes at such altitudes in the Southern Alps (and, I am sorry to say, renounces as soon as it has been brought down again into fatter ground). *Linum austriacum* was like dropped azure stars here and there ; and in stonier places there were purple splotches of *Viola heterophylla*. The *Linum* is a plant of singular loveliness ; it replaces *L. alpinum* in the southern ranges, and is incomparably more brilliant in colouring, though virtually identical in habit. For it varies in tones of azure which are really gentian-like, quite remote from the pale soft china-blues of *L. alpinum*. *Austriacum* is perfectly easy to grow ; but, by some strange caprice, it does not seem to me as perfectly hardy as one would expect. I have known a whole batch die off in a damp winter's chills ; and, altogether, I feel a great deal more confidence in *L. salsoloeides* with which

I have never yet sustained a loss, though it comes from places a great deal lower and hotter than these alpine ridges. However, I have now raised the Austrian *Linum* from seed, and hope for better results. The seedlings are very strong, and the habit of the plant is a trifle larger and more upstanding than the rather flaccid grace of *L. alpinum*. As for the Viola, I have never succeeded with it yet. These high Pansies are capricious mimps, despite their apparent heartiness. For the rest I need not paint you *Viola heterophylla*, if you are a faithful reader ; for it is, to all intents and purposes, yet another repetition of *cenisia* and *valderia*.

But now we are dropping into a wide grassy hollow, immediately under the culminating point of Rocca Longa. Here there is a little cowshed called the Casa della Rocca, or the Refuge d'Arlet, according as you choose to use the language of one frontier or another. And the mortal moment is very near. To fortify ourselves we eat our lunch, and force our trembling fingers to collect Primulas, which our souls, meanwhile, are too deeply excited to care about, or our eyes to see. Fortunately, then, it is simply a matter of kicking sods and tussocks out of the hillside that is matted with them, and then absent-mindedly cleaning the individual roots, as one separates the clumps into their component plants. Straight behind us rises a stark rosy cliff of limestone, above a rippling slope of Primula ; and, just beyond this (which is the southern face of the actual summit), there looms another, which is the actual seat of *Daphne rupestris*. For, on one cliff, and on that one cliff only, will that exclusive plant take up its residence. Neither to the right nor to the left of its chosen precipice will you see a sign of it, though the others may have exactly the same rock, and exactly the same exposure.

However, this wisdom is proleptic ; at the moment I had no inclination to wisdom of any sort ; my brain felt dissolved into an icy liquid somewhere in the pit of my stomach. The little warm hollow was filled with a silence so complete that it seemed as if the Earth-mother herself was sharing in the solemnity of the moment. A second failure could not be borne or thought of ; and already the clouds were driving noiselessly up at us over the lower rim of the bowl where we sat ; and though they were still so thin that the sun made them into a veil of gold as they drifted, I could bear the suspense at last no longer, bolted my remaining fragment of egg, and began scrambling at a slant across the slope that led to the further cliff. Up I scrambled, and up, until its crannies, and the growths in them, grew clear to view. And there, over the whole of that face, was *Daphne rupestris*.

Where should we naturally look for *Daphne rupestris*, you and I ? Where, but in places like those favoured by the rest of the family : that is to say, on ridges and slopes of hard peaty turf ? As for its name, it might easily be called the Rock-Daphne from haunting such open banks up among the rocks. And now look at that naked precipice, and give me news. For the specific name is not a blind guide as it so often is. *Daphne rupestris* is the most absolutely saxatile of all rock-plants ; it is more saxatile than anything I know except *Androsace imbricata*. Even

*Saxifraga florulenta* and *Phyteuma* occasionally seed into unlikely places, such as silt-beds and moraines ; but the Rock Daphne will practically never be seen at all, and certainly never be seen in full health, except in the cracks of a sheer limestone cliff facing due south. Indeed, it precisely matches the habit of the *Androsace*, except that it is as passionately attached to the limestone as the *Androsace* to the granite.

Here, in microscopic crannies, it roots back into chinks where no soil can be, but perhaps, a little humus at first, and then only moisture and lime. Here it forms bushes that lie tight and hard against the cliff, hugging the rock as closely as any willow or cotoneaster. Each thick little wooden twig, gnarled and pressed against the stone, is crowned with a tuft of dark green, tiny, narrow-oval leaves, solid and lucent, roughly resembling those of the common alpine *globularia*, as, indeed, does the whole look of the plant at first sight. And on these mats, in heads of two or three, are scattered the great rosy trumpets, flat and firm on the firm flat mass. They did not appear to seed, though seed one supposes they must : but one big sheet would send out a sucker, here and there, to emerge from some apparently unconnected crevice half a yard away, and there, in time, splay out into another sheet of flower and leaf, plastered close on the blank wall of the rock.

It is a marvellous sight, that little Daphne, up and up the cliff, from base to summit. It was still in flower in the highest chinks, so that I had the joy of craning up from below when I had climbed as high as I dared, to see its waxy-pink loveliness in display. The plant, of course, is very rare indeed. It is almost entirely confined to one or two small districts ; in these districts has not many stations, and is, even in those stations, narrowly restricted. For, although abundant where it does occur, it ceases, abruptly (as here), to right and left of just the one precipice that has happened to take its fancy. All along the south side of the Rocca, for instance, there are cliffs that seem made for it ; yet the Daphne won't even trouble to try them. It will have exactly what it likes, and only what it likes, this domineering small shrub. It *must* have limestone, and it *must* have a cliff both sheer and sound, and it *must* have an exposure facing full due south, it appears ; but a cliff may take pains to fulfil faithfully all these requirements, without ever succeeding in winning the favour of the Daphne.

Also, *Daphne rupestris* is quite the most difficult plant I have ever had to collect. Collecting *Saxifraga florulenta* and *Phyteuma comosum* is, by comparison, like plucking bushes of groundsel out of my moraines. The precipice is hard as iron, and solid as the British intelligence ; impossible to find a cleavage anywhere ; as you smite at it with futile hammer the rock rings derisively at you again, like adamant, chips a little, and does no more. The cracks, too, are of the tiniest; The Daphne wedges itself into them with a fanatical tightness. Its roots go far, far in, and it is also dangerously, curiously, breakable just at the neck. All along the lines of the cliff one has to clamber here and there, questing for a chink that may not prove so inexorable as the others—and a Daphne more amenable to suasion. Below you long banks of grass and lesser buttresses of limestone slope abruptly into infinity. There are cows under one's feet, near a path ; they look like fleas, or grains of pepper. And down below these again, below all the green mountains that descend and descend in successive laps—there, through swirling grey-and-golden glimpses of the cloud, one snatches a rare glimpse of Savinanza Water, lying like a sapphire pavement, among ranges that seem, from here, to be mere mole-hummocks on a lawn.

Up and up above one's head towers the wall of the cliff : and all of it, from top to bottom, is lined and seamed with flat masses of the Daphne, from the cracks at eye-level to those far up on the bare face, where no depredator can get them. Not, as you will judge, that the Daphne is inclined to be tender to the depredator, anyhow, or to give him a chance ; the Daphne has its own methods of dealing with the depredator. Unfortunately, in the vile soul of man this resistance has been held to justify reprisals ; and the depredator has, accordingly, developed a foul habit of tearing out the Daphne, in rage and desperation, by rootless masses from its chinks, thus certainly killing alike what he takes and what he leaves. He is maddened by its obduracy, as men are maddened who murder their obdurate mistresses. I have suffered under this insanity of his myself (hardly less indeed, than the Daphne), receiving moribund or lifeless twigs and rootless chunks, when I had paid good money in the hope of good plants.

After which, do I need to justify my own action ?

Many were the plants, indeed, that I collected with pious care that day ; and many were the pieces into which they were subsequently divided.   But not a piece did I attempt that was not amenable to the persuasions of hammer and chisels ; not a piece I took but had roots ; not a piece I took but has lived and thrived and surmounted the shock of removal.   And the cliffs of the Rocca certainly show no less rich than before.   This is not to say that *Daphne rupestris* is exactly an easy plant in cultivation, as you will have gathered from all this ; it is apt to damp off in the wetness of open ground in the garden ; it really wants its sunny crevice, in limy humus and vegetable soil, with perfect drainage, and rather excess of drought than of humidity.   Altogether, what with its remoteness, the altitudes and inconveniences of the Rocca, and its wild neighbourhood, the dense hardness of the rock, and the difficulty, for experienced and inexperienced alike, of getting out sound plants and starting them again when got, I am not afraid that *Daphne rupestris* will suffer from the wandering tourist.   As for the professional depredator, I throw the plant upon his mercy and sense of decency ; let him take, indeed, if he needs, and if he can, and if he must, but let him take with care and courtesy and consideration ; and realise the ugly, futile cruelty of spoiling what he cannot safely get, merely in order that some fragments of the wreckage he makes may ultimately die miserably in English gardens, instead of in their sacked home on the Rocca, when their tale of years is full.

Even when you have at last had your will of that Daphne, you have not yet by any means exhausted the riches of the slope. Among those rocks, and over those grass-slides, there are still many treasures to be seen. As one scrambles along under the face of the rock itself, to where it ceases abruptly, leaving one gazing " adown titanic glooms of chasméd fears," in the abysms cloven deep among the pinnacles, there lives with the Daphne in its sunny chinks, the very rare *Moehringia glauco-virens*, with tiny tufts of fine, iron-coloured leaves, and little four-petalled white stars of blossom. But this is only a curiosity. Here also are the Primulas, *spectabilis* and *Auricula*, hanging in wide masses on the lip of each cliff ; and, somewhere about, there is that priceless rarity *Saxifraga arachnoidea*. This had been described to me as forming a cloud of golden blossom above its cobwebbed cushions of silver-white fluff. When, therefore, my companion called me up into a dry grotto in the cliff, and showed me a pallid little dull weed of flimsy and annual appearance, I almost wept. But, sure enough, it was *Saxifraga arachnoidea*, a species confined to a few localities in the far-southern Alps, where, being implacably impatient of surface moisture, it inhabits only shallow pecked cavities in the face of sunny precipices, much like those affected by *Primula Allioni* in the Maritimes. In cultivation it is almost impossible, and (I think) altogether worthless. I have not got it, and I do not mourn it.

But a little lower down there stood out from the bank a sharp limestone tooth which sufficiently indemnified me for my disappointment over an expected Saxifrage, by yielding me an unexpected one, far more precious. For, as I drew near it from above, I saw, along its upper surfaces, a straggling mass of silver that looked very unlike the *Saxifraga caesia* to which my thoughts immediately flew. Surely this thing was too lax and untidy to be *caesia?* What, then? Another long close glance from below confirmed me in the hope I had hardly dared to entertain. For there, mercifully secure on its pinnacle, lay the lost *Saxifraga tombeanensis*—three or four plants, out of all the numbers that once glorified Rocca Longa. With feelings of deep piety, I went on my ways. Not for worlds would I have taken one of those lingering tufts. Even if worlds had been offered me, down on the nail, I couldn't have managed to touch it, either, whatever my wishes. This is a point on which I lay less stress than on the fact that I already possess such a good sufficiency of *Saxifraga tombeanensis*, that, anyhow, I should not have wanted more than one fragment from a wild clump; just as a relic and sign that I had really seen it. I did, in fact, try to get near; failed completely both from above and from below; untimately made a piety of necessity, and passed on.

Beyond the Daphne's cliff, there is a notch in the ridge, called the Col d'Arlet. By this it was to be our fate to descend over on to the northern side again, and down and down into the Val Riario, and then down and down again into the gorge of Valbonne until it runs into the main glen of the Val d'Arlet. Accordingly, when at last we had exhausted all the joys of that precipice, we struck across its base, to meet the track of the pass as it came wandering up from the Alps on the south side of Rocca Longa; where, deep down the ranges that show from here, in glimpses of the cloud, like counties on a painted chart, lies the Inn-less hamlet of Sant' Ilaria, below meadows all aflame with *Scorzonera rosea*. And, when we reached the track, we found it a meandering rivulet of loose white limestone, among which *Saxifraga caesia* was rioting, and here and there big tufts occurred of *Saxifraga mutata* just coming into blossom. But *Saxifraga mutata* is rather a disappoint-ment ; it forms, here, masses consisting of eight rosettes or more, like a rather green form of *S. Cotyledon;* and, when the spikes come up, they look as if they were going to repeat, or rival, *Cotyledon's* snowy oriflammes. Instead of which, they unfold into a quantity of squinny little orange stars, with petals so narrow that the calyx-segments are the more conspicuous part of the bloom. Add to which that each plant dies after flowering. It is an easy species to grow in any cool place, but demands a certain amount of humidity in soil and atmosphere ; and, altogether, is not worth so much attention as you feel inclined to lavish on it, when first you see the rich but delusive promise of those rosettes.

We came up on to the ridge of the Col d'Arlet, and looked over, down into the Val Riario. On our left loomed up the blank wall of Rocca Longa ; on the other side of the Pass the range rose again, no less sheer, in the dome and precipice of Marmorel. Between these giants sank beneath us a long incline of white limestone scree, towards the depths of the Val Riario, and the yet further depths of Valbonne, down in the shadow. I have rarely looked into such a profundity ; there was no actual precipice or cliff below, yet the fall appeared stupendous. It was all one could do to discern the narrow creek of the Valbonne, away beneath the Val Riario ; and, lower than this again, one narrow notch in the bowels of the forested hills alone revealed where the Valbonne flows at right angles into the Val d'Arlet, and, at that point, affords the civilised world of highways its solitary glimpse of Rocca Longa.   However, feeling too serene in triumph to quail before those distances, we began dropping down the northern wall of the Col d'Arlet, looking backwards every now and then, in gratitude, like a cat when you have given it a plate of chicken, at the peak of the Rocca which had so generously treated us ; and now, at every step we took, seemed to be shooting away up into the heavens.

But in another moment we realised that we were trampling tufts and plots of *Ranunculus crenatus*. All thought of everything else disappeared from our minds. There are no mountain plants that I love better than the white buttercups. And *Ranunculus crenatus* is twin-brother, too, to the perfectly perfect *Ranunculus alpestris*, the easiest, best-tempered, freest-flowering and longest-blooming of all high alpines—a plant which, in a cool soil and climate, you cannot easily induce to do any-thing but prosper violently. But *R. crenatus*, instead of the tri-cleft, overlapping-lobed, deciduous leaves of *alpestris*, has rounded leaves, kidney-shaped, crenelate, and delicately scolloped at the edge. They are dark, glossy and evergreen ; the whole plant never grows more than five or six inches high, and the abundant flowers, instead of being solid orbs of golden-eyed snow, like those of *alpestris*, have all the petals so deeply " échancrées,"

that the effect is rather like that of an exquisite wee white
dog-rose. Never was seen a thing so dainty and loveable.
And *R. crenatus* proves in culture to have all the good-
comradeship and affability which are such charms in
*R. alpestris.* (Its other name has sometimes been *R.
bilobus*).

*Crenatus* is a very much rarer plant, though, occurring
but locally, and only on the limestones of the southern
Alps ; whereas *alpestris* is very general over all the ranges,
on calcareous or sandstone formations, though there is
not a sign of it, for instance, on the Mont Cenis, in the
Cottians, or the Maritimes. I believe it to be naturally
as calcicole, really, as *crenatus.* In any case *crenatus* is
abundant in the stony scree all the way down the northern
side of the Col d'Arlet ; in a place, that is, very similar
to those where you would find *alpestris* in the Oberland,
on the Gemmi, or on Monte Baldo. In mossy wads on
the cliff it is not so fine, but there waves abundance of
*Phyteuma,* together with the brighter blue spikes of
*Paederota Bona-Rota*—curious and beautiful Scrophulariaceous rock-plant, which runs about in cliff crannies
like the Phyteuma, haunts the same rocks (but in much
greater abundance hereabouts), and is, in all its habit
and colouring and conformation, so generally like the
Phyteuma, that one is often, at first glance, mistaking it.

At the bottom of that first slope there comes a heathy
hollow where our feet despise acres of the plant which
M. Correvon justly calls " cette maudite *Daphne striata.*"
For no other Daphne, after *rupestris*, could expect a better
blessing. As we lie on our backs and rest for a while,

looking upwards whence we have come, so abrupt and far
rises the Col, between peaks so imperious, that one
thinks it must be all a fancy that we can ever have mounted
so high, or descended again so low.   After this the journey
begins once more, dropping through the most fatiguing
pathless scrub, till it reaches the dry bed of the Riario,
where there is such abundance of Queen Elizabeth's Silene
that one's rate of advance becomes proportionately slow.
For this loose gravel, as I said, yields perfect plants with
the minimum of trouble and danger ;  bundles of long
yellow rat-tails lie beside one on a boulder before one has
been working five minutes in a given sandbank.   And no
sign of difference is made to the luxuriance of the whole
river bed, which in another ten days, will be sprinkled
with the big blood-gouts of the Silene's blossom.

But it is when one has finished with these upper reaches
of the Riario that real trouble begins.   For now the
hillside sinks without any further laps or delays, straight
away to the tiny creek of gloom below, which is the sombre
gorge of the Valbonne ;  and all that mountain side is a
dense tangle of coppice, where the path is pretence,
getting lost every other minute ;  and perilous where it
exists, with holes or boulders buried under fallen leaves,—
while, even in more open places, it is nothing better than
the stony bed of a torrent.   The afternoon was very hot,
there was not a breath of air in the brushwood, which was
close and tangled as the Jungle.   There was never a
moment's relaxation in the slope to rest one's knees ;  we
stumbled on downward, wrestling incessantly with boughs
that flogged us savagely in the face ;  and seemed to make

no progress at all. Every foot gained was a struggle and a toil ; whenever we could see it the valley below looked as profoundly remote as ever ; though the peaks behind had shot up by now to a supernatural stature. There was no water, either, in the bed of the Riario, when from time to time we happened across it ; nothing to relieve our thirst and weariness except a strawberry here and there in a clear space.

But even the driest river falls somewhere safe into a valley. After hours of unprofitable batterings through bushes, we saw at length that the depths were getting nearer. It became evident that we hadn't been standing quite motionless all the afternoon, which for a long time had been our impression, if ever we stopped to mop the sweat from our eyes and try to gauge the advance we had made. And now there were beginning to be signs of the Riario river, too ; we came on a pool, and rested, and drank. After that the copse became taller and easier to thread. A little more and we were in a definite wood, and there was the noise of water about. At last we came down into the main bed of Valbonne, brawling in its deep channel. Another half a mile and we were fairly embarked in the gorge. For Valbonne flows under the Rocca, parallel with its northern wall, but some three thousand feet lower, until immediately beneath the Col d'Arlet. There the foolish little beck of the Riario dashes down and joins it, and the stream then coils round at right angles, running straight away from the ridge, and thus continuing the line of the Col, passes through a deep gully of cliff until the Val d'Arlet cuts across it, and receives its waters into the main river of the Arlet, hurrying to merge into the Ronca below Castellar.

The gorge was dark as night, dark and chill and beautiful. The wet precipices were hung with mosses and sleek glittering patches of damp. But there were no flowers. *Saxifraga mutata* occurred here and there, on silt, and *Phyteuma* in the rocks. But we tramped on, unheeding these. By now we were full-fed with marvels. We should scarcely have said " How do you do " to *Saxifraga florulenta.* We were a little tired, too, what with travel, and our burdens. Our feet trudged automatically onwards, rejoiced to have a path where they could do anything so unemotional. In half an hour or so we neared the end of the Ghyll, collected a few Phyteumas, just to show what we could do if we liked; and then emerged on a sunny shoulder, by the opening of the Val d'Arlet. And here we came on *Gentiana cruciata* to serve us right. For *Gentiana cruciata* roots indefinitely and very solidly down into soil that has been hardened by sun to a consistency like steel. We stabbed at the ground feebly for a while with trowels, and then decided that it was too coarse and ugly a plant to be bothered about by collectors who had just been dealing with *Daphne rupestris.* In another moment we were on the high-road. We paused for one last look at Rocca Longa, towering over the earth like the wall of Valhalla ; then turned again, and trudged away to the left, down the Val d'Arlet towards Castellar. We refused to notice anything more on the way, until my companion was seduced by the silky-grey fine foliage and the large lilac flowers of

*Scabiosa graminifolia.* I stood firm against even this myself, feeling that after the Daphne and the Silene everything else would be bathos. The Scabious, though, was beautiful, among the turf on open banks, just where the road begins to drop in a series of looping curls down upon Castellar. But when one has had sweet words with Helen of Troy, one remains easily cold to the charms of Mrs. Smith. Not even the Cyclamen could I now notice, though it twinkled pink at us from the roadsides and stone-tumbles, seeming to glow in the gathering twilight. For dusk was now beginning to fall, and darkness was almost upon us before we slouched triumphant into Castellar, not even needing words with which to congratulate each other on the richest day I had ever yet contrived in the Alps.

Under the vines in the Osteria we regally celebrated the occasion. Even the most rigid of teetotallers may relax, when he sees the village beldams washing their Isabella-coloured garments just outside the Inn, in the only drinking water of the place. And my companion, anyhow, I am glad to say, was curious in nice eating and drinking. He gave me an example which it would have been unfriendly not to follow, and had invented a dilemma which entitled us to sample every local joy without regard to fortune. As thus : having found the Daphne, we clearly owed it to ourselves and the plant, to celebrate the royal occasion royally ; but, had we *not* found it, we should no less clearly have owed it to ourselves to keep up our bruised spirits with festivity, and drown dull care. And thus the same excellent result was achieved in all cases. Not that the second, the crumpled horn of the dilemma, was ever called into use. With the one exception of *Gentiana Rostani*, which only curiosity made me wish to find, there was not a single plant this summer that I went out for to see that I did not duly succeed in seeing. But I do not think that any evening gave me a fuller joy than the evening of this day that yielded us the Daphne. I triumphed over my failure of the year before, and mocked at the mountain that had baffled me once, but not twice. We had need of our comforts too that night, for it was brief. It was our fate to leave Castellar by the diligence that starts at four in the morning, through the icy blue air of dawn in the dark valleys, to come down at length, in grilling mid-day, on Longarena, at the foot of Savinanza Water.

Here, then, I think I had better end the tale of my wanderings of this summer. I have said a good deal, and left out a vast deal more, and filled an alarming number of pages, without having said nearly all the things I wanted to, or taken you on half the journeys I intended. So the best thing I can now do, is to bring myself to a close without more words; only adding that on any other journeys I may make, in the past or the future, I shall ask no better company than yours, if you still be willing. Christmas is upon us now, immediately, and I am refreshed to bear it by having had this second holiday among the hills ; though next Christmas will be chiming, probably, before these pages burst upon a waiting world, yet good wishes never fall out of season, come they early or come they late. Therefore will I conclude by sending my heartiest good hopes, for Christmas and for every other season, to all the gardeners (and all their gardens), who diligently purchase my successive works, and put them on their shelves, and refuse to let them out on loan or hire.

*December* 16*th*, 1910.

# AFTERWORD.

Gentle Reader,

I am not more horrified than astounded to find that scandal, like a worm in the bud, has recently been preying on my damask reputation. In better words than I could devise for myself to meet the case : " I will not denige that I am worrited and wexed this day: and with good reagion, Lord forbid." For strange, stray women, it appears, have gone about accusing me of " devastating " regions and valleys of the Alps on which, in point of fact, I have never yet set foot. Is this legend worth the pains of scotching ? Come, come, let us reason. On a given range a given species dwells. But that range, remember, is very many miles long, in and out, up and down, incalculably vast and high ; and the populating species can only be counted by the million and the many, many million. What a mighty void shall I then leave in even half a mile of slope, if I pluck thence a hundred plants or so ! Look at the true pictures in this book ; and judge. The misconception of alarmists appears to be entirely based on the rooted inability of the public to realise the vastness of the mountains and the " innumerable laughter " there of even the rarer species. In the Alps themselves, however, the misconception obtains : and

I hug myself in derision whenever I see notices about the " Schutz der (or " die " or " das ") Edelweiss." Why, but almost every little mountain-hummock possesses whole lawns of the Flannel-flower ! We might just as well start a league for the protection of the Dandelion. No, what you take, or I take, or five hundred others of us might take in reason and decency from the flanks of the enormous Alps, would never be able to make a petal's difference to their glory. Nor will a lover of plants, I hope, be called upon to defend himself against any charge of rash irreverent greed in dealing with special treasures so difficult and sacrosanct as *Primula Allioni* or *Daphne rupestris*, or the most ancient king of all Saxifrages.

REGINALD FARRER.

# INDEX

Note : Capitals indicate plants collected.

ACHILLEA HERBA-ROTA, 132
Adonis amurensis, 24
ALYSSUM ALPESTRE, 29
ANDROSACE CARNEA, 38
„    GLACIALIS (A. alpina) 18,
        31, 70
„    helvetica, 81-3
„    IMBRICATA, 82-4, 170-1, 173,
        199
„    pubescens, 18
ANEMONE ALPINA, 24-5, 31-3, 86, 91,
        97, 137, 193
„    BALDENSIS, 36, 64
„    demissa, 91
„    HALLERI, 39, 58
„    HEPATICA, 22
„    NARCISSIFLORA, 90-1, 97,
        193
„    VERNALIS, 58, 94, 295
ANTHERICUM LILIAGO, 85
„    LILIASTRUM, 30, 53, 85-6,
        88, 100
„    PLUMOSUM, 85
AQUILEGIA ALPINA, 55-6, 86, 96,
        250, 252, 254
„    REUTERI, 16, 250, 252-3
ARABIS PEDEMONTANA, 89
ARENARIA LARICIFOLIA, 89
ARNICA MONTANA, 178
ASPLENIUM X GERMANICUM, 101
„    RUTA-MURARIA, 101
„    SEPTENTRIONALE, 101
„    TRICHOMANES, 101
ASPERULA HEXAPHYLLA, 18, 269
ASTER ALPINUS, 53, 131
ASTRAGALUS TRAGACANTHA, 109
ASTRANTIA MINOR, 135, 178
ATRAGENE ALPINA, 19-20, 135
Ballota spinosa, 240
BULBOCODIUM VERNUM, 36
CAMPANULA ALLIONI, 18, 59-61, 62,
        109, 255
„    BARBATA, 304
„    CENISIA, 18, 28, 60-2
„    ELATINES, 78-80, 81, 87
„    LINIFOLIA, 53, 253

CAMPANULA isophylla, 80
„    MACRORHIZA, 207-8, 210,
        243
„    PERSICIFOLIA, 204
„    PUSILLA, 54
„    Scheuchzeri, 254
„    STENOCODON, 114, 152, 253-4
CARDAMINE ASARIFOLIA, 143
CATANANCHE CŒRULEA, 227
CEPHALANTHERA RUBRA, 255, 297
CINERARIA MARITIMA, 241
CORIS MONSPELIENSIS, 229
CORTUSA MATTHIOLI, 56-7
CORYDALIS SOLIDA, 28
CROCUS VERNUS, 35, 47
CYCLAMEN EUROPÆUM, 289-91
„    hederæfolium, 289-91
„    libanoticum, 291
DAPHNE RUPESTRIS, 284, 305-10,
        315
„    STRIATA, 315
Dianthus alpinus, 277
„    NEGLECTUS, 53, 54, 98,
        113, 276-7
„    SYLVESTRIS, 53, 131, 254
DOUGLASIA VITALIANA, 37-8, 94
DRABA TOMENTOSA, 173
DRYAS OCTOPETALA, 28, 54
ERITRICHIUM NANUM, 18, 49-50, 69-
        72, 155 254
ERYSIMUM PUMILUM, 29
FRITILLARIA DELPHINENSIS, 15, 86,
        95, 97-8, 254
„    Meleagris, 97
„    Moggridgei, 254
GENISTA RADIATA, 293
GENTIANA ACAULIS, 22-3, 29, 37,
        174-5, 215
„    ANGULOSA, 29, and note
„    CLUSII, 303
„    BAVARICA, 54, 112, 113
„    BRACHYPHYLLA, 31, 66-7,
        70
„    CRUCIATA, 318
„    IMBRICATA, 70
„    Rostani, 15, 114-5

GENTIANA VERNA, 22, 23, 37, 89, 98
    109, 112, 184
GERANIUM MACRORHIZON, 255
  ,,   RIVULARE, 53
GEUM MONTANUM, 29
  ,,   REPTANS, 31
GLOBULARIA CORDIFOLIA, 29
HUGUENINIA TANACETIFOLIA, 28, 55
HUTCHINSIA BREVICAULIS, 152
HYPERICUM CORIS, 208-10, 243
IBERIS GARREXIANA, 16, 269
Iris Lortetii, 259
LACTUCA PERENNIS (Alpine Lettuce),
    131
LEONTOPODIUM ALPINUM, 62
LILIUM BULBIFERUM, 80-1, 88
  ,,   MARTAGON, 53
  ,,   POMPONIUM, 205, 212-4,
    250
  ,,   pyrenaicum, 212
LINUM ALPINUM, 53, 102, 211, 304
  ,,   AUSTRIACUM, 211, 330,
    304-5
  ,,   SALSOLOEIDES, 209, 210-11,
    254
  ,,   VISCOSUM, 250
Lithospermum rosmarinifolium, 259
LYCHNIS FLOS-JOVIS, 80, 131
MICROMERIA PIPERELLA, 244
Moehringia dasyphylla, 243, note
  ,,   GLAUCO-VIRENS, 311
  ,,   papulosa, 16, 243, note
  ,,   SEDOEIDES, 16, 243
MYOSOTIS ALPESTRIS, 186, 216
  ,,   RUPICOLA, 174
NASTURTIUM PYRENAICUM, 131
ONONIS ROTUNDIFOLIA, 20
ORCHIS LATIFOLIA, 42, 54
PAEDEROTA BONA-ROTA, 315
PASSERINA DIOICA, 243
PETROCALLIS PYRENAICA, 31, 63-4,
    109
PHYTEUMA BALBISII, 16, 269
  ,,   COMOSUM, 292-3, 294-5,
    315
POTENTILLA ALPESTRIS, 29
  ,,   AUREA, 29
  ,,   SAXIFRAGA, 243
  ,,   VALDERIA, 143
  ,,   VERNA, 28
PRIMULA ALLIONI, 16, 18, 243-9, 263
  ,,   Auricula, 295
  ,,   ,,   BAUHINI, 295, 311
  ,,   ,,   OBRISTII, (?) 295
  ,,   x Bonatii, 15
  ,,   COTTIA, 15, 44, 84-5, 108
  ,,   FARINOSA, 21, 23, 29, 39,
    42, 43, 54, 98

PRIMULA hirsuta, 93
  ,,   MARGINATA, 48, 102-3, 105-
    8, 144, 193, 215, 252
  ,,   PEDEMONTANA, 18, 43-5,
    47, 51-2, 69
  ,,   SPECTABILIS, 295, 303-4
  ,,   tyrolensis, 247
  ,,   Veitchi, 57
  ,,   VISCOSA, 93, 96-7, 108, 131,
    140, 193, 215
  ,,   ,,   cynoglossifolia, 97
  ,,   ,,   graveolens, 97
PULMONARIA ANGUSTIFOLIA, 179
  ,,   OFFICINALIS, 179
PYROLA ROTUNDIFOLIA, 20
  ,,   UNIFLORA, 21
RANUNCULUS ACONITIFOLIUS, 39, 280
  ,,   alpestris, 279, 315
  ,,   CRENATUS, 314-5
  ,,   x Flahaultii, 280
  ,,   GLACIALIS, 30-1, 64, 70,
    279
  ,,   x lacerus, 280
  ,,   x Luizeti, 280
  ,,   parnassifolius, 279, 289
  ,,   PYRENAEUS, 26, 33-4, 42-3,
    47, 68, 69, 94, 280
  ,,   Seguieri, 279, 280
  ,,   RUTAEFOLIUS, 26-7, 43
  ,,   x Yvesii, 280
RHODOTHAMNUS CHAMAECISTUS, 302
ROSA ALPINA, 39
  ,,   FERRUGINEA, (glauca) 131
SALIX SERPYLLIFOLIA, 28
SAPONARIA LUTEA, 69-70
  ,,   OCYMOEIDES, 130-1
SAXIFRAGA AEIZOON, 21, 178
    215, 226, 271-2, 281, 297
  ,,   altissima, 162
  ,,   ARACHNOIDEA, 311
  ,,   BIFLORA, 66
  ,,   CAESIA, 280, 299-300, 313
  ,,   Churchilli, 226
  ,,   COCHLEARIS, 218-225, 238-9,
    244, 250, 256-7, 265
  ,,   ,,   minor (called
    "Probynii") 111-12, 219,
    265, 266
  ,,   ,,   x "Burnati," 225
  ,,   Cotyledon, 162, 313
  ,,   CUNEIFOLIA, 178
  ,,   DIAPENSIOEIDES, 263-270
  ,,   FLORULENTA, 15, 18, 118,
    130, 135, 138 (and note),
    140, 158-170, 173, 180,
    182-3, 193-200, 217, 254,
    266, 307

SAXIFRAGA lingulata, 201, 216, 217
,, ,, australis, 217
,, ,, BELLARDI, 124,
217, 218, 220-26, 261-
63, 269-70, 272, 275, 281
,, ,, catalaunica, 217
,, ,, LANTOSCANA, 117,
214-18, 219-24, 225-6,
228-9, 262, 270
,, longifolia, 162, 223
,, MUTATA, 313, 318
,, OPPOSITIFOLIA, 31, 51, 94
,, PEDEMONTANA, 135-6, 148,
186, 201
,, RETUSA, 50-1, 71, 93, 152,
173
,, squarrosa, 266
,, TOMBEANENSIS, 266, 300,
212
,, VALDENSIS, 15, 85, 86, 101-
2, 108-113, 219, 265, 266
,, Vandelli, 266
,, Wallacei, 136
SENECIO DORONICUM, 54-5, 173-4
SILENE ACAULIS, 23, 98

SILENE ELIZABETHAE, 300-2, 316
SOLDANELLA ALPINA, 23, 35
,, MONTANA, 56
THALICTRUM AQUILEGIAEFOLIUM, 54
THLASPI LIMOSELLAEFOLIUM, 139,
152, 170, 186, 190-2
,, ROTUNDIFOLIUM, 28, 31,
63, 190-2
TOZZIA ALPINA, 142
TULIPA AUSTRALIS (celsiana), 97,
131, 196
VIOLA alpina, 132 note
,, BIFLORA, 28, 178
,, CALCARATA, 23, 29, 36-7, 89,
133, 134, 174, 176
,, CENISIA, 18, 28, 62-3, 133,
134, 187, 304
,, HETEROPHYLLA, 133, 134,
304
,, NUMMULARIAEFOLIA, 15, 141,
150, 152-3, 170, 186-190,
255
,, VALDERIA, 63, 132-4, 175,
181, 304
ULVA LABYRINTHIFORMIS, 143-4